Born in Paris in 1947, Christian Jacq first visited Egypt when he was seventeen, went on to study Egyptology and archaeology at the Sorbonne, and is now one of the world's leading Egyptologists. He is the author of the internationally bestselling RAMSES series, THE STONE OF LIGHT series and the stand-alone novel, THE BLACK PHARAOH. Christian Jacq lives in Switzerland.

Also by Christian Jacq

The Ramses Series
Volume 1: The Son of the Light
Volume 2: The Temple of a Million Years
Volume 3: The Battle of Kadesh
Volume 4: The Lady of Abu Simbel
Volume 5: Under the Western Acacia

The Stone of Light Series
Volume 1: Nefer the Silent
Volume 2: The Wise Woman
Volume 3: Paneb the Ardent
Volume 4: The Place of Truth

The Queen of Freedom Trilogy
Volume 1: The Empire of Darkness
Volume 2: The War of the Crowns
Volume 3: The Flaming Sword

The Black Pharaoh
The Tutankhamun Affair
For the Love of Philae
Champollion the Egyptian
Master Hiram & King Solomon
The Living Wisdom of Ancient Egypt

Champollion
the Egyptian

Christian Jacq

Translated by Geraldine Le Roy

POCKET
BOOKS

LONDON · SYDNEY · NEW YORK · TOKYO · TORONTO

First published in Great Britain by Pocket Books, 2003
An imprint of Simon & Schuster UK Ltd
A Viacom Company

1 3 5 7 9 10 8 6 4 2

Simon & Schuster UK Ltd
Africa House
64-78 Kingsway
London WC2B 6AH
www.simonsays.co.uk

Simon & Schuster Australia
Sydney

A CIP catalogue record for this book is available from
the British Library

ISBN 0-671-02856-1

Typeset by SX Composing DTP, Rayleigh, Essex
Printed and bound in Great Britain by
Cox & Wyman Ltd, Reading, Berkshire

Foreword

This is a peculiar novel, in so far as it has been written by an Egyptologist to celebrate the memory of the genius of one of the first and most outstanding Egyptologists, Jean-François Champollion. He was born in Figeac in 1790 and died in Paris in 1832. He is famous as the discoverer of the meaning of hieroglyphs, but it is often forgotten that his scientific and literary work also encompasses grammars, dictionaries, historical essays, explanatory notes and letters.

Between July 1828 and December 1829, Champollion experienced the most wonderful moments of his too brief life: he, who was early on nicknamed 'the Egyptian' managed at last to go to the Egypt he had been dreaming of for so long. Christian Jacq's novel tells about this extraordinary trip, its intense experiences, tragedies and discoveries. It speaks with Champollion's own voice, and sentences actually uttered or written by him are integrated where they are in the author's opinions significant. Most of the events mentioned here are in fact close to the truth. The novelist's role consisted in recreating the internal experience of a journey which was a pilgrimage to the roots of the spirit. To do this he combines several people and fills in gaps left in Champollion's own writing.

However the novel's aim is to be faithful not so much to historical truth but to Jean-François Champollion, one of the greatest geniuses of all times.

Prologue

Doctor Brousset emptied his glass of rum with a drawn and gloomy look. 'So, what is your diagnosis, my dear colleague?'

Doctor Robert wiped his forehead with his handkerchief. 'Attack of gout from the stomach, consumption, beginning apoplexy, paralysis of the spinal chord, liver disease resulting from the absorption of Nile water . . . Champollion is going to die. This time, the fiery old bird who always asked for three times his feed has used up all his energy.'

'That is an excellent analysis. His organism is exhausted. His laborious trip, the atmosphere of death emanating from the pharaohs' tomb, the feverishness of his brain, the constant preoccupations of his mind have all combined to burn up his blood and drive him to his coffin. I would even add an hypertrophy of the heart. To my mind, he will not see dawn.'

'Champollion is about to die.'

Hidden behind a curtain, eight-year-old little Zoraïde heard the terrible prediction. She knew that this time her father would abandon her forever – though he had already travelled far away many times. He had most often left France for the mysterious Orient he loved so much and from which her first name came.

Ever since his return from Egypt, Champollion had been ill. He could not bear Paris any more. He had been able to give only a few lectures at the Collège de France, where he held the first chair of Egyptology ever created in the world. Recurrent feelings of faintness had obliged him to interrupt his teaching and stifle the clear and passionate voice with which he brought forth the light of ancient Egypt.

Zoraïde did not need to hear the two physicians who, for two weeks, had vainly tried to treat Jean-François Champollion. Zoraïde was a seer. She knew that the night of 4 March 1832 would be the last one.

Taking no heed of the physicians' orders, she sneaked into the dying man's bedroom.

'Dad . . . are you sleeping?'

Jean-François Champollion opened his eyes. 'Come . . . come here quickly!'

Zoraïde ran to the bed and threw herself into her father's arms. For a long time she wept, her face on his chest.

'Bring me my Egyptian clothes,' he said in a very faint voice.

Zoraïde hurried to open the wardrobe in which her father kept his souvenirs from the Orient, long many-coloured robes, turbans and sandals. In her haste she knocked over a pile of notebooks covered with a thin and quick handwriting.

'Dad, I also found that!'

With a trembling hand, Champollion opened the notebook his daughter was handing him. It contained the first notes he had taken in Egypt, during the trip which had been the climax of his life.

'Dad . . . why did you never tell me?'

'Tell you what . . . do you mean . . . about there?'

'Yes, there, your true home. I want you to tell me everything. Everything you never told me.'

Pain made Champollion shudder. Zoraïde kissed his hands.

'I won't refuse you anything . . . put your head on my shoulder.'

Zoraïde obeyed. It was good to obey her father, whose soft voice began to tell her about a most remarkable journey.

1

'Monsieur Jean-François Champollion, I presume?'

'Himself. Happy to meet you, Commander.'

Cosmao Dumanoir, the commander of the corvette *Eglé*, was a man of average height with a pleasant smile. He had a smooth and perfectly shaven face, and the buttons of his uniform had been polished with the utmost care. He welcomed me on board his ship with real warmth.

On that very day, 24 July 1828, as the last fiery glow of sunset inflamed the Mediterranean, the voyage I had been longing to take for so long was at last opening before me: we set course for Egypt.

Maybe the journey would put me in touch with something I was meant to know, some message. Maybe the ancient wisdom of the Egyptians would be passed to me. I was on my way to just these mysteries. I had begun to decipher hieroglyphs, the words of the gods, full of magic. But an essential key was still missing; only in Egypt would I be able to find it. I would have to check my intuitions step by step and to ask the land of the Pharaohs for missing answers. After months and months of administrative worries, I had at last succeeded in setting up an expedition which would include several scientists. Together we would reach Alexandria on board the *Eglé*.

'Would you be kind enough to follow me, Monsieur Champollion?'

As I walked along the gangway of the corvette, I felt that I was reaching a point of no return. I was now to be tested to my limits and to risk my life in the unknown Orient. My life has been a constant struggle. To get the slightest thing, I have had to fight, to defend myself every inch of the way, to thwart manoeuvres, and to face calumny. Unwittingly I trigger the jealousy of people who cannot do anything or are incompetent and who then reproach me for wanting to go too far, too quickly. I have never had any protection from slandering tongues. I am like a trout alive into a pan. But I was so happy to be far away from Paris already! The air of the town undermines me. There I am like someone who has rabies; I lose my strength. Paris is horrible. Rivers of mud flow along the streets.

With the somewhat stiff elegance of men ageing under uniform, Captain Cosmao Dumanoir led me to my cabin, where he offered me champagne. The fleeting joy flickering in the liquid was unable to clear away the anxieties which had been weighing down on me during the whole journey from Aix to Toulon.

I could not stop thinking of the two dissimilar letters which had reached me in a most mysterious way and which I had hidden under my scientific notes. The first had made quite serious threats:

'Forget about your plans and stay at home. Otherwise, death awaits you in Egypt.'

Although enigmatic, the second one sounded more encouraging:

'We are waiting for you. If you have really deciphered the language of the gods, we will know how to welcome you.'

Who were they? Lunatics? Cranks? I have met so many of them, ever since the winter morning in Figeac when as a child I first laid eyes on Egyptian hieroglyphs, on this new world which teemed with rich symbols and signs of eternal life. I immediately knew it was my soul's motherland and that one day I would come to know my destiny by deciphering these

4

enigmas, words lost for many centuries. Ancient Egypt is my blood. It is my heart. It demands everything from me.

The essentials of my discoveries were in a little black case for valuables. Part of me wanted to flee. But the mere touch of the modest object and the feel of the pages where the best part of my life has been written dissuaded me from doing so. Egypt triumphed and will always triumph.

As soon as I arrived, I would go to the office of the Institute of Egypt. There, there was an old scientist, who let people call him 'the Prophet' and who had all the documents essential to my research. He had never wanted to show them to anyone before. But as he heard about my expedition, he let me know that he was waiting for me in order to give me the missing link in my research.

A woman of haughty elegance and hair of an almost unreal strawberry blond tint entered the captain's cabin. Her pale complexion enhanced a pearl grey dress shimmering from the play of light on it. Large light-green eyes lit up a face whose beauty I would describe as Egyptian. Long thin hands reminded me of drawings of queens I had saved as I had created the Pharaonic Department of the Louvre Museum, of which I had been graciously appointed unpaid curator. Aged some thirty years, the woman possessed an innate and slightly strange distinction.

'May I introduce Lady Redgrave?' said Commander Dumanoir. 'She will travel with us to Alexandria.'

I had an instinctive hatred for society life. Yet nobody ever forced me to take part in it. Driven by an impulse which surprised me, I nevertheless bowed to kiss the hand of this British aristocrat, who greeted my submission with an enigmatic smile.

'I've heard a lot about you, Monsieur Champollion.' She said in a soft sunny voice, enhanced by a slight accent. 'There is a lot of talk about you in London. My fellow countryman, Thomas Young, boasts of having deciphered hieroglyphs before you and pretends that your own system is completely erroneous.' Ill at ease, Commander Dumanoir looked at the sea. My heart missed a beat.

Thomas Young . . . a hypocritical and conceited fellow, who knew neither the ancient Egyptian language, nor Malay or even Manchu, which he taught. The discoveries he announced so pompously were just ridiculous bragging. His key to hieroglyphs had aroused my commiseration. I pitied the unfortunate travellers who would be forced to translate inscriptions in Egypt with Thomas Young's guidebook in their hands!

'I have some esteem for Mr Young, Madame, and I do not like to criticize a colleague, whatever his behaviour towards me might be. If you know him well enough, perhaps you could advise him to change profession.

'I know him well enough,' she retorted, amused. 'Thomas Young is my uncle. We will see each other again later . . .'

Staggered, I watched her leave the cabin before I could formulate a reply. It had always been like this: I was so sensitive that I felt slighted at almost any comment about my profession.

'This . . . this is a trap,' I said at last, calling Commander Dumanoir to bear witness to what had gone on.

'Calm down,' recommended the good man, who was as upset as me. 'You will soon forget the incident.'

'Thomas Young is my worst enemy,' I explained, somewhat out of breath. 'He has been persecuting me for years, fiddling with scientific papers and resorting to any means to end my work. The woman is a spy.'

Commander was deep in thought. He tried to comfort me. 'She is alone, Monsieur Champollion. And she is only a woman. You are surrounded by collaborators who will be extremely devoted to you. I am convinced that you are not at risk. This is simply a manoeuvre to intimidate you.'

Devoted collaborators . . . I was far less optimistic than the commander.

'Have the gentlemen arrived?'

'Not yet,' answered Dumanoir. 'I am expecting them in the evening.'

I felt a lump in my throat. My stomach ached. My legs were trembling. The appearance of this she-devil on the corvette taking me to ultimate goal of my life seemed like a very sinister omen. Perhaps I should give up the journey, postpone it and take more precautions.

I was shattered. The elation I had experienced as I reached Toulon turned into a kind of despair that brought tears to my eyes. My endeavour seemed doomed before it had even started.

'I intend to take you to Egypt, whatever the obstacles,' said Dumanoir. 'You can rely on me.'

'What obstacles?' I enquired.

'Our corvette,' he answered, 'is meant to escort trade vessels. But it won't be convoying anyone during your trip. People are just not taking to the sea, not because there is any danger of losing people or goods, but because trade with Egypt is in a state of complete torpor. Egypt itself is not sending any more cotton wool. So I insist,' he said as he laid his hand on my left shoulder, 'that you can rely on me.'

Seldom had I met such a display of kindness. Cosmao Dumanoir really sympathized with my distress. But his help was of no use to me. It did not rid me of the presence of the intriguer and spy.

'You should rest,' he suggested.

Hardly had he uttered these words when someone knocked at the door. It was a sailor.

'A doctor wants to see Monsieur Champollion,' he announced.

'A doctor?' I asked, most surprised. 'What does he want from me?'

The sailor opened his arms to indicate that he did not know anything. Irritated by this new mystery, I followed him.

At the bottom of the gangway a man in a black frock coat was waiting for me. Small, badly shaven, with a pointed nose

7

and a nasty look, he looked a nasty piece of work. I was immediately repelled by him.

'Are you Monsieur Champollion?'

'Yes, I am.'

His voice was as shrill as that of a nervous young girl. He stole a glance at me. 'I have an important piece of news to deliver to you.'

'Please tell me.'

He took his time, as if to enjoy his revelation better. 'Monsieur Champollion, your expedition has been cancelled.'

2

I looked at the little black-clad man with astonishment mingled with anger. 'What do you mean?'

'The plague is spreading to all the towns in the south, Monsieur Champollion. Quarantine must be declared everywhere. If you leave today, you will be condemned to stay at sea. No harbour will accept you.'

A fit of laughter shook my body. The man I had initially considered as a demon now only appeared as a ridiculous little devil.

'You spend too much time reading newspapers, Doctor!' I exclaimed passionately. 'They treat their readers like idiots. Of course people die by the hundred in Marseilles as well as here! But I think that your mind confuses physical plague with the moral plague affecting our country.'

I had already turned on my heels when he jumped at me, like a spider running on its cobweb, and grasped my arm.

'One moment, Champollion! You are expecting scientists from Tuscany . . . I have already set up a quarantine line around Toulon. Regiments man all routes from the Alps. Letters and newspapers from France are slashed and sprayed with vinegar. Your friends won't be able to pass the road-blocks. If the captain of this corvette is mad enough to go at sea, you will be his sole passenger.'

'Monsieur,' I told him fiercely, 'you are a liar. The epidemic has been invented by doctors who want to become famous. I urge you to let the Italian members of my expedition, Rosellini and Professor Raddi, board this ship.'

The demon grinned unpleasantly and took out a bunch of papers.

'These reports denounce you as a political agitator, Champollion! They are not mistaken. Nobody is above the law. The quarantine won't be suspended before the epidemic is completely extinguished. This will take two or three months, I suppose . . .'

I would undoubtedly have strangled him, had not my attention been drawn to a strange performance taking place on the quay. A priest wearing a cassock worthy of archaeological remains was harassing a loaded mule with a stick. I recognized Father Bidant, a paunchy and almost bald man of the Church, who was also passionately interested in orientalism. His natural lethargy concealed a lively and astute mind. He had been commissioned by the ecclesiastical authorities to make sure that my expedition would not transgress the boundaries of religion. They were afraid that biblical chronology might be questioned by disturbing discoveries in Egypt.

Behind the panting Father Bidant stood the great figure of Nestor L'Hôte, a talented draughtsman who was well used to sketching hieroglyphs. A fierce, strong fellow, he was unyielding and hot tempered, but I relied on him to copy the inscriptions with the necessary skill.

'Here we are at last!' exclaimed Father Bidant, as he jostled the black devil aside, to greet me. 'Do you know that we have been called plague victims? I pushed aside a bunch of rascals with my stick and a letter from the archbishop.'

'Who is this man?' asked Nestor L'Hôte in his impressive bass voice as he stared at the little doctor.

'A doctor who wants to keep us on the quay,' I answered.

'Clear off!' bellowed L'Hôte brandishing his fist.

The little devil did not hesitate. Grumbling confused threats, he scuttled backwards and fled without further ado.

'You look worried, Champollion,' said Nestor L'Hôte, with his fists on his hips.

'I have my reasons. The quarantine line may cut off our expedition from its Tuscan members, Rosellini and Raddi. Without them, we won't be able to keep to our work plan.'

'Place your trust in God,' whispered Father Bidant. 'If our cause is fair, he will come to our help.'

The priest was challenging me. He had undoubtedly heard whispers about my lukewarm devotion to the God of the Christians. I had been nicknamed 'the Egyptian' by my family, scientist and gossip columnists, who considered that my true motherland was the land of the pharaohs and that my faith was an enthusiastic and sincere belief in the gods of Thebes.

As I looked at the sea, beyond which was the land of the pharaohs, I had to admit that they were right.

Commander Dumanoir read the letter once more. It was from Drovetti, the Consul-General of France in Egypt, and it had been brought two days before by a courier from Paris. Drovetti expressed extreme reservations about the timing of my expedition. He even advocated an immediate return to Paris, for he was unable to guarantee my security in Egypt. Mehmet Ali, the all-powerful pasha ruling Cairo, was largely influenced by counsellors who hated Europeans. He would therefore certainly view the arrival of a hieroglyph decipherer unfavourably.

Should he warn me of the dangers awaiting me or not? Such a letter would have turned my discouragement into despair. I would probably have given up the trip for good rather than put the life of members of my expedition at risk.

But Cosmao Dumanoir cared about neither the Pasha nor the pharaohs. He could not give up the voyage, for it would be his last trip as corvette captain. His body was worn out by an illness which left him only a few months to live. His sole wish was to pass away on board his ship, on the open sea or in an oriental haven, far away from Europe, where he had no more connections. The Orient, the source of light . . . there Cosmao Dumanoir hoped that his fading life would find an afterlife.

Fate would decide. As might be expected with Consul-General Drovetti another official letter came, this time cancelling the expedition altogether, with a definite prohibition to embark. Fortunately, communications between Paris and Toulon were extremely slow, even though the Minister of the Interior would have used day and night mail, reserved for the government, to get in touch with Champollion before the possible departure of the *Eglé*. The journey depended on the speed of mail, the strength of winds and the arrival of my Italian collaborators.

In his letter, Drovetti mentioned serious troubles in Alexandria and in Cairo. The Pasha was threatened by virulent members of the opposition. If Egypt's largest cities were to erupt in rebellion and sedition, the blood of Europeans would be the first to be shed. But could he have exaggerated the seriousness of the situation, so as to prevent me from reaching Egypt and discovering what he was up to? Sailors had confided in Dumanoir that Drovetti was a trafficker of antiquities, who did not hesitate to abuse his authority to add to trade vessels' cargoes, statues, steles and papyri stolen in archaeological digs. The treasure went through Europe, where he would find them again one day. I, on the other hand, was regarded as an honest man, not open to financial manipulations and very keen on preserving the artistic heritage of ancient Egypt. If rumours about Drovetti turned out to be accurate, I might become a nuisance.

I had been a prisoner in Toulon for several days. The two had become unbearable. The corvette was moored at a quay, like a bird in a cage. The quarantine line had been reinforced, although no case of plague had been identified with certainty. I walked for hours, played chess with Father Bidant, who handled his bishops with unusual cleverness. Nestor L'Hôte now knew the harbour taverns, not because he was keen on drink, but because he liked to meet people. He was curious about everything. I did not see the beautiful British 'spy' again, as she had withdrawn to her cabin, where her meals were brought to her.

The sky had clouded over since the dawn of 31 July, and the wind raised a few waves. It was impossible to put pen to paper. Writing was usually a deep joy, a moment suspended between time and eternity. But I felt pangs of anguish. If I did not head for Egypt, I believed that my life would be deprived of its meaning and that I would be a man lost to himself and to other people.

Cosmao Dumanoir entered the small dining room, where I was savouring a hot black coffee. He looked haggard. 'If we do not cast off this morning, Monsieur Champollion, I am afraid our journey may be definitively in jeopardy.'

The captain of the *Eglé* was right. Refusing to accept the facts, I had not wanted to believe that the quarantine line would prevent the Tuscans from reaching the corvette. But they were only scientists, helpless in the face of administrative measures.

A sailor burst in. 'A strange man is asking for Monsieur Champollion.'

I was about to follow him to the gangway, but he gestured towards the sea. As I bent over the rail, I saw a rowing boat full of boxes. In the front sat Professor Raddi, clumsily handling the oars, his face tanned like an old herbarium, his beard neglected like an autumn garden, a magnifying glass in the pocket of his jacket and two pairs of spectacles on his nose.

'Champollion!' he shouted as he saw me. 'We are here!'

'Where is Rosellini?'

'Hidden behind my boxes of minerals. We had to come by sea so as to avoid a bunch of madmen who called us plague victims.'

Loading the scientific material Professor Raddi considered essential to his work took two good hours. He was as small and plump as Rosellini was lean and tall. Raddi himself oversaw the transportation of his precious boxes, while my student Rosellini, to whom I had taught the principles of decipherment, stepped towards me, deeply concerned.

'Master . . . we must weigh anchor immediately.'

My Italian disciple was not a man to be easily moved. Cold, distant and reflective, he would soon become a great scientist who would do honour to budding Egyptology. For the time being, though he seemed distressed.

'I received a letter from Consul-General Drovetti saying that our expedition would be cancelled. Disappointed by her failure to conquer Greece, Turkey is intent on declaring war on the Russians and drawing Egypt into the conflict. Therefore our security cannot be ensured any more.'

'Nonsense,' I said with composure, as if I could exert the slightest influence on the policy of the lunatics I hated. 'Are you prepared to follow me, whatever the risks might be?'

The joy on Rosellini's face was the most reassuring of answers. But my disciple immediately became gloomy. 'Did a written order from Paris reach you?'

'Let's leave quickly!'

I became impassioned to the point of assisting the sailors who were loading the mineralogist's boxes. Initially hesitant, Rosellini followed suit. Only two happy to be able to use his physical strength, Nestor L'Hôte joined in.

Noon was ringing from the church towers of Toulon when, taking advantage of favourable winds, the *Eglé* weighed anchor for the Orient. The westerly breeze which cooled the air would bring us to open sea in less than an hour. I let the powerful fragrances coming from the sea waft over me. Then I saw a mounted courier arriving on the jetty at full gallop. A minute figure he called to us, brandishing a document.

This was Minister Martignac's letter warning the prefect of Toulon that our expedition would not be able to take place because of international circumstances.

I waved him goodbye.

I felt sorry for the French government, but 'the Egyptian' had just set course for another world, his true homeland.

3

Because of the presence of the 'spy', Commander Dumanoir had modified the ship's sleeping quarters. He insisted that I take his cabin, and my disciple Rosellini, Professor Raddi and Father Bidant slept on mattress at my feet. A man who was keen on his sleep, it was quite painful for the latter to bestir himself at any time from his natural apathy. Raddi spent his days and a large part of his nights looking through a magnifying glass at schists, basalt and granite so as to be prepared for the desert minerals from which he hoped to obtain a bountiful harvest.

Usually the utmost calm prevailed on the ship. I worked on hieroglyphs with L'Hôte and Rosellini, who progressed quickly. Their drawing acquired a firmness of outline essential to the recording of inscriptions. They freely reproduced heads, vases, owls, lions, doors. Thanks to them the old tongue came to life again. Father Bidant tried to distract Professor Raddi from his mineral universe to play chess, but seldom succeeded.

Sometimes I felt a lump in my throat at the thought that we were getting nearer to Egypt. I leaned on a rail to watch the sky and the sea. The scene was enlivened by porpoises and the heavy appearance of two sperm whales.

True harmony prevailed between us. We formed a real expeditionary body, endowed with the clan spirit essential to face the ordeals awaiting us. Nestor L'Hôte called me 'the general', declaring that his companions and he would receive orders only from me.

As we were passing the coast of Sardinia, however, pushed by a strong wind, the usually quiet Professor Raddi burst out angrily. 'This is intolerable! I can't take it any longer! I must go back to Florence immediately!'

The worthy mineralogist seemed possessed by the devil, to such an extent that, Father Bidant traced the sign of the cross in the air. Nestor L'Hôte attempted to approach him, but was rebuked with a violence unexpected in a man of his quality. I concluded that 'the general' had to intervene to restore calm among his troop.

'What is the matter, Professor?'

'Ah, Champollion . . . if you only knew . . . I must confess to the worst of crimes . . .'

Raddi's fury had suddenly turned to despair. He agreed to sit down. Father Bidant, L'Hôte and Rosellini left the cabin silently. The time had come for confession.

'Oh my God, my study, my museum,' he lamented, taking a key out of his pocket.

'My study . . . I closed the door with three turns of the key, but I left the windows open! Do you realize, Champollion, that my wife is going to enter this sanctuary, from which she has always been banned! I am sure that she will desecrate it . . . She only dreams of feather dusters and brooms. I must go back home and prevent such a disaster. And what about theft? My collections will be plundered!'

'And what about Egypt, Professor? Have you thought about it?'

My question surprised Raddi and interrupted his flow.

'Egypt . . . yes, I want to see its deserts . . . there are invaluable treasures there! But I cannot . . . I must go back to close the windows myself.'

I calmed the professor down. A complaining Raddi would soon irritate everyone and turn our daily life into hell.

'Believe me, Professor, the Egyptian gods will look after us. Your museum and your collections are in no danger.'

I saw a gleam of trust light up his gaze.

'Tell me Professor . . . Apart from the boxes of scientific material, have you thought of taking a few clothes?'

'Clothes? Of course. I am wearing them. This Nanking costume and strong walking shoes. Add to that a large-brimmed straw hat and you know my whole wardrobe. Don't you think it is perfect?'

At dawn on 19 August, I was alone on the deck of the corvette, a telescope in my hand. In the distance, I could make out Pompey's Pillar.

We were reaching Alexandria, at last.

I could see the Old Harbour and the town, which grew ever more impressive, a huge forest of buildings through which showed white houses.

I had already forgotten the furious storm which had spread panic among my collaborators. The wind had blown so strongly that we could not hear each other. I had not been afraid; dying at sea seemed both improper and impossible.

Egypt . . . Egypt, after so many years of dreams and hopes. Jacquou, the sorcerer who had acted as midwife at my birth on 23 December, had promised my parents that their son would have an outstanding destiny. Yet my childhood had not been so joyful. I had seen the follies of the Revolution in Figeac, violence, weapons, blood, gangs of people howling the song the 'Carmagnole', people in fear fleeing and taking refuge in my father's bookshop, a treasure trove he never allowed me to enter. Yet books became my friends and confidents. I learned to read on my own, letter after letter, word after word. My best childhood memory is the heat of the large fireplace in the kitchen. I used to curl up near the hearth, a book in my hand, till I was filled by a wonderful feeling of well-being, so far away from the coldness and the grey sky. In the fire I saw the Egyptian sun.

It was so cold at the *lycée* in Grenoble! But at night, while my companions slept, I read Plutarch's biographies of famous men: emperors, rulers, all those who had carried the weight of the world on their shoulders. I wanted to know more about them. I cut out medallions in cardboard and drew their portraits, adding the dates of their birth and death. In this way I built my own gallery of famous people. As a pupil, this collection was my greatest source of pride.

As a student aged seventeen, I was able to present a study of the geography of Egypt to the Society of Arts and Sciences of Grenoble. When I was appointed a professor at the Faculty of Humanities in Grenoble at the age of twenty-one, I believed that the future would smile at me. But I had to go to Paris, to beg vainly for a position in the newly fashionable science, then come back to Grenoble to teach history with a salary just a quarter of what my colleagues earned. Then my brother and I were outlawed and put under house arrest in Figeac because we had supported Napoleon. I was twenty-six and I despaired of getting to know Egypt.

Yet I continued to fight, to search and to convince myself that I was on the right path, that I had to make this trip.

We arrived in Alexandria at sunrise, after nineteen days at sea. I did not sleep, so highly strung was I at the prospect of touching the land of Egypt at last. My good fortune had triumphed over bad luck. Like a child, I waved to the Tower of the Arabs, which marked the location of ancient Taposiris, the city which had taken up so many hours of my research when I wrote my first book, *L'Egypte sous les pharaons*.

'Are you satisfied, Monsieur Champollion?'

Cosmao Dumanoir had approached, silently. Freshly shaven, impeccable, he seemed in a confident mood. A half-smile on his lips, he seemed immune to the problems of the outside world.

'Beyond my expectations, Commander.'

'You will need a little more patience before you are able to tread on Egyptian soil.'

'Why?'

'The Europeans have imposed a blockade on Alexandria. We will enter the Old Harbour in the west. The manoeuvre won't be easy, for lots of French and British warships hamper the way in.'

The brisk morning air suddenly seemed icy. 'What are you hiding from me, Commander? Have you received bad news?'

Cosmao Dumanoir hesitated for a moment. 'Egyptian troops should soon come back from Greece,' he explained. 'They are even being allowed to bring back their spoils of war.'

'But this is marvellous! This means that French and Egyptian troops are not fighting any more in the Peloponnese! This is peace, Commander. The Pasha will welcome us with open arms.'

'That's what I hope, Monsieur Champollion, but the present situation is not to everyone's liking. The opposition blames the Pasha for his decisions. The blockade ensures that order is maintained in Alexandria. But it won't last forever. And I do not know what is happening in Cairo.'

'I'm confident, Captain.'

'I envy you.'

An expression of infinite sadness abruptly aged Cosmao Dumanoir's face by several years. I felt like encouraging him, but under the pretext that his presence was essential to run the docking procedure, he put an end to our conversation.

At the entrance to the narrows, the corvette fired a blank to greet the arrival on board of an Arab pilot. He guided us through the shoals and brought us safely to the Old Harbour. There we found ourselves surrounded by French, British, Egyptian, Turkish and Algerian vessels. The background to the chaotic scene was provided by the hulks, Oriental ships which had survived the disaster of Pylos. Everything was peaceful around us. But we were not able to drop anchor until 5 p.m.

Leaning on the rail, my companions looked curiously at the city of Alexander the Great which was about to welcome us. *Alexandria ad Aegyptum* said the ancient occupants, meaning that the city, with its Greek origin, was separate from the country.

I felt a lump in my throat and had difficulty breathing. To me, Alexandria was the edge of paradise. I was experiencing a second birth. I had the feeling that I was at last finding my true homeland after a long exile.

'A rowing boat is heading for us,' said Nestor L'Hôte.

A few moments later a small man dressed in black climbed on board. I thought he was the doctor from Toulon who had tried to keep the corvette at quay.

'I have been sent by Consul-General Drovetti,' he announced, 'to deliver a letter to Monsieur Champollion.'

The letter contained a special permit to disembark despite the blockade and the quarantine imposed because of a typhus epidemic. I did not consider it necessary to pass the information on to my companions, as I did not want to worry them without reason.

'We will follow you,' I said.

As my companions followed close on my heels, ready to board the rowing boat with me, Cosmao Dumanoir intervened. 'I think that Monsieur Champollion deserves to be the first to disembark, and that he will want to be alone.'

'You are right, Commander,' agreed Rosellini.

'May the general enter Egypt first as our scout,' joked Nestor L'Hôte.

'The Egyptian actually deserves the honour,' acknowledged Father Bidant in his turn.

Professeur Raddi stood aside, examining a piece of rock from Vesuvius.

Tears came to my eyes. My heart was pounding wildly. I had great difficulty to express myself. 'I am thankful to you . . . I—'

'Go ahead, General,' said Nestor L'Hôte. 'We are also impatient to know this land.'

Dumanoir gave me a strange look. I felt that he wanted to impart a last thought before our ways parted forever. The man to whom I was indebted for having helped me to cross the huge channel separating Toulon from Alexandria without mishap had become a friend. But there may already have been traces of death on his tired face.

'Farewell, Monsieur Champollion,' he said, shaking my hand warmly.

Standing in the boat as it slowly made its way to the quay, I confess that I forgot Cosmao Dumanoir, my companions and the corvette *Eglé*. I had been anticipating this moment with suppressed desire for so many years.

The rowing boat came alongside the quay. A sailor seized my arm to help me to climb on to the pier. I could not refrain from kneeling, and kissing and blessing the ground which fostered the greatest sages of history and the birth of a civilization to which we Europeans are heirs.

The description I had read of the town gave no real idea of what it was like. To us it was like a vision from the antipodes, a new world: narrow corridors fringed by little shops, swarming with coloured men and sleepy dogs, raucous shots arising from everywhere, mingling with the squalling voices of women, a suffocating dust and here and there magnificently dressed lords on richly harnessed horses.

We progressed as best we could in the milling crowd to the palace of the Consul-General. I walked immediately behind the Arab guide, who had to open a way for us through the human jumble of men with turbans, half-naked children clinging to our clothes, veiled women clad in long black dresses. Camels loaded with baskets full of food jostled the strollers. We passed a kiosk with jagged woodwork where three musicians played a song as heady as the heavy fragrances of rose and jasmine pervaded our clothes and concealed less sweet smells arising from the drains in the ground. Here and there at the bend of a lane minarets rose up. We progressed under arcades which sheltered us from the rays of the sun. The heat was tempered by gusts of air from the Mediterranean. Nestor L'Hôte walked beside me. Rosellini, Father Bidant and Professor Raddi had some difficulty in following the speed of our guide, who seemed in a hurry to be rid of us. It did not seem to suit him to be seen in the company of strangers.

There was the sound of galloping. Ahead of me, the crowd moved aside with astonishing speed. I saw a bearded figure with a turban low on his forehead, mounted on a donkey, charging at me. I remained stupidly glued to the spot, the steaming nose of the animal getting nearer at high speed.

Nestor L'Hôte seized my waist and pushed me out of the way, as the donkey continued to cleave its way through the crowd and disappeared in a great chorus of indignation.

'You had a narrow escape, General.'

'Let's not exaggerate,' I retorted, with false tranquillity. 'But I am grateful for your help. What about our companions?'

The priest and the two scientists had had better reflexes than mine, flattening themselves against the façades of the houses so as to avoid being trodden on. The Arab guide came to me and spoke in a broken French. 'Not injured?'

'Let's move on. I am impatient to meet the Consul-General.'

I carried with me the two mysterious letters which had reached me before my departure to Egypt. Was the incident an attack in disguise? Was my imagination beginning to run away with me?

The palace of the Consul-General was an ostentatious construction in the centre of a garden planted with palm trees. The façade, which was pierced by a door crowned with a chiselled rainbow, was embellished with a broad beam supporting a loggia with closed shutters. On the threshold knelt two gardeners.

I walked in. A steward in a white *galabieh* invited me to follow him and asked my companions to wait in a hall with stone seats. He took me to the large study of Bernardino Drovetti, the Consul-General of France.

Aged fifty-three he had been born in Leghorn and was a naturalized Frenchman. He had taken part in Bonaparte's expedition to Egypt. A barrister, a high-ranking officer and a diplomat, he was regarded as one of the most influential characters in the country. Weaving his web in the shadow, he was said to rule a huge traffic in antiquities. Some people thought that he was waiting to retire until he made his fortune. I was not in the habit of judging people from stories. I suffered too much from public rumours myself.

Drovetti sat at his desk, his hands crossed in front of him, like a judge about to pass sentence. The man was impressive: a high forehead, thick brown curly hair, bushy eyebrows, black eyes, protruding cheekbones, a straight and pointed nose and thick long moustache ending in curls.

'Sit down, Champollion, and listen carefully to me,' he ordered with the harsh voice of a man used to giving orders and being obeyed.

I remained standing, challenging him with my gaze, although I had every reason to fear him. Only he could give me the necessary permission to visit archaeological sites and buy artefacts to enlarge the Louvre collection. Drovetti could limit my expedition to a brief stroll.

'Your arrival is untimely, Champollion. The political situation is confused. I asked Paris to send an order to cancel your journey to Toulon. I suppose you did not receive it.'

The question was scathing, contrasting with the luxurious and cosy appearance of the spacious room which was in the Oriental style, with richly coloured carpets and low seats.

'Your supposition is right, sir. It was written up there that I would see Egypt this year.'

Anger coloured his cheeks, and he contained himself with difficulty. 'Well you have made your bed, so you will have to lie on it. If war breaks out between the Russians and the Turks, Egypt will be drawn into the conflict and I won't be able to guarantee your security any more. You and the members of your expedition will then face the greatest risks.'

I bowed my head. Drovetti believed in my submission.

'I can see that you are a reasonable man, Champollion. You will reside in Alexandria until the blockade is lifted, then you will go back to France. Be sure that I shall look after your comfort personally.' Judging that our meeting was over, he stood up.

'Alexandria is only a stopover for me, sir. It is my life's aim to explore Egypt. No war will prevent me from fulfilling my destiny, be it at the cost of my life.'

Drovetti was not lacking in intelligence. The strength of my determination did not escape him. He settled himself comfortably in his armchair again. He had a motive for inflicting the worst trouble on me. I had succeeded in exhibiting in the Louvre part of Salt's collection. He was the Consul-General of Great Britain and a great enemy of Drovetti. Jomard and the Earl of Forbin, the General Managers of the Museums, had done everything they could to prevent me from becoming a curator. But despite that, on 15 December 1827, I had opened the Egyptian gallery of the Charles X Museum.

'Are you a personal friend of Henry Salt, Champollion?'

'I do not even know him.'

'That's all the better for you. He will never be of any use to anyone any more. He is dead. Thorough knowledge of antiquities is a difficult art. An amateur would run the risk of spoiling the profession.'

'This is why my expedition is only composed of professionals, sir.'

'What do you want to see in Egypt?'

'The monuments of the Delta—'

'That's perfect, Champollion. I shall have the necessary permits prepared.'

'I shall need permits for the region of Thebes and Nubia,' I added quietly.

My nerves were at breaking point. I was playing for high stakes with a powerful adversary. Had he been able to read me, he would have seen how weak and emotional I felt. But an unyielding force drove me to face the obstacle. Had I not on my side my best ally, Egypt?

'Why Thebes?'

'It is the core of Egypt. I hope to start there the most significant project of archaeological digs ever initiated.'

'With what money?'

'With the money you will give me, sir. Being on an official mission, I rely on the financial help it is your duty to give me.'

'Of course . . . but this will take some time. The money will reach you in Thebes when you are ready to dig. Do you expect anything else?'

'Your trust. I am a researcher come here to check my theories on the spot and to fulfil a childhood dream. To be able to revive the civilization of the pharaohs would be a fitting reward.'

It was Drovetti's turn to bow his head slightly. I waited anxiously for the result of his reflection.

'You will stay here tonight, Champollion, in the very room where Kléber, the conqueror of Heliopolis, slept. My palace served as headquarters for Napoleon's army. You've won my protection. I like idealists.'

'One final detail . . . I would like to go immediately to the Egyptian Institute to meet an old scientist.'

'Is it the Prophet?'

'Yes it is.'

'Spare yourself the trip, Champollion. The office in which he worked has just burnt down. The papers he accumulated there have been destroyed and he died in the fire.'

The Consul-General handed me a permit in Arabic. 'Be cautious, Champollion. Egypt is a dangerous country.'

Bernardino Drovetti looked at the eccentric Monsieur Champollion, whose fierce determination had surprised and worried him, as he left his office. Was he just a scientist? A crank? Or a spy sent by the French government to discover the nature of the trade to which the Consul-General had been dedicating himself over the last few years? It was difficult to assess the threat he represented. It was out of question to take the slightest risk when he was so close to his aim.

He rang a bell. The steward in the white *galabieh* appeared almost immediately.

'Never leave by so much as a single inch the man I have just received. You will have his slightest actions reported to me. Let nothing escape you and tell your friend to be doubly watchful.'

4

I had put on my most elegant clothes after a troubled night in the bedroom once occupied by the great Kléber. Drovetti had invited me to dinner and we had talked about France, Napoleon and Egyptian art. Then the Consul-General had told me that a meeting with the Pasha would be essential to confirm my freedom of movement in Egypt. He himself was too busy to take me to him, however. He entrusted the mission to his steward, Moktar. On Sunday, 24 August, at 7 a.m., I sat in the antechamber of the palace of the Pasha in the ancient island of Pharos, waiting for an audience.

It was deliciously cool in the huge building, with a ceiling so high that my gaze became lost in the impressive sculpted mosaic sky.

I was almost desperate. 'The Prophet', on whom I had relied to guide me, had disappeared. I found myself alone in this unknown land, like an abandoned child. I had to rely on my resources alone. Would they be sufficient to take me to the end of my quest? Would Egypt consent to answer the questions which were burning my soul?

A grey-haired man sat down beside me. Elegant and aristocratic, he talked in a low voice as if he were afraid people might surprise us. My mentor, Moktar, had vanished.

'I have little time to talk to you, Monsieur Champollion. My name is Anastasy.'

'You . . .'

My surprise was genuine. A diplomat of Armenian extraction, Anastasy represented Sweden in Egypt. A true Croesus, he owned a good half of the Alexandria merchant fleet, but he was mainly regarded as a great collector. The Netherlands had bought a number of magnificent artefacts from him.

'I know your projects, Monsieur Champollion. As a personal friend of Mehmet Ali who does not consider it beneath him to resort to my financial expertise, I intervened personally in your favour. But it is impossible to know if the Pasha is well disposed towards you.'

Anastasy was being very modest. He actually held several ministers in his power and steadily bailed out the Pasha's coffers in exchange for the setting up of archaeological digs on privileged sites he had been able to spot with unfailing intuition.

'How can I express my gratitude, Your Excellency, but why . . .?'

'We share the same passion, Monsieur Champollion, but you are much more qualified than I am for deciphering the mysteries of Egypt. Do not underestimate the dangers awaiting you. You should know that my greatest enemy is Consul-General Drovetti, who holds your administrative fate in his hands. I'm deeply shocked by the way he robs the country of its treasures. Beware of him, even though he seems to yield to your demands as a scientist. Drovetti is only interested in money and power. I am convinced that he is about to conclude a huge business coup whose true nature I cannot even guess at. Your arrival may cloud an issue he has been cleverly arranging for several months.'

I felt an instinctive and immediate trust for the man. His presence alone reassured me. He possessed the wonderful calm of upright people with minds devoid of felony. A question occurred to me.

'Your Excellency . . . did you by any chance send me a letter before my departure for Egypt?'

'Me? No. Not at all. Drovetti had declared that your journey had been cancelled and that you would never set foot on Egyptian soil.'

The long figure of Moktar appeared at the end of a corridor opening on to the great hall.

Anastasy stood up. 'Beware, Champollion,' he whispered.

He walked away with small steps, turning his back on me. A few minutes later, my mentor bowed to me. 'Mehmet Ali is expecting you.'

The Pasha received me in a small room crammed with divans and cushions. Light only filtered through the wire mesh covering a small window. On a low table with a pink-veined marble top, I saw a teapot and china cups. On both sides of the master of modern Egypt stood two impressive bodyguards, armed with sabres.

'Welcome, Monsieur Champollion,' said Mehmet Ali, separating the syllables. The Pasha was a kind of colossus with a good-natured appearance. But woe betide anyone who took him at face value. A waif born in Macedonia, Mehmet Ali had set his heart on Egypt, which the British had abandoned to the Turks. He had brushed aside the mediocre authority of small local potentates to impose his iron hand on a people which had been used to many occupations since the end of the pharaonic empire. He had driven away the Mamelukes and the Wahhabis and set himself up as a respected interlocutor of European powers. In Paris, diplomats described him as a tyrant and a cruel man. People praised his acute intelligence and his determination to keep his omnipotence.

He held a pipe inlaid with diamonds. In front of him was a ruby-red hookah covered with precious gems. His eyes had a lively and penetrating expression. A splendid white beard covered his chest. His face looked gloomy, almost taciturn.

'I am being slandered in Europe,' he said, as if he had read my thoughts. 'People accuse me of being impatient, of exploiting the people, imposing over-heavy taxes and putting policemen behind every *fellah*. How can I behave differently if I am to maintain order? I am obliged to be the only landlord, to have a monopoly in rice, wheat, dates and cow-dung fuel. Only in this way can I control and order the economy. Even loose women, wandering actors and crooks pay tribute to me for the great happiness of my people.'

A convulsive hiccup interrupted his words. This apparently unseemly behaviour was the result of a poisoning attempt Mehmet Ali had survived. The best doctors in Egypt had not succeeded in ridding him of it.

'I modernize the country,' he went on. 'Trade, industry, agriculture, I work on all fronts . . . Never have so many factories been built! Don't you agree with me?'

'I hope, Your Excellency, that the monuments of Egypt did not suffer too much from the essential progress you initiated.'

The Pasha smiled in his busy beard. 'Your expectations won't be disappointed,' he replied unctuously. 'I like old stones very much.'

Mehmet Ali offered the pharaohs' treasures to merchants and diplomats, for he cared little about the preservation of non-Muslim art. Did antiquities not serve to attract wealthy people who might pay him well to turn a blind eye to their traffic?

'I am very happy about that, Your Excellency. I rely on your benevolence to facilitate my work in this land I love so much.'

'Let's hope that no war with Russia disturbs the peace I am a guarantor of,' retorted the Pasha while we were being served tea.

'Everybody relies on your wisdom. You were enough of a philosopher to joke about your defeat in Pylos, in the Peloponnese, where the Egypto-Turkish fleet was annihilated by the French, the British and the Russians.'

I had dared to cut the viceroy to the quick, but it was better to uncover now the true disposition of his mind towards me. By reminding him of the bitter memory of the battle which had put an end to his dreams of expansion, I distanced myself from the crowd of flattering sycophants to expose myself as a man who cares for truth. The approach had often brought me disappointments and deep enmities, but I could think of no other way of dealing with him.

Mehmet Ali's chest was shaken by a huge, infectious laugh.

'You are a strange man, Champollion!' he exclaimed loudly. 'It is said that you know the meaning of the strange signs the Egyptians engraved on their monuments.'

'I need to check my theories on the spot.'

'I believe you have met Consul-General Drovetti.' His gaze became more piercing.

'Yes, indeed, Your Excellency. He gave me a permit and specified that you were the only one who could validate the document.'

I perceived both the pasha's satisfaction and his weakness. He had an immoderate veneration for power. Any challenge to his authority was the worst of crimes for him. On the contrary, praises gave him the most intense pleasure.

'I like France very much,' he said. 'The most intelligent people in Cairo go to Paris to study and they are well received there. Your Consul-General, Drovetti, is an outstanding man, who helped me to set Egypt on the right path again and to get rid of ambitious people who tried to create factions against me.'

His voice grew muffled. 'Do you know, Champollion, that a French merchant prevented me from starving when I was a child? He picked me up in a street in my village and fed me as if I were his son. He is now in the paradise of Allah. I swore to myself to help any French who needed any assistance.'

I believed in the Pasha's sincerity.

'I need your help. Besides your permission to visit the sites in Egypt and Nubia, I need ships, and money to pay the porters and servants who will assist the members of my expedition.'

'That is impossible.'

I was flabbergasted. The answer was inexplicable. 'Impossible? But why, Your Excellency?'

'I grant no more permission to dig to ordinary travellers. Consul-General Drovetti is intent on avoiding plundering.'

'But . . . I am no ordinary visitor,' I flared up, indifferent to the consequences of my attitude. 'My mission has an official character! King Charles X appointed me a curator of Egyptian monuments and I enjoy the prerogatives of representing the French government, if the preservation of national honour demands it. Such is the case here! I shall have to refer the matter to the King's ministers. I know that all the antiquities traders and traffickers trembled at the news of my arrival. A cabal was set up against me so as to deprive me of any permission and prevent me from digging. Things being what they are, I shall have to let the King know why I am prevented from fulfilling my mission. As you affront me, you actually challenge him!'

Mehmet Ali remained absolutely calm. 'What would you like?'

'Access to all the sites of ancient Egypt.'

'This is a reasonable requirement . . . my best *chaouiche*, Abdel-Razuk, will come with you. He is a first-class policeman. He will be useful to you in Upper Egypt to make sure that my authority is respected. There people are sometimes hostile to the Turks. There are still gangs of brigands who do not hesitate to rob travellers. Be cautious, Champollion.'

'I shall conform to your demands as well as to those of science,' I said in the Arabic dialect of Cairo.

Mehmet Ali looked at me with astonishment. He was highly surprised. 'Do you speak our language?'

'It is essential to have a good knowledge of Egypt.'

'Of course,' acknowledged the Pasha, without enthusiasm. 'Were peasants happy under the rule of the pharaohs?'

The unexpected question hid a trap. It did not matter; I could not bear to lie. 'I believe they were. But nature was sometimes cruel, so when the Nile floods were too high or too low, the Pharaoh, who owned the whole of Egypt, made up for the deficiencies of the river. The ancient Egyptians ate to their fill and enjoyed life. Isn't it an age-old longing?'

The Pasha ordered that mint tea be served again. But we did not have time to drink it.

A group of Bedouins, surrounded by soldiers, interrupted the audience. They rushed to the Pasha, knelt down and kissed the bottom of his dress. Then moving aside, they made way for three men carrying a young panther, a white gazelle and a small ostrich in their arms. With the utmost care, they dropped their presents at the bottom of the throne.

Mehmet Ali did not utter the slightest word of thinks. The soldiers brutally drove out the Bedouins, who kept bowing as they stepped back.

'May I share my greatest anxiety with you, Your Excellency?'

Mehmet Ali's gaze became gloomy. But he did not forbid me to go on.

'It is about Thebes, the city of the god Amon, the most beautiful town in the world . . . Has it been preserved from destruction? Were its temples properly looked after?'

The questions had been obsessing me for several months. Worrying rumours circulated about the plundering of ancient monuments. The mutilation of Thebes would have deprived the world of light.

'Be reassured, Champollion. I look after the region of Thebes with the utmost care. It is my most cherished province. You will find our old capital intact with all its splendours.'

'Thanks be given to Your Excellency,' I declared, although my concern had not been totally dispelled.

The happy outcome of my meeting with the Pasha had a most favourable effect on Drovetti's behaviour. The Consul-General invited my companions to his table and accommodated them in his palace. The corvette *Eglé* had raised anchor without leaving me a chance of seeing Captain Cosmao Dumanoir again.

'Preparations for your expedition will take several weeks,' Drovetti had said. Was it a diplomatic lie? An attempt to keep me in Alexandria under various pretexts? I was sunk in uncertainty. I knew the administration too well to be surprised at bureaucratic slowness, increased by the naturally slow pace of Oriental people. Did Drovetti and the Pasha really wish to hinder my journey? Had they after all, chosen simply to allay my suspicions with reassuring words?

Such gloomy thoughts crossed my mind as I looked at the 80-foot Pompey's Pillar rising above the south-western district of Alexandria at sunset. Examining the pedestal closely, I realized that it was composed of blocks from older monuments. I even managed to decipher the name of the famous Pharaoh Seti I, the father of Ramses II. Close by had stood the famous library of Alexandria, burnt by criminal hands.

The sea breeze whipped my face. An infinite sadness overwhelmed me. The isolated column, the remains of a lost word, became a symbol of failure. Desolating and desolate, Egypt had sunk into darkness. I might never know more than this meagre remnant built on the ruins of Alexandria to celebrate a Roman. It did not speak of eternity, but of downfall. The Egypt of the pharaohs, my Egypt, lay far away, very far away from the modern Alexandria deserted by Egyptian gods. I leaned with all my weight against Pompey's Pillar, in the hope of seeing it collapse and put an end to my dream.

'What are you thinking about, Monsieur Champollion?'

Lady Ophelia Redgrave, in a yellow muslin dress with silvery facings, stood in the orange light of the sunset. I could hardly distinguish her face, suffused as it was with an ethereal luminosity. She had an unusual beauty that called to my mind a sky goddess ready to welcome the evening sun to regenerate it in her bosom.

Have you been following me, Madam?'

'Not at all. I was just taking a walk, like you. The column is the meeting point of all the travellers who have been disappointed by Alexandria. Only Greeks and Romans haunt this past. Egypt did not leave its mark here.'

'Are you turning into an Egyptologist?' I said ironically. 'Does your role as a spy require so much knowledge?'

She smiled, amused. 'You are said to be caustic, when you are only passionate. You are not the only one who loves this country to distraction. If I tell you that I am not your enemy, you won't believe me. It doesn't matter! I won't attempt to convince you. But you should know that I now belong to your expedition. Wherever you go, I shall go.'

I was dumbfounded. Lady Redgrave walked away in the sunset.

In the early morning on 22 August, I was wandering in the dunes south of the city. Alexandria had become a place of torture. My companions explored with amused curiosity the charms of the Orient, strolling the souks, sprawling in the garden of Drovetti's palace, talking with *ulemas*, who tried to convert them to Islam by mentioning the former benefits of the French presence in Alexandria.

I, however, had an overwhelming need to see the desert, breathe its air and get on my way to the south, to Cairo. I grasped some sand in the hollow of my right hand and let it flow slowly through my fingers. An old Arab leaning on a stick walked towards me. I looked around, fearing an attack. But the man was alone and progressed slowly; he was blind.

'Good morning, citizen,' he greeted me. 'Give me something. I haven't had anything to eat for a long time.'

'Citizen?' Had I really heard this rather unexpected Republican term from a man from Alexandria?

'Hurry up,' he insisted. 'My stomach cries famine.'

I rummaged through my pockets and offered him the French money I had. He touched the coins skilfully and threw them on the sand. 'This currency is no more in use here, my good man. Look further.'

The insolent old man fascinated me. I felt obliged to obey him. I managed to find a piastre. He seemed satisfied with it.

'Good,' he said. 'Thank you, citizen. You are worthy of

Bonaparte. I regret the French army is no longer here. I believe it would protect us from the pillagers who devour Egypt. There were men who loved Egypt among them. There were even scientists, people who crave for truth, like you.'

'Who are you?'

'A blind man. Keep the letter you received before your departure carefully with you. One day, people will ask for it.'

I would have liked to retain him, to ask him who he was and which letter he was referring to. But he disappeared at an astonishing speed behind a dune.

At the end of August I was summoned with the utmost urgency to the palace of Mehmet Ali. The greatest agitation prevailed. Ministers ran to and fro, shouting at each other, going out and coming in. I hurried into the crowd of sycophants and was first repelled by the two wardens armed with sabres who had witnessed my first meeting with the Pasha.

But I was finally allowed through to see him. He received me in a ceremonial room with walls covered with trophies. He wore a red and gold brocaded dress. Haughty and almost contemptuous, he wanted to appear as a head of state. The etiquette was an ominous sign.

'Ah Champollion!' he exclaimed as soon as he saw me. 'I have very bad news.'

I did not conceal my anxiety.

'French troops have just occupied the Peloponnese,' he explained, ill at ease.

Did this mean that Egypt would become involved in a conflict with France and that, as a consequence, my expedition would be still-born?

'Your fellow citizens are not reasonable,' he said, very angrily. 'I believe that I was wrong to show gratitude to them. You are putting me in a delicate predicament, Champollion. Should I treat you as a friend or as any enemy?'

I held his gaze. 'As you have already made up your mind, Your Excellency, you only have to let me know.'

A fierce smile illuminated his face. 'You are wrong, Champollion. I am making it up just now. You are insolent and proud, but you follow the aim you have set yourself. I like people of your calibre. Go and see Drovetti. I won't do anything against you.'

I forced my way into the office of Consul-General Drovetti at least ten times in the first days of September. He always received me with the utmost courtesy, deploring delays he could not be held responsible for. Because of the troubled political climate, however, he could not manage to find an escort to accompany us to Nubia.

It was impossible to take such an explanation seriously. Drovetti was playing for time. Nothing was easier for him than levying a troop of meek servants. Mehmet Ali had offered me, bound hand and foot, to his accomplice who, although officially proclaiming his benevolence towards me, kept me stuck in Alexandria.

Having uncovered their game, I decided to do what *I* wanted. I gathered my companions in the garden and revealed my plans to them, out of range of inquisitive eavesdroppers.

5

Moktar was Consul-General Drovetti's steward and Abdel-Razuk was a policeman in the Pasha's service. Both were conscientious Turks, with instructions not to let Champollion out of their sight for a second. Wherever he went, the French scientist was discreetly and efficiently shadowed. He actually made his followers' task easier for, lost in thought, he never turned round.

They wondered if they were dreaming, however, when one hot afternoon, at 1 p.m., Champollion took the direction of Alexandria's western necropolis, Kom el-Chugafa, a range of hills along the sea. The heat was such that it was hardly cooled at all by a light wind from the Mediterranean. Champollion did not seem to be suffering much from the heat. His brisk pace surprised Alexandria's coffee drinkers as they sat in the shade before the long siesta. Champollion told his companions, 'This heat is an invaluable source of health. We melt like candles and lose our unwanted fat.'

Accustomed to the coolness of Drovetti's palace, Moktar was not longer used to running in the little streets of the town during the scorching hours of the day. Abdel-Razuk did not feel much more comfortable. Yet they would have no excuse if they lost track of Champollion, who, 200 feet away from the fortifications, was leaving the world of the living to enter that of the dead. The French scientist was actually rushing on to the stairs leading into the catacombs dug in the limestone. The two

Turks looked at each other, worried. They did not like the place. Nobody knew exactly what the religion of the people buried there was. It was only known that they were neither Christians nor Muslims and that dangerous gods watched over their everlasting rest. Plunderers had succeeded in robbing corpses of their jewels, but people said that they had derived scant benefit from them, as the theft shortened their lives.

'We must follow him,' judged Moktar.

'It may not be necessary to do so,' retorted Abdel-Razuk. 'There is no other way out. We only have to wait till he appears again.'

The argument was sound. But was there really no other way? Drovetti's steward knew the harshness of his master towards incompetent servants, and it seemed unwise to take a risk.

'Stay here and I'll go downstairs to have a look.'

Abdel-Razuk whose religious fervour had increased with age, feared nothing so much as funerary sites, so he agreed to Moktar's proposal without so much as a protest. Evil spirits would not deal kindly with intruders. Moktar began to walk down the staircase. Its first steps were covered with sand. He almost immediately reached a very narrow chamber with a low vault-like ceiling. Recesses in the walls contained urns. There was an opening in the ground. Moktar uneasily slid into it and discovered a circular staircase leading to several storeys of tombs which sank deeper and deeper into the earth.

There was no trace of Champollion.

The steward found the courage to keep going. He felt a lump in his throat as he walked through the rooms where sarcophagi had been stored and families had come to hold banquets in memory of the deceased. Faced with a painting of a jackal dressed as a Roman legionnaire on a wall, he instinctively stepped back and flattened himself against a niche. Something soft hit his back. Afraid, he moved away and almost fell. His heart pounded wildly; he was convinced that he had been attacked by a spirit disturbed in his sleep. He gradually recovered his calm and realized that the niche contained a heap of clothes: they were Champollion's!

So he had taken his clothes off. Moktar hesitated. Should he go further down or go out and let Abdel-Razuk know? Why had the Frenchman behaved like that? In the end, the rarefield air of the necropolis and the fearsome figures populating it carried the day. He ran back to the surface.

Abdel-Razuk was waiting for him impatiently. 'So what about Champollion?' he asked.

'He has disappeared. Did anyone come out?'

'No. I only saw an Arab taking a walk on a hill over there.'

Moktar rushed to the place his fellow countryman had mentioned. There was the entrance to a gallery leading into the necropolis.

With a turban on my head, a brown *galabieh*, Oriental slippers and my reasonably tanned complexion, I looked like an old Muslim. I had been right in letting my beard grow ever since my arrival in Alexandria. My European look had gradually disappeared to give way to the Oriental face and figure which had tricked the Pasha's policeman. I had advised my companions to follow my example and adopt local customs, although Father Bidant had obstinately protested, and refused to leave his cassock. As for me, after I had dressed in the Egyptian fashion in the necropolis and shaken off my followers, who had little idea of the catacomb's layout, I headed for the harbour. Alexandria is said to be just a huge store. I had to walk through entire boroughs of little shops, stores and workshops sunk in the torpor of the siesta. Nobody followed me. Warehouses preceded the shipyards. Since Drovetti pretended that he was unable to charter the necessary ships for our expedition, I was going to take care of that myself.

Shipbuilding was one of the great skills of Alexandria. I was convinced that I would be able to find someone to hire us a vessel. The quays seemed empty, but I knew that dozens of eyes were spying on me. I forced myself to walk slowly and nonchalantly so as not to draw attention. I reached an area where small ships were moored. Leaning on a bollard was a warden, half asleep.

I addressed him in Arabic and asked if he could put me in touch with someone who could provide me with ships to sail south. The man hesitated before he answered. He tried to get more information, but, already initiated into oriental ways, I remained vague. Reaching out his hand, he pointed to an apparently closed warehouse. I managed to slide the large wooden door aside without difficulty and to sneak inside.

Despite the half light, I easily distinguished the sarcastic face of Moktar, Drovetti's steward, surrounded by a dozen armed men. 'We were expecting you, Monsieur Champollion.'

'What does this mean Champollion? Why are you disguised like an Arab? Why did you try to hire ships? Don't you trust me? Don't you know that I am taking care of everything?'

Consul-General Drovetti concealed his anger poorly under a flood of questions. His steward had brought me back to his palace with firm courtesy, though I had showed no impulse at all to flee. Such an attempt would have been doomed anyway, considering the impressive retinue accompanying me. My unfortunate experience had enabled me to assess Drovetti's real power over the population of Alexandria. His men were everywhere, maintaining an alternative order to that of the Pasha.

'I have a strong taste for Oriental life,' I answered. 'How can you know Egypt if you don't adopt its customs?'

Beside Moktar stood Abdel-Razuk, carrying my European clothes in a bundles.

'I suppose that you want to retrieve your clothes?'

'As you please, Your Excellency. I feel fine in my new attire.'

Irritated by my arrogance, Drovetti dismissed his servants. We remained face to face.

'You behave stupidly,' he said. 'You lower yourself to the rank of a slave. You will never have the slightest authority over your Muslim servants.'

'Please allow me to have a different opinion,' I retorted ardently. 'You use fear to rule. I use friendship.'

Drovetti cast me a murderous glance. His last vestige of social veneer disappeared. His hatred now showed through. 'There is nothing more you can do in Egypt, Champollion. Two or three years ago, your expedition would have been welcome. The country was ransacked by thieves and antique dealers who thought only of their own interest and not of the preservation of the monuments. Thanks to Anastasy and me, the situation has now changed. We have put an end to this sordid traffic. There is nothing to reform or discover. All sites have been explored and dug out.'

Drovetti turned his back on me and contemplated the garden of the consulate through one of the windows of his study. He probably thought that he had had the final say. I settled in an armchair.

'I would so much like to believe you, Your Excellency! But I have another version of the facts, supported by testimonies and personal observations. All the antique dealers in the country fear you. You and the Pasha refuse to give me the real permits I need to arrange my expedition. You forget the official character of my mission. I came here to dig for the museums of the King. I therefore wrote a note to him and his ministers to let them know about the true reasons why I cannot fulfil my duty. I explained that administrative difficulties were probably related to sordid venal intrigues. As I come on behalf of the King and on his and his government's appointment, you actually insult him by not giving me the necessary papers. If the Pasha is keen on his reputation as a protector of the arts and sciences, he should now hasten to put an end to the matter. Otherwise, European newspapers and Egyptian public opinion could very well pick up the story and harm him, as well as you.'

Bernardino Drovetti turned round, very pale. 'Are these threats, Champollion?'

'Why should you feel threatened? Have you done anything wrong?'

'I forbid you to speak to me in such a tone!' He howled. 'This is none of the Pasha's business. I am the only one who can give you the permits you request. But it would be a deadly mistake for France. You won't be able to ensure the protection of the sites. Anastasy will rub his hands in delight. He will be able to retain his concessions undisturbed.'

'This is wrong, Your Excellency.'

'What do you mean?' he asked, as intrigued as he was worried.

'Anastasy has given me his permission to dig the sites he has been controlling up to now. You re the only one who acts illegally in relation to my expedition.'

Fear distorted Drovetti's features and softened his arrogance. He felt caught in a net from which it would be difficult to extricate himself without losing his privileges. His fame and fortune were at stake. 'Let's suppose that I do the same, how can I provide you with ships? They have all been requisitioned by the Pasha.'

'The problem is solved, Your Excellency. I am not the only one who moves around dressed in the Arab fashion. My companions have done the same. Thanks to my official orders, they have managed to convince the captains of the *Isis* and the *Hathor*, who are reported to be faithful friends of Anastasy's.'

I believe there was a moment of understanding between Drovetti and me. He acknowledged me as an adversary worthy of him and recognized that he had made the mistake of underestimating me. But what I read in his gaze would have frightened the most sturdy soul. His rancour was fearsome to behold. 'You will have your permits by tomorrow, Champollion.'

*

On the evening of 13 September, my travelling companions gathered in the ceremonial room of the French consulate, in the presence of Drovetti. The Consul-General drank to the King, to France and to the Pasha and wished our expedition successful. I thanked him with the utmost seriousness for the help he had given us. A tone of sincerity ran through my speech, so delighted was I at the prospect of leaving at last for the pharaonic civilization.

'We cannot get out!' announced Nestor L'Hôte. 'Dozens of donkey owners are blocking the entrance to the consulate.'

The news of our departure, which I had hoped to keep secret, had spread throughout Alexandria. Drovetti had probably had something to do with the publicity. It added to his reputation as a liberal and generous lord. Amused, he cheered me up.

'Come on, Champollion. Don't worry about such a trivial thing! The Pasha's *chaouiche* will disperse the people. The rabble likes to celebrate every little thing, but its blood is too hot.'

The donkey owners were not really a threat. They sang and shouted, and they wanted to touch the members of the expedition and get a few coins from them. Armed with rods, the viceroy's policemen hit here and there with a violence which appalled me. Was such brutal repression necessary?

Night was falling when a long caravan followed by curious bystanders reached the Mahmudiya canal, where the two ships which were to take us to the south were moored. L'Hôte and I boarded the *Isis*, an impressive ship which the Pasha himself had not considered beneath him to use. Professor Raddi and Father Bidant climbed on board the *Hathor*. As for the staff – servants, cooks and carriers – they divided themselves according to the instructions of Drovetti's steward, Moktar, and Mehmet Ali's favourite policeman, Abdel-Razuk. They themselves had of course chosen the *Isis* in order to keep a sharp eye on me.

We were about to cast off. Two sailors were removing the

gangway when the shout of a woman glued them to the spot.

'Wait!' ordered Lady Redgrave, accompanied by four donkeys owners pulling their unfortunate animals loaded with heavy suitcases.

Beside the British aristocrat appeared Mehmet Ali himself, protected by a guard of honour. The viceroy ordered the gangway to be put up again.

'I wish you good luck, Champollion,' he said solemnly. 'May Allah protect you. Take care of my guest.'

Airily, Lady Redgrave passed me. 'I did warn you, Monsieur Champollion, and there is nothing else to say.'

The delicious noise of the bow of the *Isis* cutting through the water drowned out my retort. The real journey had begun.

6

The Mahmudiya Canal links Alexandria directly to Cairo. I was fulfilling one of my dearest wishes: I was travelling the Nile like the ancient Egyptians and making my way along the divine river which served temples and villages. Each moment brought new marvels. I discovered greening landscapes, peasants working with the same instruments as those used by their distant ancestors. I identified sites, plants, trees . . . a world of living hieroglyphs was unfolding before my insatiable eyes. I found it difficult to tear myself away from my contemplation of the marvels, even for meals or sleep.

From the first day of this cruise to the eternal past, a happy surprise had confirmed my feeling that the names of the ships, *Isis* and *Hathor*, were a good omen, placing our expedition under the protection of two of the most amicable Egyptian goddesses. A dignified Arab with a thin moustache, aged about thirty, was waiting for me in my cabin. He bowed respectfully as I came in. 'My name is Suleiman,' he said in a broken French. 'I am at your service.'

Suleiman was the name of a prince who knew the secrets of genies. A great magician, he had been able to manipulate forces from beyond this earth. The man who greeted me seemed very different from all the Arab servants I had met up to now. His natural nobleness impressed me. It seemed impossible to give instructions to such a man.

'Let's be friends,' I suggested. 'It is true that I shall need you, Suleiman. If you trust me, we will be able to work together.'

I had spoken in Arabic. Suleiman did not show the slightest surprise, but his gaze seemed absolutely frank. He bowed again, not the way a servant would bow to his master, but the way a host honours his equal, his hand touching his forehead, mouth and heart so as to express that his mind, speech and feelings were favourably disposed towards me.

It did not take me long to notice the beneficial influence of the alliance. Suleiman, who knew every inch of his land, enabled me to correct the maps used in the *Description of Egypt*, designed by Bonaparte's scientists, which had, until our expedition, been the only scientific reference. Along the Nile, at the slow pace of the *Isis*, I had the tiniest villages named for me so as to rectify mistakes and fill up gaps. Hour after hour, a new map of Egypt was traced where correspondences between ancient and modern places appeared. This first result alone was of inestimable worth.

Nestor L'Hôte, whose sturdy appetite was sated by French meals, made a fair copy of my notes with Rosellini, whose scientific passion was already satisfied. He had wasted no time in Alexandria, where he had bought numerous artefacts for the collection he was to take back to the Grand Duke of Tuscany, Leopold II.

Lady Redgrave did not deign to talk to me. Her rank as a privileged guest of the Pasha probably placed her above ordinary mortals. She contented herself with sunbathing and only mixed with the two servants provided for her. I would have to find a way of leaving her behind in Cairo.

At high noon, I was enjoying a glass of Nile water, more tasty to me than the choicest champagne, when, in the midst of an acacia grove, I noticed a tiny village with a peculiar charm. Fate willed that the *Isis* drew alongside to buy fresh fruit.

'I would like to visit the place,' I said to Suleiman, who told me the village was called Ed-Dahariye.

As I walked down the gangway, Abdel-Razuk came up.

'Stay on board,' he requested. 'The place is not safe.'

'Thanks for your advice.' I said, jumping to the ground.

I was attracted by the clay huts of the *fellahin*, which had squares carefully designed to facilitate irrigation. The poor dwellings took advantage of the shade offered by the palm trees and acacias. Huge jars where oil and wheat were stored stood against the façades of even the largest houses. Apart from the changing seasons, births, weddings and deaths it seemed as if time had stopped for good. The idea of progress had no relevance. Life was reduced to its simplest and most essential elements.

The village seemed empty, the inhabitants were working in the fields. But as I approached the largest dwelling I noticed with horror a male head with closed eyes protruding from the highest jar. Unable to move, I saw an old man come out of the house and walk towards me with a threatening look.

'Who sent you?' he asked with hostility.

'Nobody,' I answered, dry-mouthed.

'Are you French?'

'Yes . . .'

The old man spat to my feet and raised his right hand to curse me. 'Go away! Is it not enough for you to have murdered my son? Must you also spoil his rest?'

I explained to the unfortunate man that I was not involved in whatever it was he was accusing me of. As I came to understand his jerky speech, I managed to piece together the events which had led to his son's tragic death. He had stolen an antique bronze from one of Drovetti's touts. As he had tried to sell it, he had been arrested by the Pasha's *chaouiche*. His body had been retrieved in a canal. The policeman had explained to the family that the prisoner had escaped during the night and got lost in the countryside, but his father believed that he had been murdered.

Back on board, this sad story still affected me and made it difficult to continue my cartography. The help of the precise and meticulous Rosellini was a big advantage. How many generations of scientists would be required to explore the immense area of the Delta, the realm of the Red Crown, which consisted of so many holy towns under the pharaohs' rule?

The night of 16 September, which we were all awaiting with ill-contained impatience, finally came. After we had passed the village of Es-Ssafeh, ships came alongside to enable us to visit the first great site now accessible to people other than antiquity thieves: the mysterious city of Sais, which ancient people had turned into a place of great wisdom, home of the goddess Neith. After she had created the universe by uttering seven words, she had woven the fabric of life so that its secrets could be transmitted by female initiates, who produced holy fabrics for the whole of Egypt. I was consulting some maps of the site compiled from Herodotus' descriptions of Egypt, when I heard a knock on my door.

I went to open and saw Father Bidant who had rushed on board the *Isis*.

'I have a service to ask you, Champollion.'

'Please, go ahead, Father. If I can help you . . .'

He hesitated. 'Let's not stop in Sais. The place is cursed. Let's move on to Cairo.'

Dumbfounded, I laid down my quill. I had probably misunderstood.

'You are a great scientist, Champollion, but you are also a great innocent. The country is full of demons. They are not harmless, believe me; let's avoid Sais.'

I stood up, half-cross and half-amused. 'How could the old city disturb the Christian faith, Father? To my knowledge, there is no document questioning the bible here.'

'Sais was a sorcerers' academy,' he said. 'The effects of their evil spells have not yet disappeared. We run the risk of being contaminated and seeing our expedition corrupted.'

'What a superstitious man you are, Father!' I said surprised. 'Doesn't the God of Christians protect us from such illusions?'

Father Bidant gave me a rather uncharitable look and went away. Nestor L'Hôte and Rosellini followed him, both very excited at the prospect of discovering their first archaeological site. They told me that, fascinated by the study of pieces of limestone he had harvested in a quarry in Alexandria, Professor Raddi had not noticed that we had put in to land. Nobody had had the courage to interrupt his research.

'Here we are, ready to get down to work!' declared Nestor L'Hôte warmly. 'What are your instructions, General?'

'Caution before everything else. Have you brought your notebooks?'

My collaborators were ready to draw and record a large harvest of finds. We embraced each other, proud and happy to be here on a summer night which would bring back to life past wonders.

Suleiman and a dozen servants carrying torches led us to the site of San el Hagar, where once stood a holy town. Combined with the moonlight and starry sky of great purity, the light of the torches conferred a ghostly atmosphere on our exploration. I had believed that we would see a great temple, a huge divine dwelling with high walls covered with relief. As I walked through a breach in the huge enclosure, however, I discovered only a field of ruins. Sais was a destroyed and a lost city. My curiosity equalled my disappointment; it would take months to make an inventory of all the broken blocks, to measure the wall and to gather up the pieces of the statues. Silently I invoked the goddess Isis, whose veil had been lifted in this very place by those initiated into her mysteries. Who had been cruel enough to destroy this high point of spirituality, transform living stones into debris like rocks broken by lightning or earthquakes? A horrible stench arose from masses of brackish water, some of which had infiltrated a nearby and badly kept Arab cemetery. I soon distinguished, north-east of the wall, a dry area, above which I could see groups of young owls, which were considered by the ancients to symbolize wisdom and science. I walked there quickly, followed by Rosellini and L'Hôte. We were soon convinced that we had identified a funerary mound containing tombs. My companions took notes with a swiftness which reassured me about the rest of our expedition. L'Hôte was fiery. Rosellini was more methodical. If fate favoured me, I swore to myself that I would come back to Sais and restore life to this ruined site.

While my companions were drawing an accurate map of the ruins, I lingered alone in the south-western area, at the bottom of the wall, where I had located some fragmented statues. I had the feeling that this was where the famous House of Life had stood. Its science compared with that of Heliopolis, ancient Egypt's spiritual centre. Here they were said to have uncovered the mystery of immortality. But the record of it was lost in the sand. I would have to search further. Devastated by the ignorance and madness of generations, Sais escaped me. The awful emptiness which had initially discouraged me, was turning into a call to stay.

'Sais was only a stopover, Monsieur Champollion,' said a bewitching female voice. Cloaked in the moonlight, Lady Ophelia Redgrave wore an evening dress embroidered with silver threads.

'You look like a goddess,' I conceded, charmed by so much grace and forgetting my prejudice against her.

I expected a smile, but I saw only an expression of gravity.

'Don't talk like that. "Goddess" is a word which is still suffused with so much sacredness in my eyes. I am only a woman, which probably seems to you of no importance compared with Neith . . .'

'Don't believe that,' I protested.

'What do you think of this?' She showed me the small artefact she had picked up. It was a statuette of a servant in the other world, obeying the orders of the glorious people who in the fields of heaven, resorted to him to fertilize the ground. The mere decipherment of the hieroglyphs decorating his body made him alive.

'This is a pretty artefact from a late period . . . I cannot allow you to take it. It should be recorded and passed to the Museum.'

'I know. You don't have to lecture me. I don't belong to Drovetti's packs.'

Appalled, I grasped her wrists. 'Who are you really, Lady Redgrave?'

She got free with the suppleness of a cat. 'So analyse me, Monsieur Champollion!'

She was the first to leave Sais to return to the *Isis*. I stayed a long time on the site. I did not know what to think of the woman any more. My judgement of people was usually easily formed, but this time I was disorientated to the point of forgetting centuries of history slumbering under my feet.

Nestor L'Hôte tore me away form my meditation. 'You must leave this place, General. The local people are looking a bit threatening. They believe that we are disturbing the spirits of the dead.'

I let him take me to the ship. At the same time I noticed the attentive presence of Abdel-Razuk, who did not let me out of his sight.

I worked relentlessly for hours to forget Sais and Lady Redgrave. Any archaeologist would have been satisfied, but I was looking for more than the traces of a now faded glory. My mood was so gloomy that I refused to open the door of my cabin to anyone, under the pretext of meticulous research. Used to such attacks of solitude, my companions did not take offence.

Only Suleiman ventured to insist. I yielded. 'I must inform you of a serious incident. The *Hathor* is blocked at the quay by a Turkish magistrate.'

'Why?'

'Because of a tax. Two sailors have been arrested. They haven't paid tax to the Pasha.'

'Hasn't Father Bidant been able to solve the matter?'

Suleiman remained silent. Obviously not. As a 'general', I felt it was my duty to intervene without delay. Therefore I followed Suleiman and left the *Isis* for the town of Zauiyet er-Redsin.

Close beside a wall of the mosque, surrounded by a small court of loyal supporters, the Turkish magistrate sat on soft cushions and smoked a long pipe. In front of him, their hands bound behind their backs, stood the two sailors from the *Hathor*. Hanging their heads, they seemed resigned to the worst.

The Turk looked at me with a cruel and mischievous gaze as I came near him. He was extremely satisfied to have attracted me to his open-air law court. It would be a striking proof of his power to hold up a European to ridicule. The negotiation would be difficult.

Suleiman launched himself into a florid peroration mentioning the Pasha's and his servants' innumerable qualities, his subjects' total submission and divine justice. The Turk enjoyed the speech and allowed me to explain why I had come to see him. 'I want to know what misdemeanour these men committed to be thus bound hand and foot.'

The Turk answered resentfully that they owed an important amount of money to the tax people. They deserved a drubbing and probably mutilation. The crowd increased. Nestor L'Hôte, Rosellini and Father Bidant soon came to my support.

'I am in possession of official documents.' I said.' 'They bear the seal of the Pasha.'

The Turk wanted to see my permits. He examined them carefully.

'Why didn't you pay to free them?' I asked Father Bidant. 'We would have been spared this comedy.'

'Well . . . it would be a useless expense . . . The two sharks will be easily replaced.'

If we had been standing nearer to each other I do not know whether I would have succeeded in controlling my anger.

'The father is right,' added Nestor L'Hôte. 'It is useless to waste time because of two thieves.'

The Turkish magistrate handed me the documents back. They did not suit him. They certainly presented me as an important personality worthy of respect, but they did not prove the innocence of the accused, who were in danger of losing everything. I was overcome by a powerful feeling of revulsion against the injustice.

'Sirs, I won't leave the place without the two sailors. May the respected tax officer be well aware of that. Through me, he is insulting the Viceroy himself.'

The heavy threats were transmitted to the civil servant who took them very seriously and asked his sycophants for advice.

'You are much too sensitive, General,' remarked Nestor L'Hôte. 'If you want to solve the lot of all destitute people, we may as well go back.'

'These men belong to our expedition, Monsieur L'Hôte. If we abandon them, their colleagues won't trust us any more. And they wouldn't be wrong. As for you, Father,' I added, addressing Bidant. 'Please be charitable enough to rid me of your presence. Your cassock disturbs our hosts.'

The religious man's attitude turned from vague unfriendliness to patent hostility. I now had one more enemy. He went back to the *Hathor*, indifferent to the outcome of the fight.

'Don't you think . . .' intervened Rosellini softly.

'I won't reconsider my decision.'

Feeling useless, L'Hôte and Rosellini left the circle of bystanders. The Turk let me know that he was not impressed by my threats. The law was on his side and the Pasha would not disown him. A crowd of destitutes joined the fray. The incident was increasing in scale. It did not happen very often that an emissary of the tax people was challenged.

'I want to be told the amount of money owed by the accused. I take responsibility for paying it in exchange for their liberation.'

The proposal was either shocking or came too soon. It spread great turmoil in the court of the Turk who resorted to invective to restore order. I refused to answer his questions and remained motionless, thus indicating that his was my last offer. I had to wait for the outcome of the deliberation for almost an hour in the scorching sun, though in fact I put up with it quite easily.

The malevolent Turk spat out a sum which was double the amount that was owed. The difference was for him and his sycophants. I did not dispute it, at the risk of being taken for a simpleton. The two sailors were released from their ties. They thanked me with such emotion that, in the language of the ancient Egyptians, it caused my heart to swell.

'Mehmet Ali is a tyrant,' commented Suleiman quietly on the way back to the *Isis*. 'He waged war. He distributed considerable amounts of money to Europeans, and yet the people were starving and the tax collectors are more ruthless than jackals. They even take from those who already have nothing. The Viceroy owns the land, the trade, the industry. The wealth is his and misery is his people's lot. The Turkish leeches and his handful of henchmen suck the blood of Egypt. You will also be his victim, one day. Beware.'

I took his warning seriously. But as Rosellini was approaching us, I could not ask Suleiman about the precise meaning of his advice.

Lady Redgrave was observing us from the deck of the ship. She smiled, as if illuminated by some inner joy.

At dawn on 19 September, I saw the pyramids for the first time. We were approaching Memphis, the capital of the Old Kingdom pharaohs. Its name alone had fascinated me ever since my adolescence. The city was protected by the god Ptah, the patron of masterbuilders, craftsmen and goldsmiths.

Suddenly, our ship hit a sandbank and stopped. Our sailors jumped into the river to free it, invoking the name of Allah and, more efficiently, their broad and sturdy shoulders. Most boatmen are like exceptionally well-built models of Hercules, with astonishing strength. They look like newly cast bronze statues when they emerge from the river.

Without difficulty we reached the tip of the Delta where the branches of Rosetta and Damietta separate. The outlook is magnificent and the Nile is immensely wide. In the west, the mass of pyramids stands out against a background of palm trees. Some ships sail to the right into the Damietta branch, others to the left into the Rosetta branch. Others also head towards Cairo, a powerful city with its minarets, the hill of Moqattam and its austere citadel watching over the desert.

I asked that we stop abreast the village of El-Qattah so that Nestor L'Hôte could draw the sublime landscape. The other members of the expedition joined us.

'If we dismantled the pyramids, stone by stone,' said Professor Raddi, whose ecstasy increased by the day, 'what a wonderful contribution to mineralogy it would be!'

'These monuments are of no great interest,' contradicted Father Bidant. 'They were built by tyrants who were responsible for the deaths of thousands of people, doomed to slavery.'

How could I avoid flaring up when I heard such stupidities? 'You will have to stop telling such lies, Father. Egyptian religion never produced slaves. The pyramids are a symbol of knowledge.'

'Nonsense,' grumbled the religious man, moving away.

'I wonder if we will find any inscriptions there,' said Rosellini hopefully.

Leaving everyone with their dreams, I let the unearthly sight of the pyramids in the distance at sunrise pervade me.

A long, fine hand in tawny leather gloves rested on mine. I was unable to react, even though I should have protested vehemently.

'Did you imagine a light like this could exist, Monsieur Champollion?' asked Lady Ophelia Redgrave in a whisper I was the only one to hear. 'Are we not the most fortunate of all people?'

The beautiful aristocrat had once more changed, and wore a dress whose graduations of ochre hues turned her into the sort of variations seen only in the sun as it progresses through the day.

'I think I deserve this good fortune. And I do not know yet what kind of privileges it holds in store for me.'

On my heart were the two contradictory letters I had received before I left.

7

On 19 September, at 3 p.m., we entered the suburbs of Cairo. At the landing stage, an emissary of the Pasha was waiting for us. I walked ahead with Suleiman, followed by Abdel-Razuk and Moktar, to whom I had not said a word since Alexandria, and Rosellini with L'Hôte, who pointed out the long alley planted by Bonaparte's soldiers and told the story of their victory by the pyramids. Behind came Father Bidant and Professor Raddi persevering in a dialogue of the deaf, each entrenched in his special field. At Bulaq harbour, we had been immersed in the greatest shambles a disturbed mind can imagine: boats and ships were so crammed that none of them could manoeuvre. Yet, they moved in and out by a magic beyond our understanding. The quays swarmed with sailors, merchants and beggars. Nubians, Arabs and Europeans mingled. Here and there people argued over the value of a cargo, the price of transportation and other less licit business.

There were men dressed in a strange way with hats of contrasting colours, shaped like sugar loaves, displaying white tow beards and huge moustaches. Tight-fitting narrow cloths outlined all parts of their bodies. They had wrapped themselves in huge lengths of twisted white linen. The attire, the insignia and the grotesque postures evoked the old fauns painted on ancient Greek vases.

We stopped in the courtyard of a dilapidated and rather

unattractive building. Parts of entire walls were about to crumble. On the threshold, a soldier in a dirty uniform was sound asleep, his gun beside him. The emissary of the Pasha begged us to wait, entered the building, remained there a few minutes and came back with an inscrutable face.

'You are forbidden to enter Cairo,' he said in Arabic to Suleiman

'Why?' I asked in his language.

'Because of the customs,' he answered, surprised. 'Some papers are missing. Have you got permits?'

I called Rosellini, who kept the documents signed by Mehmet Ali and Drovetti. Our interlocutor seized them and disappeared again into the customs office.

'The matter should be solved easily,' I said to Suleiman.

'Maybe,' he answered evasively.

His reserve worried me. What did he fear? No expedition had ever enjoyed recommendations such as ours. To kill the anxiety I began to feel, I walked a few steps in the courtyard, while my companions put up with the delay and drank the green tea a disorderly officer was offering. I looked at veiled women drawing water with their jars from a large tank resting on wooden blocks. Intrigued by its shape, I came near and, to my surprise, saw that it was actually a magnificent basalt sarcophagus belonging to a priest of the Saite period! I brutally pushed aside the housewives to decipher the hieroglyphs of the late period, which seemed like those of the time of the pyramids. They mentioned immortality as well as the stellar destiny of one who had been recognized as a 'fair man' by the court of the other world. I could read and read easily! Signs talked to me! I feverishly copied the main inscriptions and hastened towards L'Hôte and Rosellini, who looked very gloomy.

'I found a masterwork for the Louvre, here in this very place!' I announced.

Suleiman appeared. 'The customs refuse to give us permission to enter Cairo,' he declared with fatalism.

'How is that possible? Is the Pasha's signature not enough for the civil servants?'

I rushed into the administrative building and immediately bumped into a fierce, paunchy doorkeeper with a moustache, who vehemently shouted at me and ordered me away. I retorted with similar vehemence. Dialogue was impossible for the man refused to explain his decision. Under the threat of an arrest, I had to go back to the courtyard, where my companions were waiting for me, mortified. I tried to find words of comfort, despite my own feeling of helplessness.

Lady Redgrave passed us haughtily. Our eyes followed her and, flabbergasted, we saw her enter the customs house.

'They will mistreat her,' worried L'Hôte.

'Don't be afraid,' said Suleiman. 'My fellow countrymen usually don't attack women.'

'What is the matter?' Professor Raddi asked at last. 'We're wasting time!'

Father Bidant explained the situation to him. Rosellini was biting his nails. I could read his thoughts: would our expedition fail at the gate of Cairo, because of a narrow-minded civil servant?

'We must let the Pasha and Drovetti know,' suggested Father Bidant.

'It won't be necessary,' said Lady Redgrave whose violet dress shone in the sun. 'Here are your permits.' She handed me a dozen grimy sheets covered with stamps and walked away.

I caught up with her, seething with curiosity. 'How did you do it?'

'You behave too much like a European, Monsieur Champollion. There was no way that your papers would impress the head of the customs office.'

'Why?'

'Because he does not know how to read.'

I was flabbergasted. Like everyone else, Lady Redgrave had just asked for sheets stamped in advance, without showing the illiterate customs officer permits which were beyond his understanding.

'But . . . do you speak Arabic?'

'We all have our little secrets, Monsieur Champollion. So what about entering Cairo now?'

So it was that on 20 September the expedition, in full array, reached the gate of Omar in strict hierarchical order. Dressed in the Turkish fashion, on horseback, we cut fine figures. I headed the retinue, as carried away by our success as by the vision of a new world swarming with colours and smells. An enormous crowd filled the streets of the town. Hundreds of white and coloured turbans sneaked between carriages, camels and donkeys. The donkey owners of the town are probably the most famous polyglots. At first sight, they can distinguish a German, an Englishman, a Frenchman, an Italian or any other foreigner and address him with a few words in his mother tongue.

No animal is more suited to moving around the narrow streets than the small and sturdy donkeys. With shouts and goads the owners lead the animals with a precision which commands respect. Surprised to see several of them with one ear cut, I asked Suleiman the reason. He explained that this was the way donkeys caught stealing someone else's grass were punished.

The word 'donkey' should not bring to mind the unfortunate insulted and beaten European animal, an unpitied slave to the harshest tasks in the most wrecked conditions. Nor should one imagine a rebel endowed with the worst temper, throwing whoever dares to climb on his back down on the pavement. No, anyone who has not seen an Egyptian donkey does not know one of the most wonderful animals in creation. He is lively, charming and light, walks with his head held high and shows his intelligence at the slightest thing. His owner likes to take care of him, and brush and polish his coat till it looks like velvet.

'To your right!', 'To your left!', 'Your foot!' shouted the

donkey owners, avoiding with difficulty two processions passing each other, one for a wedding, and the other for a funeral! Cavaliers whose mounts were covered with gold-embroidered velvet did not hesitate to jostle whatever obstructed their way, be it man, woman or a child.

Everywhere people ate and drank to satiety. In open-air kitchens, women surrounded by swarms of children prepared hot broad beans. Cooked parsnips, pickled cucumbers and meatballs swam together in a mouth-watering spice-based red sauce. A tea merchant with brass devices of impeccable cleanliness offered his excellent drink, thus outdoing the water-carrier and men who sold fruit syrups, liquorice water, carob or date tea and raisin juice. Adolescent praised the merits of their watermelons, pomegranates, dates, grapes, tomatoes and figs. People savoured warm flat bread, lemons and onions. In large copper pots pieces of mutton were cooking. Cairo had been transformed into a huge banqueting room to greet us.

We had arrived at the right time: on the that day and the following one, the Muslims celebrated the birth of the Prophet. The huge and important Ezbekieh Square was full of people crowding round itinerant entertainers, dancers and singers. There were fine tents under which devotions were performed. Here Muslims sat rhythmically reading chapters of the Koran. About 300 religious people sat in parallel lines and constantly moved the upper part of their bodies backward and forward like puppets with movable joints, all singing in chorus '*La-Alla-Ell'Allah*', 'There is no other God than God.' Further along 500 people were joined in a circle, jumping rhythmically up and down while simultaneously letting out cries of 'Allah' from their overworked chests. They repeated it a thousand times, but the tone was so muffled and hollow that never in my life have I heard so hellish a chorus: the awful buzz seemed to come from the depth of Tartarus. Beside the religious demonstrations walked musicians and loose women. All sorts of swings were in full action. Combined with the strangeness of the figures and the extreme variety of their costumes, the mixture of profane games and religious practices were a sight from another world. Mothers dipped their children in the muddy water as much to amuse them as to wash them. They came out as black as toads and roared with laughter. Everyone worshipped the water, which was sometimes so high that it formed a lake on which floated rowing boats full of elegant men and women.

'Champollion! Look over there!'

Rosellini's horse had come abreast of mine. I looked in the direction my disciple had pointed, but I could only see a troop of dancers practising their art near a steaming cauldron surrounded by a small gathering of visitors.

'I am sure,' said Rosellini, 'that I really saw him.'

'Whom did you see?'

'Drovetti, the Consul-General.'

'That is impossible.'

'I swear that I saw him.'

A movement of the crowd obliged us to separate and progress further in single file. I did not doubt Rosellini's good faith, yet I could not believe Drovetti was here. It meant that he would have travelled at the same time as us in another ship. And to what purpose?

The rose was a thorn,' said a grave voice. 'The Prophet's sweat made it bloom.'

Just ahead of me walked a pistachio salesman whose face I did not see. 'Are you the one who knows how to read the writing on old stones?' he asked with the same deep tone.

'Indeed I think I can do that . . . But who are you?'

'The warning in the letter is about to come true. Go to Tulun Mosque tomorrow at 7 a.m.' The man hastened his pace and headed towards a lane on the left.

'Wait! Which letter?'

The pistachio salesman had already disappeared.

Cairo has been very much ill-spoken of. As for me, I felt fine there. The 8–10 feet wide streets, which have been so much disparaged, seemed carefully planned to avoid the intense heat. Here was a monumental town, still a city of the *Thousand and One Nights*, despite the destruction of most of the delicious Arabic arts and civilization by Turkish barbarity.

Why deny it? I was in love with this mixture of often very dilapidated houses, narrow streets where tanners, potters and goldsmiths work alongside itinerant pedlars and cooks. All this was ugly and sometimes sordid, yet at the same time a magic turned the repelling and almost inhuman town into a bewitching place. In Cairo you could stroll to your heart's content, provided of course you left the exclusive district where European residents and travellers took refuge behind large wooden gates, closed each night against the indigenous population, riots and epidemics. The houses of Cairo were thrown together in chaotic districts whose only empty spaces, the inner courtyards, were most of the time occupied by animals. To get some air, you naturally headed for quiet open spaces like the great Ezbekieh Square, the mosques or the citadel. From the latter, where I stood to greet the sunrise, the ugliness disappeared. In the distance in the desert, I saw a caravan form. There were some thirty camels, most of them beside huge bundles of goods. With the help of rods, the camel drivers started to gather the animals. Below me, the capital of modern Egypt unfolded its immensity. I discovered thousands of terraces, minarets and domes. In the east glowed the sunrise fires, creating the golden light of the breaking day. Like petrified rays of light the pyramids emerged from the desert. There spread the realm of death, the land of the gods: Saqqara, Dachur, Abusir and Giza, where the ancient Egyptians had dug into eternity to uncover its secret, the only secret deserving of being discovered.

God, how sublime was the vision! I felt I was in heaven, far from human trivialities, experiencing the impulse which had inspired the minds and hands of the builders. But I had to go to the appointment mentioned by the pistachio salesman.

A donkey owner led me to Tulun Mosque, a ninth-century

edifice. Although partly ruined, it was the most beautiful Arabic monument in Egypt. The elegance of its lines and the sobriety of its architecture commanded respect. As I was considering the gate, an old *sheikh* suggested that I enter the mosque. I agreed and easily passed the first gate. I was stopped abruptly at the second one, however. I had to penetrate into the holy place without shoes. I wore boots, but I had no socks on. The matter was urgent, so I left my boots and used two handkerchiefs to cover my feet. I stood on the marble of the holy enclosure, deserted at that time of the day. I waited for a rather long time. I did not dare walk around the place, whose calm contrasted with the turmoil of the streets.

Finally a tall Turk appeared with a Mameluke sabre at his side. His face was almost entirely covered by a black beard. He stopped some 3 feet from me, as severe as Anubis, the guardian of tombs. I was suddenly afraid that I might have walked into a trap. Nothing could be easier to make an intruder disappear than by accusing him of violating the meditation of a mosque? Yet I now looked like a true Arab. Even the donkey owner had taken me for one of his fellow countrymen and forgotten to rob me. If the fierce doorkeeper now attacked me, it meant that I had been denounced. Feeling as though I was caught into a trap, I was short of breath. Should I fight? At no time in my short life had I ever resorted to violence. I loathe it. Even to defend my life, I felt unable to initiate a fight.

We remained motionless, as if fascinated by each other. I should probably have tried to escape, but such an attitude seemed unworthy. Maybe the first blow would arouse a new determination in me. The Turk stepped forward with infinite slowness, sword drawn. My taste for hieroglyphs came to the fore. Their irresistible call tore me away from the resignation which had glued me to the spot. Clenching my fists, I decided to defend myself.

'Go on your way,' he ordered. 'You are expected at the Khan el-Khalili bazaar bookstall.' Putting away his sabre, he turned away from me as if I did not exist any more.

Khan el-Khalili was the most famous and most cluttered entrance to the bazaar. Shops almost blocked the way in. Men selling flat bread, beggars, smokers of hookahs and donkey owners mingled in a constant hubbub, modulated in inexhaustible swells. Confectioners shouted at athletes whose demonstrations of strength lifting blocks of stone prevented clients from approaching their stalls. A man making red leather slippers was amused by the incident.

There was no one selling books in sight. The slipper maker came to me. 'Men's actions are judged according to their intentions,' he said. 'And we are all rewarded according to our intentions.' He was reciting the proverb written on the gate of the barbers.

'So what are your intentions?' I asked.

Moving aside from the row of slippers, he unveiled a series of red-bound books. 'Take one.'

I took a copy of the Koran.

'You might be more interested in the other one beside it.'

I looked and discovered a travel book by a Venetian who had visited Egypt in the seventeenth century and rediscovered Thebes. I was keenly reading when the cobbler-librarian tapped my shoulder. I raised my eyes and saw a familiar figure in the crowd of passers-by: Drovetti! Dressed in the Turkish fashion, he walked at his determined, martial pace which contrasted with the nonchalance of Oriental people.

Forgetting the Ventian's book, I rushed in pursuit of him, intent on not losing sight of him and asking him for explanations. So Rosellini had been right. But why had the Consul-General come to Cairo at the same time as us?

A wedding procession rushed towards me. Stopping in the middle of the street, young boys and girls had erected a kiosk with four wooden poles and a strip of cloth as a roof. Musicians played drums furiously while lanterns were hung and low seats set up so as to enable guests to rest. Coffee was served to passers-by, who thus took part in the celebration. The joyful throng was a nuisance, for Drovetti had taken advantage of it to disappear. I scuttled among the crammed rows, careful not to jostle people or behave impatiently, and managed to overcome the obstacle.

Suddenly Lady Ophelia Redgrave appeared in front of me. Her violet dress was an incongruous sight among the brown *galabieh*. Motionless in the whirl of passers-by, she looked at me worriedly. 'What are you doing here?'

'I am the one who should be asking the question. Have you just seen Consul-General Drovetti?'

Embarrassed, she hesitated. 'No . . . Of course not . . . Drovetti is not in Cairo. He stayed in Alexandria.'

The lane was too narrow for her not to have seen Drovetti. They had probably had time to say a few words to each other. I was now convinced that they had made an appointment in the bazaar, hidden in the throng. My presence had probably disturbed them.

'Did you send me a letter in France, before the departure of our expedition?'

Her beautiful light green eyes expressed surprise. 'I have never had the pleasure of writing to you,' she said in a slightly ironical voice. Lady Redgrave was an exceptionally talented actress. But the situation was now becoming clearer. The Englishwoman and Drovetti had been appointed by my European adversaries to prevent me from checking my discoveries on the spot and they had made a pact. Drovetti observed me from a distance and took all the necessary measures to hinder my progress while Lady Redgrave acted as an on-the-spot spy. Thus set, the trap would not let the prey escape . . . Champollion would leave Egypt only as a broken, defeated and ridiculed man. I was doomed to fail or die in this country without having transmitted the outcome of my work to the world.

'You look very worried, Monsieur Champollion. Would you agree to be my guide in this maze? You are the only one who can help me discover the marvels hidden among the rags and fake gold and silver.'

Her smile disarmed me. Human streams walked round us

without hitting us. We formed an islet of motionlessness in the unceasing movement. Although my prejudice against Lady Redgrave remained as strong as ever, I did not have the courage to refuse her request.

She gave me her arm and took me deep into the souk, where goldsmiths worked. There, poor imitations and small master-works by timeless craftsmen mingled. Lady Redgrave actually did not need my advice to differentiate valuable artefacts from fakes. Her choice fell on a gold armband inlaid with lapis lazuli whose navy-blue colour evoked the Egyptian sky at night, where dead pharaohs' souls shine in a myriad of stars. As she examined the jewel and bargained, according to the local custom, my heart fluttered. On the block of stone used as a workbench by the goldsmith had been engraved a dozen hieroglyphs in the infinitely pure style of the Ancient Kingdom! Interrupting the business discussion, I begged the craftsman to let me look at his precious stone. Intrigued, the man agreed and took away the tools, jewels and scales which cluttered the majestic remain.

I turned pale. I could see a cartouche, an oval ending in a curl, where the names of pharaohs were written.

'I want to buy it.' I said to the goldsmith.

He refused.

'Where does the stone come from?'

'It has belonged to my family for several generations. It's our talisman. It protects us and it will never leave our workshop.'

I was sufficiently aware of the force of superstition to know that I could not triumph over it. The extraordinary block was now forever lost for science. As soon as I left the goldsmith would have no more urgent task than to hide it in some inaccessible place.

'What does the inscription say?' wondered Lady Redgrave as I was copying the hieroglyphs.

'They are both a further proof of the soundness of my system of decipherment and a memory of one of the greatest earthly kings! Look . . . the sieve ⟨image⟩ is transcribed *kh*, the quail chick ⟨image⟩ the horned viper ⟨image⟩ and again the chick *u* . . . So, like me, you can read ⟨image⟩ Khufu, the name of the pharaoh the Greeks called Cheops and whose Egyptian name means "May God protect me".'

'The builder of the great pyramid?'

'Precisely.'

'Does the stone come from his monument?'

'Probably . . . Some travellers said that a large part of Cairo had been built with blocks from the pyramids . . . I'm afraid this is the awful truth.'

Lady Redgrave was moved. Despite the self-control she usually displayed in all circumstances, I could see that my demonstration had shaken her. Probably for the first time her mind accepted that I was neither a crook nor an eccentric.

'If God protected Cheops,' she said gravely. 'May he be as generous with you.'

We visited the souks until nightfall, when the Turkish wardens closed the gates of the bazaar, in front of which they kept watch until the following dawn. In the Orient, night fell in a few minutes. With it came silence. The human flood disappeared. Dogs left their torpor to walk around the streets in search of food. The cafès were lit up with lanterns, along with the shops that remained open. The guardians of the rich dwellings set up palm beds on the threshold of the houses they protected from thieves. They would lie there and sleep till daybreak. The calls of the muezzins sounded through the warm air to invite the faithful to pray.

I had the impression that Lady Redgrave was squeezing my arm more tightly. Drunk with the sweetness of the Egyptian night, charmed by its fragrances and troubled by the presence of this attractive enemy, for a moment I forgot the demands of my quest. Happiness pervaded me like a puff of wind, like the refreshing breeze the ancient Egyptians savoured when the ardour of the sun decreased.

But what did tomorrow hold in store for me?

8

Two days after our arrival in Cairo, where our accommodation comprised pleasant villas in the European district, I offered my companions a celebration which, in accordance with the custom, lasted from 6 p.m. till midnight. Only Father Bidant refused to join in. He was convinced that licentious devilry formed the core of the festivities. He bitterly reproached me about my conduct and accused me of letting oriental life corrupt me. As my protests went unheeded, I took no notice of his admonitions. He was wrong about the nature of our Cairo entertainment. As far as devilry goes, we only had a long song recital from Nefise, the nightingale of Cairo, and the people's idol. The experience was harsh to our European ears which were used to refined harmonies. Yet the monotonous chant, with its languorous tones, eventually charmed us and even made us sink into a state of bliss. We could not help thinking of pharaonic orchestras, priestesses who were also musicians and singers whose voices delighted the gods. The incantations tore the soul away from the trivialities of the world and, through the magic of sound, immersed it in the sacred.

Father Bidant was not completely wrong, however; the Orient was beginning to take possession of us.

The celebration was an opportunity to introduce the members of the expedition to influential people in Cairo, whose favours we gradually won. The most important of them was not the most impressive; Botzari, an Armenian doctor, was a small man with a dark complexion and a lively mind. Given the respect he was granted, however, it was easy to understand that he held the fate of many notables in his hands. In the course of our conversations, I learnt that he occupied he envied position of the Pasha's favourite, and that no significant business could be achieved without his consent.

As I wondered about the best way of approaching him, he came to me, with a mocking expression. 'Let's go out in the garden, Monsieur Champollion. We will be able to talk at peace there.'

Anyone who has not experienced the sweetness of an Oriental garden on a summer night does not know that paradise exists on earth. The fragrances of roses blend with those of hibiscus and tamarisk. A pleasant freshness arises from ground watered by gardeners at sunset. One begins to dream of a universe where human beings are again in tune with the humblest of flowers.

The Armenian doctor did not let any such bucolic feelings distract him. To him, Cairo was just a business town where he exerted his power. 'Are you happy with your stay, Monsieur Champollion?'

'Each day is a revelation.'

'You reputation grows constantly . . . Do you know what you've been nicknamed?'

'I don't.'

'You are given many titles: 'son of Pharaoh', 'the man who reads magical signs' . . . but my favourite one is the most simple. You are often called 'the Egyptian', as if you were born in this land and had never left it.'

Botzari's words made me shudder. I considered them to be almost frightening, for they revealed aspects of my destiny I refused to think about.

'That is just a poetic way of phrasing things,' I said.

'Beware of this land,' said the Armenian gravely. 'The Arabs haven't succeeded in stifling ancient divinities. They are still very much alive in innumerable engraved stones, for whose messages people say that you have the key. You own a fearsome treasure, Monsieur Champollion. Can you really imagine the consequence of your deeds?'

My surprise at hearing a theological speech from an intriguer's lips was followed by fury. By what authority did he claim to question my research.

'Doctor Botzari, the decipherment of hieroglyphs is now inescapable. Nobody will be able to prevent such a contribution from soon being available to science.'

A shrew bolted graciously in front of us. The small animal, who was the sworn enemy of snakes, was an incarnation of Atum, the great creator God of ancient Egyptians.

'Science, Monsieur Champollion, science is just one more illusion.'

The disgust I read in the Armenian's expression shook my certainties for a moment. Was it really my mission on this earth to read again the tongue of the gods and save the greatest civilization from oblivion? Or was it mad pretension?

'Forget science, Monsieur Champollion,' he recommended. 'It won't be any help in great ordeals.'

I smiled, cheered. 'In that respect, you are wrong. It has been my best ally ever since my childhood. There was no pain I could not overcome through work on my cherished hieroglyphs. Work on them helped me to overcome all of life's vicissitudes.'

Botzari stopped walking and looked at me intensely, his piercing gaze digging into my soul. 'You are very fortunate,' he concluded, 'but you should put an end to your travel here.'

'Why?' I retorted indignantly.

'You won't be able to avoid all the dangers awaiting you.'

'What dangers? Please tell me. Who hates me enough to want to make an attempt on my life?'

'Let's go back,' he said.

The Armenian had succeeded in spoiling the sweet night. Anxiety brought a lump to my throat. The threats mentioned by the quiet man with the stale mind were ominous.

On the threshold of the large house, he stopped, thoughtful. 'You know the ancient Egyptians better than the new masters of the country, Monsieur Champollion. Your research disturbs them. Antiquities interest only scientists. So let human rottenness cover the ruins and swallow them up. Egypt can only offer you death.'

'I am here to revive ancient Egypt, whatever the price.'

He stole a glance at me. 'I have warned you. I'm going back to Alexandria tomorrow. So farewell, Monsieur Champollion.'

We slipped out. When I rejoined my travel companions, who were smoking hookahs, slumped on silk cushions, I was hardly able to contain my anxiety. Nestor L'Hôte noticed it. 'Are you all right, General?'

'Yes, yes . . .'

'Any bad news?'

'Yes and no. I met a messenger from the world beyond.'

'Here they are, here!' shouted Professor Raddi. From the roof of the *Hathor*'s cabin he could make out the famous quarries of Tourah, from which ancient Egyptians had extracted the most beautiful limestone in the country.

The mineralogist's cries of enthusiasm woke up the crew of both ships as well as the *fellahin* who were still sleeping in their wattle huts on the banks we were approaching.

In the evening of 30 September, I had gathered my companions on board the *Isis* to explain my plans: I wanted to explore the astonishing area from which had emerged the necropolis of Memphis and all the great edifices of the city. No obstacle would stop us, even the scorching heat. We realized our good fortune in entering the stone womb out of which so much of Egypt had been born. Tense and almost nervous, we decided to go to bed very early.

I had not found sleep before two. Like all the others, I was woken by the good professor's outburst of joy. During that brief rest, I dreamed of quarries and stonecutters extracting blocks for the temples. I believed I was experiencing their gestures, their effort and their suffering. I became their hands. Raddi tore me away from the vision but, thanks to him, I enjoyed the unspeakable happiness of moving from dream to reality which had the charm of a sumptuous dream, too. Tourah! I was indeed in Tourah, near the limestone horizon where the wind of eternity blew. At 5 a.m., we gathered on the bank, in front of the ships. Lady Redgrave had risen before us and was waiting for us on the back of a grey donkey. Dressed in green she wore a wide-brimmed white hat. I approached her. 'Madam, this is no—'

'Don't waste words, Monsieur Champollion. I know what you are going to say: this is no place for a woman. Don't continue with such nonsense. I want to know everything about the country.'

I had no means of making her go back on her decision. Furious, I passed her and followed Professor Raddi, who had not waited for my signal to head for the quarries. The pretty spy did not relax her vigilance. I should have been acutely annoyed. Yet in my innermost self I felt rather happy near our small community.

'They look like huge barracks for an army of giants,' declared Nestor L'Hôte, as he saw the quarries from a rocky crest. 'There,' he said, pointing with his finger to excavations in the rock, 'There are doors and windows.'

We were overcome by the scale of the task. How could we explore such an immense area? So as to cover the largest possible area I allotted a piece of land for each of my companions to dig. Not very keen on physical labour, Rosellini made a vague protest. Happy to release his pent-up energy, Nestor L'Hôte distributed whistles. We agreed that whoever made a major find would whistle to let me know.

'I think you forgot to give one to me,' said Lady Redgrave.

'Madam, this is no . . .'

I did not dare complete my sentence. The amused sparkle that illuminated her gaze made me look ridiculous in my own eyes. She held out her hand to get a whistle and took the area I allotted to her.

Professor Raddi worked in a state of near euphoria. He touched each block, examined it with tenderness, put fragments in a large bag, unaware of the weight he was thus accumulating. The rapidly increasing heat diminished my companions' ardour. Mine did not decline. I drew numerous inscriptions dating back to the times when the names were people who had worked in the place.

Then I heard a whistle.

It came from Lady Redgrave's area. I immediately thought there had been an accident and, taking no heed of the danger, ran on a limestone crest to join her.

'Watch out, General!' shouted Nestor L'Hôte.

His warning rooted me to the spot. A muffled rumbling filled my ears. Raising my head, I saw a huge block hurtling down towards me. I instinctively stepped back, at the risk of breaking my neck some 60 feet below. The block passed close by, spraying me with dust. I protected my eyes to follow the rest of its mad descent to the bottom of the quarry.

'Come here,' said L'Hôte, as he reached out his hand for me.

Once on a platform, I regained my breath. My heart's beatings slowed down.

'You had a narrow escape, General.'

'Where is Lady Redgrave?'

'Over there.'

Standing on a promontory, dazzling beautiful in the violent white light which seemed to emanate from the rock, mingling with the gold of the sun, she looked at us. Had she planned a crime? Had she tried to draw me into a deadly trap? I had to be certain with legs, trembling, I joined her.

'Where is your discovery?' I said with irony.

'In front of you,' she answered unperturbed, pointing to a very sleek wall on which was engraved a very unusual episode: the erection of a monolith.

Lost in admiration before the steadiness of the outline, I immediately took out my notebook to record it.

'By the way,' she added, 'it figures the name of Pharaoh Psammetichus.'

Dumbfounded, I stopped drawing. 'How have you been able to read it?'

'I used your method,' she answered with a most charming smile.

'That is impossible.'

'Why, Monsieur Champollion?'

'Because I am the only one who knows the whole of my method.'

'Are you unaware that I possess the gift of second sight? Forgive me, I feel a little weary. I'm going back to the ship.'

I looked at her as she moved away, as light as a goddess born from the ocean of freshness which, according to ancient people, surrounded our earth.

So she had searched through my cabin and seen my papers.

We had lunch in a room hewn in the rock and arranged during the reign of Pharaoh Ahmose, the founder of the Eighteenth Dynasty, which turned Thebes into the centre of the world. We were all assessing our finds. Rosellini had recovered his good mood.

'I could not connect anyone with the steep area from which the rock fell. Was anyone working there at the time of the accident?'

'Father Bidant,' replied Rosellini. 'He wanted to look at the quarry from the highest point.'

His back supported by the wall of our strange dining room, the priest was taking a siesta. He looked sound asleep, and it seemed useless to wake him up. How could Father Bidant have conceived such a criminal plan? Imagination is a bad adviser. The blow of a cannon pierced the quietness of the scorching noon. We went out and discovered the strange sight of a hundred *fellahin* and some twenty horsemen led by a bearded old *sheikh* with an olive green turban. The whole crowd was squealing. Our curiosity turned into amazement when we saw the *fellahin* lie down with their faces on the ground, pressed together in a human road for the hooves of the horses.

The *sheikh* went first. The *fellahin* howled with pain under the weight of his horse as it crushed their necks, backs and kidneys. Horrified, I wanted to run to the place of the torture, but Suleiman barred my way. 'Don't interfere. The men are willingly taking part in the rite of *Doseh*. Only those who have the good fortune to be seriously injured can have their sins remitted.'

From the human road rose the incantation 'Allah! Allah!', painfully emerging from the concert of moaning. The unshod hooves broke their bones, opened their flesh, but nobody left until the last horseman had gone. Lady Redgrave, who had come back from the ship to have lunch with us, requested my arm. Like me, she was unable to detach her eyes from the abject ceremony, where blood was shed under the pretext of crazy beliefs. How far this Egypt was from that of the pharaohs!

More or less maimed, the unfortunate men stood up with difficulty. Their clothes were smeared with blood. Yet they still had enough strength to bow before the *sheikh* with the green turban. Then everyone made their way back to Cairo, those who had been wounded supporting each other.

'Here is one still!' exclaimed Lady Redgrave.

A figure lay in a hollow, his dress a mess of blood and sand. His face was deeply pressed into the ground. His neck had been broken.

As Nestor L'Hôte turned him over, I got a shock. I recognized the pistachio salesman who had advised me in the bazaar of Cairo. His wrists had been tied with a thin rope. This man had certainly not wanted to enter the paradise of Allah so early. My shadowy adversaries could not have given me a more impressive warning.

*

The sad discovery of the ruins of Memphis only added to the gloom which had seized our small community. I did not say a word to anyone about the identity of the victim of the *Doseh*, as I did not know whom I could trust. I was even suspicious of my servant Suleiman, who had prevented me from intervening.

Into what sort of hole in time had the huge town surrounded by a white wall, once called 'the Scale of the Two Lands' disappeared? Before us, we could only see an expanse of water, from which emerged high palm trees. Around the end of the Middle Ages, temples still caused the most blasé Arab travellers to shout with admiration. Now, there was not a single block standing. Modern Barbarians had plundered everything. I did not attempt to soften my companions' dismay, but followed Suleiman, who led me to a colossus of Ramses II, sheltered from the rising water south of the ancient wall. The legs were broken but from the intact face and torso emanated a nobleness which overwhelmed my soul. Its mere sight gave me back an energy I thought I had lost.

'Wonderful!' exclaimed Rosellini.

'Much more than that, my good friend; I remember the disgust I felt in Rome before the huge heads of emperors who were killers as well as tyrants. They were just vulgar horrors. Only the Egyptians were able to combine impressiveness with humanity. On such a large scale, the slightest minor error becomes a major defect. The sculptor has had the wisdom to express the bare minimum, without excluding finesse, gravity and smile. He feeds us with this wisdom.'

The words had come spontaneously to my lips. I was almost ashamed to express my feelings like this, but I was certain that I could perceive one of the secrets of the art of the ancient Egyptians. I remained alone for a few hours' mute dialogue with the colossus, the sole survivor of the ruined Memphis.

Lady Redgrave interrupted my meditation, sitting down on

Ramses' chest. 'Are you in love only with ancient Egypt, Monsieur Champollion?'

I gave a start. 'Let's go, Madam. Saqqara is awaiting us.'

The Egyptian land I had been longing to see for such a long time treated me with the tenderness of a mother. In all probability I would retain the sound health I had brought with me. I drank as much fresh water as I wanted. It was Nile water that came through the canal called Mahmudiya in tribute to the Pasha who had it dug.

My servant Suleiman and the locals swore that I could be taken for an Egyptian everywhere. To the use of the language, which I had intended to command completely within a month, I added the local costume: a turban on my shaved head, a gold-embroidered jacket on a striped silk vest, a draped belt made of the same fabric, baggy breeches and red slippers. A thick moustache covered my mouth. It was very warm and extremely convenient attire for Egypt. It made one sweat profusely and one felt fine.

I was already used to the local habits and customs: coffee, pipe, siesta, donkeys, moustache and heat, reinforcing what my sister-in-law had said on the day she married Jacques-Joseph: 'You have too dark a complexion; please make at least your face look pale for the ceremony!'

Only Nestor L'Hôte adopted local customs like me. Rosellini retained a cautious reserve and traces of Europe. Father Bidant swore that he would not abandon his cassock. Professor Raddi hesitated between Turkish and Italian style and dressed in accordance with his morning mood. As for Lady Redgrave, she used a skilfully Oriental wardrobe, and pulled off the miracle of combining elegance with the demands of our everyday life. Nobody dared bother her: because of our attire, people thought that L'Hôte and I were her bodyguards.

The dead plain of Saqqara spread terror among the members of the expedition. We left the two ships moored in front of

Bedrachein to venture into the barren desert, the ancient cemetery of Memphis scattered with destroyed pyramids and violated tombs. The field of mummies, as the Arab call it, was a sequence of small sand mounds, the result of careless digging and plundering. And the whole place was littered with human bones. Decorated with sculptures, most of the tombs had been devastated or plundered and filled up. The rapacious barbarity of the antique traders had been carried out here with the utmost fierceness.

The fragrance of eternity went to my head. We pitched our tent in the midst of a cold immensity peopled by Bedouins with inscrutable faces. As I managed to communicate with them, I succeeded in getting their assistance to take care of house chores and mount guard in front of our camp, day and night. The local chief, Mohammed, even displayed real affection for me.

Never did I experience the weight of solitude as heavily as in Saqqara. Lady Redgrave, to whom the Bedouins had given a magnificent chestnut horse, spent most of her time riding. During the scorching heat, she slept. At meals she conversed gaily with my companions. She had not addressed a word to me for three days. Father Bidant, who probably felt the demons' presence in the desert, relentlessly read the Holy Scriptures he would eventually know by heart. Of course he tried to convert a young Bedouin, but his efforts resulted in bitter failure. Nestor L'Hôte was as happy as a mad puppy. He pranced about from crumbled pyramid to devastated tomb, penetrated everywhere, followed any available guide and brought back lots of sketches, of which only a small part had any scientific value. I thought it was better to let him express his high spirits like this so as to control them better later. Professor Raddi remained ecstatic. The desert was his realm. He only had to bend down to pick up treasures. I thought that he was piecing together the geological history of the country and, who knows, of the whole planet. Rosellini was delighted: he spent the whole day bargaining with the locals and he had already bought some beautiful artefacts, including a sarcophagus, for the museum of Turin.

In the evening, the Bedouins gathered around our tent. They came from everywhere like silent shadows and lit small fires. They told each other stories of ghosts, legends and war feats. Tired by the work, my companions went to bed early. Lady Redgrave retired to her private tent, over which Suleiman kept watch.

I could not get to sleep. Visions of mummies' shrouds, broken bones and skulls bleached by the desert dew obsessed me. My journey was hardly begun. I was still a long way from Thebes and yet I had already touched the emptiness with the tip of my fingers. No decisive inscription had yet enable me to put the finishing touch to my system of decipherment. I had not identified the way which leads to the knowledge of eternal life as the Egyptians perceived it. And I still did not know what to think of the two mysterious letters whose authors remained unknown.

I left our modest camp to venture into the desert. The night suddenly seemed less hostile. The dunes appeared like the petrified waves of a forever motionless ocean. Did marvels of the past sleep under the immobile crust? Pins and needles in my ankles signalled to me that one of the hearts of Egypt was still beating in the desolate place. How many tons of sand and stones would have to be cleared to bring back to light the treasures slumbering under my feet?

The full moon shone with its intense radiance on a deep ravine, at the bottom of which lay some scattered rocks. My instinct commanded me to explore it. The size of the stones meant that it had been an impressive building, maybe a pyramid. My foot hit a small fragment of limestone on which a cartouche in the style of the great times had been preserved. I immediately deciphered the name: Unas.

I had just discovered an unknown pharaoh.

In the early morning of 8 October, our caravan stopped in front of the great sphinx, the guardian of the plateau of Giza and the three great pyramids, perfect forms forever engraved in the eternity of humankind. We were all exhausted after travelling part of the night to avoid the heat and to enjoy these peaceful, empty spaces. A host of Bedouins rushed to offer us dates, water and bread. We welcomed the presents with great satisfaction, but I had to remind my companions of the presence of a lady among us, so that Lady Redgrave could be served first. Our seven camels were gathered in front of the great sphinx to enjoy a well-deserved rest. A mouthful of fresh water was enough to quench my thirst, so fascinated was I by the watchful majesty of the sphinx and the power of the three stone giants. I remained long moments in front of the tombs. The longer I contemplated them, the larger they seemed, carrying me towards heaven with them. Were the greatest monuments ever shaped by human hand only built to pay tribute to emptiness, as Voltaire and some other clever minds had assumed? The admiration I felt proved the contrary. Suddenly I understood. These were no heaps of stones, or absurd demonstrations of temporal vanity, but a song of immortality. Pyramids were not tombs, but houses of resurrection. Of course man is emptiness and dust, but his spirit is light. It had to be sheltered in a dwelling which matched its extent and nature.

'The pyramids should be dismantled stone by stone,' judged Professor Raddi. 'I am sure that their core must be fascinating.'

'What a monstrous expression of completely mad vanity!' judged Father Bidant. I immediately took him aside, while Rosellini began to bargain for his purchases and Nestor L'Hôte to draw the head of the sphinx. Lady Redgrave sat under an umbrella held by Suleiman and dozed. 'Father, such criticisms are meaningless. As you have the misfortune of hating Egypt, please be kind enough to shut up so that you can at least enjoy the pleasure of being silent!'

A myriad of hawks danced in an endless circle around the

summit of the pyramids. The priest avoided looking me straight in the eyes. 'Don't be insolent,' he retorted. 'You have no right to dictate my conduct. On the contrary. I am the one who should watch over yours. Look at yourself, Champollion. You don't look like man of good moral standards. If you persist in letting yourself be seduced by this country full of demons, you will soon lose religion and you will become a very harmful scientist.'

'We will mourn together, Father. The vanity you attribute to pharaohs only exists in your mind. The huge monuments are symbols. Look at them. Don't they put to shame our mediocrity, our trivialities, our poor humankind?'

Father Bidant shrugged his shoulders, and withdrew, grumbling as he went.

Nestor L'Hôte grasped my sleeve. 'General . . . come quickly! The experience is not to be missed.'

I followed him without thinking. Hauled up by his powerful arm and that of a Bedouin who was as nimble as a monkey, I climbed up the edge of the great pyramid of Cheops. Its blocks formed huge steps. Initially enthusiastic about the ascent, I had the unfortunate idea of turning round to look down halfway up. My heart suddenly pounded wildly, I swayed. To avoid the dizziness, I closed my eyes and flattened myself against the slope. I was unable to move either forward or backward, or even to let out a cry for help.

'Climb on, General!' exclaimed L'Hôte, from far above.

I remained silent. A wave of terror overwhelmed me. Had L'Hôte drawn me here so that I could give way to dizziness and the seemingly natural disaster of breaking my neck? But how could he have known about my proneness to vertigo?

A hand rested on my shoulder. For a moment, I had the impression that it was pushing me into the emptiness. 'Is anything wrong, General?'

'I feel unwell,' I muttered without opening my eyes.

'Did you look down?'

I nodded.

'Foolishness, General. Let yourself be guided. You will admire the landscape from the top. I am sure that you won't feel giddy again. Give me your hand, climb up and only think of the pyramids.'

As weak as a child, I submitted to L'Hôte's will. The blocks of stone became my refuge, the ultimate resort between my panting body and the void. It reassured me to touch them. I blindly climbed up with a steady foot and focused my energy on the goal I had to reach: the top.

'We're there, General.'

Four hundred and twenty feet above the ground, on the crown of the most gigantic edifice ever conceived by the human mind, I opened my eyes at last to enjoy an incomparable vision. To the east, I could see the edge of the plateau of Giza, the Nile and the rumour of Cairo, to the west, the desert and, to the south, Abusir, Saqqara and the two huge pyramids of Dashur, erected by King Sneferu. The work of the people of the Ancient Kingdom was offered in the form of stones reaching up towards the absolute.

'What can one say in face of this?' said L'Hôte, fascinated.

The Bedouin guide fell asleep with his head on his knees. L'Hôte drew. I contemplated. We remained for over two hours on the summit of the pyramid of Cheops, just where the pryamidion should have been. The ancient Egyptians had not wanted to complete their work. The last stone could only be the Creator's.

On the evening of a day which had been both exalting and exhausting, we were invited to a meal presided over by Sheikh Mohammed under an acacia grove between the desert and cultivated land.

'There is no other God but God,' he declared, after he had requested us to sit on sparsely embroidered but comfortable cushions.

The meal was only composed of flat barley bread, but friendship compensated for the austerity of the food.

'I had a wonderful time,' said Lady Redgrave, who sat on my right, in a low voice.

'I didn't expect to hear the sound of your voice any more,' I reproached her.

'Don't you know that a woman wilts in solitude?'

My right-hand neighbour, a Bedouin, begged me to look at Sheikh Mohammed, who was about to make another speech.

'Blessed be your expedition, Monsieur Champollion,' he proclaimed pompously. 'Men have been brothers ever since Adam and Eve, yet they do not know it. May you help them discover what your heart has come to find here.'

He did not say anything else and concentrated on his meal. I would have liked to question his enigmatic words, but Oriental propriety forbade me to do so. We were eating silently when a series of shots startled all the guests.

The Bedouins signalled the arrival of a horseman. He immediately entered the tent and bowed to the *sheikh*. Dressed in the Turkish way, he had both the imposing bearing of Rosellini and the strength of Nestor L'Hôte.

'Is Champollion here?' he asked.

'Here I am,' I said standing up.

'I was keen to meet you. My name is Caviglia.'

Caviglia! I looked at him as if he had come from heaven. The man who had come to me was the one I most wanted to meet on my journey.

Caviglia knew everything about the plateau of Giza. Eleven years before, he had cleared the sphinx, explored the pyramids and initiated numerous excavations whose results were known only to him. A strange and not very amenable man, he refused to talk to the other members of the expedition, he only wanted to speak with me face to face. For three long days he described his work. He forbade me to take notes for fear of seeing them disappear. We had lunch and dinner in the open air and ate dates and bread brought by the Bedouins, who worshipped him. At night I slept in the tent of Sheikh Mohammed whose camp was constantly on the move. Each dawn Caviglia reappeared with renewed energy. He displayed a passion equal to mine for the slightest remnant of Egyptian antiquity.

I learnt as much in three days with him as I had in years of libraries. I was both sad and happy to be rid of the constant watchfulness of Lady Redgrave. What obscure scheme was she hatching in my absence? Why had the Pasha's and Drovetti's watchdogs, Abdel-Razuk and Moktar, disappeared? How did links between the members of our community develop when deprived of its 'general'?

'You are worried, Champollion,' said Caviglia as he sat down in front of me.

The sun was setting. We were drinking carob juice in front of Sheikh Mohammed's tent.

'I am very grateful for your help, but . . .'

'But solitude weighs down on you.'

'No. But I must do my duty to the members of my expedition.'

An expression of disgust coloured Caviglia's face. 'What a venture. Bidant is a sly priest who only wants your death. Rosellini is a merchant, like so many fake scientists. L'Hôte is a lout who only dreams of cuts and bumps. Professor Raddi is a dangerous crank. As for Lady Redgrave . . . They will all betray you, Champollion.'

I turned crimson. 'You have no right to talk like this!'

'Have you found King Unas' cartouche?'

His question caught me unaware. 'How do you know . . .'

'Chance does not exist in Egypt, Champollion. The sign was probably placed in your way . . . Bonaparte had a similar experience.'

'What?' I asked, intrigued.

'Bonaparte entered the great pyramid with his guide. He stayed inside for a very long time. When he came out, he was extremely pale. "What happened?" asked his aide-de-camp. "Nothing I could explain," answered Bonaparte. "Why talk about it? You would not believe me. In addition, I swore to keep it secret." '

Surprised by these revelations, I tried to discover more. But Caviglia remained inflexible. 'Bonaparte was only one follower among others. Take care of your own destiny, Champollion. My friends and I have been awaiting you for a long time. The tradition has not been lost, but your discoveries are essential. We would like to work with you.'

Caviglia remained grave. I felt both attracted and suspicious. 'What do you want from me?'

'Your knowledge of hieroglyphs.'

'And what do you offer?'

'Keys which are still missing, as well as knowledge about your destiny,' he answered, looking at the desert in the distance. 'You are the one who has to decide. Come tonight to the bottom of the step pyramid of Saqqara with Unas' cartouche.'

He stood up. I thought I was dreaming. What did the mysteries mean? If the man had not been a well-known archaeologist, I would have considered him as a crank and a charlatan. But the seriousness of his words and attitude contradicted such a judgement.

'Wait . . . did you send me a letter in France?'

Caviglia did not turn round. 'I may have,' he acknowledged before he climbed on his horse and disappeared into the sunset.

I was not afraid of anything, except human stupidity which can turn the most noble endeavours into failures. Ever since my childhood I had been faced with the unknown and I had tried to accept challenges. Yet the one suggested by Caviglia had enough to puzzle me. He demanded a trust which was beyond reason. There was only one certainty: Caviglia was the author of one of the two letters. But which one? Had he refused to give details to draw me more easily into a trap?

The plain of mummies. Agonizing Saqqara . . . Would it be my last stop on earth? I did not feel ready to give up this life until my research had succeeded. Caution dictated that I stay with the members of my expedition. Yet a pressing curiosity pushed me to ride a donkey to Saqqara without letting anyone know. What sensible man would have refused the opportunity to know his destiny and obtain the treasure he was so eagerly seeking?

I saw the Saqqara step pyramid for the first time. Before I had not been very impressed by the somewhat shapeless mass buried in a heap of sand and rubble. In the moonlight, it appeared in its antique majesty. I wanted to clear it with my hands so as to restore its splendour. As I knelt down, a huge shadow stood up before me.

9

They ate delicious dates at breakfast. A north wind made the morning pleasant. The vision of the three pyramids of the plateau of Giza produced an unforgettable memory. Lady Ophelia Redgrave, however, felt no hunger. Nor had she any further inclination for contemplation. She had been riding in the desert for over an hour and daringly ventured into hostile Bedouin camps.

Back at the tent where the members of the expedition had been sleeping, she had a glimpse of Father Bidant who was drinking mint tea with his missal within reach. Rosellini was studying lists of hieroglyphs he was unable to decipher without the help of the master. His chest bared, Nestor L'Hôte was doing limbering up exercises. Indifferent to the outside world, Professor Raddi was making an inventory of fragments of limestone which he examined with a magnifying glass.

Lady Redgrave dismounted and walked towards Rosellini. 'Have you seen Suleiman?'

'No,' answered the Italian.

'Any news from Sheikh Mohammed?'

'No. According to the Bedouins, he headed south. And what about you . . . did you learn anything?'

Lady Redgrave bit her lip. 'We are now certain that Champollion has disappeared.'

I thought that the step pyramid was crashing down on me. Its huge shadow enveloped me like a shroud. I turned around quickly, feeling a presence behind me. It was Caviglia.

'Are you ready to follow me, Champollion?'

I agreed.

Caviglia passed before me. We walked along the step pyramid and headed for the middle of the north face. The mass of rubble was enormous and almost reached for summit of the monument, thus ruining all perspective. Caviglia climbed halfway up the wall of sand. He removed a large block with a long and considerable effort, and uncovered the entrance to a very narrow gallery, hardly large enough for a body to slide in.

'The gallery leads to the bottom of hell,' he declared. 'It's up to you, Champollion.' Is there any more exalting experience than to go to the core of a pyramid? I slid into the narrow opening and followed Caviglia, who took good care to replace the block. The slope was very steep. I slid down on my back, my nose to the ceiling. I had to bend my legs to progress. Caviglia remained at a distance so as not to hit me when I used my heels to slow down. I scraped my calves and knees, swallowed dust and knocked my head, but I hurried, eager to see the grave of the pharaoh who had built the first pyramid.

Just I was beginning to run out of air, the gallery suddenly widened and became horizontal. At this depth there was a bluish light which immediately soothed the hardships of the exploration. Progressing into the funerary edifice, where a whole family had probably been gathered, I stopped and marvelled in front of a faience panel representing the journey of the Pharaoh, an oar in one hand, during the celebration of the regeneration in the course of which, nourished by divine magic, the ruler regained new strength so as to fulfil his task better.

'This is where Egypt was born,' said Caviglia. 'It is the tomb of Djoser, the first pharaoh to celebrate the union of the Two Lands. Some day, it will be discovered. The huge area around it will be dug and masterworks will emerge from the ground.'

'Why has this fabulous find not been revealed to the whole world?'

'Because we were waiting for you, Champollion, and because the time has not come yet. I ask you to keep everything you will see this night absolutely secret.'

'What if I refuse?'

Caviglia did not answer. His gaze was eloquent enough. 'Keep the revelations in your heart. Remain silent until we decide otherwise.

' "We". Whom do you mean?'

'The Brotherhood of Luxor.'

The Brotherhood of Luxor . . . I had heard about it in Paris. It had been mentioned as a sect collecting the teachings of ancient civilizatons, especially in India and Egypt. The information had seemed so ludicrous that I had not paid the slightest attention to it.

'We have always known that you would come. One of our brothers, Henry Salt, predicted that a young Frenchman would discover again the secret of the hieroglyphs.'

So the British Consul-General in Egypt had been a member of the brotherhood!

'I spent many years exploring the pyramids, clearing the sphinx and discovering underground galleries linking the plateau of Giza to the site of Saqqara,' continued Caviglia. 'That is the way we will take – once you are blindfolded.'

'Why? Don't you trust me?'

'That is our rule, Champollion.'

'I refuse.' My whole being rebelled against the absurd show.

'You would be wrong to,' said Caviglia calmly. 'Have you forgotten what is at stake?'

'Be more specific,' I challenged him sharply.

'You will be transformed so as to be initiated into the spirit of ancient Egypt. If you don't get the vision right you will only remain an onlooker without proper understanding.'

'And you pretend to offer such a treasure to me?'

'Me? No, of course not! Only Egypt can do that . . . if it judges that you are worthy of it.'

The true meaning of the words was beyond me, but I was most impressed by Caviglia's serenity. I was bad at pretending to be indifferent. It was obvious that the man had a secret. How could I forget the sight of Djoser's marvellous relief? How could I not believe a man who had revealed such wonders to me?

'For the last time, Champollion, I ask you to keep secret everything you will see, hear and experience tonight. Use it to decipher Egypt, but do not reveal the key which will be offered to you as a brother. The day will come when, in line with what I am doing now, you will have to pass it on to your own successor and request the same commitment.'

I hesitated again, preparing at least ten contra-arguments, and struggled with my fear. Then: 'I swear.'

'Now come.'

He blindfolded me with a white cloth which smelt of jasmine. The fragrance soon went to my head. I regretted not to be able to stay longer in front of Djoser's bluish figures and had to trust the hand which guided me in the underground gallery between the pyramids. I was unable to assess how long our journey took, but it was mostly over uneven ground. Suddenly, the slope became very steep. Caviglia hauled me briskly on. The warm air of the night filled my lungs. We had just reached the outside world.

'Have you heard about the Prophet?' I asked.

'The old scientist who worked at the Institute of Egypt? Of course.'

'Did he not say that he had discovered the secret of the hieroglyphs?'

'It is true,' answered Caviglia, 'that he declared himself in possesion of a lost science.'

'Why didn't he become a member of the brotherhood?'

'We were to welcome him shortly before your arrival. But his office burnt down.'

'And he perished in the fire, didn't he?'

It took Caviglia a few seconds to reply. 'No body was retrieved from the rubble. Some witnesses declare that they saw Moktar, Drovetti's steward, escaping in a lane shortly after the beginning of the fire.'

A criminal fire . . . The Prophet wanted to give me essential information. Drovetti wanted him murdered so as to prevent him from talking to me. 'Is he still alive?' I said enthusiastically.

'Nobody knows. His presence was reported in Thebes, where he is said to be in hiding. Some people claim that he has taken refuge in Nubia, a long way from Drovetti and his henchmen.'

'If he is still alive,' I said with clenched jaws, 'I shall find him again. I must find him.'

'He cannot go unnoticed,' stated Caviglia. 'He is over six feet eight. He has a very thin white beard trimmed into a point and never goes anywhere without a long acacia stick with a gold knob. Now concentrate, Champollion. We must resume our journey.'

The fire of hope was rekindled in me. New ways were opening. I was ready for the struggle.

Caviglia removed the blindfold. I first made out the stars and then, lowering my gaze, saw two huge stone benches which I soon identified as the two legs of the sphinx. Turning round, I understood that I was standing in front of the chest of the guardian of the necropolis, under its chin.

'Be careful,' said Caviglia. 'Let's go to the great pyramid.'

So the tomb of Cheops was the final goal of our strange expedition and the place where the Brothers of Luxor intended to perform on me what the ancient Egyptians called 'the opening of the mouth and eyes'. We walked side by side to the immense monument, whose mass stood out in the darkness.

An Arab faced us, a gun in his hand. Caviglia interposed himself between him and me and uttered a single word, whose meaning I did not grasp. The Arab bowed his head respectfully.

'He is keeping watch,' said Caviglia. 'His presence proves that there are no uninitiated interlopers.'

Probably neither prowlers nor wandering dogs . . . The Brothers of Luxor were so efficiently organized that they kept everybody away from the great pyramid. Following Caviglia, I entered it with a lump in my throat. I had to go through a dark area before I was able to distinguish the light of a torch high above me. I slid into a narrow gallery where I had to bend to progress. Very soon there was a lack of air. The light disappeared. There was no more noise behind me, as if Caviglia had disappeared. I instinctively felt that I would not be allowed to go back. So I stepped forward, convinced that I would be stifled to death. Heat and dust combined to burn my lungs. I stopped resisting. I let go. Why should I oppose the inescapable? Why should I try to retain what must disappear, be it even my own life? Isn't it a most fabulous destiny to die in the core of the great pyramid? My tension vanished. I yielded to the centuries accumulated in the eternal stones. I moved on calmly, as if the ascent was to have no end. Light appeared again as I stepped out the narrow tunnel. I stood up and discovered an immense gallery ascending to the core of the pyramid. Torches stuck at the bottom of the walls spread a fawn-coloured light, out of which the huge blocks of granite seemed to be born. I had the impression that it was both in the centre of the earth and in the middle of the sky, in an unknown space and time rather than that of human beings.

Caviglia put his hand on my left shoulder. 'This is the last stage, Champollion.'

The way seemed easier, almost effortless. I certainly had to concentrate to walk on the slippery stone ground, but some energy emanated from the gallery drawing my body upwards and making it less heavy. The place was a dazzling passage to the universe of the gods. It purified me from whatever was useless and artificial. Step by step, I walked out of a shell which I had not been aware of until now.

After I had taken a huge step to cross a threshold, I penetrated the sarcophagus room. It was lit by a single candelabra similar to those used by ancient Egyptians. The wick produced no smoke. At the bottom of the sanctuary eight men, whose faces remained in the shadow, were waiting for me. As I came near I recognized Anastasy, who had helped me in Alexandria, as well as my servant Suleiman. I knew none of the others, who were dressed in the Turkish fashion, although they belonged to different nations. I would have liked to talk to them and ask them questions, but Anastasy did not leave me time to do so. 'Step into the sarcophagus,' he ordered.

The funerary tank of Pharaoh Cheops had been hewn from a single block. No trace of a lid had ever been found. I stepped into the opening of the most venerable sarcophagus in Egypt and lay on my back. I instinctively crossed my arms over my chest, like Osiris.

A wonderful sensation of heat diffused throughout my back. It was not the everlasting rest of death, but the radiance of life itself. Closing my eyes to enjoy the extraordinary pleasure which had a taste of resurrection, I heard the deep voice of Anastasy chant a kind of ritual.

'The sarcophagus has never been closed,' he said. 'No lid was ever been laid down. In the chamber of metamorphosis, our brothers have been regenerated ever since the time of King Cheops. Here in the centre of the world, the light from within has come to illuminate their destiny. Welcome among us, Jean-François Champollion. You will spend the night in the sarcophagus. What you request from the pyramid will be granted to you.'

The light of the only torch disappeared. I did not belong to myself any more. I let visions invade me. Thoth with an ibis head, the patron of scientists and scribes, and Anubis with a jackal head, the one who opens the paths of the other world, removed a veil of blue-green hieroglyphs decorating the vault of a pyramid. I began to decipher them by applying the essentials of my method. Thoth rectified each mistake I made and filled the gaps. This is how I came to know the ultimate destiny of Pharaoh, his constant transmutations in the heaven of the fair ones, his travels in cosmic spaces, his fusion with the light of the sun out of which he had been born. I passed on the other side of life and promised myself to give back to the gods all they had given me.[1] So the pyramids were talking! What I had seen that night may have really existed somewhere, in a place excavations would discover one day.[2]

I lost all idea of time. Was that how you became Osiris in your own lifetime? Was it how you encountered the divine power, lying at the bottom of a sarcophagus, your eyes open on a heaven of stone?

'The Pasha's police have been warned,' announced Lady Redgrave gloomily.

At the foot of the pyramid of Cheops, at full noon, the community of the vanished general was becoming concerned. Even Professor Raddi realized that something unusual had happened.

'Look!' exclaimed L'Hôte, as he saw Suleiman coming to the great tent, pushing before him a donkey loaded with bunches of dates.

His face hollowed by a sleepless night, Rosellini rushed to the servant. 'Do you know where Champollion is?' he asked aggressively.

[1] Champollion kept his word. In the few more years of life he was granted, he managed to write the first grammar and the first dictionary of hieroglyphs. It is difficult to imagine that such colossal works were conceived and written by a single man.

[2] Champollion was right. The pyramid of King Unas, the last king of the Sixth Dynasty and several pyramids of kings or queens of the Sixth Dynasty do contain significant religious texts. The great Mariette did not believe in the reality of these pyramid texts, whose existence he only heard of on his deathbed.

'Just raise your eyes,' answered Suleiman, quietly.

Everyone followed the servant's gaze, and saw the figure of Jean-François Champollion flooded by the light of the God Ra, on top of the great pyramid.

10

I ate the sunniest lunch of my life on top of the great pyramid of Cheops, on a large platform where over forty people could have been seated. In the middle was a heap of large blocks which looked like a kind of small ruined pyramidion. Lady Redgrave, who turned out to be a remarkable mountaineer, Nestor L'Hôte, Rosellini and Suleiman had come to join me with honey flat bread and fresh water. Father Bidant had refused to climb on a monument he considered as not far from satanic. As for Professor Raddi, he was studying a fragment of limestone whose exceptional character he was the only one to see.

'What happened?' enquired Lady Redgrave. 'How did you disappear?'

Dressed in white, her head wrapped in a shawl from which her eyes hardly emerged, the British spy appeared like a fearsome accuser, determined to know everything.

'I did not disappear. I was working with Caviglia on sites he agreed to show only to me.'

'Which ones?'

'The plain of the dead in Saqqara and its surroundings.'

'I thought you hated the place,' observed Rosellini, sharply.

'Caviglia made me revise my opinion.'

'You should beware of the man,' said L'Hôte incisively. 'He will try to extort money from us. I'm sure of that.'

'Don't be afraid, Nestor. You won't see Caviglia again and he won't harm us in any way.'

My companions were confused.

'Does that mean—' said Rosellini concerned.

'Caviglia has left Egypt,' I explained. 'He thinks that his mission as an archaeologist is completed and that our expedition opens a new era for the knowledge of ancient people. He wishes us good luck, and he asked me to leave as soon as possible for the south, for the heart of Nubia. To him, the country is deteriorating day by day. Even the monuments are in the utmost danger.'

'Then let's not waste time!' declared Nestor L'Hôte, who, suiting the action to the word, threw his last bread in the air and started to walk down.

'I'll follow you!' announced Rosellini tensely.

Suleiman followed close behind them, after first asking my permission. We all seemed happy to seek some coolness at the foot of the great pyramid.

Lady Redgrave barred my way. 'I don't believe a word of your children's tales,' she said with passion. 'You gave us the slip with the help of Bedouins to arrange your own traffic of antiquities. Caviglia is just a minor part. Didn't you spend most of your jaunt in the company of Consul-General Drovetti, out of range of eavesdroppers?'

The accusations were so surprising that they took my breath away.

'I was right!' she insisted, triumphantly. 'The great, the noble Champollion is just a plunderer like all the others!'

'Madam,' I managed to answer in a trembling voice. 'You are mistaken.'

Angry, she took her shawl off. In the midday light, her face radiated a purity I had only seen in the wives of pharaohs. 'Would you dare swear on what you most value? On your Egypt?'

'In the ancient Egyptian language, the word for oath is 'life' ... Will you allow me to swear on what I most value now, that is to say the lives of those who make up the expedition?'

My proposal troubled her. 'Let's put an end to the game,

Monsieur Champollion. You will eventually confess the truth to me, if you care a little for me.'

The tigress was becoming tender, the fearsome lioness Sekhmet was changing into the soft cat Bastet. Ancient people said that no man could ever resist her charm. 'I may care very much for you . . . but I promised to keep the secret.'

Yielding to an impulse which surprised me, I took her in my arms. Our faces were so close that our lips almost touched each other. Her skin, scented with jasmine, had a delicious fineness. Her inscrutable gaze remained distant.

'You don't love me, Lady Ophelia, you spy on me . . .'

'That's nonsense!' she exclaimed as she freed herself.

An unpleasant surprise awaited me at the bottom of the pyramid of Cheops. Abdel-Razuk, the Pasha's *chaouiche*, was accompanied by a dozen Turkish solders. Behind them stood Drovetti's henchman, Moktar, a vague smile hovering on his lips. Abdel-Razuk stepped towards me. 'I have received instructions from the Pasha, Monsieur Champollion. Please follow me.'

'Why?'

'I don't know.'

'Is His Excellency here?'

Abdel-Razuk remained silent. Lady Redgrave and my companions were kept aside by horsemen with their swords drawn.

'Please follow me immediately,' ordered Abdel-Razuk.

It seemed silly to oppose armed force. My three-day adventure had caused enough scandal to inconvenience the master of Egypt. I had to answer for my fault before him to regain his favour.

I was hauled on to the back of a camel. This was an uncomfortable position, but I tried to keep it with dignity during the two-hour journey to a palace surrounded by palm trees in the suburbs of Cairo. Once we had passed a row of trees, we discovered a garden full of acacias and bowers covered with roses. Not far from the entrance was a small marble pavilion near a pond with waterlilies on it. Under the shade of a eucalyptus two gardens were sleeping. The palace was composed of two wings joined by an arch. The first had a long façade with windows covered with mesh and small balconies enclosed by grilles. A porter kept watch over the entrance. We greeted each other, touching our foreheads, mouths and chests with out right hands to let the other know that mind, speech and heart were open. Following Abdel-Razuk and Moktar, I entered a room with columns, which opened on to a courtyard with a fountain in the centre. The place was deliciously cool. The floor of marble mosaic hardly reflected the light. The master of the place sat on a divan, dedicating himself to the delicate art of watercolour.

He turned to me. 'Welcome, Champollion.'

It was not the Pasha, but the Consul-General of France, Bernardino Drovetti.

'You have become as Turkish as one can be,' he declared as he examined me.

'I followed your example,' I retorted.

With our turbans, beards, tanned complexions and baggy breeches, we were far away from the mists of Europe.

'Thank you for having come so quickly, Champollion.'

'You did not leave me any choice . . .'

Moktar clapped his hands, producing a dance of servants who brought sweets and drinks. I remained standing, refusing an invitation to kneel on cushions.

'I am your friend, Champollion.'

'Then why did you use the Pasha's police?'

'To protect you.'

Drovetti himself poured the mint tea in china cups.

'You mix with dangerous people, Champollion. They may abuse your generosity. I heard that Caviglia tried to extort money belonging to France from you.'

'Your informer gave you false information. You should pay less attention to Lady Redgrave's words, sir.'

Drovetti turned crimson. 'Your insinuations are stupid!'

'I'm glad to hear that. To err is human. So I can now trust Lady Redgrave again.'

Drovetti gave me a challenging look and drank some tea. 'Caviglia belongs to a secret society of plotters. The Pasha and I intend on removing the cancer from Egypt. Activists will be expelled . . . as well as their sympathizers.'

'I don't care,' I said, indifferent.

Drovetti was surprised. 'Haven't you met Caviglia?'

'Of course. He took me to visit the archaeological sites he was granted by the Pasha.'

'Do you deny that you disappeared for three days in his company and met his associates?'

'Disappeared? How romantic, sir! I was on a strictly archaeological pursuit. I have a witness, Sheikh Mohammed whom I believe to be a friend and a favourite of the Pasha.'

I took care to emphasize the last words. Drovetti's inscrutable face proved that the precautions I had taken were good. This time Lady Redgrave's intervention turned out to have had no effect. I understood why, fearing the Pasha's police and Drovetti's militia, the Brothers of Luxor had dispersed, leaving the weight of their mission on my shoulders. I had become the man who was to discover and pass on the ancient Egyptians' secrets, by combining the brotherhood's revelations and my knowledge of hieroglyphs.

Drovetti may have read my thoughts. He felt the strength of my determination. 'You could be considered as a plotter, Champollion. Your deeds might threaten the authority of the Pasha!'

Moktar seemed ready to tie me up and throw me in a dungeon.

'I don't think so. I'm only interested in the task I was entrusted by the King and which the Pasha and you approved: the discovery of ancient Egypt; to make it known to the whole world. I shall do only that, whatever obstacles I may have to face.'

Drovetti became animated again. 'Obstacles! You do not realize the risks you are running. Well, fulfil your task! But do not disturb the order of this country. Don't question the interests of those who preserve it.'

His tone had become brusque. My 'protector' controlled his annoyance with difficulty.

'That is not my intention,' I insisted, 'as long as those interests don't disturb my work.'

With a nervous jerk of his hand, Drovetti ordered Moktar and Abdel-Razuk to leave. His expression immediately softened. 'What do you think of the palace, Champollion?'

I was somewhat surprised by the question. 'It is magnificent . . . a true *Thouand and One Nights* palace. It reminds me of the dream Orient I discovered in the tales I read secretly at the lycée.'

'It is a bewitching place. Be my guest! Stay here as long as you want. Settle your companions here. Lady Redgrave will appreciate the luxury, which will suit her beauty better than dubious ships and dusty roads. And . . .' Drovetti's gaze coloured with a secret understanding.

'. . . I could easily give my support to your scientific report and even help flesh it out. I am in possession of several manuscripts of travellers who came before you. You will only have to make a copy of them. As for antiquities, don't be afraid. I take responsibility for getting some for your Louvre Museum. Does the arrangement suit you, Champollion?'

I thought aloud. 'Who could refuse such a tempting offer?'

At last Drovetti relaxed. A raptor's satisfaction illuminated his face. 'You are now being sensible. You have the makings of a great man, Champollion. Fortune will smile on you.'

I turned on my heels, ready to leave. Alarmed, Drovetti stood up. 'But . . . where are you going?'

Turning round, I looked at him serenely. 'I'm resuming my journey, of course.'

*

It was dark when we entered the town of El Minya, where the market was still busy in the light of torches. We passed a cotton mill where women and children worked, bent over hanks. The sight distressed me.

'The Pasha,' explained Suleiman who was walking just behind me. 'He has no respect for anyone but himself.'

An adolescent with wild eyes ran out of a lane. He crashed headlong into Professor Raddi, who stood gaping, and fell on to Lady Redgrave. They both collapsed in the dust. Furious Turks immediately appeared, arms in hand. They hesitated for a moment, noticed the boy who was standing up with difficulty and grabbed his collar. He shouted with fright. One of the Turks cut his right hand with his sabre. The blood splashed on Nestor L'Hôte, who was petrified and vomited against a wall.

A steel hand seized my arm. 'Don't interfere, brother,' recommended Suleiman. 'You cannot do anything for him. He tried to escape the soldiers who wanted to enrol him in the Sultan's army. He is now only a traitor and a rebel.'

Still dizzy, Lady Redgrave had not seen anything of the horrible scene. Father Bidant helped her to her feet while Suleiman poured water on the forehead of Professor Raddi who was still half-conscious. Shocked, Rosellini looked at a procession of veiled women who were in tears as they followed the soldiers taking the deserter away. The blood was soaking into the ground. A wandering dog lapped it up.

'The Sultan is a cruel man,' said Suleiman in a low voice. 'His power was born in bloodshed. On 1 May 1811, he invited the local landlords, the *beys* to the citadel of Cairo. They came in sumptuous attire, riding their best horses, harnessed with precious stones. They had to go through narrow lanes to reach the citadel. There was a massacre. The Sultan's killers, Albanians, shot the guests through narrow windows. The slaughter lasted half an hour. It is said that there was only one survivor who dared jump on his horse from the parapet of the citadel. He became mad and escaped forever into the desert.

The Mamelukes, who were considered as enemies, were slaughtered in their dwellings. This is how Mehmet Ali became the sole master of Egypt.'

'Let's leave this place,' I said.

Rosellini protested. 'We should rest and have dinner.'

I absolutely refused. I was in a hurry to leave El Minya and reach the next site we had to explore. There was only one way of forgetting the tragedy we had just experienced: to contemplate the art of the ancient Egyptians again.

'Beni Hassan,' said Rosellini, in a grating tone. 'There is nothing really fascinating to study there. Half a day should be enough. Especially if you are in a hurry to reach Nubia.'

We had hardly boarded the ships when we faced a violent gale. I caught hold of Lady Redgrave as she was about to fall.

'I don't need you . . . You were not with me earlier when . . .'

'Forgive me. I forgot my duty to you.'

Her nervousness seemed to subside. 'Are you a little human, Monsieur Champollion? Do you feel other affections than those for old stones?'

I would probably have slapped her in the face, had I not been too moved by the softness of her light green eyes, which seemed devoid of perfidy. 'Do you understand, Lady Ophelia—'

With a glance she signalled Rosellini, who was observing us. 'Keep silent and think. Are you sure that the unfortunate boy didn't rush to bring you a message?'

11

The squall pushed us so vigorously that we reached Beni Hassan around midnight. Yielding to tiredness, we allowed ourselves a few hours of sleep. Shortly before dawn, I wok Rosellini and sent him to a scout a cliff, where we could just make out some tomb entrances. He came back less than an hour later, vexed.

'There are only caves,' he declared. 'There is nothing to be got from them. Let's leave.'

How could I not trust such a scrupulous colleague? It is true that Beni Hassan had not made any great impression on the memory of travellers who had been there.

'Let's listen to Ippolito,' recommended Lady Redgrave who had just got up, her loose hair dancing in the breeze.

I hesitated. On the one hand, the major aim of my mission was still to head for Thebes and the far south. On the other hand, a vague premonition commanded me not to leave the site without giving it a look. 'Let me think.'

I disembarked. The early day was so mild that it had a taste of eternity. I had hardly walked a few steps, when a hand gripped my right leg.

I quickly lowered my eyes to a little girl in a long blue dress splashed with mud. 'They're waiting for you,' she said in nasal voice. 'They're waiting for you!'

I tried to ask her for some explanation, but, as quick as a cat, she vanished in the abundant vegetation concealing a canal.

Was it an important message? Should her words lead me to some essential discovery? I climbed back on board, thoughtful.

'It would be stupid not to examine the tombs briefly,' I said to Rosellini. 'I'll go and have a look. I won't be long.'

What constant happiness it is to walk in the desert sand! It crunches under the foot, undulates with the slightest caress of the wind and forms a supply body that is both forever changing and yet forever in similar forms. The sun had risen. I had to ascend to the caves dug in the cliff. I felt irresistibly attracted to them.

A herd of goats suddenly appeared in front of me, some white and others black, none of them aggressive. Sitting on a block on the threshold of a tomb, the goatherd slept soundly, his slumbering young girlfriend beside him.

What a surprise it was to penetrate one of the holy caves and discover a large space with wonderful columns, some of which undoubtedly dated back to primitive Doric! Here was the proof that Greece had not taught anything to Egypt and had, on the contrary, been inspired by it. Coming close to a wall, I distinguished an inscription hastily scribbled with a chalk: '1800, 3rd Regiment of Dragoons.' I used black ink to add the trace of my own visit above: JFC 1828. As I completed my modest task, my eyes became accustomed to the darkness and I thought I could discern some astonishing figures. Seized by a mad hope, I ran to the ship, jostled Rosellini, who was purchasing funerary figures from a *fellah*, leapt on deck and grasped a sponge which had been dropped by a sailor sleeping against the rigging.

Back at the tomb, I delicately wetted part of the wall and very slowly removed the crust of dust that covered it. Paintings! There were wonderful paintings . . . My companions rushed up to discover the cause of my enthusiasm and we set to the task. Thanks to our ladders and to that most significant achievement of natural and human industry, the sponge, we discovered a very ancient series of figures depicting civil life, the arts, the professions and the military caste.

The daily life of Egypt was reappearing under our very eyes. Four-thousand-year-old soldiers paraded again with a joyful step more reminiscent of banquets than of war. Carpenters made seats, beds and chests; goldsmiths worked rhythmically to orders chanted by foremen. And the desert was filled with hares, jackals, hyenas and gazelles.

I took notes and drew sketches for hours without feeling the slightest tiredness. L'Hôte and Rosellini started to work. At noon, Suleiman brought us a lunch composed of small pieces of mutton, a jar of curd to be used as a sauce for the meat and watermelons. Lady Redgrave paid us a brief visit in the early afternoon. I commented on the figures revealed by the sponge and read to her inscriptions inviting craftsmen to turn raw matter into something beautiful and harmonious. She listened silently and returned to the daylight, where Professor Raddi was taking advantage of Father's Bidant's muscular force to carry small blocks to his cabin.

At the bottom of the jar of curd, I found a small fragment of limestone on which was engraved in Arabic: 'Don't go to Thebes. Death awaits you there. You demonstrated your courage. Too many innocent people have already suffered.'

I trod on the modest fragment, reducing it to dust. From whom did the message come? Was someone still trying to discourage or warn me?

I decided not to tell anyone.

At sunset, exhausted, L'Hôte put down the piece of reed he had used to write and his sketchbook. 'That's enough,' he said. 'There is too much to record here. We had only planned to stay half a day.'

Ill at ease, Rosellini stopped copying inscriptions. 'That was my understanding too.'

'We'll stay as long as necessary,' I said firmly, while agreeing to take some rest.

We walked out. From the elegant portico of the tomb of a monarch called Khnumhotep, we overlooked a magnificent plain which was partly green and partly flooded. Everything was bathed in the golden light of a late sun foreshadowing the coming darkness. After nightfall, we went back to the ship for dinner.

The next fourteen days were spent at Beni Hassan. I became absorbed in my dialogue with the ancient Egyptians. Hour after hour they appeared more alive through the eternal images of themselves they had left. Soon weary of such a prolonged stay, Nestor L'Hôte protested several times. Rosellini discreetly joined in the protest on the pretext that, confined to her cabin, Lady Redgrave was in an increasingly foul mood. But none of them found good enough reasons to force me out of the tombs, where the radiance of eternal life in the present nourished my heart.

Suleiman was the one who prompted our departure, using typically few words. 'Don't forget your commitments,' he reminded me. 'You promised to reach Upper Nubia as soon as possible.'

It was a sad day on 7 November justifying the Brotherhood of Luxor's concern about the state of the country and the authorities' lack of care for antique monuments.

I had expected a lot from pharaonic el-Ashmunein and Greek Hermopolis Magna, the city of the God Thoth, the patron of scribes and the creator of hieroglyphs. I expected to get significant confirmation of my own system of decipherment and solve another part of the enigma. But I was hugely disappointed: the holy city was no more than a field of ruins and the debris of columns.

Seething inwardly, I decided to resume my journey, unable to bear such desolation. Anxiety gripped me. Would it be like that in all southern Egypt? Had human folly and stupidity succeeded in destroying the most prodigious heritage ever left by any civilization?

A shout of fright from Lady Redgrave tore me away from my gloomy meditation. Petrified with horror, she stood at the bow of the ship, her hands clenched around her face as she contemplated a most ludicrous sight: stark naked and dripping with water, a young man smiled broadly at her.

Judging that she was in no serious danger, I did not ask for assistance, but asked: 'What is the matter?'

'He ... he swam to the ship,' explained Lady Redgrave. 'He climbed on board with extraordinary nimbleness and addressed me in an unknown language! Hold him back, Monsieur Champollion!'

I stepped between the man and the lady. The unknown language, in which he expressed himself jovially, was a Coptic dialect. I answered in the same idiom, to the man's utmost satisfaction.

'What does he want?' asked Lady Ophelia, hidden behind my shoulder.

'He's a Coptic monk. He wants alms.'

To emphasize his request, the naked man held out a powerful right arm on the fleshy side of which was tattooed a blue cross.

'Let him take that and go away!' she exclaimed, outraged, as she offered him a silver coin.

The monk nimbly seized it, put it in his mouth, and turned his back on us without further ado and dived.

'He'll drown!' Lady Redgrave bent over, concerned.

The monk's head soon reappeared in the middle of the Nile, however. He did a kind of somersault and disappeared to return to his cloister.

'What an incredible country!' whispered Lady Redgrave.

'What a wonderful land,' I said, 'where monks have nothing to hide.'

I do not know whether the beautiful British woman's gaze indicated dislike or amusement. But I felt some kind of complicity. The sight of a stark naked monk in the country where Christianity was born creates links.

*

The ruins of the city of Antinoopolis sunk me into despair again. It was an awful series of mounds, rubble, fragments of pottery, broken granite columns. Under a palm tree, a Coptic scribe knelt on a worn mat, with a reed for drawing in his hand.

I greeted him with the respect due to his rank. He mumbled aggressively and I had to call Suleiman to clarify his demands. He was claiming a high tax on behalf of the Sultan. I asked him where all the monuments he was supposed to be in charge of had gone. With a cynicism that made my blood boil, he explained that the Sultan had ordered the destruction of ancient buildings to feed lime ovens, whose development he valued above anything else. Had Suleiman not been present, I would probably have choked the bandit in the service of such a bad master. To contemplate the suffering of vanished Antinoopolis, we had to pay a tax, for which we were given a receipt.

Wiping his forehead, Father Bidant came to my side. 'The country is all desolation,' he whispered. 'It is in the hands of infidels. Our expedition is a failure, Champollion. It is not what you dreamed of. It won't teach anything to the world of scholars and it can only arouse the Lord's anger. Yield to reason and let's go back to Cairo. I hate the squalid and stinking countryside.'

Rosellini came up, jostling the priest without apologising in his excitement. 'Master, come!'

Behind my disciple, four *fellahin* carried a granite head: a sublime portrait of Ramses.

'I purchased it for seven piastres,' declared Rosellini proudly.

It was indeed a masterwork, but a painful one. The head had been torn from the body, as the result of destruction to which we were now adding plundering. Yet if we abandoned it here, it would be offered to other pillagers. This is why, ashamed, I gave instructions to carry it to the ship and to add a few piastres for the transport.

'I could do with some bread,' declared Professor Raddi, suddenly tearing himself away from the study of his beloved stones. In his hard-wearing Nanking suit, he loped to a village alongside the river under the shade of some date trees.

'Wait a minute!' I implored vainly. Raddi did not know Arabic, so I had to follow close behind.

Bleating goats and braying donkeys greeted me. The sun was spreading a golden light on the high palms, drowning the hills of the desert in light. As Raddi arrived, women in black hastened into their shabby dwellings. Naked children continued to play in the dust as if we did not exist.

'Where is the guest house?' complained Raddi who walked to the right and to the left like a lost traveller.

Leaving the tiny village without even realizing it, the mineralogist was amazed to discover *shaduf* machines used to draw water. There were three of them on top of each other. Thanks to a rudimentary system of counterweight, the first three pails drew water from the canal and poured it into a basin about one third up the embankment. The next three heaved it to another basin, and the last three distributed it into irrigation channels which brought life to the fields. The results were remarkable, at the cost of a constantly repeated but limited effort. The nine *shadufs* were arranged in several rows connected by poles. On one of them stood a child with a stick to keep his balance.

'Water, at last!' exclaimed the professor.

'Don't step forward!' I shouted.

I managed at last to catch up with him when he reached the platform on which the *shadufs* stood. Just as I had feared, he slipped on the damp ground and fell forward. Taken aback, the peasants made no move. Raddi's heavy body tumbled down the first slope. I slipped and managed to grasp his sleeve. At last aware of the danger he was in, he did not struggle.

I drew him to me. Then, to my horror, I saw some heavy pots which had become detached from their rope crashing down towards my head.

12

Here in the heart of old Egypt, I was the happiest of men. Its greatest wonders were here, near to my ship. For the time being, I was right in the centre of them: at Tell el-Amarna, the city of the heretical Pharaoh Akhenaton, the apostle of the divine sun. My companions and I settled in a devastated palace whose remains had been abandoned to the sand and wind. We were all sitting on blocks or fragments of wall. A silent circle had formed around me. I hadn't spoken for several hours.

Draped in copious folds of cotton cloth, Lady Redgrave was enjoying the light. Ippolito Rosellini was drawing. Armed with a pike, Nestor L'Hôte was digging carelessly in front of his feet. Professor Raddi was examining a piece of limestone. Father Bidant was reciting his rosary. Moktar and Suleiman were standing to the side, with rifles, as the area was not safe, often being crossed by gangs of pillagers.

When I had discovered the boundaries of the sacred site of Tell el-Amarna, I was amazed to find representations of Akhenaton and members of his family with long heads, swollen stomachs and distended shapes. Sunrays ending in hands offering the sign of life to sovereigns made a very curious symbol! I could sense a world torn apart and on the brink of oblivion restored each day by the powerful sun god. He revived the flower-covered palace, the villas of the nobles with their sumptuous gardens, the large roads where carts travelled, the ponds of fresh water reflecting the sky with their pleasure boats, all an affirmation that no pharaoh can ever die. These God-men engraved their marks too deeply in the flesh of time for men to erase it.

Akhenaton must have been the happiest of sovereigns. He created his town, asserted his faith and expressed the sun he sheltered in his heart. He remained alive among us through the modest remnants of bricks, walls and temples sunk in the ocean of origins. I would have liked to devote myself to his memory, but other worries concerned me.

'I gathered you together,' I said, 'to tell you that someone has tried to kill me.'

Rosellini was the first to react. 'This is terrible!' he said. 'Abdel-Razuk should be informed immediately.'

'It will be difficult,' I objected. 'Because he is the one who tried to murder me. That is why he disappeared. I could see his face perfectly when he threw a large piece of pottery which was meant to break my skull.'

'Could you have been mistaken?' suggested Lady Redgrave.

'I had a witness: Professor Raddi.'

Ill at ease, the mineralogist did not raise his eyes from his modest piece of limestone. 'Alas,' he confessed, 'I did not see anything . . . I was looking at the ground. Scientific honesty forbids me to say more than I saw.'

'The General's word is not to be questioned,' intervened Nestor L'Hôte. 'If I ever find Abdel-Razuk again, I'll break his neck.'

'Don't do that,' interposed Father Bidant. 'I forbid you to answer violence with violence. You would be imprisoned and sentenced to death.'

'Whose side are you on, Father?' I asked with annoyance.

'I'm not on anybody's side,' he retorted. 'Reason calls for caution. If you are really in danger, so are we. I think it is time to put an end to the expedition if the master of Egypt is hostile to us.'

I felt pervaded by the spirit of Akhenaton who was incensed by priests mired in their own ambition and vanity.

'We will not be diverted from our path by this, Father. We will carry on as long as I'm alive.'

The priest gave me a challenging look. 'Foolhardiness is unforgiveable, Monsieur Champollion. From now on, God will hold you responsible for anything that happens to any one of us.'

We spent only a brief day at the Amarna site, looking for inscriptions and sketching maps. I realized that it would be a considerable task to decipher all the inscriptions on the site, to say nothing of the numerous tombs which were certainly hidden in the mountain east of the town.

We had to go to Thebes, to the south, to the mystery, without knowing whether the gods of Egypt would grant me the privilege of coming back to these places, so full of ghosts and the language of the sun. But I refrained from critizing the wishes of the others, as they had already given in to me so much.

Lady Redgrave avoided me as if I had offended her, and I had no intention of making the slightest move towards her. Suleiman did not take his eyes off Drovetti's henchman, Moktar, who behaved like a good and faithful servant. His spying mission was more difficult now, with his accomplice Abdel-Razuk nowhere to be seen. Perhaps the latter had taken refuge in darkness to give himself a better chance in his next attack on me. I must have been a major thorn in their sides to produce such violent action. Now Mehmet Ali knew that I had seen part of the depredation he had inflicted on Egypt, and he was trying to prevent me from going further inland and seeing even worse things. Of course, my death would have to look like an accident, far from the presence of witnesses, so as not to annoy France.

I have no more courage than other men, but I am more stubborn. I was not afraid to die in the beloved land of the gods, in the country to which I was attracted by a burning passion. Europe felt like a cruel exile. Here I was at home, and had always been so. I had only one fear, one weakness: I was afraid of dying before I understood the message of ancient Egyptians in all its purity. I was afraid of leaving this universe without having found its key.

The terrible threat uttered by Father Bidant, his ruthless judgment, weighed down on me. The priest had struck at my heart and he knew it, not so much because of the God of the Christians, who had no place in these living temples, but because of the love I felt for my travel companions. It is true that I was responsible for their safety, which caused me more serious concern than my own. The Sultan had no reason to harm them, but I had no idea what schemes his Oriental imagination would hatch to force me to give up.

The incident happened when we passed the impressive cliffs of Abu-Feda. The weather had deteriorated. The stormy Nile rose up in furious waves, and a kind of tornado increased the fury of the river tenfold. Nestor L'Hôte, who was bravely standing on the port side, raised his hand to signal that everything was all right. I yelled at him to come and take shelter. In the penumbra of the setting sun, I had the impression of a figure pushing L'Hôte in the back. He gesticulated, but did not find anything to cling to and fell into the water.

'Help!' I shouted with all the force of my lungs, but the noise of the storm drowned my voice. I rushed to the place where L'Hôte had disappeared, picked up a rope and threw it into the water.

I felt a resistance. Had he seized the end of the rope? Blinded by a wave, jolted by the ship, I could not drag him back to the ship. Then the rope tightened and I knew that my companion could be saved. His fate was in my hands. Somehow from beyond myself I found the strength. The palm of my hands burnt. The deck slid under my feet. I weakened, and began to wonder if I would succeed in saving him. But I still hung on to the rope, even though I knew it might be my life for his. I was about to topple into the water in my turn when a new and unexpected power pulled back on the rope. I

117

stood still and, recovering courage, managed to walk back. Step by step, I went back to the centre of the ship.

At last Nestor L'Hôte's head appeared, dripping with water. The hearty fellow was still fit enough to haul himself up on board.

Exhausted and breathless, I turned around and saw Suleiman. He was the one who had saved L'Hôte. He had taken over from me when I had loosened my grip. Without a word, he withdrew. The river was becoming calmer; we had crossed the dangerous narrows.

Wet to the skin, Nestor L'Hôte undressed and dried himself off.

'You were pushed, weren't you?'

'I do not know, General. I didn't see anyone. It is true that I felt something like a blow in my back, but it may have been a gust of wind. I had already been thrown off balance several times.'

I turned away to vomit. The tragedy had upset me. I would have been devastated if I had lost L'Hôte. My journey would have ended on the rocks of the Nile. Father Bidant had succeeded in turning me into my own worst enemy.

When the last squalls subsided over the damp green fields, bordered by grooves of palm trees, a deep silence settled over the land. The bare rocks of the mountains which loomed over us gave way to peaceful banks bathed in the dazzling but misty morning light. We were arriving in Asyut, the Greek Lykopolis, the city of the god Anubis who, after having mummified the glorious dead, led them along their paths in the other world.

My feverish eyes discovered with pleasure a less dusty and miserable town than the previous ones. Sycamores, palm trees, blossoming bushes, roses and magnolias brightened the streets of Asyut. My companions carried me there in a sedan chair like a pharaoh. Numerous minarets rose in an immaculate blue sky. Innumerable cats slid around the streets. Suleiman explained that the city was their paradise. They killed rats and mice and protected the food reserves. That was why the inhabitants never disturbed a cat sleeping in the shade and preferred to walk in the sun so as not to disturb him.

We passed a dilapidated and partly open café. Rags hung from the ceiling. A Venetian lantern lit up the back, which was crammed with men smoking pipes in front of an orchestra of various flutes and cages containing small wriggling monkeys. Suleiman asked Lady Redgrave, Father Bidant, Professor Raddi and Moktar to drink jasmine tea and wait for us there. He talked for a long time with the owner of the café and asked him to make sure that his distinguished guests should be treated as such.

'Where are the antique monuments?' I asked him.

'None of them remain,' he confessed, impassive. 'Only a column standing on a heap of rubble has been left. The temple stones were transformed into millstones, troughs or thresholds. Blocks of limestone were used as material to build lime ovens.'

Indignation silenced me. Asyut suddenly appeared much less pleasant. We passed Syrians, people from Asia and Africans coming through along caravan routes.

'What about the tombs?' I said. 'I want to go to the tombs.'

'It would not be prudent, Master,' objected Rosellini, 'We should take you as soon as possible to a doctor.'

'The tombs,' I said again.

Nestor L'Hôte tried in his turn to make me change my mind, to no avail. Suleiman carefully avoided interfering.

'I want to walk,' I said. 'You will support me.'

Guided by Suleiman and supported by L'Hôte and Rosellini, I climbed the sandy slopes to the necropolis dug in the hill overlooking the town with difficulty. A few years before, General Desaix had set up his headquarters and his cannons there to subject Asyut to his rule. In the luminous morning, there were no more weapons. The peace of the world beyond reigned supreme and immediately relaxed me. Each time I left the world of the modern Arabs to return to that of the ancient Egyptians, a new dynamism took hold of me.

The walls of the holy caves were covered with scenes like those of Beni Hassan, though, as far as I could see, not their equal. But I did not have the miraculous sponge I had used before and my head was spinning. Nestor L'Hôte noticed it. 'You can hardly stand up any more, General. You must take care of yourself.'

I had seen the tombs. I asked to stay here a few more brief moments before I was led to the centre of Asyut, where we visited the Turkish baths. We went into a rotunda-shaped room. The ceiling was open so that air could circulate. We left our clothes on a platform around the walls, wrapped our loins in a towel and put on sandals. We followed a kind of narrow corridor where it was warmer. A door closed behind us. We entered a room with marble walls. I felt good.

'I'll leave you for a moment,' said Suleiman. 'Don't be afraid, it won't hurt you. I'll be back soon.'

I did not have the courage to protest. My beard was beginning to drip with water. What would happen if Suleiman left me in the hands of my enemies? A colossus with greasy flesh appeared. He took me by the hand. I slipped. He held me back. A strange torpor overwhelmed me. I did not feel like struggling any more. If Suleiman, who pretended to be my brother, had betrayed me, whom could I now trust?

The colossus guided me to another spacious vaulted room. He helped me lie down near a bath and placed a small cushion under my head. A cloud of fragrant vapours penetrated my body. I relaxed.

The man turned me over and began to massage me delicately. Then, with a glove, he rubbed my back vigorously. I was led to a private room with hot and cold water and washed myself with pleasure. Then the servant offered me a fragrant bed where I lay again, relaxed, released of all impurities, my chest expanded, feeling several years younger.

An old man with a white beard, dressed in a loincloth, came

slowly to me. He knelt down and put a sheet of papyrus and a gold inkstand on the marble floor.

'Take the inkstand,' he said in Arabic, 'and shake it over the sheet.'

I obeyed like a robot. The old man considered the papyrus with the utmost attention for long minutes.

'Your illness is not serious,' he concluded. 'Sleep and tea will be enough to cure it. But your life is not yet saved . . . There is an evil spirit around you, a spirit which tries to destroy you. If you do not manage to identify it, you will be its victim.'

The seer crumpled the sheet of papyrus put it in his mouth and swallowed it. Then he disappeared with the same solemn slowness, making way for Suleiman.

'What should I do?' he asked.

'Take me back to the ship, shut me in my cabin and let me sleep for twelve hours.'

I slept until sunset the following day. Then I felt wonderful. At the head of my bed was a bowl of tea with a pleasant smell of lilies. I drank it with delight, and after some ablutions knocked at my own door which had been locked from outside. Suleiman opened it.

The evening was wonderful. A shooting star shot through the sky. We had anchored abreast of Sawadiyeh, a very quiet peasant village. After a brief meal of broad beans and bread, we gathered in the large area of the ship Rosellini had pompously called 'the living room' to savour coffee, play cards and listen to a flute concert given by the sailors.

Suleiman interrupted the peace. 'A rowing boat is coming near,' he said.

L'Hôte seized a rifle. The crew was alerted. It is unusual to travel the Nile at night. None of us heard anything about pirates, but the Pasha's declared hostility made us fear the worst.

We had lit torches, and their flames veined the dark blue Nile with red. The rowing boat came slowly. At the prow, a servant with a turban launched feverishly into a florid speech which reassured me. He was here on behalf of his master, Mohammed Bey, the governor of the province, who invited us to dinner in his palace. As a token of his friendship, he had also sent us this boat full of food.

I took care of the discussion with the emissary and offered him a crate of wine to thank him for the invitation, which I had to turn down. Annoyed, the man insisted. But I remained inflexible; the idea of social intercourse delaying my arrival in Thebes was intolerable.

'It may be unwise to refuse,' whispered Suleiman.

'It doesn't matter,' I retorted. 'We'll leave tomorrow, as planned.'

In the middle of the afternoon of the following day, we were about to cast off from the bank when a host of horsemen and soldiers stopped us with a hubbub of shouts and clouds of dust. The little army was led by the son of the *bey* himself, who had a slight speech impediment. This time, he brought a lot of meat. The musicians accompanying the soldiers launched into a serenade.

Impressed by such marks of deference, my companions begged me to accept the invitation. But, to the great displeasure of the *bey*'s son I did not alter my decision. My decision did at least bring me the satisfaction of enabling me to recover my energy. I gave the order to leave, intending to sail until nightfall.

Still clad in his cassock, however, Father Bidant rushed up to me, panting. 'Wait, Champollion, wait!'

'Why should I wait?'

'Professor Raddi and Nestor L'Hôte have disappeared.'

'You are distracted, father.'

'Go and check for yourself!'

Having examined the cabins and all the recesses of the boat, I had to except the facts: L'Hôte and Raddi were no longer on board. Nobody had seen them disembark.

Although still distant, Lady Redgrave seemed worried, Nervous, Rosellini could not stay still.

'Where does Mohammed Bey live?' I asked Suleiman.

'There are a dozen of his people on the bank. You just have to ask them.'

'Let them take me to him.'

'I'll come with you.'

'I shall go alone, Suleiman. You will stay here to take care of the others. If I do not come back, Rosellini will be the head of the expediton.'

'Aren't you taking a great risk?'

I looked deep into my brother's eyes. 'I am in charge of our community, Suleiman. I am fully and completely responsible for those who take part in it, be they my allies or my opponents, whether they want to betray me or help me. I am sure that our two companions were kidnapped by the *bey*, a henchman of the Pasha's, no doubt. If I am the person he wants, I won't disappoint him, on condition that L'Hôte and Raddi regain their freedom.'

'Unless he puts the three of you into custody . . . or has an even harsher treatment in store.'

'I have no choice, Suleiman. I won't become a coward in my own eyes.'

He bowed respectfully. 'It is undoubtedly written that nobody will be able to oppose your will . . .'

At the end of a brief journey, the *bey*'s men took me to a white house, standing in superb isolation and brightened up by a large garden planted with lemon trees. From the main door, which was open, came out a flood of monotonous music. High candelabras lined the approach and dispensed an increasingly bright light as the last glow of the day faded away.

This was a most attractive ambush. Everything indicated luxury and voluptuousness. But how could I forget that the potentate who ruled over this haven of peace held two of my companions hostage?

Much more anxious than I seemed, I asked a steward to announce me and stood still at the bottom of the flight of stairs leading to the entrance. A few seconds later there appeared on the threshold a fat man with a crimson face, dressed in flashing silk.

'Champollion!' he exclaimed in a thundering voice. 'Come quickly!'

Surprised by the greeting, I had no other choice but to obey. I raised my head to the sky of Egypt, afraid of not being able to see it again for a long time.

The imposing character took my arm.

I stiffened. 'I request that my two friends be released immediately.'

'Released? Who keeps them in custody? Come here!'

I would have liked to protest more vehemently and obtain what I wanted first . . . but my host lead me vigorously into his dwelling.

I discovered a huge banqueting room, where guests lay idly on cushions and conversed gaily. In the mist from the pipes everybody was smoking, I identified Nestor L'Hôte and Professor Raddi, side by side, having a good time, savouring huge gherkins.

'Are they free to do as they please?' I asked, taken aback.

'Absolutely,' answered Mohammed Bey. 'They are my guests, just as you are. They arrived here and announced your coming visit, which rejoiced me immensely. The place of honour is yours, beside me.'

It was certainly an ambush, but set by my own allies.

'General!' exclaimed L'Hôte as he saw me. 'I was sure that you would not abandon me!'

He staggered towards me. 'General . . . You must not offend our host . . . Suleiman told me that he could have prevented us from resuming our expedition . . . I sacrificed myself . . . and I attracted you here . . . I beg you to understand!'

'And what about Professor Raddi?'

'He followed me. I wanted to send him back, but he said that he was dying to take part in a Muslim celebration. With his wife in Florence, he does not have fun very often . . .'

The honourable professor was unable to answer the simplest

question. Blind drunk he was only able to hand over to his neighbour the large jar full of liquor that went around. Everyone drank in his turn. Despite my reputation for that kind of spirit, which is as sweet as pernicious, I had to take a sip. As soon as the jar was empty, the *bey* had it filled again. He himself drank in large gulps and smoked a very long pipe. In a formidable outburst of generosity, he declared an amnesty for all delinquents and distributed coins to the destitute people who had massed in front of the house.

We were served over twenty dishes: mutton served in various ways, melons, anchovies, salads. We wiped our hands on gold embroidered napkins. Two singers formed the artistic highlight of the evening. The first, a seventy-year-old Greek gratified us with some sweet romances. The second one, an Arab over eighty, sang a traditional monotonous chant. When he stopped singing, most of the guests dozed. Nestor L'Hôte woke them up by striking up 'La Marseillaise' followed by odes to freedom from a fashionable but insignificant work, *The Mute* by Portici. The tunes, unusual in the palace of a *bey*, aroused little enthusiasm.

The celebration lasted all night. When the sun rose, only Mohammed Bey and I were still awake. Despite the huge quantity of alcohol he had absorbed, the potentate remained master of himself. His hand did not tremble and his eyes shone brightly.

'I wish I could keep you with me for several days, Champollion. Your presence is a gift from God. Why not continue to celebrate?'

'I have a mission, Your Excellency, and I must continue to fulfil it.'

'You want to see old stones, I know . . . So explore the mountain. It abounds with them! I put a hundred servants at your disposal, who will bring you each day innumerable baskets full of stones!'

'Be thanked for that, but—'

'You want antique stones with indecipherable signs. What

for? Happiness, Champollion, consists in celebrating with friends, drinking and eating together, listening to music, keeping the memory of the dead before we die leaving our friends to celebrate our memory.'

The sincerity of his tone touched me.

'Nothing is better than long-lasting friendship, Champollion. You must learn to taste and savour it second after second . . . Stay here and let's become old friends. You will forget your stones and your vanished world. Stop running useless risks. Choose true peace, the peace of my little realm, of the every-unchanging sun, and of the Nile, indifferent to human passions.'

The *bey* was putting me to a tough test. He was certainly suggesting something invaluable. I just had to stop the course of time, giving up my ambitions, sit on a stone in front of the river and age with it.

'You're right, Your Excellency, but I do not think that I can be released from my destiny.'

Mohammed Bey stood up. 'Come with me Champollion.'

We stepped over sleeping bodies and left the white house to walk to the bank. A soft wind erased the strain of the night.

'You talk like a predestined man, Champollion, like a man who knows only one way, one love.'

'The Egypt of the pharaohs,' I said, 'is stronger than all the gods, more tender than all loves and more alive than all friendships. In the face of the such mysteries, neither you nor I have any importance.'

A hoopoe left the top of a tamarisk and flew away into the light.

'Go, Champollion,' said the *bey* in a grave voice tinged with emotion. 'But take that.'

He gave me a beautiful ring of red jasper. 'May the jewel protect you. And stick to your path, brother.'

13

Fate was cruel a few hours later. I had looked forward to discovering the holy city of Abydos, the realm of Osiris, judge of the dead and master of the transformation that enabled the fair ones to tread the paths of the world beyond. But nature decided otherwise. That year the flood was magnificent for those who looked at the countryside and admired it, but not for the poor *fellahin*. The river had overflowed and ruined several harvests. In order to avoid starvation, the peasants would be obliged to eat the wheat left by the Pasha for next year's sowing. We saw entire villages drowned by the Nile. The wretched huts of string and board dried in the sun offered no resistance. In many places, the water spread from mountain to mountain. Where the highest mounds had not been submerged, we saw *fellahin*, women, men and children, carrying baskets of earth to repair 3- or 4-inch dikes from the huge river, thus saving their houses and few remaining provisions. It was a distressing and heart-rending picture.

Standing on the roof of the cabin, I saluted antique Abydos from a distance. The Osirian world of death repelled me, as if my time had not yet come. Yet it was from this sacred place that one of the inscriptions essential to my discoveries had come, and it certainly contained other hieroglyphic tablets, offering keys to the sacred tongue, a tongue which still refused to give me its ultimate treasures, though they have been held by a man hidden somewhere under this blazing sun, the Prophet.

We reached Guirgeh on a cool morning. The north wind stirred the Nile. Now decaying after a period of glory under the Mamelukes, the town of Saint-Georges stood at a turn of the river, almost crushed by a high cliff. Herons, crows and sparrowhawks criss-crossed the sky.

People had gathered on the quay and talked loudly. After he had harshly treated a few onlookers, Moktar told me that Anastasy's excavator had asked to see me.

'Anastasy's excavator?' I asked, surprised. 'On what site does he work?'

'I don't know.' With stubborn look on his face, Drovetti's servant did not like my question.

'Where is the man?'

'At the monastery of the Brothers of Saint-Georges,' answered Moktar.

'L'Hôte will come with me,' I declared.

'So shall I,' intervened Father Bidant. 'Since it is possible I might meet true believers at last, my presence cannot be dispensed with.'

'As you wish,' I said.

The way to the monastery turned out to be very difficult. We had to be hauled by a pulley, which took us to a considerable height. The monks had found no other way of protecting themselves from the thousand ills inflicted on them by the Arabs.

Guirgeh's Coptic church and monastery were dying. The refuge was not different from the other village dwellings. The monks obeyed a vow of poverty beyond reason. Comfort and gaiety had been banished for a long time from the lives of the three or four survivors, who hung about in a church as dark as a crypt. They wore black caftans and turbans, with no indication that they were priests.

'My God, so much misery and stench!' said Father Bidant indignantly.

L'Hôte, who shared the priest's reaction, preferred to stay at the threshold. As for me, I went boldly into the tiny room, for

I had identified the man who had stood up to greet me: he was the naked swimmer who had frightened Lady Redgrave so much.

'I am Anastasy's excavator,' he declared in Coptic, a language which neither L'Hôte nor Bidant could understand. 'I have an important document to give you. My brothers do not know about it. They won't betray us. They only speak Arabic. In a very short time, this place of worship will disappear. Let's meet tonight in Qena. Ask for the *zar*.'

Without further explanation, he bowed again and returned to the other monks, sunk in an endless torpor against the damp wall.

'What did he say?' asked Father Bidant.

'That the excavations have produced no result,' I answered. 'And that he has no means of carrying on with them.

'What a wretched country, letting its religious men die and rejecting true faith,' he cursed.

Day by day, I was becoming a little more Egyptian. There was no longer a barrier or screen between me and the country. The sky had become my sky and the soil my soil. A sweet magic dissolved my European character and French habits. My thoughts flowed at the pace of the Nile but still retained the spurts of dawn and the quietness of sunsets.

'Are you dreaming, Monsieur Champollion?'

Lady Redgrave had sat down near me so delicately that I had not felt her presence. She wore a long, almost transparent, white tunic. She had a lovely scent of jasmine. Side by side on a wooden bench, we watched the passing bank, along which a young boy very slowly rode a donkey.

'Shall we make a truce?'

'Are you at war, Monsieur Champollion?'

I felt my black beard. 'I've always been at war, against idiots and liars. I have probably already lost, but I persevere. The Egypt of the pharaohs didn't survive them, did it?'

'Why does Egypt obsess you so much? Don't you think there are other philosophies and cultures which are as impressive? You should study the doctrines of India or Persia and leave your pharaonic citadel!'

'I've already done that, Lady Ophelia. Many years ago, I studied the religions of India, Persia and China. I learned the language of these civilizations. I even started writing a dictionary of old Persian, of which I had rather a good command. For a long time, I believed there was a close link between China and Egypt and the hieroglyphs of the two great nations came from the same source. I was wrong. But I have been deeply attracted by India, Iran and China. They even made me waver, and almost succeeded in weakening my love of Egypt. But it eventually triumphed, as always. Comparisons favour it. Hieroglyphs are the most beautiful language in the world and pharaonic thought is the most complete, coherent and brilliant. I am drawn to it like a child to his mother. It is my duty to serve it, but it is not a heavy task. In fact it is a joyful one. Even if I have to walk a path of loneliness to the end of my life to pass on my faith, I won't regret it.'

'Are you so lonely in this world?' she asked.

'No. I have a brother, Jacques-Joseph. He tirelessly helped me, encouraged me and rescued me from the pitfalls into which I fell. It is thanks to him that I am here today. A hundred times I almost gave up and a hundred times he convinced me to carry on. For a long time he has shown that he is also me. We'll never be two separate people. Cursed be the day which might separate us! Any difference between us is impossible, because it would imply my own ungratefulness. The present and the past, what I was, what I am and what I shall become, everything will prevent that.'

Increasingly numerous dumb palms announced the town of Qena. Their slender trunks divided into branches unfolding into fan-shaped leaves. They were loaded with nuts as large as duck eggs. The *fellahin* ate their sweet-tasting fruit and used the leaves to cover their huts.

'What about you, Lady Ophelia, are you alone in this world?'

There was no answer. She was gone.

Qena was devoted to pottery. Crammed with rows of jars of all sizes, the town contained numerous potteries. The roofs of the houses and dovecotes were built with pots. A large flotilla carried the local products to other cities.

I asked my companions to stay on board, under the pretext that the town was not safe. As I wanted an official audience with the local potentate, I only needed Suleiman's assistance.

Our progress through the streets of Qena was most picturesque. In front of each house stood mounts of pottery, some of which was used as seats by unveiled women who smiled and waved to us. Barefoot in black dresses, they wore heavy silver armbands which sparkled. These charming figures, sitting among the masses of fallen rocks and rubbish tips, were decked out with the riches of Qena as a sign of their importance. Suleiman asked one of them where the *zar* took place. Then he took me to a narrow lane winding through cracked dwellings. The stench was almost unbearable.

In front of us an old fat man with a scimitar stood up. 'What are you looking for?'

'The *zar*,' answered Suleiman.

The man let us pass and pointed to the low door of a partly ruined house. We had to push our way through rubble and litter and crawl on all fours through the opening. We entered a very dark room where disturbing figures flickered. We sat down and gradually got used to the gloom. The place was squalid. The clay walls sweated dampness. Rotten straw had been strewn at the four sides. At the far end of the room sat five women beating little drums.

A man stood up abruptly, whirled round and fell to the ground, with spittle on his lips. An old woman drew him to her. There were over twenty people of both sexes.

'They are all sick,' explained Suleiman. 'They come to the *zar* to be healed. They are possessed by demons. Only magic can release them.'

131

A fat man entered the room, panting. He stood up with difficulty after he had passed the door and immediately came to us. 'Be welcome,' he said.

The drums stopped. 'Don't move,' recommended the man. 'If your demon has not penetrated too far into your soul, he will be afraid and flee.'

At a sign from him the band began to play again. A tall, bony and almost emaciated woman came to the centre of the room and started a lascivious dance. She opened a toothless mouth to offer a weak, encouraging smile. The onlookers stamped their feet. Someone suddenly went into a trance and rolled on the ground. The band tried to echo his convulsive movements.

The fat man knelt down and took the sick man's face in his hands. He chanted a monotonous song which was overwhelmed by the sound of the drums, and for a long time he mesmerized the unfortunate man, whose convulsions gradually decreased. The doctor covered his head with a damp cloth and began to turn it in all directions almost as if intended to separate it from the body. When he removed the cloth, the possessed person opened white bulging eyes. The doctor subjected him to an extraordinary violent cure: he twisted his ears, hit his forehead and almost dislocated his limbs. I wanted to interfere to put an end to the torture, but Suleiman held me back. The worst was still to come. The doctor pinned the sick man to the ground face down, stuck his knee in the middle of his back and tugged his head as if to break his back. Appalled, I closed my eyes.

There was a heart-rending shout. I clenched Suleiman's left arm.

'Everything is all right,' he whispered.

I dared to look again at the painful sight and saw the man stand up and go back to his place. With the help of two veiled women, the doctor set up a small wooden altar with candles and a small jar of incense, whose fragrance immediately delighted our noses. The drummers stopped and came to form a circle around the master of ceremonies who recited incomprehensible litanies, in which I thought I could recognize the names of a few Egyptians divinities. The toothless woman brought out a gagged black sheep that had been hidden under tarpaulin. Tears of indignation came to my eyes when the doctor laid the blade of a long knife on the throat of the unfortunate animal. A moment later, its blood dripped on to the altar while an incantation broke out to chase away evil spirits.

The sight of the sacrifice produced a collective trance. Most people joined in a frantic saraband, jostling, knocking and hitting each other. Leaning against the clay wall, I saw the doctor smear himself with the sheep's blood, raise the animal's corpse into the air and make the patients kneel down. Raising his arms to the sky, questioned the evil forces about each person possessed. To be cured, one of them had to offer a silver ring, another a coat, another meat.

Taking advantage of the confusion, a man had sat down beside me. It was the Coptic monk who had made the appointment. 'Take that,' he said in a very low voice, presenting me with a wooden tablet covered with hieroglyphs. 'On behalf of the Prophet.'

'The Prophet?' I said, startled. 'Is he here?'

'He has left for the south. Don't linger here. People might become dangerous. Some of them are really mad.'

Several possessed people took a sip of the blood. Excited, they began to insult each other. We crawled out of the room, glad to be in the open air again.

'Leave a few coins on this stone,' recommended the Coptic monk. 'It is the doctor's pay.'

Back on the ship, I looked to the tablet the monk had given me. It was covered with dust and I had to clean it carefully, uncovering cartouches with royal names. The drawing seemed to date back to an important period.

I felt a very violent emotion. It was a list revealing the names of kings of the most ancient dynasties. The invaluable document threw a new light on the origins of Egyptian civilization. Several signs were unknown to me. I was sure that the Prophet knew the missing elements. They had probably been passed on to him by an oral tradition that would disappear with him.

The door of my cabin opened with a crash. Father Bidant came in, furious and red-faced. 'This is unbearable, Champollion! It is being said that you took part in satanic rites!'

I was facing a grand inquisitor about to burn me at the stake. 'Don't exaggerate, Father . . . Out of duty, I had to take part in a somewhat pagan ceremony.'

'And with what result?'

'This extraordinary document,' I said, showing him the tablet.

'Why is this appalling fragment so valuable?'

'It helps to trace back the origins of history and human thinking, Father.'

Father Bidant turned crimson. 'You utter horrible blasphemies!' he shouted. 'There is only one history, the one taught in the Bible! The rest is just lies! Give up your fake science, Champollion, and repent.'

I answered with a smile which infuriated the priest.

'Other people have tried to destroy the Christian religion before you! They all failed, thanks to God, and so will you!'

I stood up and walked a few steps. 'I understand your fears, Father, but what about the documents? And what about the young science . . . of Egyptology?'

'Egyptology does not exist and cannot exist! Egypt is dead, for good, and you won't revive it. Hieroglyphs have no meaning whatsoever. They are just pagan, evil signs which must remain in nothingness. Destroy the tablet, Champollion. To the eyes of God, it is worthless.'

I faced up to things. 'Leave me at least a souvenir . . . do you see the document as so dangerous for your faith?'

I had the impression that there was very little charity in

Father Bidant's ardent gaze. Beads of sweat formed on his forehead. 'You don't grasp what is actually at stake in your expedition, Champollion,' he explained in a tone that had now become calm and almost smooth. 'The Church has been following your work very closely, ever since you started publishing. Ancient Egypt certainly does not threaten the existence of the Vatican, but it would be stupid to run the slightest risk. We are surrounded by infidels and pagans. Everything that might support their cause must be destroyed, whatever the scientific value of the documents. Science is evil when it contradicts faith. And you will become an incarnation of the devil if you defy Almighty God. Observe and study as long as you please. But keep silent. Let Egypt and its satanic monuments rest under the sand. God wanted the downfall of this self-conceited civilization and of its divinities. Let's not go against his designs and let's hold the Bible as the only science worthy of respect.'

'I was brought up in your religion, Father, but it often appeared full of hypocrisy and lies to me. I don't care. Human beings may believe what they want. If Providence exists, it entrusted me with the task of reviving the Egypt of the pharaohs, whose heirs we are. The Bible is just one text among many others. Faith in a single god, expressed in various divinities, existed before Christianity was born. Egyptian history goes back much further than biblical history. Such are the truths, as I shall soon be able to prove.'

Father Bidant crossed himself. He had become extremely pallid. 'You are worse than the devil, Champollion. You are the Antichrist.'

I smiled again. 'You give me too much credit. I am probably just an old Egyptian back in his homeland and wanting to pay it tribute. I experience the adventure of the country like my personal history. It is my blood. I share the faith of the pharaohs, their desire to build, to create and to erect temples to the glory of God.'

The priest stepped back, appalled. 'You are talking

nonsense, my son! You are falling into the clutches of the devil!'

'When the world knows how to decipher hieroglyphs, Father, it will discover the highest spirituality ever conceived by any society. And it is true that on that day, our conventions and beliefs will come into question.'

With expected speed, the priest rushed to the tablet and tried to break it. Unable to control myself, I fought wildly and managed to snatch the precious document from him.

'Get out of here,' I ordered, trembling with indignation.

Father Bidant pointed a threatening finger at me. 'Now Champollion, God himself is your enemy.'

I did not expect anything more from Qena and I would have liked to leave the town as soon as possible to follow the tracks of the Prophet and study the tablet with the help of my notes while the ship was sailing the Nile. But Rosellini told me that not far from there, in Maabdeh, was a catacomb full of crocodile mummies and maybe papyrus we might be able to purchase cheaply. This aroused the insatiable curiosity of the researcher in me, so I organized a quick expedition with Nestor L'Hôte and him.

Maabdeh's sinister watchtower indicated its position to the travellers. To our great surprise, the villagers were not very welcoming. Their faces were inscrutable, and some of them fled when we arrived or shut themselves up in their houses. A blond adolescent showed us the location of the catacombs.

We had to enter them from the top of a hill which L'Hôte climbed with his usual agility. He told us that the descent into a kind of vault would not be dangerous. Sliding through a rather narrow opening, we reached a hot and dusty room with an unpleasant smell of resin and pitch. Our torches were not burning well. On the ground or in small holes were the remains of crocodile corpses, some of them still wrapped in bits of bandages. There was no papyrus.

'General,' warned Nestor L'Hôte. 'This is horrible. Don't come any further.'

At his feet lay another corpse, that of a man with a smashed skull: the Coptic monk who had offered me the Prophet's tablet.

14

'How did you get in here?' I asked indignantly when I saw Lady Ophelia moving about my cabin.

'With the help of Rosellini, Monsieur Champollion. You cannot remain shut away.'

'I have my reasons.'

'I know them. Rosellini and L'Hote told me about your awful discovery.'

'It is even more awful than you think. The naked swimmer to whom you gave alms, the unfortunate Coptic monk, was in Anastasy's service. The rival gang. Drovetti's, killed him.'

'You have no proof. It may be a local gangland killing.'

'If I am right, war has been declared. We are all in danger and I have no right to expose you to such risks.'

'We are no longer children, Champollion. Let's decide and act as a group, but each one of us must take responsibility.'

The pretty British woman showed a determination I did not find unpleasant.

'I am the head of the expedition, Lady Ophelia, and I have no intention of sharing my authority.'

'A chief who has doubts about himself,' she said ironically as she waved her fan. 'A chief who withdraws into solitude instead of going into action.'

Cut to the quick, I grasped her wrist and pushed away the fan behind which she concealed her face. 'Don't be mistaken, Lady Ophelia. I just had a moment of weakness . . . Thank you for restoring my courage. Will you be my ambassador? Ask our companions if they want to carry on, knowing Drovetti's henchmen are after us, and that they will not stop at murder. If anyone wants to give up, he should come and see me here.'

'I accept the mission. Jean-François. I shall fulfil it immediately.'

One hour later I left my cabin.

Nobody had given up.

Night had fallen when we arrived in Dendera. It was a fragrant and peaceful night with magnificent moonlight and, according to my calculations, we were only an hour away from the temples. Who could have resisted such a temptation? We had dinner and left hurriedly. Alone, with a guide, our heads wrapped in white burnouses and armed to the teeth, we strode across fields, singing the latest opera marches to soothe our impatience. But we did not find anything and we were afraid we might have got lost. We walked through a grove of palm trees followed by tall grass, thorny bushes and brushwood. The plain was empty and endless.

Should we retrace our steps? That was out of the question. The temples were certainly somewhere close by. I could feel their comforting presence.

Lady Ophelia suggested that we shout together to signal where we were. Only the barking of wandering dogs answered. Full of enthusiasm and caught up in the game, L'Hôte exhorted us to carry on. He was not afraid of night demons.

At the turn of a stony path we saw a *fellah* sleeping under an acacia. Wrapped in black rags, he looked like a walking mummy. He ran away but L'Hôte caught up with him. Terrorized and trembling, he listened to our questions and agreed to guide us to the holy place. Thin and lean, the poor devil had mistaken us for a Bedouin group. A European would have thought we were a chapter of bellicose Carthusian monks. The *fellah* put us on the right track and eventually agreed to walk with us. He guided us well and we treated him the same way.

At the end of a hard two-hour walk, the Dendera temple appeared at last. What an extraordinary sensation it was to stand there, in front of the huge portico bathed in celestial light! Of course it could be measured, but that would not convey an idea of it. Grace and majesty combined in the extreme. An indescribable peace and a mysterious magic prevailed around the huge columns, sunk in the pitch-black darkness contrasting with dazzling moonlight.

L'Hôte lit a fire of dry grass inside. A cry of enthusiasm arose from everyone. We were overwhelmed by a fever of excitement. We embraced each other, exalted that we had discovered a wonderfully well-preserved temple and were reliving the meditation and prayer hours practised by Egyptian priests for millennia. Even Father Bidant seemed enthralled.

We spent two ecstatic hours in the temple, hurrying through the large rooms with our poor lanterns, trying to decipher scenes and inscriptions.

'We should spend the night here,' recommended Rosellini.

'No. We do not have the material we need to study the place. Let's go back to the ships by the right path and come back as soon as possible.'

Heads full of dreams, we headed for the Nile in a procession, me in the rear, torch in hand.

A shadow appeared behind me. I unsheathed my sabre.

'Are you afraid of a woman, Champollion?' The fawn-coloured light played on Lady Redgrave's fine face.

'Don't stay behind, Lady Ophelia. It might be dangerous. There are probably prowlers.'

'I'm not afraid of them,' she said, raising her head to the starry sky. 'I do not fear anything any more. You made me experience the most intense moment of my life. Inside the temple, in the presence of divinities, I felt the reality of another world, far more real than the one our eyes offer us. You are the one who brought me here, Jean-François Champollion. Whoever you may really be, I shall never forget.'

I would have liked to question her about the meaning of these strange words, as well as to remove any doubts she might have about me, but she had joined the procession.

We went back to the temple at 7 a.m. with the necessary gear for sketching maps and drawing text and scenes. What had been magnificent in the moonlight became even more so when the rays of the sun enabled us to distinguish all the details. I realized that the temple was a masterpiece of architecture, but that it had been loaded with sculptures of indifferent style compared to those of the ancient sculptors. Dendera's bas-reliefs date back to a time of decline. Dedicated to Hathor, the goddess of joy, who was able to engender the brilliance of stars, the edifice had been begun, at least in its present form, by the Ptolemies and completed by Roman emperors. I even succeeded in determining, thanks to the royal names in cartouches, that the main builders had been Cleopatra, Cesarion and Augustus. The sculptures had decayed, but the architecture was less prone to degradation, and because it is a mathematical art, it had remained worthy of the gods of Egypt and all the admiration it had received over the centuries.

We contemplated the huge columns of the portico. They actually looked like immense music instruments, sistrums crowned by four faces of the goddess Hathor. When the initiated played them, they produced a sound that spread the divine vibrations round the world. I wondered if the whole temple was not just a network of resonance, influencing our souls and bodies. Alas, vandals, among whom were fanatical Christians, had disfigured several portraits of the goddess of love as if she could have interfered with their beliefs. As she is the one who welcomes the dead on the bank of the other world, I am not sure that they would be very well received there. I believe that our actions produce a result in the invisible world. Whoever destroys, will be destroyed.

'Give me a spade and leave me here!' suggested Nestor L'Hôte. 'The temple is half buried in sand! We can only see the upper part of the columns. What a sight we will have when everything is cleared!'

Sand had truly been the ally of Dendera. Hiding a large part of the reliefs, it protected them from iconoclasts. We would have to remove it and restore the edifice to its initial splendour.

Accompanied by Rosellini, I walked to the far end of the sanctuary, progressing step by step into the mystery of the temple, without forgetting to raise my eyes to the ceiling, where astrological charts, maps of the sky and cosmic divinities were depicted.

'What a huge task awaits us, Master! It will take many years to copy and translate this huge book.'

'And even more to understand it, Rosellini. I can now grasp the meaning of Napoleon's words.'

'So you met him!'

'Yes, in Grenoble, on his return from Elba. My brother, whom he had appointed as his secretary, had arranged the meeting. During the reception of constituent bodies, the Emperor saw me in the crowd and promised to have my dictionary of Coptic language printed. He even wanted Coptic to become the official language of modern Egypt. Napoleon was fascinated by Egypt. He wore a talisman and believed that the magic of the pyramids protected him. He was convinced that the ancient Egyptians possessed extraordinary knowledge. He knew Egypt, I only dreamt about it.'

The *fellah* in rags, our excellent guide, came to me, wanting to show me another marvel. Lifting a slab, he opened the way to an underground gallery which led to a crypt. In the light of the torches I could see extraordinary figures on the walls showing the production of spiritual gold. In addition to astrology on the temple ceiling there was alchemy in its secret foundations. Only Pharaoh was allowed to study the sacred sciences.

I sat with the *fellah* in the dust. We were both fascinated by the symbols – a vase, an erect snake, a falcon head – which explained how man turned into light.

'Have you met the man who is called the Prophet? I asked.

'Only God is God and Mohammed is his prophet,' he answered, shocked.

'He is a tall man with a white beard trimmed into a point,' I insisted. 'He walks with a long stick with a gold knob. He understands the signs of figures of the ancient people.'

The *fellah* lowered his head and, resting it on his knees, thought for a long time.

'A man like that came here two moons ago . . . As for me, I did not see him. But people say that he spent a whole night on the roof of the temple.'

'Did people see him leave?'

'People say that he boarded a *felucca* and headed for Thebes.'

Following an ascending gallery, on the walls of which figured priests in immortal processions, I reached the roof of the temple. I was immediately intoxicated by the beauty of the view. The countryside, the Nile, the hills of the desert formed a picture of absolute serenity, of which the temple was the core. Astrologers, called 'priests of time' by the ancient Egyptians, came here to learn their art.

The sunset's glow was already beginning to bathe the stones in a warm golden light. Lady Redgrave sat on one edge of the roof, gazing at a palm grove, over which flew ibis with outspread wings. She had taken her hat off. Her Titian red hair fell in curls on her shoulders. Her skin, so white at her arrival in Egypt, was now tanned, giving her an Oriental charm. In a yellow shirt and a black skirt, she had never looked so beautiful.

Dendera, the temple of the goddess of love . . . was she incarnate in the mysterious woman with a perfect face, whose softness concealed passion? Was she a vision of an impossible happiness or one attainable now while the sun was setting over the horizon?

Lady Redgrave turned her head with infinite slowness. 'I knew that you were here, Jean-François. Come and sit beside me.'

'Lady Ophelia, I would like to ask you . . .'

'Keep silent. We'll talk later. Give me your hand.'

The sunset flared. The last fire of the sun played with the green of palm trees and spread an orange cloak over the fields, from where there arose the sound of a flute.

Only a single day in Dendera . . . what a sacrilege! But I had to be on my way and get to Thebes, where the Prophet had probably taken refuge. In my cabin, on my desk, were the notebooks in which I had recorded my latest research. I was certainly beginning to read hieroglyphs, but by trial and error, like an apprentice reader who picks out letters, sometimes words, seldom sentences. A coherent key was still missing. My thoughts wandered between death and life, both offered by the two letters to me before my departure to Egypt. Although Abdel-Razuk had disappeared and Moktar was playing the self-effacing and obedient servant, the shadow of Drovetti and his master, the Pasha, still hovered over us. But there was also the benevolent magic of the Brotherhood of Luxor, the Egypt of the temples, the sublime nature of a journey which satisfied me beyond hopes . . . this was real life, renewed life, the most precious of treasures.

What did Thebes, the older sister of all towns and the core of all my dreams since adolescence, have in store for me? What remained of the largest and most famous capital of the ancient world?

There was a knock on my door. I opened it. Professor Raddi requested a meeting, which I immediately granted.

'We haven't had any opportunity to talk since the beginning of our trip,' he started as he sat down on my bed and on the few papers strewn there. 'I want to tell you that I am extremely happy with the stones I have gathered and with what I understand of the scientific relevance.'

'I am most happy about it, Professor! Your work is such a lonely one that I did not want to disturb your research.'

'Thank you for that, Champollion . . . I have actually got into the habit of not communicating too much with human beings. They bore me. I feel closer to stones. They also teach me to observe,' He added gloomily.

'What do you mean?'

Professor Raddi looked fixedly ahead of him, as if I did not exist. 'You not only have friends around you . . .' His voice was almost fading.

'You are revealing either too much or too little, Professor! Who are you accusing?'

'I just make scientific observations. Do you really believe Rosellini to be a faithful disciple?'

'I am convinced of it. He is absolutely sincere and devoted. He certainly has a few flaws . . . He probably spends too much time bargaining and purchasing. But his eagerness to discover and learn cannot be questioned.'

Raddi nodded as he dusted his crumpled suit. 'You can be a genius and still be naive,' he sighed. 'I bet he will betray you. And what about Nestor, L'Hôte? What is his aim?'

'He wants to express his talent as a draughtsman and take part in an unusual adventure,' I answered firmly. 'Isn't that a noble enough design for you?'

'Your disciple Rosellini only wants to take the place of his master and brave soldier Nestor L'Hôte wants to become a general . . . As for charming Lady Redgrave, only God knows what she is capable of. She is certainly a spy . . . but she is also a woman in love. She may destroy or kill, according to her heart. I hope that things will turn out well for you. I myself haven't had that good fortune. Mrs Raddi is a tigress of the worst sort. I should have refused to marry her, but I did not dare. She always frightened me. She is always right. In this lost country, I have had a good time for the first time in twenty years. I almost forgot mineralogy. This is why I shall not return to Europe. There are too many regulations, too much discipline and too many wet blankets there. Here people take me for an old crank and leave me in peace. I owe no explanations to the desert. I talk freely. The desert provides answers on what is essential. I know why the country fascinates you, Champollion. It is magical. It belongs to another world. You won't go back either.'

I remained silent for along time. Raddi stared fixedly at my right hand. 'You have a wonderful jasper ring . . . may I examine it?'

'I'm sorry, Professor. I will never part from it.'

'Ah! So you believe in talismans too . . . and magic! Science seems so ridiculous and so childish with its measures and figures in the face of the desert. Protect yourself, Champollion. There is no better strategy against unhappiness.'

'Why didn't you mention Father Bidant?'

Professor Raddi's forehead creased. Piqued, he stood up and opened the door of the cabin. He was about to leave when he stopped. 'You are the greatest genius I have had the good fortune of meeting, Champollion. You are driven by your destiny and you cannot do anything to change that. Yet don't forget that, even with a cassock, man can become the worst of wild beasts.'

The wind has been annoying us for two days and preventing us from entering the sanctuary of Thebes. The name and the city obsessed me to the extent that I had become hateful to my companions. I studied the maps and descriptions of former travellers over and again. Suddenly an idea crossed my mind. I rushed on deck. I did not find the man I was looking for there. He was smoking a hookah on the bank, in the shade of an acacia. I strode up to him with a determination which frightened him.

'Have you ever been to Thebes, Moktar?'

'No, no, I don't think so.'

'You're lying. How many times did you come here with Drovetti?'

'Whenever he needed me.'

'Did he order you to destroy any monuments?'

'No, he didn't . . . He is very respectful of them. But we are all faithful servants of the Pasha . . .'

A shiver ran down my spine. 'What did he want?'

'Thebes is full of old monuments . . . The Pasha considered that some of them should be demolished to build sugar refineries and cotton factories.'

I grasped his shoulders.

'How many temples have been destroyed?'

'A dozen . . . maybe more.'

'Maybe more . . .' I repeated, shaken to the depth of my soul.

I moved away from Moktar who was completely indifferent to the fate of Theban monuments. He began to smoke his hookah again, watching me out of the corner of his eye.

A gust of wind whipped my face.

The wind! At last the wind would open the road to Thebes.

The sky of Upper Egypt is the most beautiful you will ever see. The sun god rules supreme but it knows how to create such a perfectly pure blue that anyone who gazes on it drowns in delight.

On the banks of the Nile lies the wealth it leaves, a black, rich, light compost. The desert winds spread a dry heat like the heat from ovens when the bread is taken out.

Although I never tired of this sight, it did not still my impatience. The ship was drawing alongside. Thebes appeared.

'It may be wise to go further,' said Suleiman who was standing beside me.

I looked with alarm at the man who claimed to be my brother.

'Neglect Thebes? Are you mad, Suleiman?'

'Look to your left, the big tree . . .'

A giant sycamore shaded part of the bank. Its foliage almost

147

reached to the ground. It probably offered delicious shelter in the scorching hours.

'The tree is magnificent, but—'

'Look more carefully.'

Despite the distance, I thought I was able to discern feet jutting out from under the leaves above the ground.

'Hanged men,' explained Suleiman. 'Innocents murdered because they displeased the Pasha. Others had their heads cut off. There were over three hundred victims whose crime it was to protest against Mehmet Ali's tyranny. People say that, among the questions they were asked before the torture, some concerned the Prophet and the place where he is hiding . . . Do you still want to see Thebes?'

I clenched my fists. The decision was mine only. I should probably have weighed the pros and cons, assessed risks and thought clearly, but I relied only on the inner voice which dictated my behaviour. 'Thebes is waiting for us, Suleiman.'

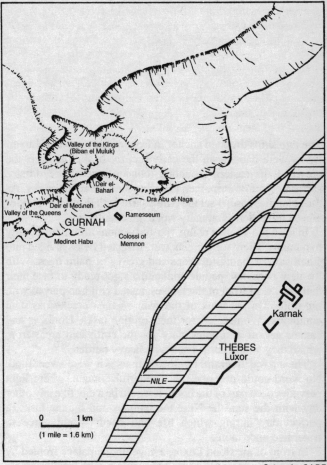

Cartography : C.A.R.T.

15

The two ships dropped anchor in front of the temple of Luxor. Larks were dancing in the early breeze. In the distance, the crests of the eastern mountain took on a red tinge. First a saffron-coloured strip, then a blazing aura invaded the sky. As the solar disc rose, it set the Nile ablaze with dazzling sparkles whose reflections gradually woke the countryside.

In his huge Theban realm, the god Amon offered his bounty to humans. There were green, well-irrigated fields divided into small square, bountiful crops and groves of palm trees. With the new-born day, people and animals got ready to face their daily tasks. In front of the houses, naked children played with rag dolls. On the bank of the river *shadufs* creaked as if in complaint. Women left for their routine tasks. Donkeys and camels set off at a quiet place for the cultivated areas from which they would come back with heavy burdens.

The air was fragrant. I gulped it in as if it were sweet food. No word could describe the wonderful climate, where light pervades each part of the body. It would be a day like any other day with the sun, the Nile, the temples and human tasks, a perfect day during which life and death would agree to fraternize once more.

In front of me stood Luxor, a huge divine palace fronted by two obelisks, perfectly carved in a single pink granite block, and surrounded by four colossi buried to the chest. I immediately recognized the art of the great Ramses. The Nile threatened the building. If nothing was done to protect it, it would soon be surrounded by water and fall to pieces.

The locals had not respected this glorious past. They had erected terracotta walls on the ruins to separate the miserable dwellings they built among the capitals of the columns. Pigeons and hens moved around among stone lotuses. Dogs ran among bas-reliefs and their excrement covered divine figures. The right part of the great entrance pylon was completely blocked by dovecotes. In front of what was the façade of a perfectly designed temple camels were kneeling, waiting for their owners to complete endless transactions.

The inside of the temple was even more devastated; there were ovens with roasting chickens, children's playgrounds, a Turkish captain's house, the remains of a Christian church and even a mosque concealing a large part of the monument. Luxor must be the most profaned of all Egyptian sanctuaries.

Overwhelmed by the heart-rending vision of a Thebes not at all like my dreams, I hid myself to weep behind a column covered with lampblack. This sad meditation may have lasted several hours, but Nestor L'Hôte found me again. I managed to conceal my sorrow and welcome him with a serene face.

'Hurry up, General! I shall be able to clear the obelisks.'

'By what miracle?'

'It should be enough to demolish the string-board and brick huts leaning on them.' L'Hôte's eyes gleamed with excitement.

'I forbid you to do so.'

'Why?' he asked, surprised.

'We would leave several poor families without a roof. We have no right to do that.'

Nestor L'Hôte did not understand my decision. As a disciplined soldier, he did not rebel, but I perceived that his friendship with me had been seriously damaged. 'I shall content myself with drawing.' He announced.

'Keep at it,' I said. 'The architecture and the relief belong to the best style. We should at least save that.'

The day was laborious. I took notes here and there and imagined the huge excavation campaign that would be needed to rid the temple of its unfortunate appendages without wronging poor people. My heart rebelled at the idea that human beings could be so unaware of the wonders at hand. A superficial investigation enabled me to discover that Luxor revealed the mystery of divine birth, how Pharaoh was formed by the gods to become the ruler of Egypt and the mediator between God and man. Would the sublime revelations, stifled by the garbage of humankind, ever be revived?

In the evening, Luxor, despoiled still though it was, had a splendour reminiscent of its former beauty. A light wind brought a new stillness. Warm colours covered the walls and columns. The orange veil of the sunset spread over the stone giant, erasing brambles, little and hovels. The squawking of poultry faded. The locals stopped moving around the ruins and went back to their huts to prepare meals. Rosellini and L'Hôte had gone back to the ship.

I was alone in the sanctuary, alone in what had been a huge reception room where gods and men united in luminous joy. Yet my thoughts were unable to reach beyond the concerns aroused by Professor Raddi's comments. Was I really only surrounded by traitors, incompetent and envious people, all in the service of the enemy? What plan had that enemy conceived against me and how did he intend to implement it? It could be that Professor Raddi was a gifted liar; after all he had wanted to take my protective ring.

In the temple, pacified by its beauty, I realized what had happened since my departure from Grenoble. The expedition, which should have just been an archaeological adventure, had aroused hatred and passions and compelled me to enter a struggle I was not prepared for. I was now the opponent of the almighty Pasha of Egypt, of ruthless Drovetti and their hordes of pillagers and murders, barring their way and determined not to back down. These men had decided to plunder Egypt, ransack and destroy it before anyone could discover their deeds. They were probably preparing even worse things. To them I was just a wisp of straw, but an official wisp sent by the French government, the very government against which I had fought so much in the past . . .

'You look as if you're lost in the past. Are you?' Lady Ophelia Redgrave had approached me with a light and silent gait. She remained standing behind me.

'The stones will be revived one day in all their beauty,' she said. 'I can feel it.'

'Scientists are too stupid and too cowardly . . .'

'You haven't been very friendly with your colleagues . . . my uncle described you as a man with a sour temper who accused his rivals of stupidity and incompetence.'

'He was not wrong. If you only knew the French scholars. They are unable to perceive the importance of Egyptian civilization. They are pretentious old bourgeois, restricted by their mental habits and hostile to any new discovery. I wonder if they could have worked as we did, day and night in the small library I kept with my brother, Jacques-Joseph, in Grenoble. We filled our two rooms with books, bought and devoured as if they were delicious food. At the same time I learned grammar, Latin, Greek and Hebrew with him, and completed my learning with Aramaic and Coptic.' The sunset had flooded the temple. The soft light and lukewarm nightfall turned us into accomplices, whispering so as not to disturb the gods.

'My uncle claims that you have not discovered anything and that you are just an impostor.'

'Young is a jealous liar!' I flared up. 'On 14 September 1822; at noon, for the first time I began to understand how to read hieroglyphs. "I have taken the keys in my hand", I told my brother, and then I sank into a fainting fit which lasted three days. But I had already dictated several principles of decipherment for Sacy, who was one of those fake scientists, and a miserable translator. I convinced Jacques-Joseph to forget him and send the paper to Dacier, the Curator of the

Bibliothèque Nationale, who held my brother in high esteem. Unfortunately . . .'

'Unfortunately?'

'I confess that I did not enjoy doing it very much, but it enabled me to carry on my research without worrying about money and accommodation.'

The silence of Egyptian evenings is incomparable. Humankind becomes silent and the countryside gradually sinks into sleep. Temples begin to look like wise men of stone, uttering words of eternity. The peace of Luxor dimmed the strange memories jumbled in my mind. Lady Redgrave made me talk and I let her do so. This was the first time I had spoken about the difficult times, when my life had not been so favoured by fortune. My only good fortune had been my unshakeable wish to make Egypt talk so that the huge voice at the root of all civilization could be heard.

'Have you ever been arrested?' asked Lady Redgrave, suspicious.

'Arrested, no; sent into exile, yes . . . and I am proud of the sentence. The White Terror obliged my brother and me to live in Figeac. There we were constantly harassed. Despite its bad faith, justice could not charge us with any crime. All this seems so trivial now . . . There is only one memory that really matters to me: the memory of nights of secret work in the dormitory of the school in Grenoble where I translated Greek and Latin authors by candlelight. My companions were sleeping. I was already alone . . . alone with texts, thoughts and words snatched from silence and death.'

'Come,' she said. 'I want to take a walk.'

Some of the Luxor bas-reliefs were so finely engraved that they had become invisible. Night was taking over rapidly, leaving the bright moon to illuminate the temple. Hand in hand, we went to the sanctuary sheltering the sacred boat carried by priests when the god Amon demonstrated his presence to the people.

We were just two figures lost in the secrecy of a sacred

place where, in the presence of the creator, Pharaoh became one with his great royal spouse in a ritual wedding. Hieroglyphs on the walls made the occurrence live for ever. That night the temple of Luxor seemed to sparkle with love.

'Wake up! Please, wake up!'

Without violence, but with determined vigour, Suleiman shook me. He was the only one who had a copy of my cabin key. It took me a few seconds to come back to earth. During my brief sleep, I had been dreaming of grandiose excavations, temples cleared of sand, renovated bas-reliefs . . . I had actually been rebuilding the whole of Egypt.

'What is the matter, Suleiman?'

'Mehmet Ali, the almighty Pasha of Egypt, has just arrived in Thebes.'

I sprang up, now completely awake. 'Suleiman, arrange a meeting with him.'

Mehmet Ali had taken up residence in a large dwelling in which half the windows had been blocked. He received me at noon, surrounded by numerous sycophants smoking hookahs and drinking green tea. Sitting on an armchair in the Empire style, he was smoothing his long white beard, which a servant had just perfumed. 'Delighted to see you again, Champollion. Does your journey bring you the joys you expected?'

Standing at a respectful distance from the throne, I bowed with deference. 'May you be favoured by heaven, Your Excellency, for having granted me an audience.'

The Pasha ordered that honey pastries and tea be served to me. I took my time savouring them, as I had no wish to hasten a conversation in the course of which I was going to make a very dangerous challenge. I thought I had found a way to defeat the tyrant without making him lose face. If my endeavour failed, it would be the end of my adventure.

'Your Excellency's health seems to be blooming.'

'I am in the best of my health, Champollion. Never have I been more determined to fulfil my duties and make my people rich and happy. The industrialization of the country is very urgent. I am very much aware of the necessity of preserving some of the ancient monuments, but I must first take care of the present.'

The warning was obvious. Mehmet Ali forbade me to mention the buildings that had been dismantled on his instructions.

'Who would blame you for that, Your Excellency? I am very attached to the Egyptian people and having seen their conditions in the course of my journey I feel that no measure in their favour can be too generous.'

The Pasha had expected a protest which did not come. His insight made him foresee an attack on another field. 'Were there any serious incidents during your trip, Champollion?'

'Some violent deaths, Your Excellency, but none of them concerns me . . . In Egypt like anywhere else, human passions are sometimes expressed most brutally. Conflicts of interest, I suppose. But I am an Egyptologist and not a policeman. I have neither the desire not the opportunity to probe. I am only interested in archaeology.'

The Pasha's piercing gaze became fixed. The master of the Egypt assessed each one of my words. He knew that I was not taken in. He appreciated my unexpected moderation, which was reassuring for his own interests. I did not say a word about Abdel-Razuk, his *chaouiche* who had tried to murder me. Neither he nor I wanted to mention that fearsome figure.

'If you want to pursue your expedition, Champollion, how can I please you? I would like to grant a favour to an eminent ambassador of France.'

I sipped my tea and thought for a long time, as if I was hesitating to voice a wish. I was actually rehearsing the stages of my argument.

'Is it true, Your Excellency, that the British refused to take home the Alexandrian obelisk you gave them, under the pretext that they would have to build a road at a cost of around three hundred thousand francs?'

Disconcerted, the Pasha answered with a nod.

'Of course,' I continued. 'The road to the new harbour is essential. But it is a serious and unforgivable offence to refuse the present of the Pasha of Egypt.'

Mehmet Ali tried to remain inscrutable, but I heard a very light sigh of satisfaction.

'For the same amount, Your Excellency, I have something much better to offer you, provided, of course, you give me your support.'

'Go on,' he ordered, intrigued.

'I am most satisfied,' I said, 'that the knowledgeable British engineer had the wonderful idea of estimating a cost of three hundred thousand francs to put off his government, and as an indirect consequence ours, from taking the miserable Alexandrian obelisks! They look so pitiful now that I have seen those in Thebes. I have a stronger and more impressive idea . . . what Great Britain disdains will be enthusiastically accepted by France! Paris needs an obelisk, Your Excellency. It would be good for our nation to see something superior to the knickknacks, frills and flounces we call public monuments. These are just boudoir decorations fit only for the little men we call our 'great' architects, meticulous copyists of the trivialities of the Lower Kingdom. Whatever people might say, greatness will always dwell in greatness and nowhere else. Only something massive really impresses people. A single column of Luxor is more of a monument in itself than the four façades of the courtyard of the Louvre. An Egyptian colossus on the platform of the Pont-Neuf would be more impressive than three regiments of horse statues the size of that of Lomot. Our capital looks gloomy. Modern art has killed art. Paris has entered the age of barbarity. When I saw obelisks erected in honour of Ramses, the greatest conqueror in his time, I knew that one of them could wonderfully commemorate the indissoluble friendship between Egypt and France.'

The Pasha did not conceal his surprise any more.

'So what do you suggest, Monsieur Champollion?'

'For three hundred thousand francs, I am sure that I can take charge of the transport of one of the two obelisks of Luxor temple, the one on the right, to Paris. The nation will be honoured and eternally grateful to you, Your Excellency.'

'What a surprising request, and what a fabulous endeavour,' said the Pasha. 'It will probably be necessary to cut the huge monolith into three pieces . . .'

'I want everything or nothing, Your Excellency. The obelisk must remain intact, so as to shine in all its power on French soil. The transport will succeeded provided it is entrusted to a man of the field, an architect or a mechanic, and not to a desk-bound scientist!'

One of the most perfect masterpieces of Egyptian art had been spoiled by vandals day after day and was doomed to speedy deterioration. This was the only way to save it. Mehmet Ali stroked his beard in perplexity, stood up and abruptly ordered his sycophants to leave. He waited until we were alone before speaking.

'You are a very active man, Champollion. Egypt lived in peaceful oblivion before you came. I am afraid you might arouse too pressing an interest in an old country which must proceed slowly towards progress.'

'Your Excellency, is not Egypt's *raison d'être* its spiritual message?'

'You see temples, sculptures and divinities. I see factories, machines and dams. We are engaged in a merciless struggle. Only posterity will be able to judge.' The Pasha stopped in front of an open window and turned his back on me. As far as he was concerned, our meeting was over.

But not for me. 'Forgive me for interrupting your meditation . . . but I did not hear your reply about my plan.'

The master of Egypt remained as motionless as granite. For a long moment, I was afraid he might have adopted an equally stony silence. 'Your obelisk will embellish Paris, Champollion.'

Drunk with my victory, I found the courage to make the final step still separating me from the core of Thebes, and entered Karnak, the palace of Amon Ra, the master of the gods.

Karnak, the hundred gates, had ruled over the universe for many centuries. What did it hold in store for me? What remained after the Assyrian, Christian and Arab destructions? Would it be reduced to the same wretched state as Luxor? Unable to wait any longer, I walked quickly in the sun. A donkey owner offered his assistance, which I readily accepted. We soon covered the distance. When we left the bank to enter the countryside, the donkey owner announced proudly, 'Al-Karnak!'

I closed my eyes. Was I going to experience the greatest joy or the greatest disappointment in my life? The donkey stopped. I climbed down, almost losing consciousness. At last I opened my eyes.

Karnak . . . Karnak stood before me, huge and superhuman.

There appeared all the pharaonic magnificence, and the greatest things ever imagined and shaped by men. Everything I had seen in Thebes seemed miserable compared to the huge conceptions which now surrounded me. I cannot describe it, for either my description would only amount to a thousandth of what should be said about such masterpieces or, if I gave even a brief dull outline, I might be taken for a crank. It is enough to say that no ancient or modern people has ever conceived the art of architecture on such a sublime and grandiose scale as the Old Egyptians. They conceived men of 100 feet when we are only 5 feet 8. Imagination, which, in Europe rises to our porticos, remains helpless at the bottom of the 140 columns of Karnak's hypostyle hall, a forest of giant flowers, a world beyond man lit by a celestial light filtering through windows of stone.

In the marvellous temple, I contemplated the portraits of most of the pharaohs who had shaped the glory of the empire. In these columns and on the walls, Egypt used the power of the spirit and succeeded in turning matter into spirituality.

Karnak also suffered from the neglect of Arab invaders for

whom Egypt was just a foreign land. Here were crashed colossi, mounds of sand to clear, lintels about to fall into ruins and camps of locals in the sanctuaries. But the genius of the ancient people had not yielded to the attacks of time and men. With its great size, Karnak could defy cataclysms, among the first of which was human foolishness.

The gods had led me to what was most sacred in the world and the vision made me forget the stupidities and vileness of life.

'Master . . . so you are here!' Opening the door of my cabin, which I had forgotten to lock, Rosellini was flabbergasted to find me sitting at my desk littered with papers.

In Karnak I had written page after page. Back to the *Isis* at nightfall, I immediately began to try to write a chronology of the kings who had left traces of their rule. On the day when the Prophet gave me the elements of oral tradition he possessed, I would be ready to write a grammar, dictionary and a general history of Egyptian civilization.

'We have looked for you everywhere, Master . . . We were very worried. Are you ill?'

'My health is excellent. The climate suits me wonderfully and I feel better than in Paris. I worked a lot today . . . I hope you did the same.'

Rosellini seemed piqued. 'Forgive my saying so but you seem in a bad mood.'

'That is true,' I said, throwing my quill away. 'I am furious.'

'Because of me?'

'Not at all. Because of France, because of all those who pretend to be closed to me or to be my friends. I haven't heard anything from them since our departure. There hasn't been even a letter.'

'It is probably difficult to send mail . . .'

'Don't try to lie, Rosellini. I know that you have received letters from Alexandria. L'Hôte, Bidant, Raddi . . . you have all received news. I haven't.'

'Drovetti probably withheld your letters to you so as to make you desperate. Don't let his malevolence succeed.'

I was alone, absolutely alone, but the spirit of ancient Egypt penetrated me, hour after hour. Links with Europe and my past broke one after the other. Deep in my heart, I did not feel any sadness. Karnak marked the climax of my destiny, relegating the past to the rank of vanities blown away by a wind of sand. I had just passed my point of no return.

L'Hôte's concerned face appeared behind Rosellini. 'General, I have bad news. I have just caught sight of Abdel-Razuk on the quay. At first I thought I was wrong, but I am a skilled observer. I shouted his name. He turned round and fled. His presence should be reported to the authorities of Luxor.'

'It is useless,' I said. 'Abdel-Razuk is at the service of the Pasha, who will prevent any action against his servant.'

As I went to enjoy the light of the sunset on the deck of the *Isis*, I bumped into a sumptuous-looking Lady Redgrave, dressed in a red silk evening dress with a three-tiered pearl necklace. She looked so radiant that she would have convinced any hermit to renounce solitude.

'I am afraid I must tear you away from your studious work,' she said, mischievously.

'Why?'

She looked at me critically. 'You look like an explorer back from the wildest desert. You should dress up to impress your guests.'

'I have nobody to impress, Lady Redgrave. I want to get some fresh air for a while and then go back to my cabin. It is more important to me to make a list of pharaohs than to have a social dinner.'

'Yet you won't be able to avoid this one.'

'Why?'

'Because the great people of Luxor want to be invited at your table . . . which is now laid on deck.'

I was about to rush to check, but Lady Redgrave barred my way. 'Not in that attire, Monsieur Champollion!'

The table had been set under a canvas cover stretched on four posts. A delightful breath of wind enchanted the evening, erasing the fatigue of the day. Lady Redgrave was a wonderful hostess, embellishing our usual setting with oil lamps and floral arrangements.

She had not deceived me with the quality of our guests. There was a Turkish *aga*, commander-in-chief in Gurnah; the *sheikh el-beled* of Medinet Habu, who ruled over the local temple and the Ramesseum and, last, the *sheikh* of Karnak, before whom everybody bowed in the colonnade of the old palace of the kings of Egypt. They ruled over an army of insignificant people and small jobs, and it was impossible to take a step in Thebes without their consent.

The conversation was reduced to an exchange of trivialities and mutual congratulations. At steady intervals, I answered '*thaibin*', 'I'm fine' to the question '*Ente-thaïeb*', 'Are you all right?' My guests smiled heartily, as I offered them pipes and coffee in profusion. Suleiman told some funny Oriental stories about demons cheated by human beings. We were showered with presents: a herd of sheep and some fifty hens. This fortune on legs delighted Lady Redgrave. It would guarantee excellent food.

Receiving an allotment of gunpowder that would give him supremacy in war, the *aga* of Gurnah gave me a large staff to help the work in the great temple. He poured out a stream of flirtatious compliments on Lady Redgrave, on whom he conferred the title of 'your spouse'. I should have reacted, had it not been that Egyptian manners prevented one from contradicting a guest abruptly.

Lady Ophelia smiled.

My heart was full of hope when, the following morning, I entered Karnak again, as if Amon's huge estate had become mine. The *fellahin* the *sheikh* had promised me were waiting in the great courtyard behind the massive entrance pylon. Accompanied by Rosellini and L'Hôte, I enthusiastically addressed the group of workers, who were led by a foreman who fixed their salary at half a piastre per day. The excavations started immediately. Rosellini was trembling with curiosity at the prospect of unearthing statues. L'Hôte was happy to leave his drawings and dedicate himself to the task of leading the men.

Suleiman brought the man I had asked him to find: Timsah, 'the crocodile', the personal excavator of the French Consul-General Drovetti and the French authorities' local representative. He was small and stocky, with a low forehead and thick hands, and he hardly opened his eyes.

'May you be blessed, Timsah. Did the Consul-General tell you of my visit?'

'Yes.'

'Did he give you money for the excavations?'

'I am expecting the money.'

'Do you mean that you don't have anything?'

'I'm expecting the money,' he repeated.

'When?' I asked impatiently.

'Tomorrow, maybe the day after tomorrow.'

'It must be tomorrow. I make it your personal responsibility.'

'The crocodile' bowed and walked away slowly.

'How shall we pay the workers tonight?' asked Rosellini.

'With my own money.'

The day was a succession of marvels. I gave instruction to measure the highest Egyptian obelisks. A young Nubian managed to reach the top of the stone peak with the help of a post wrapped in ropes. While he climbed, the foreman knelt down to implore Allah and the toilers recited verses of the Koran. Elsewhere, people dug to clear the bases of columns and unearth late bronzes. I rushed from one temple to the next, from a reception room to the holy of holies, from an alley lined with rams to monumental porticos. I devoured Karnak eagerly, convinced that the building that was founded on the same scale as the universe had never been shut. Masterbuilders had embellished it and developed it right to the end of their lives.

And I was their humble successor, now ready to revive the holy body of Egypt, where hand and spirit had created with the same genius.

I was copying an offering scene engraved on one of the columns of the hypostyle hall when the foreman came to fetch me. His uncoordinated gestures betrayed intense excitement. I ran behind him to the shrine of Seti I, in front of which a sinister struggle was taking place: L'Hôte and Father Bidant were fighting. The priest seemed to have the upper hand, and hit with the flat of his hands. L'Hôte was compelled to step back to protect his face.

'Stop immediately!' I intervened, so powerfully that it immediately brought the fight to an end. 'Have you gone mad, Father? And you, L'Hôte, have you lost all your dignity?'

'Bidant is a criminal, General.'

'L'Hôte is a lunatic,' countered the priest. 'He attacked me while I was examining the bottom of a wall.'

'He was not examining it,' protested L'Hôte. 'He was damaging it! He was trying to erase figures with stones.'

Bending over the bone of contention, I saw a touching scene: Pharaoh as a child on his mother's lap. I understood Father Bidant's reasoning. 'The virgin bearing Christ . . . this is what you were thinking of, isn't it? You wanted to destroy the Egyptian motif that served as model for medieval painters. The divine birth before Christianity is rather annoying to your eyes. Your fight is useless, Father. You will have to admit that Christianity was born in this land and drew its symbols from the oldest Egyptian heritage!'

'It is a sacrilege!' shouted the priest, furious. Shaking his dusty cassock, he left the sacred enclosure.

Karnak bewitched me. I did not need to sleep and hardly ate. I did not even think of danger any more. I had the impression that I had always lived here, that I had already walked through the alleys and seen the rooms.

Lady Redgrave had left the ship to settle in a comfortable dwelling in Luxor, full of zealous servants. An impassable barrier had arisen between us again. Father Bidant shut himself up in his cabin, where he had his meals served. Professor Raddi had taken a campstool and spent hours in meditation at the edge of the desert. He did not hear anything nor see anyone. Surprised by my stamina, L'Hôte and Rosellini assisted me to the point of exhaustion. My health, which had been a constant cause of worry in the cold and mists of Europe, was improving under the Egyptian sun. In addition, Karnak was able to obliterate fatigue. Divine energies flowed from the ground making the body as good as new again. I understood why the builders had been able to lift stones of such size and build on such a huge scale. They were imbued with a superhuman power from the ground on which temples were built.

The monuments did not belong to the past. They were the everlasting present of consciousness, as serene as on the first dawn of the world. Thebes had become the core of the universe and the place where my destiny was fulfilled both in external life and in the mystery. If I were allowed to dig in Karnak, I wouldn't move from here. I would even forget the Prophet and the decipherment of hieroglyphs. I would content myself with being the most modest of workers and removing sand and dust till the end of my life.

I dreamed of Karnak restored to life as I sank into sleep.

There was an intense bustle in the temple of Mut, south of Amon's sanctuary. In the bright early-morning light, the site of the divine mother appeared in all its strangeness with its scattered blocks, weeds and sacred lake shaped like a moon crescent. A number of *fellahin* had gathered around L'Hôte, who had insisted on carrying his pick in an isolated place which had been shut up in silence and oblivion for centuries. I would have let myself be seduced by the charm of the plain full of hidden treasures, but when I saw L'Hôte struggling with a hostile mob, I had to help him.

I pushed aside a few workers and addressed the *sheikh* of

Karnak who was brandishing a short rod threateningly. 'What is the matter?'

'Look,' said L'Hôte, pointing to a hole, from which emerged the black head of a statue of the lion goddess. 'The *fellahin* are convinced it is a demon. They want to destroy its face before they unearth it. It brings the evil eye.'

'They are right, they are right!' shouted Father Bidant, brandishing a cross over their heads. 'The cursed statue should be put back into the sand!'

Rosellini forced him to shut up, but the *sheikh* of Karnak retained an inscrutable and hostile face. He could not allow himself to lose face in front of his men.

'There is an evil spell,' he declared. 'The lion will jump at our throats. Yesterday in Qena, fish greedy for human flesh attacked people who were swimming and ate their genitals. In Akhmin, children cut a snake into pieces. He was immediately regenerated and bit them. There is an evil spell. We will get the evil eye.'

He could have told many other fabulous stories containing remnants of Egyptian mythology. I did not have time to tell him about the uraeus snake, which was in charge of the protection of pharaohs or about the myth of Osiris, whose genitals had been swallowed by a fish.

'I can remove the evil eye,' I said. 'I am not afraid.'

Intrigued, the *sheikh* pushed two *fellahin* away with his rod. 'Prove it.'

I knelt down. With my bare hands, I removed some earth and cleared the severe face of Sekhmet. She was the lion goddess with the fiery gaze, in charge of the annihilation of Pharaoh's visible and invisible enemies, and of teaching physicians their art. I took her sturdy forehead in my hands, arousing a whisper of fright.

'Look, the goddess accepts me. It won't spread misfortune or illness.'

I kept the position for a long time. Each *fellah* expected to see me devoured by the terrifying lioness. But the evil eye did not strike me. They smiled again. A worker went back to work, followed by a second, then a third . . . At the end of the morning, Sekhmet's powerful statue sat imposingly in front of our eyes, and we marvelled at so much power combined with so much majesty.

Rosellini had difficulty in controlling his emotion. His hands were shaking.

'What is the matter, Ippolito?'

'Your gaze, Master, your attitude in front of the *sheikh* . . . Never have I seen you so determined and fierce . . . I thought you would fight the crowd of Arabs, resolved to do anything to save the sculpture.'

'Yes, I shall defend Egypt tooth and nail. I developed an instinct for justice when I was five and it has always been strong. I remember, I was passing a tumbledown house. A beggar leaned on the door, a hat in his hand. I was about to drop a coin in when a chief of the revolutionary party knocked the blind man, who was barring his way, with his stick. I rushed to the door, seized the stick and begged it not to obey the bad man any more and to beat him! The damned Jacobin guffawed and advised my mother to curb me so that other people did not have to do so later. Indeed people often tried to destroy my desire for justice. But they did not succeed and nobody ever will.

I did not linger any more, for I was seriously worried. Suleiman should have been with me a long time ago. We had arranged to meet at lunch time in front of the entrance pylon if he did not manage to find 'the crocodile', Timsah.

My brother had lost his usual impassiveness. 'I haven't been able to find Timsah. He has disappeared.'

'Wait for me here.'

A brief talk with the *sheikh* of Karnak, to whom I had to give a substantial tip, a *baksheesh*, gave me the information I was looking for. 'The crocodile' was hiding at a woman's house in Karnak town. We were soon confronting him.

'Why were you hiding?' I asked briskly.

'I was resting.'

'Where is the money you promised to pay the workers?'

'It has not arrived.'

'When shall I get it?'

'I don't know.'

'How do you get in touch with the Consul-General?'

'He sends messengers.'

'Each day? Each week?'

'It depends . . . whenever he thinks it's necessary. I haven't seen any for a long time. This is not a good reason to travel.'

'The crocodile' kept his eyes shut. My questions did not impress him. Protected by Drovetti and the Pasha, he felt invulnerable.

I immediately put an end to the useless meeting.

Four days elapsed. Time was flying. I had to stop the excavations. Drovetti's representative had received no message. He would receive none as long as I persevered with my plan. So the rumours circulating in Paris before my departure had been true. Drovetti would oppose my desire to study the sites and restore them to their former glory by all means. I was to content myself with being a traveller.

I walked sadly on the quay of Luxor. There was a glow in the west. The Nile would soon be illuminated by the thousand colours of sunset. Thebes was there, close by, and I had to give it up because of a devil who had sworn to ruin me as well as the ancient Egyptians.

As I contemplated the bank of the dead, a man rushed at me and pushed me violently towards the river.

16

Without the help of Nestor L'Hôte, I would have been knocked out and thrown into the Nile. Pulling out his sabre, he threatened my attacker. As the latter attempted to flee, he threw it at his legs, causing him to fall. He climbed on his back and pinned his face to the ground. The man struggled, but he had to acknowledge defeat. L'Hôte tore down the turban concealing his head and his face.

Abdel-Razuk, the Pasha's policeman, had tried to kill me a second time. 'Whom do you get your orders from?' I asked.

The *chaouiche* raised his eyes heavenwards.

'Answer,' shouted Nestor L'Hôte, 'or I'll break your neck.'

I translated the threat. My companion's anger frightened Abdel-Razuk. He stammered and decided to talk.

'The . . . the Prophet ordered me to kill you.'

I was dumbfounded. 'Why?'

'I don't know.'

'Where is he? Is he hiding in Thebes?'

'He left for the south . . .'

'When?'

'Three days ago. I had to let him know about your death so that he could come back to Thebes.'

'Go away, Abdel-Razuk. Don't get· in my way again. Otherwise, my friends and I won't control our sabres any more.' I ordered L'Hôte to let him clear off.

'Why don't we take him to the Pasha?'

'If he is telling the truth, it is better to leave him free. He will let the Prophet know. The latter will be shaken by the failure of his plan. We are on his tracks and we must leave for the south. We will eventually find him and discover why he wants me dead. Everything must be ready in an hour . . .'

The two ships moved away from the quay of Luxor. Thanks to the wind, Champollion and the members of his expedition were soon some distance from the prestigious capital of the pharaohs of the New Kingdom.

Bernardino Drovetti, the Consul-General of France, left the window from which he had watched their departure. He lit a faience pipe full of Turkish tobacco and took a sip of Bordeaux wine with great pleasure.

Sitting in a corner of the large reception room which served as the Consul-General's headquarters, Abdel-Razuk chanted verses of the Koran.

'This is wonderful!' whispered Drovetti to himself. 'Now that he has left Thebes, we can carry on safely, Abdel-Razuk!'

The Pasha's *chaouiche* stood up. He was afraid of the touchy man who had Mehmet Ali's ear.

'Don't forget to take the necessary precautions . . . Champollion is now facing the most dangerous part of his trip. Nature may help us. There have already been a lot of accidents in the south. Our accomplice will be able to show his mettle during that damned expedition.'

It was heart-rending to leave Karnak. I promised myself I would come back as a conqueror, sure of being able to hear the stones and revive the voice of eternal Egypt. After the days on shore, my companions resumed the journey with curiosity, speculating on the hew horizons awaiting us.

Consulting the archaeological maps I had sketched, I arranged for our next stop to be in El-Kab, a very ancient city where I hoped to see ruins from the earliest of ancient times. As we came abreast the town of Esna, night and wind thwarted my plans. The *reis* taking care of our progress recommended that we stop. I gave instructions that we sail somewhat further south. We left our heavy ships and took rowing boats to reach the site of Contralatopolis. Only L'Hôte and Rosellini accompanied me. The latter was the first to set foot on the shore.

A tall man dressed in a dirty *djellaba* with holes in it hurried up to him. He talked loudly, with a speech impediment. Rosellini pressed me to intervene. I noticed that the man was toothless, which explained his poor diction. What I understood him to say filled me with such dismay that I fainted. My pallid face alarmed L'Hôte, who was always quick to notice my slightest reactions.

'What does the bandit say, General? Did he insult you?'

'This is far worse, my dear friend, far worse.'

My breath was taken away, and I had to sit down with the help of my collaborators. The toothless Arab was surprised to see me in such despair.

'Tell us, Master,' insisted Rosellini.

I made a huge effort to speak. 'Just twelve days ago, there was a great temple here . . . it has been completely demolished by the Pasha's workmen. Some of the stones were used to build factories, others to consolidate the pier of Esna, which is in danger of being swept along by the Nile.'

Neither L'Hôte nor Rosellini were able to find a comforting answer. They knew that the determined destruction of Egyptian monuments was the most unbearable pain for me. Nothing could comfort me. The cold north wind felt icy on my head.

'Let's go back to Esna,' I said, on the verge of tears.

Another calamity was awaiting us.

Full of water, the *Isis* had run aground. Fortunately it had come alongside a shallow area and, reaching the shore very soon, it had not sunk. Yet it was necessary to empty the ship in order to repair it and plug the leak. Our provisions were wet, and we had lost salt, rice and corn flour.

For the first time I saw L'Hôte prostrated. 'This is a bad omen, General . . . the far south does not augur anything good.'

'On the contrary,' I retorted. 'This is nothing compared with the danger which would have threatened us if the leak had opened while we were sailing in the large channel. We would have irretrievably sunk. May the great god Amon be thanked!'

I was surprised at my optimism, and that it was so infectious.

'Good gracious, you're right, General! We are ruled by Egyptian gods! Let's put our fate into their hands.'

Our new enthusiasm was immediately tempered by the noisy arrival of large body of men with rifles, long guns, sabres and spears. They were under the command of a forbidding-looking giant with a moustache. I ordered my companions to stay on board. I caught a glimpse of Lady Ophelia, her face almost entirely concealed by a mauve, wide-brimmed hat. She did not yield to panic.

I walked quietly towards the commander. After I had wished him and his family many blessings, I asked the reason for the deployment of so many troops against my modest expedition which, as everyone knew, benefited from the signal favours of the Pasha.

Bad luck was dogging us. I was dealing with a narrow mind insensitive to the charms of speech. His only answer was 'Follow me', in a tone which did not invite argument. I was invited to climb on the back of a camel, from which I waved reassuringly to L'Hôte.

I was taken to a vast dwelling some hundred yards further down the Nile. The commander threatened me with a huge gilded pistol and pushed me towards a potbellied potentate in front of whom he bowed.

'I am Ibrahim Bey,' declared the potentate. 'The town of Esna and its surroundings are under my jurisdiction. Are you Russian?'

'No, Your Excellency. My name is Champollion. I am French.'

'But you may be Russian. You may be lying. Yesterday in Cairo, people said that the Russians were marching on Constantinople and that our army was preparing to fight them. Our almighty master, the Pasha, is afraid spies might travel through our provinces. He expects his governors to arrest and kill them.'

I could see only hostile gazes around me.

'The Pasha gave me permission to travel in Egypt study ancient monuments,' I said quietly. 'That is my sole mission.'

Ibrahim Bey put his hands on his belly. 'I don't believe you. Who could be interested in such old stones?'

'My official documents are on the ship. Just take a look at them.'

The potentate pulled a disillusioned face. 'It's too far. I am tired. The Pasha requested me to identify Russian spies . . . I intend to obey him. You will do, whoever you are.'

The commander and several of his men surrounded me, ready to take me by force.

'I forbid you to touch me!' I declared, furious, brandishing my right hand as a derisory weapon.

The commander drew his sabre, intent on beheading me.

'Move away!' ordered Ibrahim Bey abruptly to his men. 'As for you, Champollion, come closer.'

He examined my right hand with the utmost attention. Intense surprise coloured his face. 'Where does your ring come from?'

'It was given to me by Mohammed Bey, the Governor of Beni Hassan province.'

A wide smile spread on the potentate's fleshy lips. 'He is my beloved brother,' he declared and kissed me with such emotion that he almost stifled me. 'My brother's friends are my brothers!' The intense effusions lasted a long time. The potentate of Esna swore that he would offer me his support in this world and in the next, honour my old age with sumptuous presents and keep a place for me in paradise. I took advantage of such favourable dispositions to ask him for some explanations about the Russian spies who caused him so much worry. He answered that it was a serious matter. On the previous day, people had said that violent fights had made Cairo unreachable. Fortunately, the ill-founded news had vanished like a mirage.

'As you like old stones,' said the potentate proudly, 'I shall present you with some.'

While a peaceful army of workers was completing the repairs on our ships and a procession of servants was bringing delicious dishes to the members of my expedition, I headed with curiosity for the temple of Esna, because such was the decision of the council of gods.

I was surprised to discover a rather large building almost entirely buried in the sand, in the midst of the noisy, dusty town! Moreover it was being used as a cotton warehouse, a use which would enable it to escape destruction for sometime. The temple had been washed by the alluvium of the Nile, especially on the outside. The gaps between the first rows of columns of the pro-naos had also been filled in with mud walls, so that I needed ladders and candles to see the bas-reliefs more closely. To enter the sanctuary, I had to go down and move aside the litter barring the way. Once inside, I had to be careful to avoid jostling men sleeping on mats or reciting the Koran, barefoot on carpets, in a place which had been destined for other mysteries. The sanctuary, which had been founded in ancient times, was dedicated to the ram god Khnum, whose task it was to shape all living beings on his potter's wheel. As far as I have been able to judge, the reliefs taught wise people the process of creation, the root of all craftsmanship.

Standing between two capitals, the ladder creaked in a sinister way. Someone was coming down. The bottom of a cassock appeared. Father Bidant sneaked with difficulty into the temple, which was buried almost to the top.

'It is terrifying,' he said as he caught sight of me, a candle in his hand. 'You believe that you are penetrating the devil's cave!'

'Don't worry, Father. There are only a few infidels and me.'

'What a strange place,' he said, worried.

'If you removed the temple's gangue, it would appear to have been built at a prosperous time and completed by Roman emperors. There are surprising texts about the origin of life, here.'

'Are they in line with Christian doctrine?' worried Father Bidant.

'I'm afraid not,' I confessed. 'According to what I understand, the texts mention a divinity which transmits its creative force to other creative forces acting on its behalf . . . intermediaries between God and man in a way, which ancient people called the 'genies', beliefs which Christianity strongly resisted.'

I expected a scathing answer, but the priest contented himself with walking into the buried room.

'I was wrong to address you in such a brutal way, Champollion. I blew up beyond reason, that is true. It was not very Christian. I beg your pardon. You must understand me. The heat, the unrefined food, the fatigue of the journey, the annoyance of being so far from our beautiful French countryside, the constant contact with infidels, are like almost unbearable weights which led me to a regrettable fit of anger and intolerance.'

I was deeply moved. Father Bidant's sincerity erased our former quarrels. 'I am not without blame either, Father. As soon as the ancient Egyptians are attacked, my blood seethes. Don't take me for a sworn enemy of the Christian religion, I just believe that it is not original and that it takes root in a more ancient and larger belief which will be a new light for humankind in the future.'

Father Bidant carefully touched a relief with his finger, as if the divine figures bore a magic that might endanger him. 'I obviously can not follow you on this ground, Champollion, but I admire your endeavour and I try to understand it. Admit in your turn that it is my duty to keep you on the path of true faith.'

'And mine to convert you to the religion of the pharaohs, Father!'

The priest smiled good-naturedly. 'Don't harbour any hope! But continue to work well for science.'

He left the temple. I had been mistaken about him. He was good man who, ill-prepared for such an adventure, was really disorientated by the Orient! His tolerance became the best way of restoring a deep and lasting peace between us.

It was dark when I left the sanctuary of Esna. I had lost any idea of time, surprised by the extent of the philosophy depicted on the walls. I felt astonished and annoyed, for I was still unable to understand some hieroglyphs and could not achieve the complete decipherment which was so close.

There was a joyful commotion outside. Some bohemian girls called *ghaouzis* had pitched their tents in a small square. They were surrounded by their fathers, cattle traders who did not hesitate to sell their daughters to the highest bidder. Dressed in black boleros and white skirts showing there bare bellies, with heavy mother of pearl necklaces around their necks, the *ghaouzis* began to dance and sing. Their shrill voices were accompanied by the sound of flutes, clarinets and lutes. The monotonous music produced an immediate effect; I listened without pleasure and yet let myself be charmed. Spreading through the warm night, the music pervaded every fibre of my body.

Swaying her hips rhythmically and gracefully, one of the dancers was particularly beautiful. Free under the bolero, her breasts quivered with pleasure at each movement. Her flat, bronze belly seemed to have a life of its own. Her narrow ankles covered on the ground with surprising agility.

'Are you interested in loose women?' Lady Redgrave's voice startled me. Dressed like a boy in black trousers and brown shirt, she had put up her wonderful hair in a bun concealed under a headband. In the semi-darkness, she could pass for a young man.

'What a curious occupation for a man of science,' she went on ironically. 'Unless the man lies about his real occupation and is just a spy in the pay of the French . . .'

In this atmosphere of gaity and relaxation, I had no wish to start a quarrel. 'This is not the right place for a lad to stroll, Lady Redgrave. It is very risky to venture in the crowd.'

'Why did you abandon me to my solitude, Jean-François? Have I annoyed you?'

'It is unpleasant to be called a spy . . . but you are the one who is keeping me resolutely away!'

'You are dishonest, Mr Egyptologist. Such a lack of scientific rigour does you no honour.

'You won't succeed in angering me, Lady Ophelia. This is too sweet an evening and too pleasant an entertainment, and you are too attractive. Enjoy the dances and the songs and we will talk later.'

'Later . . . always later! Stay with your courtesans. I'm going back to the ship.'

How could I persuade her to stay with me? While the beautiful *ghaouzi* flew into perilous acrobatics, Lady Redgrave disappeared.

When I returned in the early morning, I saw a frightening sight at the bow of the *Isis*: a very large cannon!

L'Hôte, who was waiting for me with a bowl of steaming tea, explained that it was a present from Ibrahim Bey to ensure our security. He said that he had not worried about my long absence as Turkish soldiers had formed a protective ring around the temple while I was working there and then followed me at a distance to the *ghaouzi* celebration. Their commander had spent the night on board and disappeared just before my arrival.

We left for el-Kab, the antique Nakheb. There we were greeted by lashing rain, and thunder and lightning. Thus we were able to say, like Herodotus during his travels in the reign of King Psammetichus: in our time, it rained in Upper Egypt!

I walked quickly through what remained of the town and along the second wall enclosing the temples and sacred buildings. I examined everything by day, and night with a lantern in my hand. There was no longer a single column standing. Several months ago, barbarians had destroyed whatever remained of the two front temples and the whole of the temple that still stood outside the town. They had been demolished to repair a quay or some other utilitarian building. I had to content myself with examining some sculptures that remained on stones left by the destroyers. A sacred world was vanishing. Here and there cartouches with the names of great pharaohs, Tuthmosis, Amenophis or Ramses, proved that masterpieces had stood here, which had disappeared some time before my arrival. I had been right to hurry to Egypt.

My sole comfort came from Lady Redgrave who had left to explore a hill near the ancient town. She called me with a joyful cry.

'There is an unusual tomb,' she announced when I joined her with L'Hôte and Rosellini. 'It is made from just columns with texts.'

I went down on my knee to examine them. I felt familiar with the signs and could guess the general meaning. The inscription had been made by a high-ranking officer, Ahmose, who had been the head of Pharaoh's sailors. Under the rule of a monarch, also called Ahmose, he had led his troops to victory and driven Libyan invaders, the Hyksos, away. This was the longest and most revealing inscription about the liberation war at the end of which the glory of Thebes, the new capital of the empire, was to shine. Several centuries later, I felt an intense affection for the hero and regretted that he was no more among us to expel the modern barbarians from Egypt.

Moktar and Suleiman interrupted my copying to tell me that Professor Raddi had disappeared. They wanted me to search the village where a peasant had seen him with a young woman.

Suleiman did not conceal his acute anxiety. If the mineralogist had decided to seduce a local woman, the matter would probably end in the worst way.

I ran to the village. The thought of a member of my expedition being in danger gave me the most heart-rending torment. Even my dear hieroglyphs did not comfort me. There were just some hundred huts, crammed against each other to fight the sun and the heat. Merry children immediately indicated the presence of a stranger in one of them. Professor Raddi was there, bending over a little girl lying on a mat. Over her face he shook a string, at the end of which he had tied a coin.

'Don't make any noise, Champollion. The girl has a fever. I hope to cure her with my method.'

Helpless and doubtful, we watched Professor Raddi's treatment. The eyes of the parents, who had heard about someone who made miracles in our expedition, glistened with hope. The dilapidated cottage was utterly miserable. The only wealth consisted of two pewter basins which the mother cleaned relentlessly.

A long hour elapsed. The coin went to and fro endlessly. The girl stammered incoherent sentences. Then she came out of her torpor, sat upright and recognized her mother, who took her in her arms.

'I think I have succeeded,' sighed Professor Raddi, wiping his forehead.

'What did you do?'

'We have healing gifts in my family. I had forgotten about them in Italy. I recovered them here . . . It is marvellous not to be confined every day in an office, and not to be shut up with research that nobody else is interested in! I'm learning not to work, Champollion!'

The parents wanted to thank the professor who gratified them with many embraces and hugs with typical Italian exuberance. I took advantage of the distraction to address the little girl.

179

'You mentioned the Prophet earlier . . . Do you know him?'

'I'm afraid of him. He gave me the evil eye.'

'Did he stay in your village?'

'No, but he came here a week ago.'

'Do you know where he went?'

'He said he was going to Edfu . . . I am so happy that he is no longer here.'

17

Full of enthusiasm, we arrived in the early morning at the huge pylon of the Edfu temple. From a distance we had been impressed by its colossal dimensions. Yet the prodigious building, the best preserved of those we had seen up to then, was largely buried in the sand. Sacred towers rose 75 feet above our heads and sank at least 40 feet into the ground.

The great temple of the God Horus, Pharaoh's direct protector, had become a kind of seedy village where *fellahin* had settled with their families, unaware of the holy place they were profaning. They lived on the roof of the temple and damaged it. To climb on the roof, we had to progress through huts to a flight of coarsely hewn stairs. I imagined the huge esplanade hidden under the mass of rubble, the large courtyard preceding the room with the columns, the spacious rooms decorated with reliefs and texts, most of which were still inaccessible to me. Everywhere swarmed human beings who lived among poultry, cows, dogs, donkeys and overabundant vermin. We walked on foul debris and we had to disturb natives sleeping on cornices or on the drums of capitals, their backs leaning on the faces of the goddess Hathor or the god Horus. People smoked, ate and drank without paying the slightest attention to the divinities.

The temple was a summary of the universe and a collection of the sciences practised by the ancient people. Astrology, botany, medicine, magic, mineralogy, alchemy and geography were taught in its place. I dreamed it would one day be restored to its full splendour.

As Nestor L'Hôte entered the rooms arranged in the pylon, he let out an exclamation. He had identified the guardroom used by some hundred soldiers of Napoleon's old guard during the Egyptian expedition. Left in oblivion here after the El-Arish Convention, they had taken refuge in nearby villages and come back to the camp, on the walls of which they had carved names, dates of deaths and windmills with pointed roofs which reminded them of some part of France. The last of these brave men had become Mamelukes and adopted the costume of those they had fought.

'This is a fabulous place,' acknowledged Father Bidant, who was visiting the temple with me.

'It could be fabulous indeed if it was cleared from the heap of garbage and sand that stifles it.'

'And protects it from destruction,' added Rosellini.

I was overwhelmed by a deep feeling of helplessness. Did temples have to be buried and forever concealed from sight to be preserved? Was it not another way of sentencing them to death and to slow, pernicious destruction? Was it possible to rid Egypt of the barbarity which had overwhelmed it?

The bothersome administration interrupted my meditation. Moktar needed me. He took me to the end of the Arab town, to a military officer who wanted to check my permits.

I thought he was making fun of me. He led me in front of a niche closed by a curtain, between two brick walls which were about to crumble. Seeing other similar niches closed in the same way, I wondered what mystery I was facing when the curtain opened. A man with a turban sat on a stone, holding a sheaf of dirty papers. He had just unveiled his office. 'Your permits,' he said aggressively.

Instead of answering straightforwardly, which would have been a serious offence, I launched into profuse, sweet compliments about the importance and competence of the high-ranking civil servant who was doing me the great honour of talking to me. However carefully chosen, the rhetorical flourishes did not seduce the man. He stood up to lift the curtain of another niche full of papers. With a dexterity achieved in the course of a long career, he extricated a yellowed document and brandished it in front of my face. I read with astonishment the text of a local law dating back to 1650, according to which foreigners were forbidden to venture on the territory of Edfu. Offenders risked being sentenced to long periods of imprisonment. It would have been useless and dangerous to draw the man's attention to the fact that such dispositions were null and void.

The civil servant was triumphant. He did not conceal his hatred of foreigners. There was only one solution: I had to prove to him that I was no foreigner. Changing my attitude, I stressed each syllable of my Arabic and threatened him with the worst retaliation down here and in the world beyond if he dared question my quality and titles. I flared up in a vague attempt at anger.

Frightened by my unexpected reaction, which indicated that I was capable of doing the worst, the civil servant clumsily gathered his papers and folded them hastily. I was seized by a strange inspiration.

'Who ordered you to bother me like this?'

He set his lips.

'Is it the Prophet? Are you at his service?'

His silence was enough of an answer. Furious, I pulled the curtain back over the puppet.

Two men had watched the scene from a hut on a mound overlooking the town.

'Champollion has not been stopped,' whispered Abdel-Razuk.

'We did not expect anything better from the stupid police-man,' said Drovetti. 'At least he spread what little venom he had and sowed a few new worries in Champollion's mind. But he is a sensitive man, and we will succeed in frightening and disgusting him.'

Our departure was delayed by Nestor L'Hôte. The unfortunate man had entered one of the dilapidated houses on the roof of the temple to draw a capital he had cleared from a heap of garbage. It left him with pimples, red blotches and unbearable itching, and had to spend a lot of time bathing in the Nile.

Our ships reached one of the most stunning places in the Nile Valley, Gebel el-Silsila, where two deserts meet, leaving only a narrow pass for the river between two yellow sandstone hills. Gebel el-Silsila means 'mountain chain'. According to tradition, the course of the Nile was closed by a chain between two mountains. The two banks were exploited by ancient Egyptians, and travellers walking through the quarries are amazed to see how many stones were removed to build the open-air galleries. Here they live with the memory of workmen who sweated blood to bring the first stages of future masterpieces to life. The huge faults and mass of debris which are still to be seen make it possible to estimate that work went on for thousands of years and provided the material used in most Egyptian monuments. We felt as if we were entering the very side of the mountain where, block after block, Luxor, Deir el Bahari and Karnak had been born.

Professor Raddi fell into ecstasy. He had never been able to take advantage of such an amount of high quality sandstone. The voice of the Nile, swift and thunderous in this place, recalled that of the masterbuilders, foremen, stone cutters, quarries and toilers for whom the huge workplace had been their sole horizon for many years.

'Prodigious,' he exclaimed as he kneeled in front of a block. 'This is the most beautiful workplace I ever saw. Engineers from ancient times still dwell here. I can hear them! The stones had no secrets for them. Their hands knew their inner nature and their slightest vein. They could distinguish the good ones from the bad just by touching them. They live here for ever. They cannot disappear . . .'

L'Hôte and Rosellini contained their astonishment, but their looks clearly indicated that they took the mineralogist for a bit of a lunatic.

'The sun is too hot,' said Rosellini. 'It is softening our brains. We should go back to Thebes.'

Professor Raddi reacted with amazing violence. He slapped his fellow countryman so hard that he fell to the ground. 'I forbid you to say such stupidities! You are unworthy of this place . . . keep silent or go away!'

L'Hôte wanted to pounce on the mineralogist, but Lady Redgrave prevented him from doing so. 'Don't make the incident worse . . . keep your head, Monsieur L'Hôte.'

Astounded and shocked, Rosellini turned imploring eyes to me. L'Hôte was waiting for my orders. I was unable to give any. The dissension sent me into complete disarray. Our small community was breaking up. Hatred had replaced friendship. Indifferent to the tragedy he had caused, Professor Raddi walked away slowly and took out his magnifying glass to examine each outstanding specimen more closely.

'General,' said L'Hôte. 'Let me thrash the ill-mannered lout.'

I shook my head. Furious, the draughtsman seized a small block of sandstone, threw it away and sat at a distance.

Moktar helped Rosellini up. My Italian disciple, who was no fighting man, needed time to regain his breath.

'Why . . . why did Professor Raddi hit me?'

'Behave like a man,' said Lady Redgrave. 'You hurt his feelings and he reacted. If you react at the first aggravation, the future of Egyptology does not look too promising.'

Ippolito Rosellini was startled. 'Master . . . the woman is a demon. She spies on us. She is our worst enemy's apostle! Why do you trust her? Why don't you chase her away? She will soon stab us in the back!'

Moktar smiled, pleased by our dissensions.

'Leave me alone,' I said.

Masks had fallen. Gebel el-Sisila's quarries had revealed my companions' true natures. Professor Raddi was a selfish man, shut up in his visions, Nestor L'Hôte vindictive and intolerant. Rosellini was a coward without any real character and Lady Redgrave an imperious and ruthless woman. Fortunately, Father Bidant had not witnessed the rifts which had just broken our friendly relationships. I was tempted to join him on board the *Hathor* and confess to him. But the sight of Suleiman sitting at the prow of the ship dissuaded me from doing so. What sins did I have to relieve my soul of? Had I not dedicated myself to Egypt and to the spirituality pervading each one of its stones?

Work in the magical quarries restored peace. Weary of so many sculptures from the time of the Ptolemies and the Romans, my eyes delighted again in the sight of pharaonic reliefs of more glorious periods. There were innumerable traces of Eighteenth Dynasty kings and their masterbuilders. My dear Ramses, his father, the fierce Seti, and his son Merenptah, had ordered shrines of eternity to be dug in the rock. There were praises of the god Nile, identified with the celestial river bringing primeval water throughout the universe. It was natural to worship him here, as this was the place where the river seemed to come to life again after it had broken the sandstone mountains which barred its course. When the texts are fully understood, people will realize that the Egyptians had very advanced ideas about the energy flow which perpetrates life, whether of the stars or human beings. They imagined that our earth was surrounded by an ocean of vibrations where creative forces took shape, and they considered each being as a network of constantly renewed interacting waves. Beyond the ordeal, the quarries conferred a new impulse to our journey. They embodied the youth of the world and the wish to build another life. Gebel el-Silsila taught us that human society needed temples.

I had drawn comfort from solitude and dialogue with the

stones. I could now see my duty clearly: I had to restore unity to our community.

We spent two days examining the double temple of Kom Ombo block by block, one half of which is dedicated to the hawk god Horus and the other to the crocodile god Sobek. This was how the principles of air and water combined in a subtle alchemy. The place was superb. The sanctuary formed a kind of panoramic viewpoint overlooking the Nile. The sunset embellished it with a golden light which hid the poor quality of later sculptures and restored the building to its former splendour. Father Bidant remained shut up in his cabin, where he dedicated himself to prayer. Sulky, Nestor L'Hôte drew carefully and somewhat reluctantly the reliefs I pointed out to him. Feverish, Rosellini stayed in his room. Lady Redgrave read Milton's *Paradise Lost* on the terrace of the temple overlooking the Nile. Suleiman continued to watch over Moktar, for he was afraid the latter might get in touch with our shadowy enemies.

Which of my travelling companions could betray me to the Pasha and the Consul-General? Who had the duplicity to feign friendship and yet try to stifle discoveries which I was convinced would deeply change man's history and thinking?

My belief strengthened every day. Egypt was more than Egypt. It had brought forth sciences, formulated the deepest philosophies and built the most elaborate temples. Here beat the heart of the world. Here would originate the spiritual revolution to sweep away the ancient beliefs and enable men to be united with the gods again. This was the reason why, whatever the cost might be, I had to succeed in deciphering the sacred language and its explanation of how to use celestial energy. The Egyptians had no other ambition than wisdom, which did not result from belief, but from knowledge of the universe.

Fashioned by centuries of light, the mere presence of the stones elevated souls. The journey I had been longing for so long was turning into a pilgrimage to the core of my being. How could any sentient being feel a stranger in this land where every temple dealt with the essential? On the height overlooking the Nile, I could put my life into perspective for the first time. It appeared in all its misery and triviality. I was just an ant trying to nibble some food from a huge banqueting room where giants served delicious dishes. But I was a laborious and obstinate ant, with an insatiable appetite and strength far greater than its size. Providence had offered me the most beautiful present man might ever dream of: I was able to discover heaven on earth and to enter it in my lifetime. It would have been mean to enjoy its selfishly. I had to pass on the truths I had glimpsed when I had lifted the veil of Isis, and I had to work relentlessly, taking no heed of my tiredness.

The sun began to set, flooding the silver reflections of the river with liquid gold. I enjoyed the moment that was offered to me. The Egyptians called it 'fullness'. Everything was becoming quiet. Fragrances pervaded the north breeze, which wrinkled the surface of the water. People instinctively became silent. The landscape filled the gaze, dissolved thoughts into an ocean of green and orange and erased impurities.

A figure appeared through the columns. Moktar stood still at a respectful distance. 'The man you are looking for is here,' he announced mysteriously.

'Who told you?'

'News travels fast in Orient. Nobody knows who transmits it. The Prophet is hiding in the village, at a merchant's.'

'Why should I believe you?'

'How can I convince you? I am just a humble intermediary. If you want me to guide you, there are two donkeys waiting for us.'

Was Moktar drawing me into a trap? How could he, my enemies' servant, give me his help without duplicity? But from whom else could I get advice without revealing the Prophet's presence? I had to take the risk.

'I'll follow you, Moktar.'

*

The night market of the village of Kom Ombo was in full swing. The crowd swarmed among the open-air shops. With unshakeable patience, our donkeys ploughed their way through crates of grain, jostled water carriers, avoided camels, trampled heaps of pistachios on pieces of fabric. The wives of *fellahin* looked at us with curiosity, their faces unveiled. They bought food and haggled for clothing. A large number of them gathered around a seer. One howled an offer to swap a chicken for onions. Indifferent to a quarrel which had just broken out between two young men, a butcher was slaughtering a sheep. Children who had stolen some broad beans tore them to pieces with their teeth. Numerous oil lamps lit the stalls.

The donkeys stopped in front of a ruined house. Palm leaves barred the door.

'You are expected inside,' said Moktar.

I hesitated. No member of my expedition knew where I was going.

Moktar looked at me icily. It was impossible to discern the slightest emotion on his face. If I quailed in front of this obstacle, I would lose face and nobody would ever speak to me again in this country. Everybody would know that the 'general', the Egyptian, the French government emissary, was a coward.

Turning round to greet the last glows of the sunset, I did not procrastinate any longer. Stepping over a clay ledge, I entered the house.

It was completely dark inside. A heady smell of garlic attacked my nostrils.

Motionless, I held my breath. I perceived a slight breathing.

'Are you the Prophet?' I asked, tensely.

I did not get any answer. Fear gnawed at my stomach. A weak light illuminated the little room, at the end of which stood a veiled Arab woman, dressed in a delicate red shirt and blue silk baggy breeches. She was a rich aristocrat.

'Who are you? Why did you ask me to come here?'

'Who are you?' asked a voice in Arabic, disguised by the veil.

'I'm Champollion, appointed by France to discover and preserve the treasures of ancient Egypt.'

'Keep your pompous declarations for the Pasha,' she retorted. 'Who are you really?'

A thought crossed my mind. 'Take the veil off or I shall do it myself.'

I took a step forward.

'Would you dare?'

My attitude showed that I would.

Very slowly she removed the thin fabric concealing her face.

'Lady Ophelia! Why such a performance?'

'This is no performance, Jean-François. I had to talk to you, away from the enemy and from Suleiman.'

'Do you consider all the members of our expedition as enemies?'

'I am at the service of my country as you are at the service of yours. I have a mission to fulfil, too. If you like me, reveal your true aims.'

'You resorted to this masquerade . . .'

'I am glad to prove you that I can adapt to Egypt as well as you do. I know its language and customs.'

'But mainly you know Moktar . . . and probably his master, Drovetti.'

'Why should I hide it from you? The Consul-General is indeed a friend of mine. And the Pasha received me and listened to my advice. Are they therefore criminals? Am I the most despicable of women to give them their real value? You are prejudiced, Champollion. The masters of Egypt are not as devilish as you think.'

'Are you trying to tell me that they do not allow Egyptians monuments be demolished?'

She shrugged her shoulders, exasperated. 'Don't play the offended archaeologist all the time, Champollion! You work for the greater glory of France and I for that of Great Britain. We have the same profession, even though we belong to opposite sides. Duty does not make admiration nor . . . affection impossible.'

'Lady Ophelia, I am not a spy,' I said firmly. 'It is true that France entrusted me with a scientific task, but the journey went beyond all my hopes. The greatest mysteries were awaiting me here.'

Lady Redgrave smiled. 'You are a man of genius, Jean-François! You scientific cover is perfect. I almost don't doubt your passion for hieroglyphs any more. You also have an exceptional gift as an actor.'

'How can I make you except your mistake? How can I persuade you that I am an Egyptologist and nothing else?'

She put her veil on again. 'I also know how to keep my mysteries,' she said with a voice as soft as a caress. 'My dearest wish would be to reveal them to you . . . if you were sincere.'

The sublime princess of the Orient undulated towards me. Without realizing it, I took her in my arms. Her mouth came close to mine. Her skin was fragrant with jasmine.

'No,' I said as I pushed her back. 'You don't love me. You love a ghost you made up. You should first trust my word, and trust it entirely! Otherwise we will both remain silent.'

She broke my heart with her accusing, disappointed eyes.

18

We sailed to Aswan under a bright sun and in full midday heat.
The landscape changed and became softer. Palm trees,
sycamores, acacias, tamarisks and green thickets embellished
the banks. Here and there we could see the white spots of small
mosques crowned with domes or minarets. The villages
looked richer and more pleasant. The surroundings of Aswan
marked our entry into a new world. Granite gave way to
sandstone. The population mingled *fellahin*, Turks, Bicharis,
Nubians, Abyssinians and Sudanese. The market stalls
displayed elephant teeth, dates, gums, feline skins, spices and
other exotic products. Look back across the landscape, we
could see the Nile behind a row of trees, bare rocks and barren
hills which made us believe that Egypt ended there and that the
source of the Nile was very close by.

My companions were delighted by the large oasis after the
barren route of the Nile Valley. I could not rest, however, until
I was able to go to Elephantine Island to study two famous
temples dating back to the glorious period. I was faced with
more disappointment as the temples had been demolished a
few years before. Only the location remained. I had to content
myself with a ruined door dedicated to Alexander, the son of
the conqueror, some hieroglyph worship texts engraved on an
old wall and some scattered pharaonic remains used as
materials in Roman constructions. I heard something from one
of the wardens of the island which aroused my fury: the stones

of ancient sanctuaries had actually been used for the Pasha's latest palace and new barracks. Nestor L'Hôte saw my disappointment and carried on drawing in silence.

It was Rosellini who tore me away from the sadness weighing down on me. 'Come, Master,' he beseeched me. 'I think I have discovered the fountain without a shadow.'

My disciple's excitement was understandable. In this place, which was believed to be mythical, the same rays fell vertically on the day of the summer solstice. Thanks to their clever calculations, the Egyptians had been able to measure the circumference of the earth accurately here.

The fountain without a shadow looked like a wall, a kind of Nilometer opening on to the river at the bottom of a flight of stairs covered with moss. Rosellini slipped and fell heavily on his side. I helped him up but he refused to go on, for fear of another fall. I, however, recovered the strength and daring of youth as soon as I was in touch with old stones. With acute pleasure, I climbed down the old monument that had been visited by so many priests before me.

I spent a long time in the semi-darkness inside the well, which was supposed to catch light. The coolness dispelled my tiredness. I had been feeling more lonely since my break with Lady Redgrave, but my solitude was brightened by the discoveries now illuminating my days in Egypt. I had the sensation that I was walking through the rooms of a huge temple on the scale of the whole country, as I progressed towards the south. From the beginning of my journey I had understood that it was essential to see the whole of Egypt. As I reached the southern gate in Aswan, I had filled myself with landscapes and sanctuaries. My yearning for Egypt was validated second by second.

As I turned round to climb the stairs up, I saw it. The viper was gazing at me fixedly. It stood on its tail, ready to strike at me. I could neither step backward nor forward. I had to remain as motionless as the reptile. Death faced me, but strangely, did not arouse any fear in me. In the course of my research I had encountered numerous snake goddesses: the cobra that protected Egypt, the snake that rose up on the King's forehead to keep evil forces away, and the one who looked after crops and harvest. There were also the reptiles which formed essential letters in the hieroglyphic alphabet. If I was really Egyptian, what could I fear from a loving hieroglyph?

I therefore climbed one stair without looking at the viper again. It rose higher. My left leg passed less than a yard from it. Eventually I saw again the light of the sun, which had never seemed so soft to me.

The most famous sight in Aswan was the market. It was the most lively and colourful in the country. By the entrance *fellahin* slept, wrapped in their robes under the shade of sun umbrellas, watching over heaps of wheat, millet and rice. Naked children surrounded by flies ran everywhere. Magicians read the future in geomantic figures in the dust, assailed by a large crowd. I found one of them, a tall blind Sudanese, smiling with pleasure at the idea of taking advantage of so much gullibility.

'Why did you bring me here?' I asked Suleiman.

'One of our brothers has told me some alarming news. All the members of the brotherhood have left Egypt. Drovetti has denounced the Brothers of Luxor to the Pasha as dangerous conspirators. The Pasha has decided to suppress them discreetly with his usual methods. Serious suspicions hang over you. You are still protected by your mission's official character, but how long will that last? It would be better to go back to Cairo as soon as possible, complain about health problems and ask to be repatriated. It might dangerously unwise to carry on with the journey.'

We passed a street blocked by a caravan of tired, dusty camels. They panted under the weight of heavy loads of ostrich eggs, ivory, gold and silver armbands, wooden plates, animal skins, leather and drums. At the head of the procession an old man with legs so long they almost touched the ground was riding a donkey. Heady smells mingling spices and herbs rose up from the open-air kitchens.

'Do the Pasha's police know you, Suleiman?'

'I don't know,'

'Is it true that you don't know, brother, or are you refusing to tell me?'

He remained silent.

'You are running far greater risks than I do, Suleiman. Leave the expedition and go into hiding.'

'I swore to protect you. I won't go back on my word.'

Light filtered through flakes piercing the canvas stretched over the lane. The ground was wet. Men knelt and smoked hookahs, while others ate corn or dates. A little Nubian girl who wore only a necklace and rings around her ankles tugged at my sleeve, then burst out a laughing as she fled away.

'As for me, Suleiman, I won't go back on my decision. I have been longing for this journey all my life. It is my goal, the crowning glory of my life. Whatever the dangers might be, I shall see it through. People will have to destroy me to prevent me from completing it. If am to die, I will be happy if it is here in this land.'

'Brother, you are forgetting that you must pass on what you have seen and understood. You cannot live just for yourself.'

'I haven't forgotten anything. I don't know Nubia yet. I have only had a glimpse of Thebes. I haven't set hands on the Prophet . . . As long as my work is not finished and my decipherment not completed, I won't be able to pass on anything of value.'

'Let's go into this shop,' said Suleiman, suddenly anxious. 'We are being followed.'

The salesman, a fat, squat, bald man, bowed low before us. Then with great lyricism he praised the extraordinary quality of his products, known throughout the world: arrows, bows, daggers, clubs, whips, hookahs, turbans . . . The house was a bazaar in itself. We haggled for a blanket we had found at the back of the ship and left an hour later.

Suleiman looked at the crowd. 'Let's have a coffee,' he said as he knocked at a wooden shutter painted in blue.

The shutter opened vertically, uncovering a niche, inside which sat an old wrinkled man, watching over a steaming coffee pot. He poured us two cups.

'We are safe,' judged Suleiman. 'At least for a time . . . I understand your determination, but is it sensible?'

'Is this trip sensible? Is it sensible to want to bring Egypt out of darkness and the silence of oblivion? I am not convinced by your argument, Suleiman. Caution is out of place. We must act quickly.'

'It is very difficult to make you change your mind, even in face of impossible odds.

'Does Drovetti have agents in Nubia?'

'I don't think so. The Pasha's police are almost absent from the region. We only have to fear pillagers – and traitors.'

'Did you know who the agent is that Drovetti placed among us?'

Suleiman sipped his coffee. 'It would be wrong to accuse anyone without evidence. Words can't be erased once they have been uttered. No I haven't identified him or her.'

It would have been wrong to press him. I savoured the excellent coffee and waited for him to say more.

'You disciple, Ippolito Rosellini, is a strange man. He has a treacherous look. He is too deferential to you. This is not the way a student behaves.

'Have you anything specific on him?'

'He is too sly to make major mistakes. Yet he is the one who took you to the necropolis where you discovered the corpse of the Coptic monk, Anastasy's excavator. He is also the one who told you about the Nilometer, where a viper awaited you. What if he had arranged the first crime and prepared the second one?'

Dark thoughts about Rosellini had crossed my mind, but frightened, I had dismissed them.

'Rosellini is no traitor.'

'Still, you should avoid the most dangerous place in the region,' recommended Suleiman.

'That is to say?'

'The quarries.'

'The granite quarries? Such a fabulous place? Suleiman, you are my brother . . . You can't deny me that pleasure!'

Suleiman shook his head, dispirited. 'This is precisely what I feared. At least watch Rosellini's behaviour . . . If he is the one who asks you to visit the quarries, then beware of a trap.'

A gloomy atmosphere prevailed at dinner. Indisposed, Lady Redgrave ate her meal in her cabin. Father Bidant had begun to fast. Professor Raddi, who had started to study the minerals he had been gathering from the onset of our trip, had withdrawn in his domain after he had swallowed an egg and drunk a glass of wine. Moktar and Suleiman were eating a dinner of flat bread and broad beans in the servant's quarter. L'Hôte looked rather grumpy. Rosellini was eating roast chicken with a hearty appetite.

'Why do you have such a gloomy face, L'Hôte?' I asked.

'I am homesick, General. There is too much heat, too much desert, too much dust . . . I'm dreaming of green countryside, rain and clouds. I remember misty early mornings, grass damp with dew, fire in the fireplace and cold nights when you curl up in sheets warmed by a bedwarmer.'

I also remembered the icy dormitories of college, the drizzle, the mud in the towns, the low clouds masking the sun for entire days, weeks, months . . . I recalled the frozen fingers, the colds, the bronchitis, the painful limbs, the despair of leaden skies . . . but I did not regret them!

'General, you must tell me where we are going. I'm still ready to follow you, but I would like to know where you are taking me. Are we going back to Thebes or continuing our progression to the south?'

'I am not hiding the truth from you, Nestor. When I asked you to come with me, I told you about my aim: Thebes and the far south, as far as the Nile flows. We are on the threshold of Nubia and we go on.'

Rosellini intervened. 'Let's not leave Aswan without seeing the temple of Philae. The ancient people said it was a marvel.'

'So I can look forward to some beautiful drawings,' said L'Hôte, tempted.

'There is another site we should not neglect. It has great scientific importance.'

'Which one?'

'The granite quarries, Master.'

Between Aswan and Philae, the quarries stretch over more than 4 miles. Agile, energetic donkeys, led us on paths only they knew, taking us through ruined Muslim mausoleums to an ocean of granite rocks littered with naos stones, steles, columns and rough-hew statues. The works had been abandoned because of flaws in the stone. A colossus of Amenophis III, carved in the rock and then rough-hewn to be transported to the House of Gold, where sculptors, 'those who give life', would open its mouth and eyes, had been left on a path to the plain. The statue's seat was the size of two men. The most extraordinary work was a well-hewn obelisk of at least 32 yards still lying on the rock, from which it had not been completely detached. A crack had made the monolith unfit for erection. As I examined it closely, I realized that, to clear such a colossal block, the quarries had made notches at 6-inch intervals to delineate the stone surface for extraction. In the grooves, which were sometimes as long as 8 inches, they inserted wooden wedges which they wetted. The wedges swelled and this simple device was enough to make the granite crack and give the stone-cutters a block ready for polishing. Here and there lay the remains of the tools used for rough-hewing and polishing.

We had dispersed, each admiring an area of the mineral landscape, where we could still feel the presence of those master stone cutters who knew the slightest vein so well that they could give it precisely the right place in the building to come. Dazzled by the new paradise, Professor Raddi had hired L'Hôte and Moktar to gather and transport outstanding samples of granite, which he selected with meticulous care. His revived passion reassured me. Back to his first love, the good professor could now overcome the world-weariness by which he had been overwhelmed.

Father Bidant was in conversation with Lady Redgrave. They sat in the sun on a huge block of pink granite. Suleiman was not to be seen. As I walked a few yards towards a stele whose hieroglyphs inscriptions I wanted to record, I noticed that only Rosellini had stayed with me. With his usual care for details, he was taking numerous notes.

'Look at that,' I said, as I knelt down. 'There are traces of an inclined plane . . . blocks were slid on it with the help of rolls and sleighs. They were carried to a pier when the water was low. Carpenters built very big rafts under the blocks. When high water came, it lifted them and transported them throughout Egypt. Part of the colossi probably remained immersed so that they lost at least a third of their weight. What a fabulous workplace, Ippolito . . . Not only did the Egyptians know how to extract, polish and hew, but they also had a genius for organizing and sharing the work and creating sacred pieces on the scale of the whole country.'

My disciple did not seem to appreciate what I was saying. 'How can you imagine all that, Master?'

'I don't imagine, Ippolito, I see. I can see the scenes as if I were experiencing them as we talk. We will find documents to confirm what I say.'

Rosellini held a black stone which had been used as a hammer in his left hand. 'What if you were wrong? What if ancient Egyptians were only barbarians like the present ones?'

I looked at my disciple with amazement. My sight became blurred. I had the impression that he was raising his arm as if he wanted to hit me. 'I don't think I heard you properly, Ippolito . . . After what we have seen and experienced, how . . .'

The arm made an aggressive gesture. I did not move. I

199

preferred to die rather than to accept the betrayal of a man in whom I had placed my trust.

Suddenly Rosellini's expression changed. Fear overwhelmed him, as if he had seen a presence behind me. His hand opened and the sharp stone fell to the ground.

'Forgive me, Master . . . a moment of distraction. It's probably the heat . . . Let me record the text of this stele. Don't overdo it. We need you so much.'

I was unable to speak. Had I dreamed it? Had my disciple plotted to murder me? It must have just a horrible nightmare, for he had given up any murderous intent. I had to suppose the threat had never existed. The light air and the bright sun of the quarries cleared away the dark moment.

I was startled, however, when, on the mound overlooking the place where I stood with Rosellini, I glimpsed Moktar, his face as grim as that of a judge.

Moktar looked upset.

'This is utterly impossible,' he said for the second time. 'The *Isis* and the *Hathor* cannot get over the second cataract.'

Impressed to be in my cabin which overflowed with papers and statues bought by Rosellini, Moktar assumed a disappointed air as he conveyed the Egyptian administration orders.

'What do you suggest?' I asked in a conciliatory tone.

'What Allah does not want cannot be achieved by man.'

'Very well. Beyond the cataract, can we find other ships to take us to Nubia?'

'Maybe, but we would have to unload the *Hathor* and the *Isis* and transport the expedition's material on camels to the pier opposite Philae.'

I smiled radiantly. 'Well, then let's unload!'

The sacred island of Philae, the dwelling of the great magician, had a bad surprise in store for me. Painful rheumatism in my left foot prevented me from walking. Common sense would have advised rest, but how could I remain still when the temple of Isis was so close?

With Suleiman's help, I mounted a donkey to visit the pink granite quarries, with their hieroglyphic inscriptions. Once I had crossed the Nile in a rowing boat, four men helped me, while six others encouraged them. They took me on their shoulders to a small sanctuary, where a room had been arranged for me in some old Roman buildings like prisons, but absolutely sound and sheltered from the winds.

The soil of the island was extremely barren. Granite rocks protected the coasts, but it contained the best field of ruins I had ever seen in such a limited area. Some palm trees, weeds and orange and yellow flowers gave an illusion of coolness.

Father Bidant bowed to me. 'Is it very painful?'

'Painful enough to keep me glued to the spot when I should be walking around the temple.'

'Will you accept my arm?'

'With pleasure, Father. A few steps may help.'

We walked with difficulty to the central alley in the outside pylon, where Nestor L'Hôte was contemplating an inscription and weeping. Intrigued, I thought he had suddenly achieved full and complete understanding of hieroglyphs! Coming closer, however, I was disappointed.

'Come and read that, General! What a marvellous memory!'

'In the Vth Year of the French Republic, on 13 Messidor [the tenth month of the revolutionary calendar]' read the inscription, 'a French army led by Bonaparte came to Alexandria. Twenty days later, by the pyramids, the army routed the Mamelukes. Desaix, the commander of the first division, followed them beyond the cataracts which he reached on 13 Ventôse [the sixth month of the revolutionary calendar] of the VIIth year.'

I abandoned the draughtsman to his patriotic enthusiasm. The realm of Isis was devoted to worship, and access to the mysteries was only for initiates whom the great goddess saw as pure enough. They lived here until the fifth century AD and were finally driven away by persecution. I understood that the last monument erected by the Egyptians did not contain any new form of divinity. The religious system of the people was so much a whole, and its various parts so much interrelated and forever fixed in such absolute ways that neither Greek nor Roman domination produced any change: the Caesars and the Ptolemies built again in Nubia and Egypt only what the Persians had destroyed during their invasions. But they did rebuild temples where they had existed in the past, dedicated to the same gods. My explanation of the formidable vision of the sacred did not convince Father Bidant, however, attentive though he was to my words.

'My belief is enough for me, Champollion. You should not excite your mind with these old dreams. You should rather keep an eye on those around you.'

My foot became more painful. 'What are you implying, Father Bidant?'

'Nestor L'Hôte is a rather strange character. Was his drowning a pretence? I have been suspicious of him ever since the beginning of our trip. Two or three times, I thought I glimpsed him the company of rather shady Arabs, probably henchmen of Drovetti's or of the Pasha's. I am afraid he might betray us.'

Impressed by the priest's words, I tried to remember the times when L'Hôte's behaviour could have been suspect, but the pain in my foot prevented me from thinking.

'You are too naive, Champollion. Do you really believe a man like Nestor L'Hôte launched himself into such a perilous adventure just for the pleasure of drawing? Think of greed . . . this is really what drives the world. L'Hôte is no better than other people. If he was offered money to spy on us, the plot was forged in France. The initiator can only be Drovetti.'

'Take me to the south-west of the island to the door of the room with columns.'

'Why that place?'

'Because of a memory, Father, just a memory.'

Father Bidant realized that I would say no more. I had no

wish to tell him I wanted to examine a small sandstone obelisk of which I had a lithograph. It had enabled me to identify a cartouche and to decipher the name of Cleopatra, written in the way I had expected it to be. The precious inscription had been an essential stage in my understanding hieroglyphs. It was necessary to check the original and get a key, with the help of which I might be able to forget about the damn Prophet, who was constantly evading me.

There was no obelisk, but I saw Lady Ophelia Redgrave, draped in a large white cotton cloth which left her shoulders bare. Used to the sun, she wore no hat, for her thick Titian red hair was enough to protect her.

'Your obelisk is now in the British Museum, Monsieur Champollion. My uncle needed it for his work. It reached him in good condition.'

Her tone was sharp; she was delivering a blow she hoped would be fatal. But her gaze expressed something different.

Father Bidant close to avoid another quarrel and took me further away. 'Let's give up the far south and return to Cairo as soon as possible,' he recommended. 'This is a terrifying country. It will kill us.'

'Let's put ourselves into God's hands, Father . . . It is true that I hesitated to prolong the adventure.'

'Are you becoming reasonable at last?'

'Lady Redgrave pointed out the only wise decision. The absence of the obelisk compels me to search for another remnant, which I knew about before and which I must check on the spot.'

'Is it another obelisk?'

'A whole temple.'

'In Thebes?'

'No, Father, in the far south. Just where we are going.'

I did not go back to my bed immediately. I felt strong enough to stroll in the gallery of the great temple leading to the staircase in front of which boats moored. Despite the blazing sun, the place was cool and restful. Each of the capitals of the colonnade was different and pleased the eye with the delicacy of its contours. The smile of the goddess was actually engraved in the stone.

The fever was so high that I became delirious. Lady Ophelia's face merged with that of the goddess Isis receiving the dead Osiris' semen to give birth to a son, Horus, who restored the justice and other that had been disturbed by the murderer of his father, his brother Seth. Philae's reliefs swirled around me and unveiled the true nature of Isis, that is to say Nature, creating according to the plan preconceived by gods. The great goddess became Hathor, the temple of Horus, the smile of heaven, the everlasting joy of the dance of stars, the mother and source of light, Isis and Hathor, who were both the same and yet different, the smile of the world beyond, which makes crops ripe and fields green. It was the same woman, the one who never changes, celestial love.

'Master! Master! I succeeded!' Rosellini's exclamations tore me away from my dream. I sat up in my bed. 'Master, a naos stone, a complete naos stone! I found it in the underground chambers of the temple. I bought it for a modest amount . . . It is the only intact one in all Egypt!'

Rosellini launched into a detailed description of the monolithic block, the holy of holies of the temple which contained the statue of the God only Pharaoh was allowed to contemplate.

'I also have a letter from France for you!'

'Give it to me, quickly!'

It was a long letter over four pages, from my brother Jacques-Joseph. He mentioned earlier letters which had presumably been lost. He described the Parisian cold, the rains and the fog, wished me a thousand moments of happiness and even more finds to establish the new science of Egyptology and help resurrect the spirituality of the Pharaohs. He asked about my health, which he imagined to be much better than in France, and assumed me that he was impatient to read the innumerable notes I would certainly write. He kept to the end the bad news, which pained him very much: my application for the Academy had been once more refused. My reputation in official scientific circles was diminishing. Smear campaigns were in full swing. He begged me not to be affected by them and to remain hopeful for the future.

'I'm hungry,' I said to my disciple. 'Get a big meal ready for me to celebrate my recovery.'

We all gathered for a party at the site of the cataract. We sat in the shade of a santh, a rather thorny mimosa, which was the only tree around, in front of the Nile's rapids whose rustling reminded me of our alpine torrents. The majesty of the place, the absolute serenity of stones unaffected by human passions, silenced us. We prepared to cross a border, aware of the seriousness of the moment.

I asked to be dropped at the blood red granite island of Biga. The engraved memorial of Osiris coming back to life was there. Not far away the Nile was forcing its way through a mass of shoals, opening stone channels into which the water jumped on and on again in a joyful ceremony. The powerful and authoritative voice of the cataract filled our ears. Stark naked Nubians swam between the rocks, pushing bundles of reeds before them like floats. One of them headed towards us, taking little heed of the presence of a lady, and invited us to tea in his village, consisting of a few huts built around the ruins of a temple.

I felt like staying there to wait for the resurrection of Osiris. Man seemed out of place in such a desolate realm.

Nestor L'Hôte interrupted my meditation. 'What have you actually decided, General? There are rumours about your health . . . dangers . . . I need to know.'

'Let's carry on. We won't be disappointed by the far south.'

'Here is our new squadron,' announced Moktar.

The flotilla beyond the cataract was composed of a main vessel, a *dahabieh* displaying a French flag under a Tuscan flag, two boats with French flags, two Tuscan boats, a boat for provisions with a blue flag and another with our armed forces, that is to say Moktar and a few henchmen. The main ship was armed with the cannon our friend Ibrahim Bey had presented to us. The *dahabieh* was rather large, and its living space had been arranged almost luxuriously. Each of us had a bedroom and a bathroom. The common areas comprised a dining room and a living room with two divans and a piano.

Moktar explained emphatically that the *dahabieh* had been flooded for four days so as to rid it of rats and vermin. The Pasha's policemen had even mounted guard to prevent them from coming back.

'I want to see the front of the ship,' I requested.

'That is not the custom.'

'I don't care. I must know the whole ship to which the lives of members of my expedition have been entrusted.'

'Usually, travellers don't go.'

'I am no ordinary traveller. Get out of my way.'

Moktar yielded. A sailor glided into the water, a small board in his hand which he nailed under the keel near the helm. It would act as a brake.

The front part of the ship was taken up by a kitchen, behind which a squat mast with a lateen sail was tied to a huge yard. Near the kitchen was a cabin with a minute window, from which monotonous music arose. I entered it. A dozen sailors were crammed in there playing drums and flute. Others, wrapped in their burnouses lay on their sides, like bundles of old clothes. Their only wealth consisted of a wicker armchair for their chief. The men lived in dirt and in most unbearable poverty.

'I insist that decent lodgings be given to the sailors,' I said to Moktar, who did not leave my side.

'That is impossible . . . If you change their habits, they will refuse to work. The cabin is theirs. They built it with their own hands. They each have a place here. If you insult them by driving them away, they will rebel.'

I had to give in. It was stupid to want to make people happy against their own will. I had just received a lesson in humility which I would not forget.

Coming back to the deck, I discovered an extraordinary sight. Another boat had been added to our expedition. It was for Professor Raddi, who had gathered innumerable samples of stone ever since the beginning of our journey. It was too heavily loaded and risked sinking at any moment. In addition, the professor was admonishing a dozen young Nubians, trying to make them transport a palm tree some 80 feet in height! I had to be very insistent to put an end to the plan. The boat, however, joined our expedition and Raddi settled in a cabin which looked like a rock cave.

In the morning, under the blue sky of Philae, we left Egypt for Nubia. Larks danced in the light to greet our departure. The wind was our ally and enabled us to sail at a good speed. A pair of wild ducks guided us. To the ancient people they symbolized the two souls of a pair flying to the heavenly city to meet Osiris, the master of resurrection. Could the gods have given any better omen?

Elephantine
Sehel
Biga
Aswan
Philae
1st Cataract
Dabod
Qertassi
Kalabsha
Beit el-Wali
Dendur
Gerf Hussein
el-Dakka
Amada
Wadi el-Sebua
el-Derr
Kasr Ibrim
Korosko
Abu Simbel
Wadi Halfa
2nd Cataract

Cartography : C.A.R.T.

208

19

In an effort to defeat both the cold and the heat, day and night I wore flannel, furs, coat, burnous, and a thick hooded cloak. My companions soon followed my example, as since we had passed the tropic, we all shivered with cold and as soon as the sun went down.

Dabod, Qertassi, Tafa, Kalabsha, el-Dakka . . . the temples of Nubia passed before my eyes with their alleys of sphinxes, porticos and royal colossi. In Kalabsha, I discovered a new generation of gods completing the circle of the various known forms of Amon, the origin of all divine forms. Amon Ra, the supreme and primeval being, was both himself and his father. That is why he was called the 'husband of his mother'. He was also the goddess Mut, who represented the feminine inherent in his male and female essence. All other Egyptian gods were just expressions of these two basic constituents considered in their various aspects, pure abstractions of the great being. These forms created an endless chain, coming from heaven and materializing into human and other incarnations on earth. The last of these incarnations was Horus, on whom the Pharaoh was modeled, and who protected him.

Nubia was both beautiful and bountiful. It opened my eyes and initiated me more deeply into the spiritual light of the ancient people, and into the nature of the voyage into the universe before materialism.

When we arrived at el-Derr, the capital of Lower Nubia, on

23 December, I was taken up by another worry: we had to bake our bread as soon as possible. Suleiman went to the Turkish magistrate of the place to ask for permission to use an oven. I was listening to the musicians in the front part of our *dahabieh* when I saw two figures rushing into the village: Nestor L'Hôte and Professor Raddi. The latter had finally exchanged his Italian costume for Oriental clothes. Why were they hiding? Concerned, I went to Rosellini's cabin. It was empty. No one had seen my disciple since the early afternoon.

The sun was nearly setting. Dark deeds were threatening. I anxiously knocked at the door of Father Bidant's cabin. There was no answer. I found the courage to enter and saw the prie-dieu, the crucifix, a Bible and a carefully made bed, but no priest. He had also disappeared. Further enquiry with the *reis* in charge of our navigation brought no result. Only Lady Redgrave remained. She might know what was going on, or even be the instigator of the plot I was about to uncover. But Lady Ophelia had left the *dahabieh* and nobody had seen her walk away.

My companions could not have vanished without the sailors noticing. It was impossible. They were lying; a great weight suddenly descended on my shoulders. I felt like an insect vainly struggling in the centre of a cobweb. Should I stay on the ship or flee? But where to? Should I look for help, but from where? The arrival of the Turkish magistrate, a tall, lean, tense man, put an end to my predicament. Accompanied by a dozen Nubians wearing only loincloths and armed with spears, he came on board the *dahabieh* and bowed to me.

'I beg you to follow me.'

'Why?'

'I do not have to explain. You are under my authority.'

The trap was closing. Either my companions had been arrested or they had betrayed me. The image of the strange flight of two of them came back to my mind.

'I have been appointed by France,' I said. 'You can only seize me with documents signed by the Pasha.'

'I am the Pasha's official representative,' he retorted. 'I act on his behalf and I don't need any document.'

Lost in distant Nubia, what court could I turn to for help? My ultimate weapon was my derisory scientist's honour. Even eaten away by fear, I would keep face. It was unworthy of my mission to let these people see me frightened. So I followed the magistrate. None of the sailors on the *dahabieh* moved. The plot had been well planned and I had been unaware of anything up to the last moment.

We followed a dusty path to the village. The dilapidated huts were silent. There was not the slightest sound; no children laughing, nor any living soul in the dark lane leading to the centre.

I saw a fire.

'Step forward,' said the Turk.

I hesitated, convinced that I would get a spear between my shoulders as soon as I made the first step. Retaining a semblance of courage, however, I moved on.

Hardly had I moved than a huge clamour glued me to the spot. Local people came from everywhere and encircled me. They started singing a Nubian song, of which I did not understand a word.

The circle opened to give way to a procession led by a tall Turk with a turban, holding a torch in his hand. Was this a barbarous ceremony of which I was to be the hero?

Then a spontaneous laugh released my anxiety as I recognized Nestor, L'Hôte, Rosellini, Professor Raddi, Suleiman, Moktar, a veiled dancer with blonde hair, who was none other than Lady Redgrave, and a priest with a cassock! Then came the local magistrate and the sailors from the *dahabieh*. All the inhabitants of Nubia had gathered.

'But . . . why?' I asked L'Hôte.

'Have you forgotten the date, General? It's 23 December . . . and we are celebrating your thirty-eighth birthday!'

The Turkish burnous is convenient because you can pull it down over your eyes to hide tears. The night of my birthday, the most moving night in my life, was rich in laughter, songs and dances. Even Father Bidant relinquished some of his ecclesiastical reserve after midnight to enjoy L'Hôte's bawdy jokes and admire the fiery belly dance of two young Nubians.

Rosellini explained that the local potentate had almost committed suicide when he had heard that my companions wanted to arrange a big celebration in my honour. The region was so poor that there was neither fresh meat nor vegetable nor even communal ovens to bake bread. Lady Ophelia had rescued the poor man from dishonour by inviting him to join us and preside over a frugal banquet of biscuits bought in Asyut and preserves from Europe. The food did not matter. The richness of our hearts was ineffable.

The *schamali* blew with such violence that it caused thunderstorms and aroused the Nile's fury. Waves lashed the shore. The sun was obscured by clouds. The wind lifted columns of sand. But nothing could prevent our vessels from sailing across the hungry land and progressing towards Abu Simbel, which I had always considered as the ultimate goal of my journey. We had to fight the current with oars, have the ships towed, avoid shoals in the middle of the river and triumph over adverse currents.

The passion by which I was moved was infectious enough to erase any trace of depression in those around me. I expected to find confirmation of my system of decipherment and to meet the Prophet in great Ramses' main temple. If the man was to confront or help me, it would be here and nowhere else. Why had I not accepted this evidence? My intuition was based on an inscription from Abu Simbel bearing the royal name of Ramses. Fate had arranged a meeting to which I went with a young man's enthusiasm.

Life on the *dahabieh* was good. Each of us had our own apartment. Meals provided opportunities for confidences which brought us closer together. Father Bidant told us about his career and his stays in Rome. He accepted the journey into a heathen land as a godsent ordeal. L'Hôte initiated us into the art of drawing and drew a portrait of each member of the expedition. Rosellini talked about the future of Turin Museum, and about the collections of treasures and masterpieces he hoped to gather. In rather erudite terms, Professor Raddi described the first chapters of the huge history of the earth he had been writing for over twenty years. Lady Ophelia spoke about her childhood in London, her walks in the English countryside, her stern education under Thomas Young's guidance and her taste for the people of the Orient.

The coolness of the night encouraged sleep. When the storm calmed down in a sunrise that spread gold over the summit of the mountains, we saw at last a peaceful bank on which naked peasants worked in fields irrigated by bucket waterwheels. The young Nubians radiated tender, innocent beauty which relegated the Eve of paradise to darkness. Oxen with glistening hides made a wheel turn, raising buckets of water from the Nile at a slow and steady pace. Near the bank, a mother was breast-feeding her baby in the shade of some palm trees.

I was stunned by so much beauty and serenity. Here man was reconciled with God. Nature was not hostile and simply required him to offer whatever was necessary to be given a bountiful life in return.

'General! Look on the other bank!'

From a huge mound of sand, piled like a high cliff, emerged gigantic heads, the faces of royal colossi. It was impossible to know whether they were standing or sitting.

It was seven o'clock when we came alongside the foot of a temple. I recognised it as one dedicated to Hathor. She was depicted as Nefertari, the great royal spouse dear to the heart of Ramses II, in two huge statues by her husband's side. The sight of the two temples, the kings and the queen's, made me ecstatic. Hewn in the rock itself, the buildings manifested the birth of spirit out of matter and the power of light expressed in stone.

I looked for the inscription whose copy had opened the door of Egyptian writing to me on 14 September 1822. I had become so excited that I had fetched my brother in the small flat in which we were living. I had not been able to stop howling, 'I've found it!' before I fainted.

A violent pain suddenly inflamed my left knee. Short of breath and unable to stand, I collapsed.

'What happened?' I asked Father Bidant, whose face I recognized as he bent over me. 'Where am I?'

'It is a serious attack of gout. We brought you back to your cabin.'

'Have you got a plaster?'

'Yes indeed.'

'Bring me some with a sponge.'

Plaster rubbed on with a sponge is an excellent remedy to relieve pain. Forced to spend three days in bed, I took advantage of the respite to begin a dictionary of hieroglyphs and translate a text I called 'the decree of the god Ptah'. I had copied it in the large room of the temples of Ramses. My eyes gradually opened. Sentences connected with each other almost naturally. The language of the gods became more familiar day by day. I learnt to read and write hieroglyphs with texts and the magic of the land of the pharaohs as my sole teacher.

Rosellini and L'Hôte reported to me every evening. They copied historical reliefs in bright colours, some of which were unfortunately beginning to fade. I seethed with impatience and hoped that the gout would soon cease to condemn me to helplessness.

It was past midnight. Absolute silence prevailed on board the *dahabieh*. Everybody else was sleeping after an exhausting day. My dictionary progressed, almost at its own pace, as if dictated by some inner voice. I did not sleep. The illness was receding. The door of my cabin slowly opened. Lady Redgrave appeared. Her mauve dress left her shoulders bare. It was an exquisite satin evening gown in the best English taste. She stood on the threshold, her face hardly lit by the flickering light of a candle. 'Are you awake, Jean-François?' she whispered in a juvenile voice I did not know.

'Come in, Lady Ophelia. There is an armchair at the foot of the bed.'

Refusing the wicker seat, she sat on the edge of my bed, close to my left leg. 'Could we put an end to our hostility for good?' she suggested. 'We are here, lost at the end of the world, far away from civilization. We should try . . . to be happy.'

However much I tried to close my ears to the mermaid's song, I was bewitched. My conscience immediately condemned me for such weakness, but how could I resist?

'Be happy? We should at least trust each other, Lady Ophelia.'

'I trust you, Jean-François. I trust the man you are. But I don't trust the spy at the service of France.'

'I am no spy and France does not matter here. There is just Nubia, the temples, the Nile, a reflection of paradise . . . and us.'

She smiled. 'I would like to believe you . . . But we are both slaves to our missions. My uncle warned me that you were very cunning.'

'Help me to stand up, please.'

I leaned on her arm and went to the desk, on which Rosellini had put my papers into order.

'Please look,' I begged her. 'Here are the draft of a dictionary, translations of texts, checks of hypotheses I made in the Parisian cold, records of scenes . . . Is this the work of a spy or an Egyptologist?'

Softly yet firmly, she made me lie on bed again. 'You are the only one who can be convinced . . . Because you are the only one who knows how to read hieroglyphs.'

'The future will prove that I am not lying.'

Lady Redgrave took my right hand into hers. 'Let's stop this cruel game, Jean-François. I understand your mission. Please understand mine. Your love for your country and your aspiration to its glory are noble feelings. We may not be enemies. We probably aim at the same goal. Let's combine our efforts . . . provided we are sincere. If you love me, reveal the real aim of your mission to me. Then I shall be able . . . to give you everything.'

'I could lie to you,' I said in a choking voice. 'But I won't demean myself in my own eyes . . . No, Ophelia, I am no spy. It is true that the French government gave me the means to set up this expedition, but my only aim is to follow in the steps of the ancient Egyptians.'

She stood up, suddenly haughty, and walked back to the door of the cabin. 'In that case, let me wish you an excellent night, Champollion.'

It was dawn before I was able to find sleep, but I had hardly been asleep for more than a few minutes when someone knocked loudly at my door.

'Open! Open immediately!' shouted Professor Raddi.

'Push the door,' I answered in a thick voice.

A hurricane rushed at me. 'Champollion, it is a disaster, a terrible disaster! A catastrophe!

He went on like this for some time, in the most exaggerated terms. I waited until he had completed his litany, then asked for some explanation for his anger.

'My bags . . . my bags of mineral samples . . . have disappeared!'

'Where did you keep them?'

'On the front deck, under some canvas. I did not have any more room in my boat. We must investigate.'

'Ask the *reis* to come.'

The investigation was easy. Once we had questioned the captain, he immediately brought the culprit, who had come forward spontaneously.

'What did you do with Professor Raddi's collections?' I asked the tall, lean fellow.

He did not understand my question, until I mentioned the

bags. 'The bags of stones? I threw them into the water. You can find stones everywhere.'

It was impossible to explain to the unfortunate man, who had no mineralogical knowledge whatsoever, the nature of his fault. Before I reported the result of my enquiry to the good professor, I sent the sailor back to his quarters.

Raddi collapsed. I saw him age by ten years in a few seconds. 'I'm leaving Abu Simbel,' he announced. 'I go back to Cairo, I shall piece my collections together again, stone after stone.

'Professor, I sympathize with your anguish, but I beg you to reconsider. You would not have the necessary strength to complete your journey. Dedicate yourself to Nubian mineralogy which has not been explored yet . . .'

'I need my samples to write the history of the world. I am a lost man without them.'

'Didn't you want to give up office work, Professor? Didn't you fall in love with the desert and the silence?'

Professor Raddi lowered his head, ashamed. 'Yes . . . But there is my work, the most immense work ever endeavoured by man! Do you realize that, Champollion: the history of the world told in minerals! Egyptian granites, sandstones, alabasters and limestones were to provide significant landmarks.'

'You can gather an ample crop here, Professor. Just keep working at it! That is the best remedy against misfortunes, however cruel they might be. When we head back to the north, you will be able to again find what you lost.'

I put so much conviction into my words that Raddi agreed to give up his plan and stay with our community.

When he left my cabin, I was exhausted and yet happy to have preserved the unit of our small community, although it seemed increasingly in jeopardy. Lady Redgrave was becoming an implacable enemy. Despite his deference, Rosellini gave hints of ambition and envy. L'Hôte stuck to the principles of his discipline and gradually became weary of the adventure. Professor Raddi was suffering at the hands of destiny. Who had decided to betray me? My only consolation was Father Bidant's conversion: he had become the apostle of a peace I had not expected any more.

I had always refused to accept fate. I denied it once again. To regain new energy I needed the rejuvenating sight of an Egyptian temple. And here was one, a few steps away from me. Forgetting illness and pain, I stood up.

The great temple of the Abu Simbel is a marvel which does honour to Thebes. The imagination overwhelmed by the work required to build it. The smile of the colossi watching over the façade and depicting Ramses the Great is one of the purest masterpieces ever carved by Egyptian sculptors. It radiates both serenity and power, and belongs to both divinity and humankind, heaven and earth.

I regretted not having a magic wand to transport Abu Simbel's huge statues to the square named after Louis XIV. It would immediately convince my French detractors of Egypt's importance.

Despite the icy wind, I wen to the sanctuary with the support of Suleiman and Nestor L'Hôte. The Nubians had set up beams and boards to reach and enter a hole. The sailors had strengthened the fragile architecture, which was in danger of collapsing. We had to clear away the sand to penetrate the narrow pass.

The miracle occurred: my pain vanished and I recovered complete use of my legs. I took most of my clothes off, just keeping on my Arab shirt and underwear and crawled to the small opening of a door, which, once cleared, would be at least 25 feet high. It felt like entering an oven. Sliding into the temple, I found myself in an extremely hot atmosphere. Rosellini, L'Hôte, Suleiman and I explored the surprising excavation, each holding a candle.

The first room was supported by eight pillars, against which leant 30-feet high colossi representing Ramses the Great. On the walls were a line of historical bas-reliefs depicting Pharaoh's conquests in Africa. I was struck by a scene showing his triumphal chariot followed by groups of human-sized Nubian and coloured prisoners. It was altogether a most beautiful and impressive composition. The other rooms – there were sixteen of them – abounded in beautiful religious bas-reliefs with unusual features.

We planned to make large colour drawings of all the bas-reliefs in the great room of the temple. The heat there, underground now that the sand had almost covered its façade, was like that of a warm Turkish bath, and we constantly perspired. It trickled into our eyes and dripped on to paper already soaked by the humidity. The expedition braved the furnace, however, only leaving the temple because of exhaustion, when our legs refused to carry us any longer.

Everything was colossal here, even the work we had initiated, which might bring us attention. Those who know the place can appreciate how many difficulties must be overcome to draw single hieroglyph in the great temple. But who could talk of work in the face of so many splendours? Tiredness and pain left me. Perched on a ladder, I copied texts, took imprints and made several copies. Texts would then be repeated on prepared drawings so as to avoid any mistake.

Face to face with a portrait of Ramses, I understood his function. He was making an offering to a god, who was also called Ramses. But it would be wrong to believe that the ruler worshipped himself. Through his symbolical persona he honoured the divine sun who he bore in his heart and whom he represented on earth.

When we had looked at all the bas-reliefs, we felt the need for some fresh air. We had to walk back to the entrance of the furnace and prepared ourselves to leave. I put on two flannel vests and a woollen burnous and Suleiman immediately wrapped me up in a large coat as I came back into the light. I sat close to one of the outside colossi, whose huge calf stopped the north wind, and rested for half an hour, perspiring profusely. Then I went back to my ship where I spent about two hours on my bed. The trial visit proved to me that we could spend two and half or three hours in the temple without experiencing the slightest difficulty breathing, just a weakness in the joints. The Turkish bath atmosphere was the best remedy for the minor and major aches and pains we were all experiencing. That is why I decided to stay at least three hours in the temple. As for L'Hôte and Rosellini, I only imposed two hours of work on them in the morning and the same in the afternoon so as not to condemn them to suffocation. So in addition to revelations about the pharaohs, the great temple of Abu Simbel brought me a wonderful present: it relieved me from gout.

I asked Suleiman to fetch Lady Redgrave. She joined me while I was meditating in front of Abu Simbel's small temple with its six colossal figures representing the royal pair with their children. I was furious with a draughtsman called Gau, who had introduced me to these masterpieces, unappreciated because of the poor quality of his work. I resented him for having drawn these slender statues with their elegant curves as heavy magots and fat cooks in the work he had dared publish.

'What do you want?' asked Lady Ophelia, in a pink muslin dress.

She sheltered herself from the heat of the sun with an orange parasol and strutted about like an elegant lady in a London salon.

'Look . . . Look at this temple, Lady Redgrave. Do you know for whom it was built? For Nefertari, Ramses' great royal spouse, the one he loved before everything . . . He asked the realm's most famous architect to come, arranged a building site and composed the most tender and noble love poem ever engraved in the stone of eternity. Could Pharaoh offer a most beautiful present to the woman he venerated?'

Lady Redgrave lowered her parasol. She walked a few steps towards the temple and stood there alone, in the middle of the esplanade.

*

Champollion the Egyptian

Abu Simbel's small temple proved to me that Egyptian civilization definitely differed from other Oriental ones, for one can only assess the true cultural level of a people through the position of women in their society. At the time of the pharaohs, women performed the highest spiritual and material functions. They could become heads of state, know the mysteries of temples, own their own property and bequest it to whoever they wanted. Their condition was one of the highest and we should draw inspiration from it. Once urgent and indispensable works like the dictionary and grammar were completed, I would devote a book to women in ancient Egypt. When Lady Redgrave eventually understood that my life was destined to celebrate the glory of a civilization of light, she might read it with pleasure.

Work went on at a sustained pace. Abu Simbel was a site which brought immediate and constant happiness. The naturally indolent Nubians good naturedly joined in the task. Find followed find. Then, around the great temple, I discovered a stele proving that Ramses had so completely annexed Nubia that it had become a province of his realm. Some monuments were so difficult to reach that I had to adopt a dangerous strategy to copy their texts: I had to stand in a boat and use two telescopes to identify each hieroglyph carved on the rocks.

In the evening we shared a frugal meal with the Nubians. We had the feeling that we had become villagers. We had forgotten the pace of life in cities, the daily toil, the noises and the turmoil. The sun set the tone, the sky provided the colours and the temple gave us a sense of eternity. Material food did not matter. The sweetness of mutual friendship turned our Spartan bread into something more delicious than the most refined dishes. We usually sat in a circle around the fire and listened to a blind man telling beautiful long stories, often about a terrifying lioness whom the sun god had asked to destroy humankind for having betrayed light and spoiled life. In one of them the goddess Hathor had intervened to pacify its murderous passion and save some beautiful people who had fled to the desert.

On one particular evening, the village chief was not there. We waited for his arrival to eat the festive dish we had been served, a mixture of broad beans and barley. There was a solemn, almost tense atmosphere. Nobody dared talk. Very soon only the spluttering of the fire was to be heard. Then the chief appeared accompanied by the surprising figure of a tall young coloured man in a white coat over a blue dress. I was struck by his headdress of curls, which formed a wig reminiscent of those worn by noble people in some Egyptian bas-reliefs. In addition to spanning the gap between the past and the present, the headgear let out sweet fragrances. The Egyptian custom for banquets required that you come with your head perfumed so as to please the gods' nostrils. To the sound of a lyre the young man started to sing a song in my honour, describing me as the 'great general sent by a powerful monarch'. His melodious voice developed into a bewitching monotonous music that induced a collective ecstasy.

The village chief, who offered coffee to me, wore a broad smile. 'You've come from very far away,' he told me. 'And you have arrived because you are a friend of God's. Our village is now open to you. Come as you please and we will celebrate each time you tread our soil. You will stay in my house. We will sleep under the same roof and share bread. This is how God's will will be fulfilled.'

I was deeply moved.

A wide hipped Nubian brought two children who were introduced to me. 'Here are my children,' declared the chief. 'May you bless them. I myself won't leave my village. But they may come and visit you. I am sure that you will welcome them and celebrate when they come.'

I immediately assured him that such would be the case. Yet I blushed with confusion. I was, alas, convinced that the two young Nubians would not be so warmly welcomed in our old Europe, where most families have forgotten ancient customs.

My life appeared almost useless. I was experiencing a peace beyond feelings and reason. In Europe, Egypt was just a dream. In this village of the far south it became a land of eternity. It destroyed anything useless and superficial in me. How could my life matter in the face of ageless stones devoid of history and the seed of death? It was not enough to love and venerate them. It was impossible to know them through the mind alone. It would be a most enviable destiny to identify with them, become a stone and penetrate its heart.

In the morning, I was summoned by the village chief, who insisted on giving us two extraordinary presents: a gazelle whom Nestor L'Hôte immediately called 'Peter' and a big Kordofan cat. To match his gift we gave him a large amount of money, to which I added a big sum for the singer who had charmed our souls.

Noisy laughter drew my attention. A group of children had gathered around Professor Raddi, who was trying to purchase a small yellow dog and a buffalo. He had found no other means of negotiating then to imitate the cries of the animals, which aroused great hilarity. To the children's disappointment, I persuaded him to renounce his purchases. Back on the vessel, I went to my cabin to sort out some papers and work on my dictionary before going back to the temple. On my table, I saw a conspicuously sheet of paper with a few Arabic words: 'The Prophet has left Abu Simbel. He is awaiting you on the Nile.'

I hardly had recovered from my surprise when an uproar and a stampede broke out on deck. When I emerged, the cause had disappeared. The *reis* explained that he had just quarrelled with one of his cooks, whom he had caught searching Lady Redgrave's cabin. The man had hit and jostled him and fled. Several sailors had run after him.

I thought the matter was of no importance but an alarmed sailor came back to tell the captain that the cook had taken refuge in the great temple of Ramses and threatened to destroy its reliefs if anyone attempted to arrest him. My presence was indispensable. I did not hesitate for a moment, upset at the thought that such masterpieces might be disfigured by a deranged man.

At the entrance to the sanctuary stood several sailors with sticks, intent on beating the man, whose others could no longer be heard. Without listening to the calls for care, I slid into the opening with a torch. The antechamber and the large room were silent. A quick investigation revealed that my precious reliefs were intact. I rushed to the end of the sanctuary which was lost in darkness. In front of the four divine statues lay a body. As I shed some light on it, I saw that his neck had been broken. The man had stumbled and hit himself on the knees of one of the statues.

The bogus cook was not unknown to us. Abdel-Razuk, the Pasha's policeman had just ended his unfortunate career, struck down by the Egyptian gods.

20

Abdel-Razuk was buried in the village cemetery. As the authorities' representative, Moktar supervised the brief and modest ceremony.

'What was the unfortunate man's name?' I asked him when he came back on board the *dahabieh*.

'Silouf. The *reis* had just hired him. Allah punished him for his crime.'

So Moktar refused to identify his colleague and chose to kill him a second time by suppressing his identity! My silence seemed to reassure him. He probably believed that I was taken in and that that I had not looked at the corpse too closely. As for my companions, they had had no opportunity.

Nubia had triumphed over Abdel-Razuk, and put an end to the sordid mission he had been entrusted with. I could discern the benevolent influence of the great Ramses, who gave me his eternal protection.

For days, I had not said word to Suleiman who constantly watched the members of our expedition. We took ourselves off to the back of the *dahabieh* as it sailed towards Wadi Halfa, and I told him that the cook who had met his death in Abu Simbel was none other than Abdel-Razuk. The news made him gloomy.

'So they followed us to Nubia . . .'

'Did you hope that they would eventually leave us?'

'Neither the Pasha nor Drovetti really care about the region.

Abdel-Razuk had his masters' complete trust. He was no ordinary policeman. If he took the decision to follow you wherever you went, that means that you are either a very precious . . . or a very threatening character.'

'The unfortunate man is now dead, Suleiman. Is there any further risk?'

'Don't be naive, brother. Moktar is still here, with a traitor who spies on us at all times. Close to you lurks the Pasha's shadow, who waits for the moment when you will take one step too far. I am worried . . . Increasingly worried.'

'What do you think of that?' I showed him the mysterious message about the Prophet.

'It is impossible to know anything for certain about the man . . . He is more elusive than the wind. I find myself thinking he has been invented by Drovetti to mislead us more easily and draw us on to false tracks.'

'The man exists, Suleiman. I can feel it. I must meet him.'

'But who wrote this? An ally or an enemy?'

'Who knows Arabic among us? You and . . . Lady Redgrave.'

Suleiman smiled. 'Don't forget the captain and a few members of the crew. Are they all ordinary sailors? Abdel-Razuk managed to be hired as a cook.'

'Let's trust to fate . . . I refuse to be anxious and to live in suspicion all the time.'

At noon on 30 December, we arrived in Wadi Halfa, half an hour from the second cataract where Hercules' columns stand. There were a few houses alongside cultivated areas on the east bank of the Nile, as well as palm trees and sycamores. Lean Nubians strove painfully to survive. The cataract was a granite barrier of small islets, some covered by scrub and bushes. Everywhere the tips of rocks emerged just about water.

The walls of the Egyptian fortress of Buhen stood like a distant keeper. Black people were forbidden to enter. I felt a pang of anguish. I could not take my eyes off that ultimate border. I had fortunately reached the final point in my journey, and I would not go beyond the granite barrier over which the Nile had been able to triumph.

I hoped that the many monuments beyond it were of no great significance, as I would not have the chance to see them. It would have meant giving up our ships and riding on camels, which were to difficult to find, to cross the desert, risking starvation. Food was already very scarce; we had been saved by our Aswan biscuits.

I therefore decided to end our journey and turn back. Unable to cross the rapids, the *dahabieh* and other ships turned their bows towards Egypt. While the news of our return spread and the necessary manoeuvres were performed, I climbed on the heights of Abusir with Suleiman. From there we saw the furious water, the waves crashing on reefs and the horizon lost in bluish hues which downed the Africa sky.

Here man was nothing. He could hardly even consider himself as a transient guest doomed to absolute silence. Above him rose the voices of the river, the sun and the rocks. Man suddenly lost his arrogance and what he believed to be his intelligence, to bow before the majesty of life.

As I left the promontory, I saw that Suleiman had engraved my name in a rock, leaving a record of our adventure and of the man who had initiated it. Jean-François Champollion. He was merely a toy in the hands of providence, but he was also a passionate man who had to express the intense fire which had dwelt in him ever since his childhood, an explorer of the invisible in search of a lost civilization. Yet nothing would remain of him except maybe a name on a rock, forever forgotten in the solitude of the cataract.

The sound of the cannon broke the silence of the Nubian air. A flock of pelicans flew off in a flutter of wings. Lady Redgrave stood at the prow of the *dahabieh*, near the weapon she had just ordered to be fired.

It was our homage to the far south. The sailors began to sing a song of farewell that was both sad and full of hope. I had the exciting sensation that my work was just beginning for real on that day, although I already had over 600 drawings in my portfolio. But there were still so many to draw that I was almost frightened. I would have liked to be able to explore Nubia for months, live in Thebes for years, stay in each temple and feel and experience its peculiar genius from inside. But anxiety was now gnawing at my mind, as if time had suddenly become short.

'Let's not waste time on the way, General,' said Nestor L'Hôte, concerned. 'I have checked the ship with our provisions. They are getting dangerously low. If we spend too much time on the sites, we may run the risk of starvation. The villages are too poor to feed us.'

I nodded my assent. L'Hôte had made the announcement in front of all the members of our expedition, so they all knew the seriousness of our situation. My own responsibility was thus fully known. But I was hurt by his attitude. My faithful draughtsman seemed to be fed up with Egypt. He was no longer charmed by the country nor by his work. And he was ready to make use of any means to hasten our return.

'We won't take any risks,' I said. 'I shall reduce our research to what is essential.'

'But Egypt is worth a few meals,' objected Father Bidant. 'Let's lose some weight for the glory of science.'

This unexpected ally was not alone. Rosellini and Lady Redgrave were in full agreement with him. L'Hôte felt isolated. He shrank into a corner of my cabin and crossed his arms to express mute disapproval.

'Let's not waste time in talking,' I said. 'We'd better dig.'

I ordered our flotilla to stop close to the site of the Beheni of antiquity. I expected to find two large historical steles whose existence had been indicated by travellers. Only an empty desert and poor ruins remained. Sand had covered everything. I did not admit defeat, however. As the sailors had agreed to come to our assistance, I formed several teams, which dug and cleared with enthusiasm any locations I pointed out.

Fortune soon favoured me. With Suleiman's help, I uncovered an impressive stele from the time of first Ramses. His eyes sparkling with envy, Rosellini came running. 'It's a masterpiece,' he said immediately. 'The Louvre is very fortunate . . . It's too bad for Italy.'

Disappointed, he walked away and fervently went in search of the second stele we knew to be buried in the area. But our efforts remained in vain. In the evening, exhausted and dispirited, we went back to the vessel. Bitterness showed on our faces. I had explained that the monument we had not been able to find would have been very important for tracing Egyptian history. So much toil had been spent to no avail . . . I despaired of being above to encourage my troops for the next day.

I had underestimated their courage, however. At dawn we were all ready to get down to the job, determined not to come back empty-handed from the excavation ground, whose detailed plan Rosellini had laid out. Keeping his usual watch over me, Suleiman once again engraved the name of the head of the expedition on a prominent rock. Everyone worked. Dressed in trousers, Lady Redgrave was as active as anyone. Despite his cassock, Father Bidant bent to dig and clear the sand in the hope of unearthing a treasure.

At noon, we had still found nothing. My companions sat down one after another, discouraged, with hot foreheads and short of breath. I still had some energy, so I left the area delineated by my disciple to go on a lonely walk in the desert I loved beyond reason. Step by step I moved away from my group until my left foot hit a hard mass that hardly struck up from the fine sand. I knelt down with a pounding heart and hastily cleared what looked like the round top of an antique stele. My happiness was indescribable. It was Sesostris' monument. I immediately called my companions, who came rushing over, Rosellini first.

He was pallid. He noticed the quality of the stele which he stroked with the tip of his fingers. 'What a wonderful piece, Master . . . do you also want it for the Louvre?'

'What do you think?'

'The law is the law . . . the discoverer keeps the results of his excavations.'

'The monument is dear to you, Ippolito. It was first mentioned by an Italian traveller. Therefore it is legitimately yours.'

I was unable to interpret Rosellini's look. Was it satisfaction? Surprise? Disappointment?

'I refuse, Master. The two monuments should stay together. They are yours and, through you, they belong to France.

I grasped my disciple's shoulders and hugged him. 'Thank you for your generosity, Ippolito. The gods will be grateful to you.'

With infectious joy, we proceeded to a brief clearing. I gave instruction that Sesostris' stele be taken on board the *dahabieh*.

While this was being done under Rosellini's supervision, we stayed in the desert, savouring our victory and thanking the divine sun, Ra, who had allowed it. Father Bidant himself was becoming sensitive to the beauties of Egypt, while L'Hôte, now more cheerful, praised our success.

True to my word, I ordered that we resume the descent of the Nile, which gradually brought us closer to Thebes. There was a powerful current and a strong north wind. Wadi Halfa and darkest Nubia receded behind us for good. Wild ducks flew in a blue sky. On the bank a buffalo shook himself after his bath. At that very moment I perceived the hidden beauty of the Egyptian landscape. Increasingly more bewitching, day after day, it never altered. The only changes were in the intensity of the light and the sparkling of the Nile. Man was the guest of a land and a sky which constantly prolonged the past and carried a breath of eternity into the future. Shaped by divinities, nature offered both solitude and fraternity: it brought my soul in touch with the ancient Egyptians, made me enjoy the slightest event, be it a felucca passing, the song of a bird, or the brightness of foliage.

I forgot myself and entered the absolute simplicity of this millennium-old life which filled my heart and flooded it with the same sun which had watched over the building of the temples. There was no place for anything superfluous. My true being emerged from what was not essential, became aware of its impermanence, and in the ensuing detachment discovered hope, the unspeakable union with the secret fire that made Egypt immutable.

In an attempt to dispel the nostalgia that had overcome me, I wrote notes about the discovery of the two steles and monuments. In the course of this task I had some doubts about the proper spelling of king Sesostris' name. Although night had fallen, I wanted to check the detail without delay. I left my cabin and headed for the front of the *dahabieh*, where I asked the *reis* where the sacred stones had been put. He was surprised by my request and said that no artefacts of such importance had been loaded on the main vessel. He called the sailors, who confirmed the fact. One of them, however, declared that he had helped load something on the ship that contained our provisions.

'On whose orders?' I asked indignantly.

His description matched that of Rosellini.

I ordered the *reis* to summon him to my cabin. I looked at him silently.

'What is the matter, Master? Is it bad news?'

'Very bad news, indeed, Ippolito. But you already know.'

'Me? How could I know?'

'I am not a public prosecutor. You should confess your fault and make amends.'

'What fault? What am I accused of? And why?'

'Keep quiet, Ippolito. Don't get yourself into deeper and deeper water.'

Rosellini lowered his head and gave up. 'I was stupid,

Master. I yielded to a most vile impulse. I longed so much for the two steles – not for me, but for the museum . . .'

'I can understand that, Ippolito, but I cannot accept that you lied to me, abused me and betrayed my trust.'

'No!' he protested. 'I was sincere! The idea only came to me when I reached the ship with our provisions – an irresistible desire to possess the two steles. I thought you would not notice anything.'

He wept tearlessly, with stifled sobs and gasps, and left my cabin without raising his head.

As soon as our flotilla had anchored in Serret el-Gharb, I summoned my travelling companions. Frightened, Rosellini hid behind L'Hôte. He was probably afraid I might reveal his disgraceful behaviour to our community.

'I forgot my birthday, but I didn't forget today's. We will celebrate the New Year together and, as the head of the expedition, I want to give you presents. I do not want to think of our differences any more. Let's be united in brotherly friendship. Lady Redgrave, please come up . . .'

At my request, Suleiman had succeeded in buying a lapis lazuli necklace which I put round the beautiful spy's neck. Moved, she thanked me with a smile that was certainly not that of an enemy.

Rosellini, who was beginning to unwind, received an *ouchebti*, a small magic figurine was said to work in the fields of the other world at the request of those who had been recognized as fair. Nestor L'Hôte I presented with a collection of charcoals which revived his desire to draw the whole of Egypt. To Father Bidant, I gave a Coptic manuscripts about the ordeals of the saints. To Professor Raddi I gave a very rare mineralogy treatise Jacques-Joseph had consented to leave to me after he had extracted it from his library.

Then I went to the prow of the ship where I had ordered the captain to summon his crew. I gave them a bonus and thanked them for their precious help. The musicians grasped their instruments and a song of rejoicing rose from their throats.

Joyfulness gripped our expedition. We set up tables on the bank. Close by, a *noria* driven by oxen emitted a bitter endless complaint. Ninety-foot high palm trees provided calm and coolness. We raised our eyes to the sky, where the first stars were born. They contained the souls of pharaohs who had returned to their light. I contemplated the tops of the high trees, which were able to face the blazing sun without losing their vigour. Peasants sat with their legs crossed and wove fibres to make cages and baskets. As a starter, we were given palm stalks that exuded a sweet juice and the mashed marrow of young trees. Slowly the herds came back from the fields, where naked children were still playing.

Who can celebrate the enchantment of life in the shade of palm trees? And who can describe the satisfaction of a New Year banquet on the Nubian bank, bathed in limpid air and full of an everlasting wisdom that continues to nourish the voice of the river? I would have liked to be a poet, a painter and a musician at such a time . . .

With a lump in my throat, I stood up, a glass in my hand. 'I would like to drink to the success of our expedition.'

'With what? Enquired Nestor L'Hôte, ironically.

'With two bottles of Saint-George wine!' I revealed, pleased with the *coupe de théâtre*. Suleiman brought the precious liquid, which had been carefully concealed at the bottom of a trunk. We savoured it reverently, although it was slightly altered by the tropics.

'Life, health, strength!': such was the triple wish that followed the name of each pharaoh. We wished our community the same, when we loudly greeted the arrival of a tall Nubian carrying the skin of a panther, ostrich feathers, a javelin and some shells. The presents were shared with an infectious enthusiasm increased by palm wine.

I received a big ostrich egg embellished with children's drawings. The upper part had been cut to form a lid. As the guests, somewhat tipsy, sang fashionable songs which the Nubians tried to emulate as best they could, I opened the egg and looked inside. There was a carefully rolled papyrus. I removed it discreetly and went to the shade of a grove to unroll it, hidden from the gaze of the others. The document had been written in Coptic by a hand that betrayed signs of age. It was signed 'The Prophet'.

> Having escorted you from the mouth of the Nile to the second cataract, I am proud to tell you that nothing must be changed in your hieroglyphic alphabet. Your decipherment is accurate. You may apply it with equal success to Egyptian monuments from Roman and Greek times and, what is more interesting, to all inscriptions from temples, palaces and tombs of pharaonic times. Your journey has enabled you to revive the tradition and your hieroglyphic work will be universally recognized. Farewell.

This was the key, the ultimate key: the structure of the hieroglyphs had not varied for the birth of civilization to its last breath, from ancient kingdom tombs to the great Ptolemaic temples. Egypt was one and indivisible. It had created a scared tongue that had survived time and death.

And my decipherment was right.

We had no more time for leisure, and, despite its frugality, our New Year banquet had diminished our meagre food reserves. The following day, we explored Machakit cave which we entered from a cliff which fell abruptly into the Nile. The weather was awful and a violent wind blew in gusts. Despite a strong headache, Nestor L'Hôte did not want to give up the ascent. His determination inspired me. I had the utmost difficulty in gathering my thoughts. The Prophet's message had upset me. When and where had I come across him? Why had he refused to meet me?

L'Hôte reached out his hand to help me several times, but our efforts were rewarded. We discovered an Eighteenth

Dynasty shrine dedicated by a nobleman called Paser to the cataract goddess, beautiful Anukis, a most gracious woman with gazelle horns. L'Hôte drew the bas-reliefs while I copied the inscriptions.

As I copied them, I deciphered them. Hieroglyphs were no longer a dead tongue, external to me, but a language from within that had become as natural as my mother tongue. I was now able to read them.

Suddenly the signs danced and swirled before my eyes. I was drawn with them into a huge wave that rose up to the sky.

An acute pain in my left cheek brought me back to my senses.

Nestor L'Hôte slapped me again. I opened my eyes. 'Ah, General! I was afraid . . . You collapsed, General! Probably from exhaustion . . .'

'Yes exhaustion . . .'

'We should not linger too long. Look outside.'

The north wind, which had risen shortly before our arrival at the foot of the cliff, had now strengthened into a kind of hurricane. L'Hôte did not let go of my hand and tugged me on the way down. Several times we were flattened against the rock by gusts of wind. I even lost my balance and only stopped myself falling by clinging to a knotty branch that cracked under my weight.

Fate allowed us to return safe and sound to the ships where our companions berated us for our recklessness. The flotilla sailed for half an hour, in the hope that the current would overcome the violence of the adverse winds. But the *schamali* became furious, the Nile was covered with white horses like the sea, and huge waves were building up. Eventually the gale forced us to the shore.

It was however a kind gale, for it left us in front of the rupestrian temple of Gebel-Adda. As we entered it in search of shelter, we saw that the sanctuary had been inhabited by Coptic people who had covered the pharaonic motifs with Christian inscriptions. Happily surprised, Father Bidant even fell down on his knees before a St George on a horse, which reminded him of his familiar churches.

'At last, Champollion! At last! Memories from the true faith!'

'I came here to meet more ancient saints, Father.'

A few moments later, I was gratified in the holy of holies. The sight was so unusual that I burst into laughter. 'Come, Father. Hurry. Here is a truth which may surprise you!'

The priest was silent. The Christian stucco had become partially detached from the wall, uncovering one of the original Egyptian figures, a pharaoh to whom St Peter was paying tribute!

'If Christianity bowed to Egypt,' I said gravely to Father Bidant, 'it was because it recognized all its greatness.'

The Nubian night was a perfect shrine for the moon's light. It shrouded the mountains and the desert in blue. I had left the *dahabieh* to walk alone in the ruins of a Mameluke citadel dismantled by the Pasha's army. The destroyed world, in which the noise of bloody battles still sounded made me painfully sad. It was heart-rending to leave Nubia. Each temple, each carved cave deserved a long stay.

In the cool night, under the twinkling stars, soul and body lived to the full, far away from all agitation. Envies and desires subsided to make way for the serenity of primeval times, when the human soul and the soul of the cosmos were still one.

I heard the sound of stones rolling not far from me. I felt a presence. Despite my fear, I wanted to know who had followed me. It might be the Prophet . . . Had he chosen this lonely place to approach me? The noise of steps came nearer. Someone fell heavily behind a brick pillar, about to collapse. I rushed to help a man dressed in the Turkish fashion to his feet. His face was covered in blood.

It was Professor Raddi!

The mineralogist was dazed. Fortunately, it was just a superficial injury, despite its spectacular appearance, just a cut. I helped him sit on the remnants of a wall and let him regain his breath.

'Champollion . . . Is that you, Champollion? Ah the desert, the desert! I walked in it throughout the night! I walked around rocks, climbed on dunes and slopes on which the limestone shimmered. The moonlight made them shine even more . . . They looked like diamonds in the sand. I picked up thousands of them, thousands . . . and I went on. I saw an island on which a huge town with colonnades was built. It had obelisks, white and red pyramids, houses with gardens . . . it was beautiful! I want to go back there. This is where I want to live . . .'

'We will go together,' I told him, 'as soon as we have had some rest.'

I took his arm. He did not resist. We walked slowly to the *dahabieh*. I laid him on his bed, and he immediately fell asleep.

Maybe Professor Raddi was losing his head, or had seen one of the mirages for which the desert is so famous – unless he had glimpsed ultimate realities ordinary men cannot see.

Our arrival at the site of Abu Simbel was a moment of great happiness for the whole expedition. We had got to know with the two temples of Ramses and his wife. The clear and radiant joy emanating from the stones, the colossi's smiles, prolonged the harmony generated by the New Year celebration in our community. Despite my own desire, however, I had to speed up the work. Our provisions would soon be exhausted. I could not put lives at risk. Therefore we checked, completed and improved our copies of texts and scenes. I noticed that, despite our care, we had made mistakes and omissions. We should have spent months checking each wall and column of hieroglyphs a hundred times.

A truly Egyptian calm had become the rule in our community. Everyone worked in silence and respected the masterpieces. Father Bidant had given up prayer to help L'Hôte, with whom he got on very well. Lady Redgrave assisted Rosellini by holding his notebooks and bringing him drinks.

Professor Raddi sat on one of the colossi's feet and remained motionless in front of the Nile, admiring landscapes that he was the only one to see.

It was almost unbearable to leave Abu Simbel. The days and nights spent on the site would figure among the happiest in my life. When on 16 January, at around 1 p.m., the ships moved away from the shore, their flags unfurled, to the sound of the Nubians singing a song of farewell, my heart broke.

In the middle of the river, I ordered that the main vessel be stopped so as to contemplate the queen's temple for the last time. Then I said farewell to the huge statues of the façade of the great temple, whose gigantic mass increased as we moved away. I was leaving behind an essential moment of my adventure, paradise recovered. I could not help feeling that I was abandoning myself as I left, probably for ever, the sublime monument.

21

On the evening of 17 January, we reached el-Derr, the capital of Nubia, where we had dinner in beautiful moonlight, under the highest palm trees we had ever seen. I got into conversation with an old native who had seen me alone on the bank of the river and politely come to keep me company and offer me date spirit. I asked him if he knew the name of the sultan who had ordered the erection of el-Derr temple. He immediately answered that he was too young to know, but that all the village's old men seemed to agree that the temple had been built about 3,000 years before Islam. But they were unsure whether the huge work had been built by the French, the British or the Russians. This is how history is written in Nubia!

Pursuing my lonely walk, I soon bumped into Father Bidant. 'You look very upset, Champollion. Has anything happened?'

'No,' I answered. 'On the contrary a great happiness, the greatest happiness.'

'Do you mean your famous decipherment?'

I was surprised by his perspicacity. He knew all about it.

'You heard about the discovery of the Rosetta Stone at the age of nine,' he said. 'At the age of thirteen you decided that you would be able to read hieroglyphs some day. At the age of twenty, you were granted the chair of antique civilization in Grenoble. You have been relentlessly pursuing your dream ever since and you have tried to convince the world that you will reach your goal.'

'You know my life better than I do!' I answered, surprised.

'I should know everything about the souls I am in charge of,' he said gravely.

'In charge of?'

'Yes, Champollion. The highest Church authorities entrusted me with the mission to redeem you from darkness if the latter threatened to engulf you. We were afraid magic decorations might disturb your mind.'

'Hieroglyphs,' I objected, 'are no vain decorations. They express thoughts. I may be mistaken, but I believe that the results of my work may be of interest for historical and philosophical studies. The language and the writing of Egypt differ so much from our usual tongues and writings systems that the history of ideas, language and arts will find endless opportunities to gather important and new data. In Egypt's most ancient times the historian will see a state that has not been improved on in the course of generations because it could not be so. Egypt remains the same at all times and it is still a great powerful source of enlightenment.'

'Can you already assess the consequences of your discoveries in relation to the truths revealed by the bible?'

'We will have to examine everything closely, Father. The Egyptians existed before the Hebrews. They taught them everything. Moses was an Egyptian who left his native country. In the future people will read hundreds of texts teaching them Egyptian wisdom, the purest wisdom ever experienced by man. It will change our vision of the world.'

The priest lowered his head until his chin almost touched his chest. He mumbled something I did not understand, seized a rosary and spoke nervously to his beads. 'Be careful, Champollion,' he advised me before he walked away.

Despite being a capital, el-Derr was just a big village of poor houses in front of which people had laid plates, jars, pots, and spoons so as to display their fortune before travellers. We were given a substantial meal served on a piece of leather cut into a circle, on which were laid dishes of saffron rice, onions and chick peas. Everybody ate heartily, realizing that the time of restrictions had come to an end. L'Hôte had recovered his good temper and enthusiasm. He drank a lot of palm wine and became rather heated.

'General,' he said loudly,' I have make a brilliant plan with the *reis*. I told to Ippolito and Lady Redgrave and they both supported it . . . I hope you will, too.'

I began to worry. My draughtsman had broached the subject in a most mysterious way. The audience was attentive.

'This is rather a strange plan,' continued L'Hôte. 'But it will be something memorable. Of course, it involves some danger, but we may reduce that considerably . . .'

I begged him to come to the point.

'This is a unique opportunity, according to the *reis* . . . He guarantees full security if we follow his instructions.'

Annoyed, I crossed my arms. 'Come on, L'Hôte! What is this brilliant plan it is so difficult to tell us about?' he hesitated a few more moments. 'A huge crocodile hunt!' he said.

Just before dawn, I granted myself the pleasure of another lonely walk among the houses surrounded by acacias and palm trees. The locals were still sleeping. Birdsong pierced the fluid early-morning air. The most beautiful embellishments of the modest but remarkably clean capital were the sycamores with glistening foliage. In their delicious shade a coloured brick mosque had been built. Close by was a *sebil*, a shelter where merchants arriving in long and patient caravans from Sudan settled. They slept there with slaves of both sexes. A civil servant in charge of the taxes on palm trees slept on a mat. I passed him as silently as a shadow so as not to disturb this age-old order, for I was just a transient witness.

I went back to the bank, where the expedition was getting ready. I had agreed with the *reis* and L'Hôte that they could requisition the *dahabieh* and six other boats with rowers, sailors and hunters with rifles. Full of enthusiasm, L'Hôte stood at the prow of the first boat. The current was so strong and the wind so violent that the ships jumped like arrows. Sometimes the *dahabieh* led, sometimes it was L'Hôte's boat. The sailors became excited at the game and launched into a mad pursuit. Appalled, Father Bidant averted his gaze. Two boats hit each other violently. There were broken oars and some painful backs. I ordered the captain to slow down so as not to put the crew and the passengers at risk. At the climax of his excitement, L'Hôte brandished his weapon, ready to shoot at the first crocodile to come his way. But the Nile remained desperately empty of crocodiles. I must confess that I was also curious to see one of the monsters in whose body the god Sobek, the ruler of life-giving water, had become incarnate. The river became wider, but islets hampered our navigation. Then L'Hôte let our such a loud cry of joy that everybody startled. Sunbathing on a small sandy promontory were big old crocodiles. L'Hôte shot immediately, sure that he would kill one of them. But the bullets rebounded on their thick hide. Frightened by the noise, the crocodiles ran to the water and hurriedly slid into it.

The hunters were very disappointed and, out of frustration, emptied their rifles at random.

Suleiman jostled me and placed himself before me. 'Don't stay here. You've just been shot at.'

A crowd of children greeted our return to el-Derr and invaded the ships. The sailors' somewhat brutal intervention was necessary to curb their exuberance. We left without delay for the temple of Amada. Suleiman's enquiries had led to nothing; a large number of people had had rifles and several hunters had shot at the same time.

The sanctuary impressed us all. Lost in the desert, in deepest silence, devoid of any external embellishments, built at a time of greatness, the temple was an image of serenity itself.

It did me good to see it at a time when I was still experiencing the nervous consequences of the attack from which I had escaped thanks to Suleiman's intervention. Although buried in the sand, the temple emerged out of time like a sacred milestone. As I went inside, I saw with despair that the pharaonic reliefs had been covered with a poor plaster by Copts who had turned the temple into a church. Until then I had been able to resist the tension that had been building up in me during our Nubian trip. But this was too much. I turned to L'Hôte. 'Bring me a hammer.'

My collaborator returned quickly. Nobody dared question me. Everybody could feel the huge anger boiling in me. I grasped the hammer and broke a large piece of stucco, bringing back to light an Egyptian relief still shining with its original colours. Father Bidant was indignant and wanted to stop me, but Rosellini and L'Hôte prevented him from stepping forward. Forcefully yet precisely I completed a task which was a tribute to the genius of that ancient people. I felt a peaceful joy. As I revived this art of light, I purified myself.

We spent two wonderful days working non-stop in Amada, uncovering most of the ancient figures, admiring columns which foreshadowed the Doric style, drawing and recording with enthusiasm. With great emotion I easily translated some writing said to be by Thoth, the master of hieroglyphs, whose words I could now understand.

When we left for el-Dakka, I felt lighthearted. After Amada, I hope there would be time to see another masterpiece. L'Hôte and I rushed towards the el-Dakka pylon as the sun rose. The first hieroglyphic inscription I saw told me that I was in a holy place dedicated to Thoth. I could no longer doubt that the god of scribes was favourably disposed towards me. I must confess that I even irreverently thought that august Thoth, the Egyptian Mercury with the caduceus, the gods' usual sceptre, was giving me a sign.

We devoted part of 26 January to the small temple of Dendur. It was modern building which had not yet been completed by the time of Emperor Augustus. Despite its modest dimensions, I was very interested in it because it was dedicated to Osiris' human incarnation, Osiris, the conqueror of death . . . death which smiled increasingly more often at me during my sleep.

After we left the sanctuary, Professor Raddi let out a cry, followed by a second and then a third. The mineralogist was as happy as a child. He had just unexpectedly discovered a wonderful echo! He distinctly repeated eleven syllables, in a sonorous voice. As enthusiastic as his fellow countryman, Rosellini enjoyed declaiming verses from Tasso which mingled with shots fired by the sailors in all directions, which through natural magic were echoed by the sound of cannons or thunder.

Alas fate had another storm in store for me, which tore apart our serenity. I needed another notebook to record some columns of hieroglyphs. Leaving L'Hôte for a few moments, I went to fetch Rosellini, who was taking measures outside the temple. As I could not find him, I walked to a nearby hill, from which came the sound of talking. I could recognize the voices of Lady Redgrave and Rosellini. My blood chilled as I heard my disciple's words.

'Champollion is no greater scientist than I am,' he said. 'It is impossible to convince him of that for the moment. I let him believe that I consider myself as his inferior, whereas I know more than him. Back in Italy, I shall become a great curator, who will create the largest museum in the world. Champollion is a dreamer and an idealist . . . He won't be able to use the results of his expedition. I shall be able to do that. I am the only Egyptologist whose name posterity will remember – even if I have to push Champollion away from my path.'

I turned back so as not to hear more.

Once we had crossed the Tropic of Cancer below Dendur, we bade farewell to the Southern Cross and in Beit el-Wali we left behind the wonderful clear nights of Nubia. Casting a last glance at the stars of another world, I remembered Don Calmet, the monk who had taught me general science in the open air. He had been the first to recognize my gift for languages. How he would have appreciated such moments of intense meditation, in which one learnt about the sky just by contemplating it from the bank of the Nile!

A soft hand was laid on my shoulder. 'What else are you hoping for, Jean-François?' asked Lady Redgrave. 'Haven't you achieved your aim, the decipherment of hieroglyphs?'

'News spread very quickly . . . but you believe me at last!'

She did not answer. I turned to her, full of hope.

'Not at all. Why do you continue the journey if your aim has been fulfilled?'

'Because I must now read! I must decipher Thebes and penetrate the core of the holy city! My work has only just started, Lady Ophelia . . . a universe is opening before me.'

'Could you be returning to Thebes to meet the famous Prophet, to whom you will entrust the information you gathered? You might be inexorably pursuing a plan which will lead you to the ultimate fight against Drovetti?'

I was dismayed. I was being betrayed by some people and misunderstood by others . . . was it so difficult to share an ideal?

'This is the most beautiful sky in the world,' she said. 'Why should we spoilt it by lying to each other? Why don't we abandon ourselves to the feelings that drive us?'

Maybe I should have taken her in my arms and confessed that her slightest word troubled me and that she had the beauty of the noblewoman of ancient Egypt . . . But I behaved like a coward. I fled. I did not want an affection which was not rooted in complete trust. Solitude was better than doubt.

Philae was looming ahead. We were coming back to Egypt and bidding farewell to poor Nubia, whose drought had eventually wearied my travelling companions. As we set foot in Egypt, we could expect to eat rather better bread than the meagre fare with which our head baker had related us every day. He was as good as the Arab cooks praised as a *cordon bleu* in Cairo.

On 1 February, at around 9 p.m., we saw the powerful granite rocks on the banks of the Nile, then the Biga cliffs and at last the wonderful entrance pylon of Philae temple. I thanked its antique divinities, Osiris, Isis and Horus, for preventing starvation from getting the better of us between the two cataracts.

The stars were shining. Several Nubian families welcomed us with joyful cries when we set foot on the shore near Trajan's Kiosk. We were greeted by a flute and drum concert in which L'Hôte joined with his beautiful grave voice while Professor Raddi, a piece of granite in each hand, danced a few jig steps, to the great enjoyment of the children. Rosellini offered his arm to Lady Redgrave to help her leave the *dahabieh* and tread once again the land of the pharaohs. Side by side, Suleiman and Moktar watched over the gangway to the vessel so as to discourage any attempt at theft.

I was savouring a coffee provided by the head warden of the site of Philae, when someone tugged at my trousers. I bent down and saw a 10-year-old little girl. She wore a beautiful red dress. She had probably just been the star of a celebration.

'You must come with me,' she said.

I smiled. 'Why?'

She concentrated, trying to remember what she had to say. 'A great friend of Mr Anastasy's is awaiting you.'

Anastasy . . . his name was a reliable guarantee. The 'great friend' could only be a Brother of Luxor. It was impossible to let Suleiman know, for Moktar did not leave him alone.

'I'll follow you,' I told the little girl.

She quickly led me to the other side of the island, where another *dahabieh*, similar to ours, was anchored. The two sailors keeping watch over the gangway bowed to me and made way. They stopped the little girl and presented her with a doll, which she immediately adopted.

A servant guided me to the cabin of the master of the place. It was sumptuously furnished with leather armchairs, a divan, a mahogany table and oak bookcases. A 60-year-old man of great bearing stood up and walked to me. He wore a white suit and smoked a pipe. Furrowed by deep wrinkles, his face had been seamed by the sun.

'I'm pleased to welcome you, Champollion. I'm Lord Prudhoe.'

'And you are a great friend of Anastasy's . . .'

'And your brother . . .'

We spontaneously hugged each other, both moved.

'You will be the last of us, Champollion. Mehmet Ali is after us. He is identifying us one by one. Denouncement works well. Most of us have already left Egypt. We are being confused with a revolutionary sect. I shall begin a long exploration of Nubia and Arabia. I shall die there under suns that never disappoint me. In fact I shall leave tonight. As for you, you will go back to Thebes, the highlight of the universe. Drovetti and his men are awaiting you there. You should know that your life is in danger.'

'Who is the traitor among the members of my expedition?'

'I don't know, Champollion. I am certain that everything was arranged before your departure from Toulon. I have no hope of making you give up your stay in Thebes; I shall not even attempt to convince you. You have been longing for it for too long. But you should be aware that you are as much in danger in your community as with other people.'

Although I remained apparently calm, I was shaken by Lord Prudhoe's warnings. 'I no longer have a choice,' I said. 'My job was to decipher hieroglyphs.'

A long silence followed.

'I haven't been able to meet the Prophet,' I added, 'but I received a message from him confirming the value of my discovery.'

'Well,' said Lord Prudhoe. 'We only have one final precaution to take: we must share your secret. In this way, if you disappear, I shall pass on the mysteries which, until now, have been in your sole possession.'

I felt a lump in my throat. He was asking me to entrust him with my most precious treasure, the essence of my life, on our first meeting. I had often been too gullible and trusted people who had then harmed me . . . Lord Prudhoe's piercing gaze analysed my inner predicament. He patiently drew on his pipe.

'Give me some paper,' I said. 'I shall explain it to you.'

He smiled good-naturedly. 'That is unnecessary, Champollion. Your trust is enough. I would be unable to understand it anyway. You are the only one who is able to transmit your prodigious discovery to future generations. But there is one more detail . . . I have a present for you.'

He extracted a very old book from the bookcases. It was a treatise on hieroglyphs by an Egyptian priest, Horapollo, who had lived at the time of the Greeks.

'You have already read the text . . . But this copy has been completed by handwritten commentaries which will be useful to you. They were written by an ancient man whose competence you will judge for yourself. To our Brotherhood, it is an indispensable key whose use has been reserved for you.'

I excitedly perused the venerable document, which brought me the essential revelation of the three meanings – literal, moral and symbolic – of the hieroglyphic language. They mostly related to levels of reality. It was not just a language that was unveiling, but also an entirely new philosophy a vision of life which would appear as an essential creation in the future. I held an extraordinary revolution in human thinking in my hands.

Would Drovetti and his henchmen be enough to prevent it from happening? Seeing my emotion, Lord Prudhoe offered me port. 'If the gods favour you, Champollion, your expedition will have invaluable consequences. You will found a science, resuscitate a civilization and revive a wisdom of which future men will have great need.'

'Why don't you stay with me?'

'Our rule is to scatter all over the world. You will head for the north and I shall head for the south. That is right.'

'Does the famous Prophet really exist, in your opinion? Is he a friend or an enemy?'

'You often met him on bas-reliefs, Champollion! He is a haughty man with a beard and a long stick . . . the accurate portrait of a great dignitary at the court of Pharaoh, one of the stewards who are responsible for making harmony prevail on earth!'

I had been very careless. The Brotherhood of Luxor had set me a most salutary trap, a trap that harmed my vanity.

We spent the night talking about our past and our projects, forgetting that there would be another day and that dawn would soon break.

'I hate farewells,' declared Lord Prudhoe, 'but I don't want to be late. As for you, you have no more time to waste. We will see each other again . . . in another life.'

Without further ceremony, he left his cabin to go to the front part of the *dahabieh* and give instructions to the captain. I waited on the bank for his departure.

The little girl with the red dress was sleeping under an acacia, clutching the doll against her chest. I did not want to wake her up, but a stone rolled under my left foot. The little girl rubbed her eyes, stood and grasped my arm. 'Have you got a present for me?' she asked

'Would you like this?' I gave her an embroidered handkerchief.

She used it to dress her doll.

'I would like to know . . . who gave you this beautiful dress?'

'The man on the ship which is leaving . . . they call him the Prophet.'

22

According to the information gathered by Suleiman in Aswan, Drovetti had left the region some time before for Thebes, where his men were said to be spread everywhere under the pretext of conducting archaeological digs. I would have wished to leave as early as possible for the ancient capital, but we first had to mend our two ships, the *Isis* and the *Hathor*, which had been neglected during our Nubian adventure. My companions used the break to sleep to their heart's content and eat to their fill. Feeling fighting fit and not at all tired after so many successes, I studied once more the weathered remains of the ancient temples.

We bade farewell to ancient Syene on 8 February, but fortune was against us. On 10 February we were still a long way from Ombos, which is usually a nine-hour journey from Aswan. The violent north wind that had blown constantly for three days made us dance on the waves of the Nile, now as swollen as a little sea. We dropped anchor near Melissah, a sandstone quarry of no interest. Otherwise, we were in sound health and full of courage to explore Thebes from top to bottom. I looked forward to the prospect of receiving letters. I found letters form Paris somewhat too short. People forgot that I was thousands of miles away from France and that evenings might seem long when one just spends them smoking or playing *bouillotte*. We needed a supply of small packages from Paris. It should not be thought that I was too demanding;

I was almost entitled to that after having written twenty-seven pages, which I would complete as soon as possible for fear of people saying that the most talkative people in the world are those who come back from the second cataract.

A strange torpor had overcome our community. Father Bidant had shut himself up in his prayers. On the deck of the *Hathor*, Professor Raddi contemplated the Nile and the mountains in silence. Rosellini filed scientific notes. L'Hôte retouched sketches. As for me, I progressed with my dictionary and my grammar book. I worked in a sort of daydream dialogue with the god Thoth, who helped me improve my knowledge of the sacred tongue.

Our trip continued without mishaps. We were now a short distance from Thebes. Our hearts were longing for the sight of its imposing ruins. Our stomachs were also concerned, for a ship full of fresh provisions was reported to be in Luxor. It was another courtesy from our worthy Consul-General Drovetti, and we were in a hurry to take advantage of it. But an extremely violent north wind stopped us during the night between Hermonthis and Thebes, and we only reached the latter on the early morning of 8 March. Our ships were anchored at the foot of the colonnades of the Luxor temple which we had decided to investigate more thoroughly.

Alas, the state of the magnificent divine palace had not improved. It was still blocked by the *fellahin*'s huts which disfigured its beautiful porticos, not to mention the tiny house of a Turkish captain on a platform savagely damaged by pickaxes to make way for the man's litter. The sanctuary provided neither a convenient nor a clean room in which to settle. So we had to stay on the ships until we had completed our records in the temple. The provisions offered by Drovetti, who was reported to have gone back to Cairo after extremely disappointing archaeological digs, were served at a big banquet celebrating our return to Thebes. Despite my opposition, Suleiman insisted on tasting the meats, vegetables and fruit we ate. Nothing seemed suspicious until he forced himself to take a sip of Bordeaux wine. A moment later, his stomach was on fire. Professor Raddi immediately treated him with magnetism while a sailor brought a bitter tea. The pain receded, but Suleiman remained feverish for several hours. 'Poison,' he whispered. 'Poison . . .'

We crossed over the left bank on 23 March. There were took the road to Bilan el Muluk, where the tombs of New Kingdom pharaohs were dug. Narrow and stony, the Valley of the Kings is enclosed by high mountains without any kind of vegetation, and the heat is sometimes unbearable. Our caravan immediately settled in the most magnificent lodgings ever to be found in Egypt. King Ramses, the sixth of the name, was our host. We stayed in his magnificent tomb, the second on the right as one enters the Valley. In a wonderful state of preservation, the hypogeum got enough air and sun for us to be wonderfully accommodated. We stayed in the first three rooms, which run on for about 75 feet altogether. The 15–20-foot high walls and the ceilings were all covered with painted sculpture whose colours had almost retained their original brilliance. It was a princely dwelling, except for the inconveniently linked rooms. The floor was entirely covered with mats and reeds. Our bodyguards and servants slept in two tents by the entrance of the tomb. Such was our settlement in the Valley of the Kings, a true place of death, for no blade of grass, nor living being were to be found, with the exception of jackals and hyenas which, the night before the previous one, had devoured the donkey carrying our provisions, a 100 feet away from our palace.

Fortunately the Kordofan cat and L'Hôte's gazelle were both safe and sound. They had both settled in the sarcophagus room where I had set up my campbed to sleep peacefully in this dwelling of eternity by a pharaoh's soul. My venerable bedroom closed with a wooden door from a *dahabieh*.

Each night, I waited until everybody was asleep, softly stroking the gazelle, which was sunk in blissful slumber. As soon as I heard the steady breaths of the sleepers, I lit a somewhat smoky lamp to prepare the next day's programme. People waited for my instructions and I had to be ready to give them clearly and without hesitation. Outside there was an almost absolute calm, sometimes interrupted by the howling of jackals or hyenas. Used to them and shut up in their tents, the workmen did not wake.

These were my most beautiful work hours. I had entered the tomb the Egyptians called a 'dwelling of eternity' in my lifetime. I enjoyed its mysteries and symbols without feeling the need to analyse them. The teachings of the pharaohs did not make use of the mind. One had to let them pervade one and live with the bas-reliefs of strange figures who only talked about what was essential.

My companions' rest pleased me. They were serene and relaxed. The energy emanating from the sacred walls almost allowed me to overcome sleep. As I wrote and thought of further tasks, I dispelled my tiredness. I was aware of the exceptional character of these moments and I did not want to miss one iota. It was my duty to protect my companions and workmen and watch over their peaceful sleep. My ineffable pleasure and supreme reward consisted in enjoying solitude without community and in feeling connected to the minds of ancient men as well as to those of men who were gradually beginning to rid Egypt of its shroud of sand.

Morning always came too soon. The cat and the gazelle bluntly stirred me out of my contemplation, both expressing a touching affection, each in its own way. Moved by the manoeuvres of the two accomplices, who pretended to be hungry, Rosellini fed them a second time and whispered sweet Italian words to them. The cat, which spent most of its time sleeping, had passed the habit to the gazelle whose undisputed master he had become.

Our two guests of honour did not appreciate the visits of the peasants who came to the door of our royal home with sheep, goats, donkeys and hens. Neither the cat nor the gazelle could bear the intrusion, so we turned them away.

Day by day our lodgings seemed more adequate. The long gallery with a soft slope to the sanctuary was sunk in pleasant shade during the hot hours of the day. An enjoyable coolness enabled us to work easily. Following L'Hôte's advice, we piled up clothes, arms and provisions. Ramses' tomb soon looked like a thieves' cave! With our moustaches, beards, Oriental costumes and sabres, we looked like fearsome adventurers, ready to cut the throat of whoever came.

To celebrate our new arrangement, I gave a small party washed down with old Burgundy wine. We drank to the Ramses dynasty which was hosting us so cordially. To our table we invited Signor Piccini, Anastasy's agent in Thebes, whose gaiety increased ours tenfold.

After a Neapolitan joke he bent towards me. 'I have a request,' he whispered in my ear.

'I am listening.'

'Do you intend to dig?'

I hesitated to answer. Piccini's good-natured face suddenly appeared hostile and inquisitive. Was he trying to get some information to harm me? Was he an agent of Drovetti's hiding under the mask of friendship? I wanted to be clear about it in my own mind. I decided that I might as well reveal my plans and assess his reactions.

'Yes, I intend to dig.'

'Here or on both banks?'

'On both banks.'

'With whose money?'

'Mine, for the promised funds haven't arrived yet.'

'In that case, I would like to make a request. I would like you to keep my children.'

The request had been made in a trembling voice, with his head lowered.

'Your children? But how old—'

'My children . . . I mean my workmen, those who have been

digging with me for fourteen years. If you could keep them, it would be a great relief.'

I poured him a large glass of wine. 'Be reassured, Signor Piccini. Our expedition is not rich, but we will hire as many workmen as we can.'

We immediately settled the matter with Rosellini. Our finances enabled us to keep thirty-six of the Italian's 'children', who would start work the following day, under Rosellini's supervision. Piccini was moved to tears. My disciple, whose practical mind never lost its fine edge, began to give instructions, emphasizing the necessary discipline.

Nestor L'Hôte sat down beside me. 'I have the best of stories to tell you,' he said ribaldly. 'A Turk revealed to his wife a teaching he had been given at the mosque. The Imam had mentioned holiness and the sacred duties of marriage. Husbands who comply with their marital duty at nightfall, he had said, perform as meritorious a deed as if they were cutting the throat of a sheep. Those who pay a second tribute in the middle of the night perform as much in the eyes of God as if they were sacrificing a camel. The men who pay a third tribute to the holiness of their union at sunrise act as generously as if they had freed a slave. The wife, whom everybody knows is only concerned by her husband's salvation, said at nightfall: 'Let's sacrifice a sheep.' The husband obeyed and fell asleep, his duty done. But his wife woke him up in the middle of the night and said: 'Let's sacrifice a camel.' The husband obeyed for the second time and went back to sleep, exhausted. At daybreak, his faithful and religious wife warned him that the time had come . . . to free a slave. Reaching out his arms to her, he implored her: 'Now darling, I am your slave! Please free me, I beseech you.'

Once the laughter had stopped, L'Hôte addressed me gravely.' General, what kind of work do you intend to give me in the next few days?'

'We shall bury ourselves alive in the kings' tombs and study them thoroughly.'

'Have you made a choice?'

'A most appropriate one . . .'

'In other words,' retorted L'Hôte who was beginning to know me well, 'we study all of them. How long do you intend to keep me from the sunlight?'

'Three or four days—'

'Let's say at least two weeks, General, if we work quickly!'

I did not dare contradict him, he had guessed my secret intentions. Gloomy, he moved back, preferring to listen to Professor Raddi, who had launched himself into a long monologue about the classification of granite.

'To your health, Champollion!' said Lady Redgrave with a challenging look. 'May the valley of tombs favour you!'

At dawn the following day, our community of donkeys and scientists took possession of the royal necropolis of the illustrious New Kingdom pharaohs. We were fascinated by the dryness, the steep rocks, the mountains breaking in large faults created by extreme heat or inner falls, streaked with black strips as if they had been partially burnt. No living animal ever frequented this valley of death, except the flies, foxes, wolves and hyenas, which were attracted by our settlement and by the smell of our cooking.

As one enters the most remote part of the valley through a narrow, obviously man-made, opening, which still offers a few remains of Egyptian sculptures, one soon sees, at the foot of the mountains or on their slopes, square doors, most of the time blocked by rubble, with decoration which is only noticeable from close. The doors all look alike and give access to the tombs. Each tomb has its own door, for in the past none of them was related. They were isolated, and the links we saw were ones forced through by ancient or modern treasure hunters.

The unchanging guardian of the valley is a high mountain that ends in a kind of pyramid, which looks as if it had been hewn by man. It reminded me of the mother pyramid, the step pyramid of Saqqara, from which was derived all sacred architecture. The summit is the keeper of the silence which any living being penetrating the place must observe. Overlooking a petrified scene, it gives access to the landscape of the other world.

I visited the old kings of Thebes in their carved palaces. There from early morning to evening, in the light of torches, I walked through series of linked rooms covered with sculptures and paintings, most of them surprisingly fresh. I felt fully happy and reassured, as if all danger had disappeared. Each tomb expressed a particular genius and unveiled an aspect of the mystery engraved in the place. I sat on some of the remains of mummy bandages strewn around, to meditate before I explored the underground palaces. What an unspeakable emotion . . . In this Egypt built by and for eternity, I could feel in my flesh the wisdom that incorporates all aspects of life. Tombs are dug in a world that differs from our world of appearances, as if they were the dwellings of ancient gods. Perhaps the primeval power chose them in the core of the universe as an ultimate place of retreat, to sink into luminous slumber and look after the destiny of humankind.

As I penetrated for the first time one of these deep caves with Nestor L'Hôte, who held a candle, he began to tremble and stepped back, strongly impressed by representations of snakes, men with their heads cut of and phantasmagorical characters with knives.

'I won't go any further,' he said. 'It's hell.'

'It's just the beginning, Nestor, just the beginning . . . Let's go on.'

Despite his fears, my draughtsman agreed to go further into the huge tomb of Seti I, which disappeared deep into the bowels of the earth. He was soon rewarded for his courage. The most wonderful scenes appeared in the candlelight. The opening of the mouth, the crossing of the gates of the other world, the resurrection of the body of light, the vision of paradise reserved for the fair ones – the dazzling blues and reds gave us a hint of what perfection might be. I asked L'Hôte

257

to draw everything so as to have an accurate copy in our portfolios. I fumed against previous publications, which betrayed the Egyptian genius in a most scandalous way. The Egyptian commission, Gau and the British who dared publish such shapeless sketches of beautiful great compositions should be whipped publicly. L'Hôte, on the other hand, rendered with scrupulous accuracy the varied styles of monuments of different times. At the bottom of the tomb, under the great astronomical painting decorating the ceiling, I thanked him warmly for being of so much use to Egypt.

Moved, and aware of the importance of his task, his enthusiasm increased. 'The sculptures are even more refined than those we saw in temples,' he acknowledged. 'But why did they reserve such perfection for places doomed to silence and darkness?'

'Maybe because beauty can only bloom secretly,' I answered. 'Here we are not taught art as we conceive it, but we are taught the secret of eternity.'

L'Hôte was overwhelmed by the magic permeating every inch of wall. Empty rooms became alive. Figures over forty centuries old came to life under our careful gaze. Everything lived another life, untouched by human baseness.

'It is impossible to reproduce such beauty,' complained L'Hôte. 'Everything has been revealed here and is now lost.'

'I don't think so, Nestor. In their eternal dwellings the, pharaohs engraved a message of hope.'

L'Hôte walked to the empty sarcophagus. The king's mummy had disappeared. Only the spirit survived. His face lit by a flickering light, the sturdy draughtsman looked like a modern Aladdin discovering the treasure trove.

'It's a supernatural work,' he judged. 'Supernatural indeed . . .'

Leaving him to his thoughts, I stood in front of a bas-relief depicting the goddess Hathor welcoming the king. A facsimile of the incomparable masterpiece had been exhibited in Paris in 1828 at the Belzoni exhibition, but nobody had believed in the perfection of the original. This time we could force the point on the whole world that Egyptian art was far greater than the poor drawings that had been hitherto published. I called L'Hôte. 'Nestor,' I told him. 'I must commit a sacrilege. I must disfigure the tomb to help Egypt shine in Europe. Forgive as an artist and as a man of honour.'

Dumbfounded, L'Hôte was unable to utter a word.

'Give me your saw.'

The draughtsman brought me the artefact he often used as a ruler.

Carefully, with tears in my eyes, I cut the bas-relief, daring to lay a profane saw on the most accomplished Theban royal tomb. I handed it over to L'Hôte.

'Wrap it,' I said, trembling with emotion. 'I am more attached to it than to my own life. It at least must reach Paris intact.'

I was in a hurry to discover the tombs of the other Ramses. That of Ramses II had been visited ever since antiquity. Idle nosey-parkers had spoiled the walls. Like modern ones, they believed that they would become famous by scribbling their names on the paintings and bas-reliefs. Stupid people of all centuries left their mark there. First came Egyptians of all periods, who wrote initially in hieratic and then in demotic. Then, judging from the writing, there were ancient Greeks, proud republican Romans or Romanos, early imperial Romans, New Kingdom unknowns, lost in the superlatives attached to their names, Copts, who wrote humble prayers, and finally European travellers brought to these lonely tombs by their love of science, by war, by trade, by chance or by idleness.

I particularly looked forward impatiently to entering the tomb of Great Ramses, the Pharaoh who had introduced me to hieroglyphs and whose visible work was evident all over Egypt.

As soon as I entered it, I was attacked by bats. Frightened by the light of the candle, they flew in all directions, threatening to blow out the weak flame. One of them hung on my beard. I gave it a hard knock to make it loosen its grip. Once the bats had been become, I prepared myself to be dazzled by the treasures the most powerful of all kings had accumulated during his 73-year reign.

Two vipers fled before me, leaving the trace of their threatening undulations in the sand. I was not afraid of them. Or did I feel any fear when I saw a huge scorpion taking refuge in a crevice. But they still caused me acute pain: they dishonoured what should have been a splendid tomb, even though it was full of rubble almost to the ceiling.

The entrance to the funerary chamber had been blocked. I ordered two workmen to make a way thought for me.

'Don't go, General,' said L'Hôte. 'It is too dangerous. You run the risk of being bitten by one of these beasts. They have been settled here for a long time. It is now their domain. I am afraid they may have chased away the great Ramses himself.'

I refused to accept such sinister warnings. The suffocating heat was choking the workmen, however. L'Hôte could not stand it any more. 'Come with me, General. Don't stay here. There is nothing more to see. Everything has been devastated.'

Obstinately, I crawled into the narrow, painstakingly dug opening. My disappointment was devastating. Judging by the remains, the tomb had been grandly designed and decorated with fine sculptures, and a large-scale archaeological dig might have discovered the illustrious conqueror's sarcophagus. But there was no hope of finding the royal mummy because thieves and pillagers have devastated everything. Where did the great Ramses now rest? Would his corpse be recovered some day. Fate dogged his last dwelling. The huge riches it contained had disappeared. But he survived in temples and his name still illuminated the whole of Egypt.

There was a joyful bustle around the tomb of Seti I. Servants walked to and for with a succession of dishes which they arranged in proper order at the entrance of the vault, where

Rosellini stood, dressed in the latest Theban fashion for Turks.

He first welcomed Professor Raddi who wore his European suit for the occasions, then Nestor L'Hôte who had smoothed his beard and carefully trimmed his busy moustache, followed by Father Bidant, who had cleaned his cassock, and last by Lady Redgrave, who looked gorgeous in a dark red evening dress enhanced by gold jewels and by the lapis lazuli necklace I had given her as a present.

I took my guests to the heart of the tomb, where Suleiman and Moktar had set up the table. With a white tablecloth, embellished with fresh jasmine flowers, the celebration was almost worthy of our illustrious host.

I was glad to sense the guests' happiness. Fascinated by the perfection of the pictures, they respected the silence. Never had we seen a more sublime reception room. Egypt offered us one of the eternal banquets for which it was famous.

I stood up with a glass in my hand. 'I drink to the heath of Belzoni, who discovered the tomb. Without him we would not be able to share food in this exquisite resurrection dwelling.'

Deep in my heart, I also thought of the community of the Brothers of Luxor, who had opened new ways to me.

Suleiman drew the assembly's attention to a dish which I claimed was exceptional.

Everybody tasted it and was disgusted! I had wanted to offer our young people a new dish, which would enhance the party: it was a piece of young crocodile in spicy sauce, for I had unexpectedly been brought one that had supposedly been killed on the previous morning. It had, however, gone rotten and it would probably give us all indigestion.

Our good temper restored with a mutton stew which L'Hôte had cooked with loving care, I stood up again. 'I organized the celebration at which I am pleased to see our community gathered, in honour of the person who is dearest to my heart.'

Surprised, they all looked at me questioningly. Lady Redgrave held her breath.

'I mean my daughter Zoraïde. I should have celebrated her

birthday on 1 March, but there was not enough food in Nubia . . . Now we can eat as much as we want without depriving anyone.'

My guests warmly drank to her health. Thanks to the delicious food from Cairo we did not have to ration ourselves. As joyful songs burst out under L'Hôte's direction, Lady Redgrave came to me. 'You hadn't told me that you were a father . . .'

'Is your uncle's information incomplete, Lady Ophelia?'

'He does not care about your private life. His sole concern is to demonstrate that you are not a serious and credible scientist.'

'I am sorry to disappoint him.'

'You did not mention your wife, Jean-François.'

She looked at me with the tenderness she was so good at expressing. It was like a net from which the soul could not escape.

'I mentioned my daughter, whose presence I can feel here, beside me. It should be enough.'

'Forgive me for having hurt you . . . but I prefer not to have a rival for you.'

She walked away. I did not see her again face to face during the whole evening. She managed to sail from room to room, her beauty admired wherever she went.

When dawn broke we had shared jokes, memories and hopes. In my heart was the smile of a little girl. It was so warm and intense that I thought I was holding her when I closed my eyes.

'Hurry up, General!'

Waking quickly from my brief sleep, I saw L'Hôte.

'I did not want to sleep,' he explained. 'So I started work with the workmen . . . and I think I may have discovered an undescrated tomb!'

Now fully awake, I shared his enthusiasm. We hurried to the location of the find, where Rosellini, who had heard the rumour, was already awaiting us. The workmen had gathered in a dense and talkative mob, mentioned the fabulous treasures for which gangs of pillagers in the Theban region, and Drovetti's henchmen, were constantly on the look out.

A quick clearance brought to light the entrance of a small tomb, which really was undesecrated. The excitement reached a climax.

'General,' said L'Hôte passionately, 'I have a favour to ask you. I would like to go in first.'

'This is out of question,' objected Rosellini, caustically. 'You are just a draughtsman. The scientific directors of the expedition are Champollion and me. We are the only ones who are entitled to exploit an archaeological find.'

'No Italian will give orders to a Frenchman,' bellowed L'Hôte.

'That is enough,' I intervened. 'Ippolito, you will be given the artefacts we find in the tomb. As for you, Nestor, you will be the first to enter it. It will be your most beautiful memory. You've done enough for our community to enjoy this happiness.'

L'Hôte could not contain his impatience any longer. Clearing the entrance by hand, he slid a candle into the opening.

'What can you see?' I asked from outside.

'Furniture . . . and mummies, a man and a woman wearing gold masks . . . and there at their feet wheat sprouts in a hollow statue shaped like a trough . . . There are even some long stalks!'

Following L'Hôte, I recognized the symbol of the plant form of Osiris: from the body of the god emanates a new life, the resurrection of the dead grain revived by the mysterious celebrated in the tomb. There were marvellous find: sarcophagi, vases, and statuettes. A modest remnant moved me more than everything else: it was an intact shining metal disk which had been used as a mirror. It reflected the rays of the sun and bathed the faces of those who contemplated themselves in rapture.

As I left the tomb after several hours of exciting work, an imperious voice shouted at me: 'Are you satisfied, Monsieur Champollion?'

Dressed in the Turkish fashion, his moustache trimmed in large upturned curls, cheeks covered with bushy whiskers, Bernardino Drovetti, the Consul-General of France, was eyeing me with a dark and scornful look.

23

'I'm Happy, Consul-General. I am more than happy, I am mad with joy! Nubia fulfilled my hopes and much more. As for Thebes, it is a constant delight. I shall soon be able to tell you about my main discoveries. You won't regret having placed your trust in my expedition. You've still heard nothing about the funding I'm still waiting for?'

'Right, Monsieur Champollion. But I have heard that it is time to put an end to your digs. The king has told me that your return to Paris is essential.'

'Have you received an official letter?'

'Don't your trust my word?' he asked, offended.

'Of course I do. But the document concerns me personally, and I would like to see its terms. Memory is not to be trusted. When can I read the king's letter?'

'I left it in Alexandria to give you a few more days before you have to pack up. I shall await you in Cairo to prepare for your return to France.'

Without waiting for a reply, Bernardino Drovetti put an end to the conversation and strode hastily towards a group of men on horseback. He climbed on his mount and disappeared in a cloud of dust.

We had exchanged our travellers' cloaks for local attire and settled comfortably into a house in Gurnah, close to the wonderful temple of Seti I, whose relief-covered columns glowed in the sunset. Herds of goats wandered among sycamores groves and date palms. The house that had been reserved for us overlooked the road to the Valley of the Kings. We were between the world of the living, with its green fields, children's cries and *fellahin*'s derelict houses, and the world beyond, made visible on earth in its temples and tombs. There was not a blade of grass around, just stones and divine sun.

I loved the house in Gurnah as soon as I entered it and I knew that I would love it more than the most sumptuous of castles. It made me feel like working and labouring non-stop. Built on the bank of the dead, it smiled at those who were alive. Pleasant, cool and silent, it gave us the energy necessary for the next day's work. Although poor, it turned us into princes. We were all delighted by our modest bedrooms, furnished with cushions and carpets.

Rosellini, who had seen me talk to Drovetti, had a worried look. While I was arranging books and manuscripts on rudimentary bookshelves, he approached me hesitantly. 'Master . . . how long are we going to stay here?'

'As long as we can.'

'The Consul-General looked annoyed . . . Did he give any instructions?'

'Have you heard anything about them?' I asked, intrigued.

Rosellini stepped back, afraid. 'Not at all . . . It's just an impression.'

'Drovetti has his own requirements, I have mine. Only think of working and constantly improving your knowledge, Ippolito. Leave other concerns to me.'

'As you wish, Master.'

Piqued, Rosellini left my bedroom. He was replaced by Father Bidant, who asked for a meeting. 'News not too good, apparently.'

I looked at him, intrigued. 'What bad wind blew it over to you, Father?'

'Ah, Champollion! It is my duty to confess souls . . . News reaches me without my having to ask for it. And . . . Moktar's attitude is significant. He wants to see you in the utmost secrecy and entrusted me with the negotiation.'

'What about?'

'He will only confide in you. He will spend the whole day waiting for you at the Ramesseum.'

Tamarisk groves surrounded the Ramesseum, Ramses the Great's ruined temple. It was the noblest and purest of Thebes' wonderful monuments, despite the damage it had undergone. The first pylon displayed war scenes, where the representative of divine light, Pharaoh, brought the rule of chaos and darkness to an end. At the back of the first courtyard lay a broken colossus, the most gigantic ever created by Egyptian sculptors. Hewn in a single granite block, its face expressed both power and serenity. Its beauty outdid any conceivable perfection. I spent a long time stroking the formidable shoulder and thinking of the glorious time when it was still standing and contemplating the horizon where the sun rises.

I walked respectfully in the hypostyle hall, where the elegant majesty of some thirty columns would charm the eyes of the most prejudiced against architecture that is neither Greek nor Roman. There I copied the names of the great Ramses' numerous sons gathered here to celebrate their father's everlasting resurrection. Behind the hypostyle hall I discovered two small rooms with columns. On the back wall of the first one there was a wonderful image of Pharaoh sitting on his throne under a persea, a dark green tree with heart-shaped leaves. Divinities were writing the king's sacred names on them. Entering the second room, which, according to texts, had been covered with solid gold, I was greeted by two strange figures sculpted at the bottom of the door: Thoth with an ibis head holding a palette and a brush, and the goddess Seshat, the writer of divine books, who also held a palette.

I was sure that I was entering a library . . . the library of the Ramesseum, Ramses the Great's palace! The major books of Egyptian culture had been kept here. I could also see some symbols: the ear welcoming the word, the eye which is able to recreate the world, the god of speech and the god of intuition. In this room, where few people had been allowed, were details about rituals, the protection of the temple and priests' duties, lists of material goods and religious artefacts, the movements of the sun, moon, planets and stars, festivals, magic rules about the conjuration of evil forces, the protection of the divine boat, times of resurrection, and about alchemy. All the sacred science on which Egypt's daily life was based had been fathered here. It opened infinite paths of research for future Egyptologists.

Although I suddenly felt dizzy, I explored further behind the colossus, beyond a big acacia which concealed the remains of a pylon on which unfolded scenes of the battle of Kadesh against the Hittites. Abandoned by his troops, Ramses faced solitude as he was encircled by thousands of enemies. About to surrender and see civilization collapse under the barbarians' attacks, he beseeched the deity: 'My father,' he said, 'why did you abandon me? Never did I betray you.' The miracle occurred. God's spirit descended from heaven, became incarnate in Pharaoh and gave him extraordinary powers. Standing alone on his chariot, he broke the circle of his enemies, tore them to pieces and drove them to the Euphrates, in which they drowned. Fascinated by the mystical battle, I understood that Christianity had been born from ancient Egyptian thought.

Suddenly I realized that I had forgotten Moktar. Bewitched by the Ramesseum, I had let the story of living stones permeate me. He was not far away. He sat under the big acacia, smoking a long pipe. He had probably followed me with his gaze while I was walking around the temple. I sat beside him after I had brushed aside some tall grasses that concealed us completely. 'What do you want to tell me Moktar?'

'Allah is merciful . . . He reveals his faults and errors to man. He enlightened me, when I was in the wrong, especially about you. My master, Consul-General Drovetti, described you as a harmful and ambitious man, ready to do anything to quench his thirst for glory, without the slightest consideration for other men, and contemptuous of servants . . . a real jackal of the desert. But I saw the way you lived during the long journey and I discovered who you really are.'

I was dumbfounded. Could I credit his words? Could I believe in the sincerity of Drovetti's steward?

'I admire my master,' he went on. 'He gave me a house and enabled me to have a family . . . He trusted me, I trusted him, I killed for him because I thought that his orders did not contravene Allah's will. This time, it is different. You are a fair man. Only God can decide to bring the life of a fair man to an end. Nobody can pretend to substitute himself for him. I refuse to be the instrument of a fate that would not come from him. This is why I disobeyed my master for the first time. I did not attempt to murder you, nor did I tell him anything about your discoveries, your projects or your encounters. I remained silent as if nothing had happened. But my master is clever. He will soon realize that I lied to him as he lied to me. Yet if he wants it, I shall continue to serve him. There are not only friends around you. Leave Thebes as soon as possible. Your presence puts important interests in jeopardy. As for me, I shall disappear. We won't see each other again. Farewell. May Allah protect you.'

Without leaving me any opportunity to question him further, Moktar left the shade of the acacia and disappeared in the ruins of the Ramesseum.

Invisible, with his back against the forehead of the collapsed colossus, Suleiman was keeping watch.

I had only a few more days to explore Thebes, a site that reassured, bewitched and elevated me. I should have taken Drovetti's ultimatum seriously. But time did not exist any more. There were too many things to do.

The head workman had recommended me to investigate the site of Deir el Bahari. I left my collaborators to their digs and, taking advantage of a very docile donkey, I went ahead in the light early morning air.

With its unique style, the sanctuary offered a thrilling sight.

Despite the accumulation of sand, I was sure that I could identify a succession of terraces linked by a central ramp ascending towards the upright cliff. The masterbuilder who had conceived the simple and luminous plan had used the cliff as a back wall for the holy of holies, thus uniting in an indissoluble way the man-made temple and the mountain created by God.

Step by step I progressed reverently among the monuments, with their extraordinarily fine sculptures. The bas-relief were so subtle and impalpable that I had to wait for the precise time when the sun fell on them to decipher them. The slightest detail or hieroglyph, the faces of gods, the colours of their dress were just a profusion of breath-taking masterpieces. There was a divine grace her unspoiled by the activities of the early Christians. And the sand covered so many other marvels that I would never be able to have them cleared!

Another surprise awaited me: as I read the inscriptions, I was amazed to discover a king unknown in ancient lists, a pharaonically correct king with a beard, about whom words were used in the feminine gender, as if he was a queen! I spent most of the day investigating the matter and came to the indubitable conclusions that a woman called Hatshepsut had ruled over Egypt as a pharaoh, with the same rights and duties as a male sovereign. My records compelled me to change my conception of Egyptian history.

The soft light of the sunset bathed the pillars of Deir el Bahari in gold. The goddess Hathor's profile was outlined against the deep blue of the sky, taking on red and orange hues. It was the most beautiful and pure face I had ever contemplated. I was deeply moved by the softness of her features, and by a stone which had been so finely carved that it shone like a sparkling jewel. Tears came to my eyes. How had a sculptor been able to express the genius of his hand to the point of creating celestial beauty on earth?

A song arose from the roof of the temple, near the final sanctuary. It was a very sweet song relating the birth of love between a *sheikh* and a young Bedouin girl. It expressed the poetry of a desert people who, over generations from the birth of time, had transmitted stories around a fire. The voice was light and undulating. The curves of the melody followed the dramatic turns of the story. The *sheikh* had seen the young girl surreptitiously. Madly in love, he described her large black eyes, as lively as those of a gazelle, her straight and supple waist, her pomegranate-like breasts, her words as sweet as honey. Devoured by passion, the *sheikh* could no longer sleep. He struggled hard to win his beloved. He had to convince her parents, get rid of his rivals and touch the beauty's heart. But the story ended well. Hand in hand, the two young lovers headed for the tent of the girl's father to celebrate their union.

The last notes of the song faded away with the last glows of a blood red sun, which disappeared behind the mountains. For a few minutes, the bank of the dead wavered between day and night, bathed in the thousand sparkles of gold, red and purple hues blending in infinitely tender embrace.

I wanted to know to whom the bewitching voice belonged! Climbing over the scattered blocks, I saw a young Bedouin girl sitting at the foot of a column, under a capital with the head of Hathor. She was playing a little flute with a shrill sound which hardly disturbed the contemplation of the last moments of the day. In a long green dress with a white headdress surrounded by golden thread, the young Bedouin chanted a languorous old aria.

As I came nearer, I could see her fact at last. 'Lady Redgrave! Is there no metamorphosis beyond your reach!'

She continued to play the flute, as if did not exist. It would have been criminal to interrupt her. I waited till the last notes vanished, enjoying the simple pleasure of the ageless music.

'It is my favourite place,' she said, gazing at the sunset. 'Here love rules supreme. Is not its goddess the most demanding of all? Doesn't she ask us to reveal our most intimate being? Whoever refuses to trust her, only deserves death . . .'

'Is that the case for you, Lady Ophelia?'

'I have been waiting for you, Jean-François. I knew that you would come.'

'Did you ask the head of the workers to tell me about the site?'

I immediately regretted my aggressiveness. She did not answer and continued to look fixed at the horizon. 'Why do you refuse to talk about your wife?'

'Are you married, Lady Redgrave?'

The north breeze rose and brought the breath of life Pharaoh had to provide all living beings with day after day.

'Yes, I'm married.'

'Will you speak about Lord Redgrave?'

'He is a perfect man. He runs his estate, hunts, reveres God and the British crown. He doesn't make the slightest error of taste. There is nothing more to say about him.'

'Does he know that you are travelling in Egypt?'

'Lord Redgrave hates heat and I cold. This creates an insurmountable gap between us.'

'Do you have children?'

'Lord Redgrave and I only met once: on the day of our wedding. We both obtained what we wanted: he had my fortune, I had a title and freedom, the freedom to serve my country as I understood it and to travel. And you, Jean-François, what did you expect from Madame Champollion? Why do you remain bound to her?'

She walked down from her promontory to kneel before me and take my hands.

'Why do you look for anything more than the present, Lady Ophelia? Why do you demand more from life than the happiness, the temple, and the divine love which surround us?'

'Divine love is not enough for me. Until now, we have lied to each other out of fear. We have escaped . . . love, true love does not know such tricks. The temple is yours. Keep the secrets of your past, if you wish. My mission is in danger of becoming a failure . . . but what does it matter if we stay together?'

'The temple is Hathor's, the goddess of the sky. We are only transient hosts. We do not have to impose our desires.'

'What if you left science to the desert wind and agreed to be an ordinary man like everyone else?'

'It would not change anything,' I said. 'The sanctuary would remain in the celestial world and we would remain in the human one.'

She moved away abruptly. 'You are a monster!'

Seizing her flute, she broke it in two pieces and threw them away. Then she ran to the valley, which was adorned by the long thread of the Nile that shone in the last light of the day.

The following day, Rosellini insisted on leading me to the site of Amenophium, the huge funerary temple of Amenophis, the third of the name, whom the Greeks had wanted to assimilate to the Memnon of their heroic myths.

Amenophis III had been the most outstanding ruler of Thebes. He reigned over the richest city in the world. I expected his temple to be a marvel, but the disappointment was awful.

Imagine an 1800-foot long space levelled by successive deposits of the Nile, covered with long grass, whose rugged surface still revealed fragments of architraves, colossi, columns and huge bas-reliefs, which had not yet been buried by the river's silt, to be forever concealed from the curiosity of travellers. There stood over eighteen colossi, the smallest ones some 20 feet high. Made of various materials, all had been broken and we could see their huge members scattered here and there, some at ground level and others at the bottom of modern excavations. From the mutilated remains, I copied the names of a great many Asiatic people whose captive chiefs were depicted around the bases of the colossi. Greek and Latin inscriptions were far too modern for me and I ignored them to go to the nearby village of Deir el Medineh, the next Theban site to explore before the delay granted by Drovetti expired.

I had been intrigued by Deir el Medineh for a long time.

Numerous artefacts from there had passed through my hands. Rosellini had purchased a large number of them for his museum. He and L'Hôte came with me. We progressed slowly, at the pace of our donkeys. Behind came Suleiman and a dozen workmen, ready to clear the entrance to a tomb or a sanctuary.

L'Hôte came alongside me. 'General, you are hiding something from me. You don't do that usually. It must be serious.'

'What do you think, Nestor?'

'Threats. You've received new threats. People are plotting against you and you refuse to accept it. Why do you refuse my help?'

'Because I don't now anything about these intrigues, except that they have been instigated by Drovetti, probably with the Pasha's consent.'

'Where is Moktar?'

'He left the expedition on his own initiative. We won't see him again.'

'What do you intend to do?'

'Nothing except working and digging. We came back from Nubia, where the worst dangers awaited us, safe and sound. Thebes should not be more dangerous. Be trustful, Nestor . . . and beware.'

Nestor grumbled, turned his head and walked away.

The peaceful caravan took a narrow footpath that led to a barren ravine overlooked by rocks. In a hollow had been built workers' houses, now almost buried in the sand. A small temple surrounded by a wall dominated the desert on the edge of which grew a mimosa. On a branch a bird was singing.

From the temple's entrance, I could see again the desert where the soul unfolds to meet God in an immediate and pure way. The trivialities of life disappeared. Part of the veil shrouding the mystery of life was lifted and I had a glimpse of the nature of montionless eternity, so similar to that of the dunes.

As I entered the workmen's temple, where all the great

Egyptian architects were depicted, another veil fell from my mind. I understood that the arts of ancient Egypt did not aim to represent the beautiful shapes of nature. They intended to express only a certain set of ideas. They were not to perpetuate the memory of forms, but the memory of people and things. The huge colossus was the immutable sign of an idea as much as the tiniest amulet. Whatever their degree of finesse, their goal had been achieved. The perfection of forms was only secondary, whereas forms had been everything in Greece, where art was cultivated for itself. In Egypt it was just a powerful means of depicting thought. The tiniest adornment of Egyptian architecture was a straightfoward expression of the idea behind the construction of the whole building, whereas the embellishments of Greek and Roman temples all too often only appealed to the eye, without touching the mind. The genius of these people was fundamentally different. In Greece writing and the arts of imitation were separated early and for ever. But in Egypt, writing, drawing, painting and sculpture constantly developed towards the same aim. If we considered the peculiar state of each of these arts and their purpose, it was adequate to say that they blended into a single art, the art of writing. Temples, as is indicated by their Egyptian name, were, as it were, just magnificent large characters representing celestial dwellings. Statues, images of kings and individuals, bas-reliefs and paintings depicting scenes of public and private life came into the category of figurative characters. Images of gods, emblems of abstract ideas, embellishments and allegorical paintings, and the long series of hieroglyphs were directly related to the symbolic principle of writing.

Egypt wrote life.

It also wrote my life.

In Deir el Medineh the world beyond appeared in the poignant scene of the weighing of the soul, taken to be the heart by ancient people, and thought to be the measure of true conscience of man. The great judge Osiris stood at the back of a chapel I lit with a candle. At the foot of his throne rose the lotus, the symbol of the material world, topped by an image of the God's four children, the ruling genii of the four points of the compass. Osiris' forty-two judges sat in two rows. On a pedestal at the front of the throne stood the Egyptian Cerberus, a threefold crocodile, lion and hippopotamus monster, which opened a wide mouth to threaten guilty souls . . . Somewhat further on stood the scales of hell. The gods Horus, Isis' son with a sparrowhawk head, and Anubis, the son of Osiris with a jackal head, put on one side of the scales the man's heart, and on the other an ostrich feather, the symbol of justice. Between the fatal instrument, which had to decide over the fate of the soul, and Osiris' throne stood Thoth, the ruler of divine words. The divine scribe wrote the result of the test undergone by the dead Egyptian's heart and presented his report to the supreme judge.

Despite the surrounding darkness, Rosellini could feel my uneasiness. 'Are you all right, master?'

'Leave me alone, Ippolito.'

'Are you sure that you don't need me?'

'Go away as I ask.'

'When should I come back to fetch you?'

'Go back to Gurnah and don't worry about me. I shall copy the texts and scenes. I'll make sure I complete everything. I just need absolute silence to listen to my ancestors' voice.'

I had moved out of time. I spent five days there, consumed by my work, eating what Suleiman brought me in the evening.

I faced my death and my own judgement. I had learnt the list of faults which could condemn one to a 'second death', and to the annihilation of the soul, and I had confessed mine to the God Thoth and the goddess Maat, the keeper of universal order.

Tearing myself away from the shrine, where an immutable destiny had now been sealed, without taking the slightest rest, I went to the temple of Medinet Habu, where Nestor L'Hôte was proceeding to a general record under Rosellini's instructions.

'How did my disciple bear my absence?' I asked Suleiman.

'Both well and unwell.'

'Well?'

Because he was able to manage the workmen.'

'And . . . unwell.'

'He takes himself to be you. He believes himself to be a boss. As he steps aside from what he believes to be his rightful position, he deviates from truth and he will eventually hate you.'

'You are too severe Suleiman.'

'And you are too generous.'

The vision of the huge temple of Medinet Habu, the greatest in Egypt after Karnak, brought an end to our conversation. Once again, I was captivated by Egypt. Ramses, Amon's beloved, the third of the name and the successor of the great Ramses, had created the huge building, in front of which was gigantic pylon and a royal pavilion with a unique shape.

Carried away by my enthusiasm, I walked for several hours to try to understand this new universe, which was a summary of monumental Egypt. Here, almost buried under the remains of private houses, built on top of each other for centuries, were a number of very important monuments. They were among the greatest historical memories, demonstrating the state of the arts in all major periods of Egyptian history. Here superimposed on each other was a temple of the most glorious period, that of the Eighteenth Dynasty, a huge palace of the conquerors' time, a building from the first period of Egypt's decadence under the Ethiopian invasion, a shrine erected by one of the princes who broke the Persian yoke, a propylon from the Greek dynasty, a roman propylaea and, most recently, in the courtyard of the pharaonic palace, columns which used to support the roof of a Christian church.

Thirsty, I saw a group of Bedouins sitting in the first great courtyard. They would not refuse to give me water if they had some. Considered as a gift of God, it did not belong to men. Whoever asked for it should be satisfied. A few steps away from them, I saw a snake charmer and his assistants. The man was old, with a pockmarked face. Around his torso and his neck coiled and uncoiled a viper with a flat head. In front of him was a big basket from which emerged two cobras who stood erect on his command. One of the assistants was a woman, who knelt on a dusty carpet with a child in her arms.

I was offered water by a young boy while the magician continued to charm his cobra, which everybody seemed to consider as harmless. Only Suleiman looked worried. To be honest, the unusual performance appeared more like a taming exercise than a magic session. I was most interested in the incantations the man constantly repeated in a low voice. Careful not to disturb the cobras, I came near and bowed to him so as to hear him better. Suleiman followed me like a shadow.

The trap worked.

Frightened, the cobras nestled in their basket. But the viper left its master's neck and stretched out at lightning speed. Paralysed, I closed my eyes and waited for the fatal bite. I did not feel anything but I heard the noise of people rushing away in flight.

When I opened my eyes again, I saw the snake charmer, his assistants and the woman with the baby running as fast as their legs could carry them. They had left the basket with the cobras. Suleiman lay face down on the ground, holding the viper he had caught by the neck a few inches away from his face. It was coiled around his arm.

'Find a stick,' he said calmly, 'and crush its head.'

Intrigued by the commotion, a Bedouin did so. Suleiman stood up and dusted himself off.

'I was afraid of some trap of the kind,' he said. 'Snake charmers don't work here usually. It would be better to go away.'

'Don't think of it! That is impossible as long as we haven't explored everything . . . This is an extraordinary temple.'

Resigned, Suleiman followed me as I headed for the strange

tower of Medinet Habu, which appeared to be the only royal palace preserved in a temple.

It was a pleasure to walk up the stairs to the royal apartments after the danger I had escaped. I admired frescoes painted by a genius, glorifying birds playing among papyrus clumps, blue and pink lotus flowers and flying ducks. The king and the queen would have spent happy days here surrounded by their children and their intimates, without ever forgetting the nearby sacred temple with its immutable presence.

Then I climbed up the inner staircase of the great pylon, whose reassuring mass had turned Medinet Habu into a refuge from pillagers a long time after the extinction of the pharaonic dynasties. From the roof, I had a striking view over the Thebes region. To the east stretched the green cultivated areas, the Nile, the Luxor colonnades, and the Karnak obelisks and pylons; to the north the Ramesseum, Deir el Medineh, the huge necropolis with the districts of Gurnet Murai, Dra Abu el-Naga, Gurnah and Deir el Bahari, and in the west, the Valley of the Queens and the Libyan cliff. I was overwhelmed by this universe and filled with an intense joy which tore me away from myself and my individual limitations. How could I think of death and of the past in the face of so much light and life? How could I remain insensitive in the face of so much magic pervading the smallest block and the humblest statue?

Suleiman sat beside me. 'This is the true reality,' he said. 'Our eyes hardly see it.'

'It should also be deciphered, Suleiman and thoroughly understood. All this is a symbol of the world beyond, our true homeland. I want to pass on what I perceive. I want to offer other people the opportunity of following this path.'

We were both aware that the task would overwhelm us. We granted ourselves the selfish pleasure of enjoying the incomparable sight, oblivious of everything else.

As we left the temple at sunset, children surrounded us. They were all trying to sell us a scarab, an amulet, a statuette, crude imitations, hastily produced in a workshop which was unable to reproduce true Egyptian beauty.

A little girl stood aside. Despite her rags she had a touching charm. The purity of her face recalled that of the goddesses. Indifferent to her companions' commercial transactions, she was playing with a blackish artefact. Breaking the circle of traders, I looked over her head.

She was playing with the dry hand of a mummy.

Beyond horror, my mind was enlightened, and at that moment I understood why I was really in danger.

24

I gathered the members of the expedition in the living room of our house in Gurnah. They were all aware that I had important news to break.

'My friends, the Consul-General of France had given me very little time before I have to leave Thebes. It is probably already over, but nothing has happened. We have received no official order, and I'm still awaiting the promised funds. We have explored sites and set up a plan of archaeological digs for the next centuries.'

'This is perfect,' concluded Father Bidant. 'As God has favoured us, let's not tempt the devil. Let's go back to Cairo and prepare ourselves to head for Christian ground at last.'

'Nobody knows where Drovetti is,' said Lady Redgrave. 'People even wonder if he has not left Egypt.'

'A man like him does not admit defeat so easily.' said L'Hote. 'You held him up to ridicule, General. He is preparing his retaliation. Father Bidant is right: let's consider ourselves fortunate to have survived so many dangers. Let's thank providence and go back home.'

'That sounds like reasonable advice,' approved Rosellini. 'We must make an inventory of the artefacts we have discovered. Only in Europe shall we be able to work properly.'

Only Professor Raddi did not give his opinion. He had gathered his day's harvest, a dozen butterflies he was examining carefully.

'Your words are full of good sense,' I said. 'They are reasonable, nor would I consent to be. I still have an essential task to perform: I must go back to the tombs.'

Sighs of exasperation arose from the assembly. I had expected such a reaction. Work in the tombs would not be easy. We would have to find more energy and put up with bodily suffering to discover the splendours of the sacred vaults.

'Why carry on?' asked Father Bidant, surprised. 'Haven't you seen enough sepulchres? I saw two with Lady Redgrave. That was enough. It was difficult to move. There was no air and I felt mummified and almost dead with heart.

'And you have no idea of the ordeal imposed on the draughtsman!' added L'Hôte. 'The light is dim, you get dust in your eyes, and you have to adopt positions which make your back ache, not to mention the tension you constantly need to avoid errors . . .'

'That is rather unfair, Nestor! Are you forgetting the messages we saw, the transcendent concepts we perceived? Egyptian spirituality hides old truths, which we believe to be very young. We need your representations. I must discover all the symbols to find the key to the enigma.'

'What enigma are you referring to?' asked Father Bidant.

'The meaning of life.'

'Come on, Champollion . . . do you really believe that this dead religion could be superior to our faith in any way?'

'Monsieur Champollion is not called "the Egyptian" for nothing,' intervened Lady Redgrave.

'Bossuet, whose sound Christianity you won't contest,' I said to Father Bidant 'only dreamed of studying Egyptian theology. That had to wait until our time, and nobody will prevent me from completing the task.'

'It's useless to oppose the Egyptian's will,' said Lady Redgrave enigmatically. 'It is stronger than all our wills together.'

Dumbfounded by this unexpected assistance, I smiled at Lady Redgrave, who remained stonily indifferent.

*

'I am exhausted, Master,' said Rosellini. 'I would have been happy to come with you, but I have no more strength.'

'Take a rest, Ippolito, and begin your inventory as soon as possible.'

At dawn I left the house in Gurnah, whose other occupants were still asleep. My disciple went back to his bedroom, yawning. As for me, I was endowed with an almost inexhaustible energy, which only three or four hours of sleep full of hieroglyphic dreams were enough to restore.

Outside, two donkeys were waiting for me with Nestor L'Hôte, the only adventurer who had not yet given up. 'Which tomb shall we first visit, General?'

'That of Ramses IV.'

What bliss to be up at dawn, moving slowly along a desert path to a sacred place where wise men discovered everything about the transfiguration of the human soul! The ancient words of the salutation hymn to the rising sun naturally came to my lips. Was it not right for the creature to thank its creator for such moments of happiness?

Hardly had we settled in the tomb than L'Hôte burst into a violent temper. 'My God, hieroglyphs are so boring! We are all fed up with them . . . I am like a man who walks on fire and only has a quarter of an hour more to live! I'm fed up, General. Your Egypt is not mine. I need rain, green and humid plains, coolness. I'm leaving.'

'And where are you going, Nestor?'

'To France. Keep my drawings. And may God protect you, General, if you are still a little Christian. You are the best of men, that's for sure, but I wonder whether you are still living among men. The Egyptian . . . yes, that's right . . . you've become an ancient Egyptian.'

Dropping his pencils and his portfolio in the sand, L'Hôte climbed on his donkey and left the Valley of the Kings in a cloud of dust.

So he was abandoning me. I knew that I would not see him

again. I had liked the man's faithfulness, his juvenile strength and trust. I did not feel any resentment, for I was convinced that he had not betrayed me.

He was not wrong. Egypt had made me understand that I was only a passer-by on this earth, a stranger in search of the original light in which all beings originate and in which they will all be united again beyond the ordeal of death.

I was entering death as I progressed further into the depths of the royal tomb.

Complete solitude brought me a power of concentration I had never experienced before. Ideas, translations, and interpretations constantly came to my mind spontaneously. I was penetrated in my life by that other world depicted on the walls of the tomb, I experienced in my flesh the symbolic journey indicated by divinities with whom I had established a brotherly relationship.

A hundred times I almost lost consciousness. A hundred times I overcame fatigue and suffocation. A hundred times I experienced the journey of the soul. After a fairly simple door, I entered large galleries or corridors covered with perfectly refined sculptures, largely retaining the vividness of bright colours, and leading to rooms with even more decorated pillars, until I eventually reached the main room, which the Egyptians called the 'golden room'. It was more spacious than the others and in the middle lay the king's mummy in a huge granite sarcophagus. The plans of the tombs published by the Egyptian commission give an accurate idea of the scale of excavations and of the immense pick and chisel work they required. Almost all the valleys are full of mounds of little stone splinters from the impressive works inside the mountain.

The royal tombs' decoration had been systemized and what I found in one of them could be found in almost all the others. The top of the entrance door was usually embellished with a bas-relief which was actually just a preface or a summary of what followed: a yellow disc in the middle of which was the sun with a ram head, that is to say the setting sun entering the lower hemisphere and worshipped by the kneeling king. To the right of the disc, that is to say the east, stood the goddess Nephyts 'the ruler of the sacred place' and to the left (west) the goddess Isis, at the two ends of the God's journey in the upper hemisphere. Near the sun was carved a huge scarab, here as elsewhere the symbol of regeneration or successive rebirths. The king knelt on the celestial mountain, on which the two goddesses' feet also rested.

The general meaning of the composition referred to the dead king. In his lifetime, like the sun which moves from east to the west, the king had to give life to Egypt and enlighten it. He had to be the source of all necessary earthly and spiritual goods for its inhabitants. Therefore the dead pharaoh was naturally compared with the setting sun descending to the dark lower hemisphere, through which he had to travel to be reborn in the east to restore light and life in the superior world (where we live). Similarly, the dead king had to be reborn either to pursue his transmigrations or to live in the celestial world and be engulfed in the womb of the universal father Amon.

The secret of life was taught by the movement of the divine boat on the celestial river, on the primeval liquid, the principle of all existence, during the twelve hours of the day. At the first hour, the boat set off and received the eastern spirits' devotion. Among depictions of the second hour figured the great snake Apophis, the sun's brother and enemy. In the third hour the sun god reached the celestial region where the fate of souls was decided in relation to the bodies they would dwell in for their next transmigration. The creator sat in court, weighing the human souls that came to him. One of them had just been sentenced. It was brought back to earth in a boat moving towards a gate kept by the jackal god Anubis, led and being beaten by monkeys, the emblems of celestial justice. The culprit was depicted in the shape of a huge pig, above which had been engraved 'greed' in large characters. In the fifth hour, the God visited the paradise where blessed souls rested from the pains and ills of their journey on earth. On their heads

285

they wore ostrich feathers, the emblems of fair and virtuous behaviour. They made offerings to the gods or, under the supervision of the lord of the heart's joy, they picked fruit from celestial trees. Further along other souls held sickles to cultivate the fields of truth. The caption said: 'They indulge in water libations and offerings of grain from the glorious country. They hold sickles and harvest the fields allotted to them. The sun god tells them: Take grain to your homes, enjoy it and make pure offerings to the gods.' Elsewhere I could see them bathing, swimming, jumping and frolicking in a huge basin full of primeval celestial water, under the Nile god's supervision. In the later hours the gods prepared to fight the sun's great enemy, the snake Apophis. They armed themselves with pikes and took nets because the monster lived in the river.

Souls that had been sentenced, their hands bound on their chests and their heads cut off, walked in long lines. Some of them, their hands tied behind their backs, dragged their hearts, which had been taken from their chests. In large boilers souls were burnt alive, either in their human shape or in the shape of birds, or just as heads and hearts.

In each place, I could read the torture victims' sentences. 'Evil souls do not discern the rays of the sun god. They do not live in the terrestrial world any more, nor hear the voice of the great god when he goes through the area.' On the opposite walls, where blessed souls had been depicted I could read: 'They found favour with the great god. They live heavenly life in glorious dwellings. The body they left behind will rest forever in their tombs, while they enjoy the supreme god's presence.'

This is one of the thousand proofs against those who persist in believing that Egyptian thinking was improved by the Greeks. I am positive: Egypt is indebted only to itself for the greatest, purest and most beautiful things it produced. Whether scientists who make a religion of believing in the spontaneous generation of arts in Greece like it or not, the truth is different. Greece slavishly imitated Egypt when the first Egyptian colonies came in contact with people from Attica and the

Peloponnese. Without the pharaohs' civilization, Greece would not have become the classical land of fine arts. This is my belief on this major issue. I wrote these lines in front of bas-reliefs the Egyptian made with genius two millennia before the Christian era. Egypt is the mother of our civilization, the origin of our thinking in its highest and the most crucial dimensions.

I was absorbed in the study of a fascinating painting representing the birth of a new sun, of a new consciousness, when some stones hurtled down the slope to the vault. Someone had just entered the tomb.

A strange feeling pierced my heart. I was afraid, yet without feeling the slightest fear. I was both afraid of my existence being interrupted before I had done enough work, and absolutely calm at the prospect of dying in this dwelling of resurrection. What could I expect from life after all the revelations that detach man from himself, blend him with the cosmos and dissolve him in the stars?

The steps came closer, slow and heavy. I expected to see a merciless being from the world beyond with a knife, asking for explanations and making a list of my faults.

I was ready. I understood that the faith of ancient Egyptians relied on knowledge and not on belief. It was no use believing in gods, but it was essential it know them, give them a name and discover what creative power they represented. Hieroglyphs were in fact the words of power which accessed the necessary knowledge.

What demon would appear? Would I be able to defeat it just by giving it a name? In a few seconds it would stand before me . . . I felt a lump in my throat. My heart pounded wildly, but I remained serene, although the thought of Drovetii's killers came to my mind.

The visitor eventually appeared in the candlelight. Father Bidant.

He shook his dusty cassock and sat on a stone bench along the wall. He wiped his forehead.

'Damned heat . . . How can you breathe in this steam bath?'

'Look, Father, look around you! You will see hell, purgatory and paradise! What Christianity announced already existed here and much more!'

I expected a dramatic reaction, but the priest continued to mop his forehead with a handkerchief.

'This is exactly what I have been afraid of, Champollion . . . this and the rest. Before our journey, the Catholics and the Protestants agreed on one point: never should Biblical chronology be upset. Never should Christian revelation be questioned. Nobody should know the traces of civilization before the sixteenth Egyptian dynasty. In this way the Holy Book's truth would remain complete and absolute, including its historical view.'

'I am now able to prove the contrary, Father. The chronology recognized by the Church is wrong. You will have to date the appearance of thinking much further back in time. People will have to admit that the Bible could not have existed without Egyptian inspiration.'

'I know all that, Champollion. I also know that your discoveries will cause troubles you can't even imagine.'

'You don't talk like a priest any more . . .'

'Because I am not just a priest. I have been studying orientalism for many years in Rome and keeping up with your works as well as with that of other scientists who want to decipher hieroglyphs. I judged very quickly that you would be the first to reach the goal the Church is afraid of. Why did you need to lift the thick veil that covered mysteries that had been forgotten for centuries?'

'The answer is on the walls of this tomb, Father! The secret of the human soul, that's what the Egyptians understood!'

Bidant nodded. 'I began to worry when, as a teenager, you declared, and later wrote, that Egypt had an idea of divinity which was at least as pure as that of Christianity. It was a challenge to faith which nobody ever took seriously enough. And you have now deciphered hieroglyphs . . . you open the gates of several millennia of religion through which will pass gods and goddess.'

'That was not a challenge, Father. Just a simple truth.'

'Don't play with words, Champollion! Haven't you made it clear that the Egyptians believed in a unique god and in the immortality of the soul? Won't you write tomorrow that the meaning of human life is to be united with God after a trial at the court of the other world?'

'It is my duty to describe what I have seen. This is the scientific ethic.'

'You're not an ordinary scientist any more. You are the Egyptian.'

'And what about you, Father. Are you a spy in the service of Drovetti?'

Father Bidant stopped mopping his forehead for a while and looked at me for along time with interest. 'You also understood that . . . You are definitely much less naive than my superiors thought.'

'I had an intuition the first time I met you . . . And the beginning of a confirmation when you acted as an intermediary between Moktar and me. On the other hand I want to be certain of the sincerity with which you expressed yourself in Nubia. I believed you.'

'You were right . . . but you have become my worst enemy, Champollion. You almost upset my beliefs. I even almost killed you when I insanely shot at you. That is why the time has come for me to move away from you and Egypt as soon as possible. God knows what inner turmoils you would make me endure if I had to hear you talk about your gods and your religion. Although the old divinities are dead and confined to the depths of tombs, I sometimes wonder whether they are not more powerful than some of our dogmas. Champollion? Are you listening to me, Champollion? Champollion!'

The sun was at its zenith when Father Bidant left the tomb of Ramses IX, panting under the weight of the unconscious Jean-François Champollion on his shoulders.

25

On 18 May 1829, on the summit overlooking the Valley of the Kings, I have been thinking of you, my brother Jacques-Joseph and writing to you. Forgive my feverish and hasty handwriting. I had to tell you everything and yet there was so little time, considering the immense task awaiting me! I have recovered from my faintness in the tomb of Ramses IX. Father Bidant, who took me to Professor Raddi so that he could heal me with his hands and magnetism, has left Egypt. He did not bid farewell to anyone and slipped out in a great hurry.

I haven't heard anything about what is happening in the world, nor for weeks about you and those whom I love. It has been difficult, very difficult. For, despite my philosophy and the fact that the emptiness of human concerns is written everywhere around me in powerful characters, despite the fact that I meditate from time to time on the summit of the barren mountain overlooking the great body of Thebes, I am still attached to this poor earth, to its insignificant inhabitants and mainly to those who shiver with cold on the other side of the Mediterranean . . . in France! Let's not mention it, it makes my heart ache . . . yet I must confess that my mind will have no other home than the Valley of the Kings, where I immersed itself in the mysteries of life and death. I must now leave my dear tombs, dwellings of resurrection, to meet Rosellini.

You should consider me as a newly revived man. I have been living in these underground palaces where one does not really care about secular matters for many days. I shall now live in our chateau in Gurnah, a mud-brick one-storey house, which looks magnificent in comparison to the dens and furrows in which our friends, the Arabs, nest. But I shall only stay there at night. As soon as dawn breaks, I shall get up, climb on my donkey and go slowly along the paths, breathing in the morning coolness in search of the numerous tombs I know to be still buried in the sand. Rosellini wants to persuade me that I am exhausted and wearing out my body. Don't believe a word of that. I hope that I shall prove to you that I am still capable of achieving great things.

The Gurnah headquarters had a certain elegance now that Rosellini, who had an acute sense of administration, had arranged them. A dozen servants, supervised by a dragoman called Boutros, looked after our slightest wishes, for we were the lords of the country. The dragoman was a military-looking steward who more or less knows four or five European languages which he happily mixed up. He was ruthless to his subordinates, ready to steal anything that fell under his hand, completely servile, careful about food and wine so as to take the best advantage of savoury dishes and good wines. He knew how to make other people work without sweating himself. He let out heart-rending sighs to show his sympathy when he saw us tired, and yet inertly despised us. He lied with a smile on his face. He was a brigand within the limits of his own moral standards.

In my absence, Rosellini had set up a rigid schedule: he woke up at six, did scientific work from seven to twelve, had lunch and rested till two, and worked again until four. It was real museum director's schedule, but that did not bother me. As soon as the day's tasks were completed, I left the chateau and mounted a donkey with a saddle and a bridle which was waiting for me by the door, under the watch of two Arabs who were chasing flies away. In the company of Suleiman, who was still worried, I granted myself the rare pleasure of working leisurely in the Theban necropolis, and filling my heart with the silent landscapes I now knew to be landscapes of the soul.

One evening, as I came back from my usual ride, I arrived just in time to see a fight between Professor Raddi and Rosellini. Both clumsy, they were no danger to each other, but I thought such a struggle unworthy of two scientists and energetically interposed myself between them.

'Gentleman! Are you crazy?'

'Monsieur Champollion,' declared Professor Raddi emphatically. 'Rosellini prevents me from doing my scientific work. This is unacceptable and I request you, as the chief of our expedition, to punish the troublemaker.'

Rosellini was flushed with anger. 'The professor is mad!' he bellowed. 'He decided to turn the house into a zoo! Our gazelle Pierre and the cat are not enough for him. He has just introduced a donkey, a cock, a goat and some lizards, not to mention a baby panther he found God knows where, which has just used its claws on my inventory notebook! It is unbearable!'

'He is exaggerating,' objected the mineralogist. 'Anyway I don't recognize his authority.'

'And what about your butterfly collections?' Rosellini went on. 'The bugs are now littering all the bedrooms! Champollion will even find some in his own!'

'Science always progressed thanks to martyrs,' stated Professor Raddi, turning his back on Rosellini. 'Things being what they are, I'll leave this wretched house and settle at a native's. My collections will grow despite ignorance and intolerance. Even today, I know I'll catch specimens so rare it will shut you up.'

With great dignity, and with a butterfly net in his hand, the Professor left to hunt.

'I am sorry,' said Rosellini, whose anger was now subsiding. 'But I can't stand him any longer.'

Each evening, on my return from my walk with Suleiman, with whom I shared silent emotions, I received important and unimportant Theban dignitaries in the 'reception' room of our Gurnah palace. Despite Rosellini's hostility to such meetings, which he deemed to be useless, I regarded them as extremely important. Neither Professor Raddi, who came back to sleep in Gurnah in between his hunting parties, nor Lady Redgrave, who indulged in long rides in the countryside, attended them.

Usually the village *sheikhs* told me about their complaints and asked me to intervene with the highest local authorities to get more food or clothes. I did my best for them and asked them, in exchange, to find me some good workers. Once again ignoring Rosellini's opinion, I entrusted the *sheikhs* with money so that they could pay the men who came to work on my excavations. The system worked wonderfully, all the more so because I did not hesitate to give numerous little presents to the small potentates, who were happy to see their importance thus acknowledged. This was actually the truth, because archaeological digs would have been impossible without their consent. Of course they kept a significant share of the sum I distributed, but on the other hand, they ensured order and security.

One day I had dealt with the usual matters. Only a silent old *sheikh* with a beard remained. He had been waiting for me, motionless, for over an hour.

'Forgive me for having imposed this ordeal on you,' I said, with a feeling that the meeting would differ from the other ones.

'My tribe and I have been waiting for centuries. One more hour is not even the blink of an eye in the light of eternity.'

The man was fierce and proud. I was intrigued by his speech. 'What is the name of your tribe?'

'I belong to the Ababdeh, the noblest and the most courageous of tribes.'

'May God favour it and keep it prosperous!'

The Ababdeh language was one of the most ancient and extraordinary tongues. I had only studied it superficially and I was grateful for the opportunity for such a conversation, which I wanted to last as long as possible.

'Do you know Egypt well?' he asked inquisitively.

'As well as a few months here and a forty year passion enable me to know it.'

'Why do you help the *fellahin*?'

'Because they are men, like you and me, and because it is a most unworthy vice to believe yourself superior to anyone.'

He made a doubtful face. 'Do you know that they are lazy, lie and often despise your generosity?'

'I don't care. I act according to my conscience. And I know that they live under wretched circumstances whereas the Pasha's innumerable villas are lit with gas and have the latest comfort. I am outraged by this. The role of a head of state is to offer his subjects the opportunity of living in freedom and happiness. You can't do that in poverty. It is the enemy of civilization. In Pharaoh's realm, there could be no celebration as long as anyone suffered famine.'

'This is rather dangerous talk,' stated the Bedouin.

'They are just words of justice. People won't make me keep quiet.'

'Our existence hasn't changed since the time of Abraham,' said the Bedouin. 'We live in the desert and we were prosperous until the arrival of the Mamelukes. Our tribe shed blood to fight them. When Mehmet Ali took power he used us and relied on our support. He is now as cruel a tyrant as those he executed. As for us, immemorial sons of sand and wind, he deigned to grant us a right of asylum on Egyptian territory. As you listen so readily to *fellahin*'s petitions, you may want to listen to my tribe?'

This was becoming a delicate issue. Bedouins did not have much sense of fun. To them a word that had been given could not be taken back under any pretext. The *sheikh*'s nobleness made up my mind.

He was able to read it in my gaze. 'Come with me to our camp,' he requested. 'I shall explain my plan.'

I was greeted like lord in the tent of the Ababdeh chief. Two silent young girls, as bright as lightning, offered me honey cakes, dates, figs and mint tea.

My host waited until we were full before continuing our conversation.

'We fought the Mamelukes. We shall now fight the new despot.'

'How?' I asked.

'With our courage, our sabres, and rifles that will be sold to us, that you will sell us.' I was staggered.

'But . . . I am no arms merchant.'

'That is not what we were told.'

'Who dared accuse me?'

'Someone who claims to know you well,' said the Bedouin as he stood up and introduced Lady Redgrave into the tent.

She ran to me, full of passion.

'What stories have you been making up, Lady Ophelia?'

'These people want to rebel against the Pasha, Jean-François. That is a fair cause! They need us, our two countries and the support we must give them. Don't waver any longer.'

The Bedouin and the British spy were staring at me gravely.

'This is sheer madness! I am just an Egyptologist, but I can assure you that you are heading for disaster if you try to fight the Pasha's troops. He will crush you without mercy and annihilate the whole tribe. You underestimate his cruelty. He is totally attached to his absolute authority and reacts with extreme violence to the slightest threat to his throne.'

'Show yourself as you really are,' insisted Lady Redgrave. 'You proved a hundred times that you cared for the poor and destitute people's lot. You have no right to abandon these men. Give them something to fight with and triumph, as I do.'

Anger swept through me. 'So that was your mission. You were to stir up the Bedouin tribes to overthrow the Pasha or compel him to call on Great Britain for help . . . Even if I was able to do so, I would never join in such a criminal plan. You would send entire families to their death. Their sole protection is the desert where the Pasha's troops do not venture easily. You would destroy a precarious balance to generate a turmoil in which as usual the weakest would be the victims. This is infamous!'

'You're just a coward!' cried Lady Redgrave. 'I shall manage on my own.'

She left the tent of the Ababdeh chief, who sat like an old scribe, his legs crossed. My fate was in his hands. A single word from him could send me to my death. He clapped his hands.

The two servants brought more tea and sweets.

'There is a time for anger,' he said. 'And a time for joy, as my thoughts are now clear again, let's enjoy this friendly drink together.'

A long silence ensued. I knew I should not interrupt it at any cost.

'Lady Redgrave was most convincing,' he continued at last. 'I think she would even have fought with us. Her feelings for you are so strong that she was certain she would convince you. You rebuffed her and hurt her pride.'

'Did I behave like a coward to you?'

'These honey cakes are our sweetest pleasure. My father, my father's father and their forbears savoured them. In the evening, when men are silent, the desert begins to sing. This is right. This is God's will. And it is only right that it should continue. Mehmet Ali will disappear, but the desert won't. You reminded me of this truth. You saved my tribe from madness.'

We did not say anything more. When there was only one honey cake left on the silver tray, Allah's share, the two servants came back and knelt on each side of the entrance of the chief's tent. The latter stood up.

Our meeting was over.

As I bent to leave, he spoke again. 'A gift for a gift, such is our law . . . I have a piece of news to give you. Drovetti has been back in Thebes for several days. He is spying on you. If you care for your life, leave. But if you want to prevent him from harming other people, look for the tomb of the vines.'

Under the rule of the pharaohs, Egypt was a great civilization of the vine. The ancient people enjoyed famous vintages which were given the names of rulers and the year of their reign. To enjoy a 'Ramses the Great, twelfth year' was probably a event of the greatest importance in the banqueting lives of Theban nobleman. Then Islam rooted out the stocks, even those on tombs. Yet the Bedouin's clue meant that he knew the location of one. He refused to tell more, for he had deliberately chosen to put me to the test. I therefore had to prove to him that I was an able researcher in such matters.

Our chateaux in Gurnah enjoyed an almost constant temperature of 95°F, which was a real blessing for my health. Rosellini suffered from it, however, for he enjoyed the morning warmth, as soft as a spring breeze, and the cooling north wind which often blew at noon and in the evening. Outside the temperature often rose above 123°, which turned the examination of steles, sarcophagi and statues, which my disciple recorded with his usual meticulousness, into a harassing task.

I walked with Suleiman around the necropolis. We talked in vain of vines and grapes with the *fellahin* we met.

'We won't achieve anything this way,' said Suleiman. 'It must be a tomb that was filled after it had been plundered. Let's question the old people, village by village. We might find one of them who remembers some detail which will put us on the right track.'

After several fruitless attempts, we were told that a 110-year-old man from Sheikh Abdel Gurnah, behind the Ramesseum, could tell us about most illicit archaeological digs in the area – he might actually have arranged them himself. We met him on the bank of the Nile, where he was watching over the children bathing in a place he knew to be devoid of crocodiles, still the cause of numerous deaths in areas they infested. The man was antagonistic and sour-tempered. A large amount of tobacco was necessary to loosen his tongue. With infinite slowness he recalled his memories. There was indeed a tomb with the remains of a vine. He drew a rough map of the necropolis of Sheikh Abdel Gurnah to show its approximate location.

He had not remembered totally correctly. We had to clear several entrances leading to modest, undecorated vaults which had been profaned a long time before. But we eventually reached the tomb of a Theban nobleman named Sennefer, who had been the head gardener of Pharaoh Amenophis III. It had been his duty to embellish Amon's estates. A steep gallery led to the tomb, a large room with square pillars. Everywhere there was wonderful decoration, in which the deceased and his wife, a magnificent young woman whose gaze reminded me of Lady Ophelia's, were depicted as celebrating rituals to ensure their survival.

Raising my eyes to the ceiling, which was lit by Suleiman, I saw that we had reached our aim: the roof of the tomb was a luxuriant vine arbour with black grapes! Sennefer and his wife, who helped the main shoot to sprout from earth, lived in a paradise of juicy grapes, branches and interlaced vine leaves.

Alas, the sight of the antechamber was less happy. Brownish bandages, broken bones and sarcophagus wood that had almost crumbled to dust, these were clues that fully confirmed my first hypothesis. I inwardly thanked the Bedouin chief for giving me the proof I still lacked.

'It will be a rough game,' I told Suleiman. 'But we shall try to win.'

Back in our chateau, I was welcomed by a gloomy-looking Rosellini.

'I had bad news for you, Master . . . A letter was sent to me from Paris so as to avoid too much of a shock for you.'

I turned pale and immediately thought of my daughter and my brother. 'Tell me, quickly, Ippolito!'

'Your application for the Academy has just been rejected for the sixth time . . . a certain Pardessus was elected.'

I burst out laughing. 'I was judged less worthy than Pardessus . . . that doesn't surprise me. I would have been flattered to be appointed to the Academy at a time when my discoveries were still disputed, out of good or bad faith, it doesn't matter. I would also have been flattered to have the Academy think of me while I was still completing my studies and beginning to gather a harvest in the ruins of Thebes. I would have considered my appointment as a kind of national award. The Academy judged it appropriate to refuse me such satisfaction. I shall not make any further move and when the Academy calls me, I shall be in as little hurry to come as a connoisseur to drink a bottle of musty champagne. Even Nile water may be disgusting when you are no longer thirsty. In the meantime may the Academy enjoy God's peace and mercy.'

'There is also a better piece of news,' Rosellini went on. 'A present from the Pasha, brought by a special emissary.'

My disciple gave me a remarkably heavy gold sabre. I accepted it without a word and shut myself in my bedroom.

I was usually delighted by the evenings in Gurnah. No words could describe vividly and tenderly enough the splendour of the night sky over the plain.

But that night, I was not able to enjoy the peace and silence which usually regenerated me. The Academy, official science and its stupid asses, the tyrant's sabre, it was all too much . . . The fire of rebellion which had stirred my youth overwhelmed me again.

I began to write a memorandum to Mehmet Ali, the almighty master of Egypt. Aware that the ancient people sometimes represented their country in the form of a cow, the Pasha did not hesitate to milk it and exhaust it without mercy. Here was the result of Drovetti's noble advice. I explained my grievances at length.

How many times had my expedition found emptiness, for the most important pharaonic monuments had been destroyed and razed almost under our very eyes. I made a list and appealed to the Pasha's infinite wisdom to preserve the huge heritage, which was in danger of being soon annihilated. Stones suffered, as well as men. I protested against the *fellahin*'s awful misery and beseeched the Pasha to feed and educate them so that poor people could eventually leave this state of slavery. It was necessary to fight the true enemies of Egypt, that is to say those who destroyed temples, looked for saltpetre, built sugar factories or plundered tombs, the overabundant flood, the *fellahin*'s illiteracy and antiquities collectors.

My memorandum would leave at dawn for Mehmet Ali's palace, and I had no doubt that it would reach it without delay. My brother Jacques-Joseph would have recommended me to be more moderate, so as to preserve my own security, but I did not care a fig.

In the flood of excitement, I assessed my action as a curator and a scientist. In my exploration, I did not forget the Louvre Museum, a museum that had been entrusted to me without decent means to develop it. Yet I had gathered monuments of all sizes, the smallest certainly not the least interesting. As for large ones, I had chosen from thousands three or four mummies will peculiar decorations or Greek inscriptions, as well as a beautiful painted bas-relief of the tomb of Seti I, in the Valley of the Kings. This latter piece was a major one, worth a whole collection in itself. It caused me a lot of trouble and it would certainly lead to a court battle with the British in Alexandria, who also claimed to be the rightful owners of the tomb. Despite this, my bas-relief would reach Toulon or sink to the bottom of the sea or the Nile rather than fall into foreign hands. My mind was made up. In Cairo, I had purchased some beautiful sarcophagi. One was made of green basalt and covered inside and out with cameos of unbelievable perfection and fineness. It was the most perfect thing of its kind one could imagine, a jewel that would embellish a boudoir or a reception room, so fine and precious was the sculpture. The lid figured in half-relief a wonderfully carved woman. This sole artefact would pay my debt to the House of the King, not from the point of view of gratitude, but from the financial angle for, compared with those which fetched 20,000–30,000 francs, the sarcophagus was certainly worth 100,000 francs. The bas-relief and the sarcophagus were the two most beautiful Egyptian artefacts ever sent to Europe. They should rightfully belong to Paris and follow me as trophies of my expedition. I hope they would then both be kept in the Louvre for ever, in my memory.

As the cool wind of dawn rose, I wrapped myself in a woollen coat and left our chateau to walk to the edge of the desert. In the distance, a caravan was leaving for the south.

A white figure on a horse came towards me, raising small clouds of sand. Her features tense, Lady Redgrave stopped when she came alongside me. 'You like to win on all fronts, Champollion . . . I hope you are satisfied! My uncle, Thomas Young, has just died, on 10 May 1829, in London. He worked at his hieroglyphic dictionary till his last moments. His pencil fell on the ground as he breathed his last. Are you happy?'

'How could I rejoice in the death of a researcher?' I answered emotionally. 'I would so much have liked to meet him to explain to him why he was wrong.'

'He was not wrong. You are the one who is mistaken! Posterity will have forgotten you soon, and it will celebrate the fame of Thomas Young, the true decipherer of hieroglyphs!'

She turned east and left at full gallop.

We were having lunch when Suleiman came to tell me of a troop of Turkish soldiers had arrived, headed by an officer who gave the Pasha's name as a reference. I was asked to go forthwith to one of Mehmet Ali's Theban palaces, where he had just arrived.

'What does this mean?' worried Rosellini. 'Why such a hurried summons?'

'Some domestic troubles,' I answered, feigning calm. 'If . . . if I did not come back, warn the French authorities and go back to Europe without delay.'

Alarmed, Rosellini stood gaping while I left our dining room in Gurnah to enter Mehmet Ali's clutches.

Never had the expression 'to be full of yourself' been more appropriate, as I, Jean-François Champollion, attempted to look confident as I entered the private apartments of the Pasha of Egypt. Inside, however, I trembled like poplar in the wind.

Mehmet Ali sat in a high-backed armchair which made him look like an emperor. He smoked a long amber pipe and ran his hand through his carefully trimmed, thick, white beard. He was motionless, like a wild beast waiting for its prey.

'Please allow me, Your Excellency, to thank you for your magnificent present.'

'I read your memorandum with the utmost care, Monsieur Champollion. It mentions many strange things.'

Contrary to the usual oriental practice, the Pasha was going immediately to the heart of the matter. It was a bad omen. The Viceroy was forgetting his diplomatic qualities, and behaving like a warrior.

'You mention temples that have been demolished and razed . . . isn't that just an ill-founded rumour? Isn't such devastation the work of time?'

'No, Your Excellency. It is indeed under your rule that such serious events happened. Major sanctuaries like el-Kab, Antinoopolis or Contralatopolis have disappeared completely as a result of the work of iconoclasts and profaners. It was my duty to let you know about such deplorable activities, which may be imputed to barbarians. They could only have acted without your knowledge.'

'Of course,' he approved icily.

'In my memorandum,' I went on, 'you will at last find clear and comprehensive information. Now Your Excellency, you must act firmly. Your honour as a head of state and your reputation in the world are at stake. Promise me to protect the monuments that still remain and to prevent further deteriorations.'

Mehmet Ali nodded ambiguously. It was impossible to be more insistent.

'Tell me about Ramses the Great,' he asked in a dry tone.

Concealing my surprise, I launched into a description of the extraordinary pharaoh's rule, recalling the incredible number of monuments he had erected or restored. I mentioned the formidable state of advancement sciences and arts had reached in ancient Egypt. As I mentioned cartography, the Pasha interrupted me.

'Could you draw a detailed map of the pharaohs' Egypt? It would make it easier to watch over the sites.'

'I shall complete it as soon as possible, Your Excellency.'

'You did not confine yourself to the past, Monsieur Champollion . . . Your memorandum emphasizes the *fellahin*'s condition, as if I was responsible for their misery.'

'I did not write that, Your Excellency. The people should receive an education only you can give them. The Mamelukes drove the country into poverty and unhappiness. It falls to you to be the ruler who will put an end to such injustice.'

The Pasha smoked for a long time and remained silent. Then a mischievous smile lit up his face. 'So,' he said. 'Ramses was indeed the greatest of pharaohs, was he?'

I do not know whether divine intervention prevented me from choking the hypocritical tyrant. Aware of the rage that was building up in me, he was poking fun.

Mumbling a meaningless platitude, I took leave of him.

When I reached Gurnah I was still upset. Yet it was quickly replaced by the most acute anxiety when I saw that some servants had gathered in front of the main entrance. I had to jostle them to get in.

My blood was chilled by what I saw. Ippolito Rosellini lay on the ground, his eyes rolled upwards. Professor Raddi was bent over him trying to make him drink a potion.

'He was bitten by a scorpion,' explained the mineralogist. I knelt down, appalled. 'Ippolito.'

'He will live,' diagnosed Professor Raddi. 'But I cannot guarantee him the best of health in the years to come. Help me carry him on his bed.'

'Where is Suleiman?'

'He left to fetch the healer. The two of us will save your disciple.

Rosellini remained unconscious for two days and nights, during which I did not get a wink of sleep. Eventually, looking awful and racked with pain, he returned to consciousness. Professor Raddi and the healer had done miracles with herbs and magnetism. Rosellini ate a little and sank into a refreshing sleep.

'You should do the same,' recommended the mineralogist. You are beyond even the point of exhaustion.'

'Probably you too, you used up a lot of energy healing him . . .'

'It does not matter any more, Champollion. I have now completed my collection of minerals. I know the history of the earth and I can write it. But I have lost interest, ever since I discovered butterflies. They are so soft, coloured and fragile . . . I was wrong to hunt them. I should have contented myself with observing them. We ruin life, we are guilty of carelessness in the face of a world that is far beyond our understanding. The desert, Champollion, this is the source of true wisdom and true love . . . the great journey means to leave for the desert in the company only of the wind.'

Afraid that I understood him only too well, I stood before the main door of our castle-like home.

'It's useless to try to hold me back, Champollion . . . you know that I do exactly what pleases me, as you do. Who would care about an old lunatic? Since I have met the desert, I no longer have attachments, family or homeland. It calls for me, it calls for me so loudly . . .'

'Stay here tonight, Professor. We are both too tired to have a long conversation. We'll talk tomorrow morning. I have many things to tell you.'

Professor Raddi lay down on a mat and immediately fell asleep. I resisted as long as I could, but my eyelids betrayed me. I collapsed in my turn.

Suleiman woke me. Startled, I saw that Professor Raddi's mat was empty.

'He left before dawn,' explained Suleiman.

'Did he tell you where he was going?'

'To the Delta, through the desert.'

'And you did not stop him?'

'Nobody can prevent anyone heading for his own destiny in this part of the world.'

We never saw Professor Raddi again and nobody ever found his body.

26

A little red-faced man in European dress arrived at the entrance to our Gurnah palace while Rosellini and I were having lunch in almost complete silence. My disciple was recovering from the scorpion bite with difficulty. He complained of diffuse pains which hindered his thought and work. He had not been affected at all by Professor Raddi's disappearance, and even declared himself happy to be alone with me, two Egyptologists in charge of teams of workmen running archaeological digs which he meticulously supervised.

Suleiman introduced the visitor.

'Monsieur Champollion?'

'Yes indeed.'

'I am Monsieur Mimaut's private secretary,' announced the little man pompously, as if he was referring to the Pope or the King of France.

He was deeply disappointed by my lack of reaction.

'Well, who is he?' I asked.

Piqued, our guest puffed himself up. 'Monsieur Mimaut is Bernardino Drovetti's successor.'

The sky of Thebes seemed to fall on my head.

'But . . . since when?'

'The decision was taken on 5 January. A letter was sent to you in Alexandria.'

'I never received it.'

'That is impossible! It was an official document addressed

to Consul-General Drovetti, who was to convey it to you! An administrative investigation is necessary.'

'Did the Pasha know about the change?'

'Of course,' answered the secretary. 'He is the one who punished Drovetti, even though he had been on excellent terms with him until your arrival in Egypt. Mehmet Ali heard that the Consul-General had initiated many intrigues against you, especially in holding up permissions he should have given you without delay. The same thing happened with the money for the archaeological work. I am now bringing you the ten thousand francs that were requested for archaeological work in Thebes for sixteen months and were blocked by Drovetti.'

Rosellini forgot the heat, the tiredness, the scorpion and his pains. I was overwhelmed by a delicious feeling of triumph. Alas it was not to last, for such unexpected change had disturbing consequences.

'So Drovetti knew for several months that he would be replaced.'

'The former Consul-General,' said the little man dryly, 'is an emotional man. He protested against the decision and he was very bitter when he was compelled to accept it. But he displayed goodwill and agreed to continue here for several months longer to enable Monsieur Mimaut to succeed him unhurriedly. The transition is now coming to an end.'

'Do you know where Drovetti is?'

'Here in Thebes. He will leave tonight or tomorrow with a large convoy.'

'Have you checked his luggage?'

The little man was horrified.

'Don't think of it, Monsieur Champollion! Bernardino Drovetti is a diplomat. He is free to come and go as he pleases and take whatever he likes.'

'That is exactly what I feared. I only have a few more hours to put an end to an appalling traffic!'

Leaving the emissary and Rosellini, both astounded, I rushed outside, with Suleiman on my heels.

'We must intervene as soon as possible,' I said. We must hurry to the necropolis of Sheikh Abdel Gurnah.'

'Take this,' he recommended, handing me a rifle.

'I don't know how to use it. Ask two reliable men to come with us.'

This time our donkeys had to quicken their pace. As we reached the hill in which the tombs had been dug, I did not feel any fear. I thought I knew what I would see as I uncovered Drovetti's secret. I thought my presence alone would prevent any violence.

I asked my little troop to stop at the bottom of a hill pierced by numerous holes which, in the past, had sheltered vaults now emptied by pillagers. Usually no human presence haunted these devastated places.

'There!' exclaimed Suleiman.

A fleeting figure had just disappeared into a vault about halfway up the slope.

'Let's go.'

'Let me walk first,' suggested Suleiman. 'You would be too much at risk.'

We walked abreast to the dark opening we had located. It was the entrance to a real cave, which could be reached by a steep underground gallery. It was probably the beautiful and spacious tomb of a great Theban dignitary, which had been plundered with a long time before. We had only just entered the gallery when we were attacked with stones, which narrowly missed us.

Suleiman took aim and fired a shot which produced a commotion in the depth of the tomb.

I had to explain to the two armed Arabs who had accompanied us, that these were neither genies nor evil spirits, but thieves of the worst kind.

We ran to a first, rather large room. The scene which met us as well as the smell, was so horrible that I had to stand in the way to prevent our companions from running away as fast as their legs could carry them. There were over twenty mummies, some standing against the wall and others lying on the floor. Some were still wrapped in bandages, but the blackish flesh of most of them was more or less rotten. Heads, hands and feet lay about in baskets.

'Here is the trade of Drovetti and his gangs,' I said to Suleiman, hardly able to contain my emotion. 'They sell mummy's flesh to amateurs. The load was to leave with him for Europe. You now understand why he so badly wanted to keep me away from Thebes, and even plotted my disappearance. He had a premonition that I would discover his crimes against the ancient Egyptians.'

Suleiman, usually so quiet, was losing control. 'I thought the evil traffic had stopped.'

'It reached its climax in the sixteenth and seventeenth centuries,' I explained. 'People believed in the medicinal qualities of mummy's flesh. Peasants unearthed them and took them to Cairo and Alexandria. From there traffickers sent them to Europe, either in the shape of whole mummies or in pieces. When they were short of mummies, they made them by murdering *fellahin*.'

'The scoundrels who do such things should be arrested. Where have they gone?'

A few minutes were enough to clear the entrance of a very narrow gallery which had been hastily concealed with stones. I ventured into it, almost suffocated by dust, but Suleiman held me back by the waist. 'It is now my turn to resist you for once. I am armed.'

He pushed me back abruptly and began his difficult descent. More mummies had been stored in the gallery. As we passed them and leaned on the corpses, they crumbled into dust. Our faces touched those of old Egyptians who had been dead for centuries. A head rolled under my feet.

Suddenly I heard two shots. Suleiman collapsed before me.

I tugged him by the shoulders with difficulty and hauled him to the upper room. Infuriated by their chief's injury, the two Arabs rushed into the narrow gallery.

I laid Suleiman on the ground. His chest was covered with blood. It was an unbearable suffering to breathe.

'Don't try . . . to comfort me . . . it was good, Champollion . . . good to have a brother . . . like you.'

Suleiman died in my arms with a smile on his lips.

I had too much sorrow to cry. The Egyptian I had most loved had died because of me.

Supporting Suleiman's corpse and accompanied by the two silent Arabs, I remained prostrated for an infinity. My mind wandered in a world without shapes. Curiously the mummies confirmed the certainty of resurrection. They testified to another life, which Suleiman's soul would enter in full glory.

As soon as I had recovered my thoughts, the two Arabs asked me for permission to go down to the bottom of the vault to fetch the corpse of the man Suleiman had killed. It was not Drovetti, but his faithful steward, Moktar, who had served him until death.

The Pasha had left for Alexandria. My meeting with his representative was useless. Of course he promised to initiate a thorough investigation into the bandits who had been hired by Drovetti. The latter had already left for Cairo. It was impossible to get in touch with Monsieur Mimaut's secretary, who had also gone back to the capital. But why should I complain? I at last had the necessary money to start serious excavation, my disciple was still with me and Drovetti could not harm me in any way now . . . The death of a servant was just an unimportant incident, swept away by the desert wind.

Yet nobody knew that I was grieving for a brother, someone who had watched over me for the whole expedition, and who had given his life so that I could pass on what the gods had given to me.

On the night before Suleiman's burial, I worked solidly at my dictionary and grammar. It was the best tribute I felt I could pay him. The burial ceremony began shortly after dawn so as to avoid the heat of the sun. I had insisted on having the corpse watched over in the large room of the Gurnah chateau, in the modest dwelling where we had lived so happily.

A group of noisy mourners appeared on the threshold. They wore dust on their hair, beat their breasts and cried incantations in the hope of repelling the destructive forces of death. As there were no relatives, Rosellini and I acted as such. But unlike the other mourners, we remained serene and motionless.

Two priests undressed the corpse, washed it carefully and wrapped it in an immaculate white sheet. An *ulema* recited prayers from the Koran. Then the modern mummifyers placed the body in a wooden box with no lid and covered it with a red shawl. I was asked to break Suleiman's seal, which had been used for his signature and was now useless in the human world.

The procession formed, headed by young children, who enjoyed the celebration. In the Orient the colour of death is white. The grief of loss mingles with the joy of knowing that the beloved is in the heaven of the fair ones. Before the procession set off towards the cemetery, officers poured rose water and suffused it with incense. Did they remember that the word 'incense' is a synonym for 'to make divine' in the old Egyptian language? Thus shrouded in a fragrance of holiness which would enable him to go through the gates of the other world without difficulty, my brother Suleiman was hurriedly taken to his last dwelling while the mourners covered themselves with dust, raising a chorus of howls.

It was a very humble cemetery with just a few gravestones near the village in the full sun. Without wasting a second, as if death was in a hurry to deprive us of Suleiman's material aspect, his corpse was drawn from the wooden box and buried with his head to the south. The priest filled the grave with stones and sand and recommended the deceased to answer accurately to the two angels who would welcome him on the other side and submit him to questions which would decide over his ultimate fate, in heaven or hell. As I listened to the words, how could I not think of how it might be if my dear Egyptian religion was extended into today's ceremonies?

The mourners and the priests became silent. The poor necropolis returned to silence. Destitute people came. The villagers and I gave them bread and dates in memory of the banquets celebrated by families in antiquity in the tomb shrines, thus indissolubly united the dead and the living.

I remained alone and laid a palm and a reed on my brother's grave.

Was it a trick of my senses? I thought I could see his soul flying away in the shape of a bird on the wing. It ascended to the sun at lightning speed and merged with it.

A young Arab girl came and dropped a lily on the tomb. Her face was concealed by a veil, but the figure enabled me to identify Lady Redgrave without difficulty.

'I must leave Egypt, Jean-François. I've been denounced to the Pasha. Shouldn't you think of going back too?'

'Going back?'

'You're not going to spend the rest of your life here, are you? I shall find a way of taking you back, if you feel some love for me . . .'

Her words broke my heart. She had aroused passion in me, but she had allowed another kind of love to act against it.

'Have you ever experienced exile, Lady Ophelia? Do you know the unbearable pain of being away from your homeland, from the land where you want to spend each hour of your life? I endured exile for almost forty years. I had to wait so long to go back to Egypt and to my true homeland. You may take me for a lunatic, but this is where I was truly born. It is my real country. I feel so well . . . all my pains and ills vanish. I am moved by a new and inexhaustible energy. I feel that I can do anything and overcome all fatigue. The ever-shining sun nourishes my body and my soul. If I leave the land and monuments, I shall die.'

Lady Ophelia was weeping. 'So, because of you, I lost everything . . .'

'Don't believe that, Ophelia. With me, you would never have experienced the happiness you hope for. Egypt is too demanding a mistress.'

'Let me be the judge of that, Jean-François Champollion.'

27

On 1 August 1829, Rosellini and I decided to leave our Gurnah chateau, where we had spent so many pleasant hours and settle on the east bank, in the very enclosure of great Karnak. After the universe of tombs and so many departures and separations, I needed the temple of temples to regain a new serenity.

I settled our new headquarters, as L'Hôte would have said, in the Ptolemaic temple dedicated to the goddess Opet, whose secret role, according to texts engraved in the walls, was to act as a celestial matrix to resuscitate Osiris, the new sun.

The small sanctuary turned out to be a very convenient home with its corridors opening on various rooms and a long room with columns. The cooks and servants lived outside in tents.

Is there any more beautiful dream for an Egyptologist than to reside in a temple? The coolness, the vivid memory of the initiates' presence, the magic power of sacred words around us were most beneficial to our work and research. My only annoyance was my new feeling towards my disciple. It was a sort of distrust I was not used to. The scientist's passion was undeniable, but it dried up the man's deep sensitivity. How much I missed Suleiman's silent brotherly feeling, L'Hôte's warmth, Professor Raddi's wise madness and even Father Bidant's anxious faith . . . their shadows swirled in the darkness of the temple where, far too often, I could also see the smile of a woman blending with that of Isis.

Karnak was the most inexhaustible world that could ever be conceived. The Egyptians called it, with reason, heaven on earth. The temple was actually a sacred town composed of several areas, a living body that had been constantly growing. No architect ever completed his work on this site. Future builders spent centuries restoring monuments, setting collapsed columns upright, repairing pylons, and brining back to light beauties concealed by sand, litter and human stupidity. I had just heard that the Archbishop of Jerusalem had charitably decorated me with the cross of Knight of the Holy Sepulchre. The diplomas had reached Alexandria, where I could collect them in exchange for the usual fee, 100 gold louis each. On the banks of the Kidron, people did not know that on the banks of the Seine scholars were not Croesus, and the Wheel of Fortune did not really turn in their favour unless they were also businessmen. So however great my eagerness to display the cross of a knight fighting infidels, I had to renounce the tribute and content myself with the fact that I had been thought worthy of it! It was not part of erudition to support secular fees.

I was sitting at the back of the temple, completing a chapter of my grammar, when Rosellini, asked to talk to me. 'Master,' he said. 'I have taken an important decision. I cannot work properly under these circumstances. I must go back to Italy and start arranging a museum. The journey will be long and painful, some artefacts may be broken or even lost, but a major task is awaiting me and my health is poor. The success of an expedition like this one depends primarily on the scientific exploitation of the results achieved on the field. Otherwise, it would just be a leisure trip.'

'A trip in the course of which some men died, Ippolito, and others saw their destiny fulfilled.'

'I'm not concerned by such details.'

'You are free to do as you please.'

Rosellini was about to leave the sanctuary when he turned back. 'May I ask you one last question, Master: have you really succeeded in deciphering hieroglyphs?'

'I think so and I shall provide the evidence.'

'In that case, why didn't you give me all the keys you possessed?'

How could I answer, except by lying, which I refused to do, or questioning his character, which he would neither have admitted nor understood? I was unable to say anything. Only God knows how he may have interpreted my silence.

So I was now alone with my *fellahin* and Karnak. The scribes had described the sweetness of Amon's estate and countryside so well that I wandered there with delight for a whole day, leaving my beloved stones to mingle with the peasants. In the fields where women walked without veils and children played naked, people interested in my presence and welcomed me most warmly. It was true that I did not look like a European any more and spoke the language of these poor people, who repeated millennia-old practices, scratched the soil, sowed, watered, raised crops, grazed herds, and lived in the company of camels, donkeys, buffaloes and watchful yellow or black dogs, which slept in the hot midday sun, but knew so well how to watch over villages at night.

I sat on the coping of a well in the fields and granted myself some sweet hours of meditation. Close by, in the shade of a tamarisk, a mother had laid her baby on a faded rug and was playing with him. I learned to enjoy the warmth of the sky and the breath of the earth singing its love for the Nile, a human being in the cycle of seasons.

I would have liked to abandon myself to the pleasure of being idle and devoid of thoughts, but . . . we must go on tormenting ourselves till death, and toiling to extract the best of ourselves, otherwise our earthly life would be meaningless compared with eternity.

You might think that I spent my time among the dead, shaking off the dust of history. But a lot of this work brought me in touch with beings that lived an eternal life. Ordinary people think that their lives exist, whereas they are only, like me, shadows devoured by time.

When I saw the herds coming back in the green plain on the edge of golden crops, I thought I was dreaming. Was the day already turning into evening? The north wind rose and moved the dark clusters of palm trees. The ineffable sweetness of the breeze permeated my whole body. I gradually emerged from my torpor to experience the resurrection of the end of the day. The burgeoning green was becoming dark. The temperature dropped and the heat lost its harshness to caress my skin. The hills lost their dryness to glow in the rays of the setting sun.

The sky burst into dozens of colours applied in large brushstrokes. Birds flew in orange, azure, dark-red and purple furrows. There were sailors on the river, *fellahin* drawing water, and women returning to the village joined in their songs. The celestial and the terrestrial Nile would soon blend into a single route to the world beyond. The landscape of this world vanished to give way to that of the soul. It was time for me to go back to Karnak temple and wander in its alleys. Acacias, mimosas, palm trees, barley and wheat fields sank into darkness. They enjoyed the coolness of the night and awaited the miracle of the new morning the sun might grant them if it succeeded in defeating the demon of underground abysses.

The peace of Aton, the secret light of the sunset in which life begins, spread over everything. The creaking of a *shaduf* making melancholic complaint could hardly be heard in the evening air. As I passed the great pylon that gave access to the temple, the sun had set, but strange lights still filled the invisible horizon. The shadow of night spread from the west like an iridescent scarf cast over the river, displaying silver sheens.

It was in that sanctuary that we might see light overcome darkness and give birth to a new sun. The stars were shining with that unique close warm sheen which typifies Egypt.

I walked through Tuthmosis III's reception room, where the

pharaohs were initiated into their duties, and walked up the stairs to the observatory from which astrologers deciphered the laws of the sky. Thanks to the constellations and the swallows which carried the spirits of the ancient kings, the mystery became visible. In the lapis lazuli night it elevated the soul in a joyful drunkenness and took it into an ethereal dance to the Milky Way.

Karnak gave more than it had promised. I let the serenity of the stones pervade me, meaning to spend the night on the roof of Khonsu temple. Then, rising up from the field of ruins like a ghost, a man came to me.

Was it death? Was it *Don Giovanni*'s Commander come to invite me to the banquet of the other world?

He walked at a steady pace. Thanks to the moonlight, I could see that he was holding a kind of three-pronged hoe in his hand. He knelt in front of the entrance of Khonsu temple and prostrated himself several times in front of a divinity hidden in the night. Then he stood up and sat beside me.

'What a beautiful night,' he said. 'It is so calm and mild . . . I am the gardener at Karnak. I come to hoe the plants in around the sacred lake while the sun is sleeping. In the daytime, I carve little flutes in reeds and play them so that the flowers don't die. My great-grandfather, my grandfather and my father were gardeners, too. They taught me the tricks of the trade. I shall teach them to my son.'

The voice was grave and bewitching. It had interrupted my meditation just when I was taking the decision to leave my own expedition, to abandon, Jean-François Champollion, the Egyptologist, and stay in Egypt, where I would live as an unknown *fellah* to my last breath in the land that had been mine for ever.

'Have you got children?' asked the gardener.

'A daughter.'

'Then you must go back. She needs you. A father does not abandon his child.'

He was reading my thoughts.

'I know how you feel,' he said. 'Leaving Egypt is like dying. But your daughter will draw her own life from yours. You have no right to deprive her of your presence. This is the only fault God would not forgive you.'

He was piercing my heart. He was tearing me away from myself, as if he were digging up a simple flower. My daughter . . . I would leave my nourishing ground for her, the air that gave me life, the heat that healed me, the temples and tombs in which the meaning of life became so obvious that it eliminated everything superficial and useless. I was about to lose the paradise of Karnak and go back to the hell of Paris.

'When you leave,' said the gardener, 'villagers will come from everywhere. They will leave their dwellings and gather on the bank near the huge sycamore under which your ship is anchored. A procession of mourners will let out cries of despair. As for you, you will look fixedly at the temple. You won't see nor hear anything. You will try to let the life of these stones pervade you to the marrow. And you will leave, brother, and never come back.'

Epilogue

'Tell me more, Father,' said Zoraïde. 'Tell me . . .'

'You know the obelisk . . . it has arrived in Paris. I do not like this modern Babel which ruins my health, but I am happy to be near the magic stone. And I made my contribution to posterity with my grammar.'

'Tell me more . . .'

'I would like to be granted two more years,' said Champollion, touching his forehead. 'There are still so many things inside!'

Zoraïde looked at him so intensely that she was sure she could keep him a little longer. He found new resources to pass on his faith to her.

'Remember . . . only enthusiasm really matters in life. The heart has to be inflamed and the inner being moved by a desire which is beyond it and absorbs it. Be faithful to your enthusiasm. Nurture it . . . and may you say, when you breathe your last, that there is not a single hour of your life of which you can be ashamed.'

Then he stopped talking, exhausted by the ultimate effort.

And his head dropped on the pillow, lifeless.

On 4 March 1832, at the age of forty-two, Jean-François Champollion died.

Zoraïde did not cry. Despite the pain that burnt inside, despite the fire she knew would never go out, she felt a strange joy for her father. She had seen his bird-soul fly away to Egypt, where she would join him some day.

She walked round her father's bedroom. She looked at the family diary where the words of the healer who had brought Champollion into the world had been written: 'I prophesy the birth of a son promised to the highest fate. He will be the light of centuries to come.'

Then she touched all the objects her father had brought back from Egypt and to which he had been so attached. She stopped at a papyrus of the Book of the Dead, which she placed on his heart. She climbed on the bed and fell asleep beside him, her head on the papyrus, whose hieroglyphs, translated by Champollion said: 'A god similar to light has come. He will live for ever.'

Glossary

Bey: a title below that of prince and pasha. The *bey* manages civil servants called *effendis*.

Chaouiche: policeman

Dahabieh: a boat used as a house on the Nile.

Fellah (plural *fellahin*): peasant.

Galabieh: traditional dress worn by men in Egypt.

Mucharabieh: small balcony closed by a grid.

Reis: boss, chief.

Schamali: north wind.

Shaduf: simple lever device for lifting water to irrigate the fields. It is operated by hand.

Sheikh: title of reverence

Ulema: Arab scholar.

Zar: traditional ceremony usually arranged to free a woman over thirty from the evil spirit possessing her.